# One Day in Lebanon

## *A Hostage Rescue*

# Lawrence Scofield

## Acknowledgments

This book would not have been possible without the efforts of Judy, my wonderful editor. My thanks and love go to my family for everything they do to enrich my life: Jennifer, Elizabeth, Daniel and John. They're the best.

Neither products nor brand names used in this novel represent or imply any relationship with, or endorsement by, the author or publisher.

## Copyright Notice and Disclaimers

# Books by Lawrence Scofield

**"The Laura Messier Files"**

Three Days in Tripoli

Two Days in Moscow

One Day in Lebanon

# One Day in Lebanon

## *A Hostage Rescue*

# Table of Contents

Prologue ..................................................................1
Chapter One ...........................................................14
Chapter Two............................................................32
Chapter Three..........................................................38
Chapter Four............................................................47
Chapter Five ............................................................51
Chapter Six...............................................................59
Chapter Seven .........................................................67
Chapter Eight ..........................................................72
Chapter Nine ...........................................................78
Chapter Ten..............................................................83
Chapter Eleven.........................................................85
Chapter Twelve ........................................................88
Chapter Thirteen.......................................................91
Chapter Fourteen ...................................................102
Chapter Fifteen ......................................................107
Chapter Sixteen ......................................................109
Chapter Seventeen..................................................113
Chapter Eighteen ...................................................115
Chapter Nineteen....................................................122
Chapter Twenty .....................................................135
Chapter Twenty-One...............................................137
Chapter Twenty-Two ..............................................143
Chapter Twenty-Three ............................................147
Chapter Twenty-Four ..............................................153
Chapter Twenty-Five...............................................157
Chapter Twenty-Six ................................................164
Chapter Twenty-Seven............................................169
Chapter Twenty-Eight.............................................175
Chapter Twenty-Nine..............................................177
Chapter Thirty .......................................................182
Chapter Thirty-One ................................................187
Chapter Thirty-Two.................................................191

Chapter Thirty-Three.................................201
Chapter Thirty-Four ................................203
Chapter Thirty-Five.................................204
Chapter Thirty-Six..................................207
Chapter Thirty-Seven ...............................209
Chapter Thirty-Eight ...............................211
Chapter Thirty-Nine ................................213
Chapter Forty ......................................216
Chapter Forty-One...................................220
Chapter Forty-Two...................................230
Chapter Forty-Three.................................234
Chapter Forty-Four..................................237
Chapter Forty-Five .................................249
Chapter Forty-Six...................................257
Chapter Forty-Seven ................................260
Chapter Forty-Eight.................................266
Chapter Forty-Nine .................................267
Chapter Fifty ......................................270
Chapter Fifty-One ..................................273
Chapter Fifty-Two...................................275
Chapter Fifty-Three.................................282
Chapter Fifty-Four..................................285
Chapter Fifty-Five .................................286
Chapter Fifty-Six...................................287
Chapter Fifty-Seven ................................291
Chapter Fifty-Eight ................................296
Chapter Fifty-Nine .................................299
Chapter Sixty.......................................301
Chapter Sixty-One...................................304
Chapter Sixty-Two ..................................305
Chapter Sixty-Three ................................310
Chapter Sixty-Four..................................315
Chapter Sixty-Five .................................320
Chapter Sixty-Six ..................................321

Chapter Sixty-Seven.................................................324
Chapter Sixty-Eight................................................326
Chapter Sixty-Nine.................................................327
Chapter Seventy ...................................................330
Chapter Seventy-One ...............................................332
Chapter Seventy-Two................................................334
Chapter Seventy-Three..............................................338
Chapter Seventy-Four ..............................................340
Chapter Seventy-Five...............................................346
Chapter Seventy-Six................................................349
Chapter Seventy-Seven .............................................351
Epilogue ..........................................................355
Author's Notes ....................................................362
About the Author...................................................367
Sneak Peek ........................................................368
Prologue ..........................................................1

# Southern Lebanon and Surrounding Region

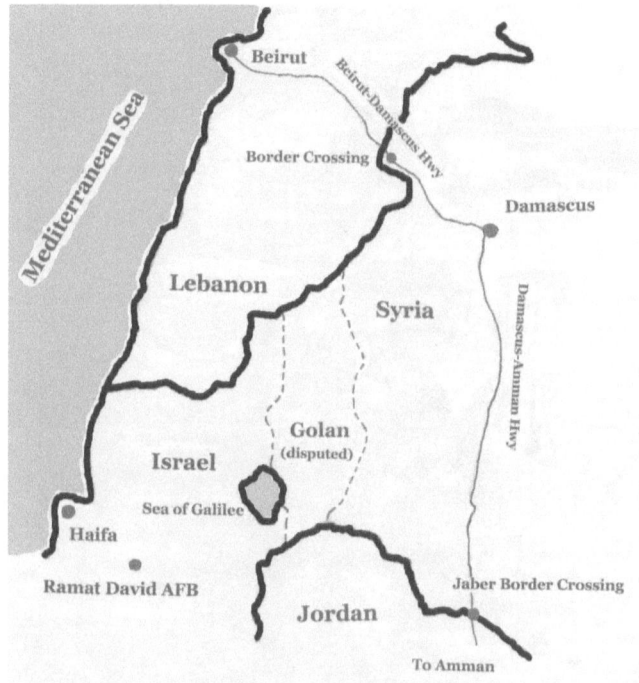

# Prologue

*September 22, 1988*

AS WILLIAM SHARP drove to work on Thursday morning, he had no way of knowing this day would be unlike any other. Traveling from his rented townhouse in the diplomatic section of Damascus, Syria, toward the American Embassy downtown, he considered the security situation in the city. With a civil war raging over the border in Lebanon and the Israeli occupied Golan Heights only a few miles to the south, Damascus was a dangerous place for those sympathetic to Israel. The Russian KGB and the Iranian MOIS had strong intelligence operations in Damascus as did the Israelis and the Palestinians who battled each other daily on the streets of the city. The Americans, however, did not scale up their intelligence efforts, preferring to withdraw staff to lessen the risk to their personnel.

I'll bet the intelligence briefing report will be late again today, Sharp thought. Yet another code red bulletin written by an analyst at Langley who hasn't a clue about the current conditions on the ground. Sharp glanced at the cars waiting beside him at an intersection. We need to infiltrate those militia groups. I need to know who's planting a bomb today, who's standing around the corner waiting to take a shot at me. If we don't get better intel, sooner or later something's going to happen. Sharp let his thoughts trail off as traffic began to move again. He was cognizant of the risks and alert to dangerous situations, but sometimes that wasn't enough.

After arriving at the heavily fortified American Embassy and parking in his usual spot behind the building, Bill, as his friends called him, took the stairs two at a time up to his small office on the second floor. He threw his briefcase on the desk, hung up his jacket and walked down the hallway toward the front of the building to check in with the duty officer and retrieve messages left for him overnight. "What's up this morning, Richard?" Sharp asked the clerk.

"Morning, Bill. Brooks left this for you," Richard said, handing Sharp an interoffice envelope. Franklin Brooks was the Ambassador and Bill, in his mid-thirties and a former Army Delta Force officer, served as his assistant.

"Thanks," Bill said, grabbing the envelope. "Where's the intel briefing report this morning?"

"It comes out at noon, Bill, just like yesterday."

"It used to come out at nine."

"Not anymore," Richard said with a shrug.

"Langley needs to get their shit together, Rich." Bill said over his shoulder, walking back to his office.

Bill sat down behind his desk, propped up his feet and opened the envelope. It was a one page itinerary with a handwritten note from Brooks scribbled across the top. "Cover this for me. I've got a conflict," the note said, signed "FB."

Nicholas Buck, the Under Secretary of State for Political Affairs, was flying in from Brussels this morning for a secret meeting with President Hafez al-Assad. Brooks wanted Sharp to meet Buck at Mezze Air Force Base, accompany him to the Presidential Palace and return him to the airport after the meeting. Bill immediately picked up the phone. "Rich, I thought Brooks was supposed to babysit the Secretary today," Sharp said.

"Apparently, something came up, Bill. Brooks is already gone."

"Are the Israelis going to shadow us?"

"They don't know about the meeting, Bill."

"Jesus, you mean we're going to be alone?"

"You'll be fine," Rich said in a condescending tone. "No one knows about the meeting."

"Why don't we take an unmarked car?"

"Can't do that. The Secretary expects a limo. Mezze is right next to the palace, Bill. It's a ten minute drive over there."

Bill looked at his watch. "All right. Tell Henry to bring the car around back and I'll be out in a couple of minutes."

"Henry went with Brooks."

"Who's my driver then?" Bill asked, surprised that the Embassy's best driver was unavailable.

The clerk looked at a list. "It says here it's Ahmed."

"Who the hell's Ahmed?"

"A new hire. He's a local guy."

"Come on, Richard," Bill said, frustrated at the violation of policy. "You know we never put local drivers with visitors. Can't one of you guys drive us?"

"Everyone's busy this morning, Bill. Ahmed will be okay. He knows the city."

"Does he even speak English?"

"Of course he does. You won't have a problem."

"Damn it," Bill said with disgust in his voice. He slammed the phone down and stared at the itinerary. This is a risk, he thought, shaking his head.

Bill grabbed a cup of coffee from the cafeteria before finding his driver, a diminutive young Syrian man, leaning against a black Embassy limo in the parking lot.

"Are you Ahmed?" he asked, approaching the car.

"Yes, Sir."

"You got a last name, Ahmed, or are you one of those rock stars with only one name?"

"It's Kalami, Sir. Ahmed Kalami."

"Are you related to Safa?" Bill liked Safa Kalami; she worked on the housekeeping staff at the Embassy.

"Yes, Sir. I'm her brother."

"That's the best way to get a job, my friend. Connections. I'm gonna ride in front with you. We're going to Mezze Airport. You know where it is?"

"Yes, Sir."

Ahmed pulled out of the Embassy gate and Bill watched Ahmed closely as he negotiated his way through traffic.

"How long have you been working at the Embassy?" Sharp asked, seeking to ascertain the risk of using a local driver.

"A week," Ahmed said.

"You certainly speak good English."

Ahmed chuckled. "I studied in America for a while. A foreign exchange student."

"Really? Where did you go to school?"

"Harvard University."

Sharp whistled. "No shit? Damn, you must be smart."

"Just an average student, Sir," Ahmed said, glancing over at Sharp.

As they swung around the cloverleaf in front of the airport, Sharp pointed toward the north end of the terminal. "You need to go to that end, Ahmed. You're looking for a gate with a guard shack."

Ahmed found the gate where the guard pointed toward a Syrian military Jeep parked inside the gate. "Go ahead and pull behind it," Sharp said. "They know where we need to be."

Sharp and his driver were led around the terminal and onto the tarmac where the Jeep abruptly stopped. Ahmed kept the engine running and the air conditioning on high during the wait. The day promised to be sunny and hot, typical early fall weather for Damascus. Sharp watched the plane land ten minutes later, a white Boeing 747 with the words "United States of America" printed in black on a blue stripe above the windows. "When they get off the plane," Sharp said to Ahmed, "walk around and open the back door."

"Yes, Sir."

Airport maintenance workers wedged blocks under the tires and rolled portable stairs up to the plane's door. Sharp heard the whine of the engines decrease as the door opened and two men and a woman appeared in the doorway, pausing briefly before walking down the stairs. Sharp met his party halfway across the tarmac, extending his hand to the older man. "Bill Sharp, American Embassy here in Damascus," he said, shouting over the wind and the din of other aircraft taking off and landing.

The older gentleman, in his late fifties with wire rim glasses, raised his voice in response. "Nicholas Buck. This is my assistant, Melissa Clarke," Buck yelled, gesturing toward the woman, "and Harry Acker, my interpreter."

"Come on. Let's get you off the tarmac. Would you step this way?" Sharp held his hand out toward the limo. All three visitors climbed into the back seat.

The entourage made a U-turn, proceeding out of the gate and onto the expressway ramp that led to the private, two lane road between Mezze Airport and the Presidential Palace.

Buck glanced at his watch. "How long is the drive, Mr. Sharp?"

"It should be just a few minutes." Bill pointed out the windshield. "This road takes us directly to the Palace."

The air base and the palace sat beside each other on a plateau northwest of the city. The Syrian escort led the entourage onto the Palace grounds, three large modern buildings set around an elongated roundabout driveway. The entourage pulled up to the steps in front of a tall façade of gray marble and glass. Sharp led his contingent up the stairs into the palace foyer, a huge gray marbled room with a red carpet running the length of it. A man walked toward them smiling broadly. "I'm Foreign Minister Masoud Fakhoury. Welcome to the Presidential Palace, Secretary Buck," the man said in fluent English. "Would you step this way, please?"

He led the party to the Presidential Office where he motioned toward a waiting room. "Please have your associates wait here."

Buck turned. "I need my interpreter," he told the Minister.

"Of course."

Melissa and Bill were ushered into a side room where the guard motioned them toward seats along the walls. Bill settled in for what he thought might be a long wait. He looked briefly at Melissa on the other side of the room. *Maybe early thirties? I should talk to her.* He was about to speak, when she looked up and gave him a blank stare. *Maybe not.*

Bill glanced at his watch when the door opened again. It had been an hour and fifteen minute meeting. Outside the waiting room, Bill saw Buck and President Assad standing face to face in the hallway shaking hands. *They're not smiling,* he thought. *It must have been a tough meeting, probably about the Palestinians, those poor bastards.*

Ahmed stood by the car holding the rear passenger door open as Sharp's entourage exited the palace. Once they'd climbed into the limo, Ahmed turned and looked back at Buck. "Back to the airport, Sir?"

"Yes," Buck said impatiently as though the question was unnecessary. "Where else would we be going?"

"Sorry, Sir. Just asking."

Bill leaned over and spoke softly to Ahmed. "Let me do the talking. Okay?"

"Sorry," Ahmed replied.

The Syrian Jeep started down the long driveway toward the exit and Ahmed accelerated to catch them. Sharp glanced at the sprawling city below the cliff that provided a measure of protection for the Palace. The wind had kicked dust into the air, clouding his view.

Bill heard Buck speak to his aide. "Melissa, hand me the briefing book, would you? SecState will want a report as soon as we get back to Brussels."

"Yes, Sir," she said.

As soon as the car reached its full speed between the Palace and the airport, Bill saw a disturbance ahead of them in the roadway. The Jeep in front of them began to brake.

"Slow down," Bill said, looking at Ahmed. "There's a traffic accident ahead."

The Jeep pulled close to the accident; a box truck lying on its side blocked the roadway. The soldiers climbed out to assist the truck driver who staggered around, dazed and bleeding. Ahmed stopped the limo a hundred yards back from the scene. Although the truck didn't appear to be on fire, smoke was coming up from underneath the hood. Two soldiers assisted the driver while another walked around the truck doing an inspection. A fourth soldier ran back to the Jeep and began talking on the radio.

Buck looked up from his briefing book. "What's the problem? Why are we stopping?" Bill looked back. "There's an overturned truck in the roadway. We should drive around it on the shoulder. Okay with you, Sir?"

Buck looked at his watch. "Go ahead. Let's get on the way."

Bill became nervous whenever he experienced something out of the ordinary. He turned his head side to side, studying the landscape for approaching danger. "Ahmed, do we have room to pull around on the shoulder?" Ahmed said nothing.

Bill rolled down his passenger window and stuck his head out to get a better look. In the distance, some yards away from the roadway amid the brush and trees, Bill watched two men stand up from behind a bush. One of the men rested a long cylindrical object on his shoulder. Bill turned toward the back seat. "We've got trouble.

Everyone duck down in the seat. Now!" Bill shouted. He quickly rolled up the window. "Get the hell out of here, Ahmed," Bill screamed. Ahmed made no attempt to drive away. The car sat motionless. "Ahmed!" Bill gave Ahmed a shove in the shoulder. Ahmed sat there looking straight ahead.

The man holding the object kneeled and pointed what looked to be a weapon at the Syrian Jeep. Bill recognized it and shouted, "Everyone down! Down! RPG!" as the men fired. The projectile screamed toward the Jeep leaving an exhaust trail behind it. A huge fireball of yellow and red enveloped both the truck and Jeep, followed by a thunderous sound. Metal shrapnel flew into the air in all directions. The blast threw the remains of the Jeep completely off the roadway. A wave of sound, fire and air hit the limo, lifting it off the ground and slamming it back down askance in the roadway. Large chunks of smoldering metal crashed against their vehicle, one large chunk glancing off the bulletproof windshield, putting a large crack across it. The occupants were thrown against the roof and landed hard on the floorboard as the limo dropped to the ground.

"Fuck!" Bill shouted, lifting his head to watch the aftermath. A second explosion, not as strong as the first, erupted and sent clouds of thick, black smoke into the air.

Bill ducked down again, then raised himself up and looked in the back seat. "Anyone hurt?" He waited. The occupants seemed to be in a state of shock, stunned and shaken. No one answered. "Is anyone hurt?" Bill asked more forcefully. Bill put his hand on Ahmed's shoulder and shook him. "Ahmed!" He waited a second, then repeated himself. "Ahmed! Is the car still running?"

Ahmed didn't answer. "Ahmed!" Bill shouted. "Is the car still running?"

Ahmed looked at the dashboard. "Yes."

"Get us the fuck out of here. Now!"

Ahmed pressed the accelerator and the car lurched forward, bare metal grinding on the pavement. Ahmed let up on the pedal.

"I think the tires are blown," Ahmed said.

"I don't give a shit. If it'll move, get us the fuck out of here," Bill shouted.

Ahmed pressed the accelerator and the car began to lurch forward. Ahmed aimed for the shoulder attempting to drive around the burning wreckage.

"I can't see where we're going."

"Drive, damn it!" Sharp pointed at the shoulder. "Get far enough off the road to get around the wreckage. If we hit anything, keep going. Move!" Bill put one hand on Ahmed's shoulder and the other on the dashboard to brace himself as Ahmed drove completely off the roadway, churning up dust and debris. The car tipped at a precarious angle as the wheels fell off the roadway, pushing large chunks of metal aside as it made its way around the burning mass of wreckage. Debris became lodged underneath the car and the grating sound caused Bill to wonder if they were even capable of getting to the airport. Bill glanced at the men who'd fired the RPG. They were running toward them with the weapon aimed at the car. "Get your ass going, Ahmed!"

Ahmed pulled back onto the roadway but could go no farther. He stopped, seeing a white pickup truck sitting sideways in the roadway blocking their path. A 50 caliber machine gun mounted in the bed of the truck was pointed straight at them. Four men in green military uniforms and black masks walked toward them with AK-47s pointed at the car. A fifth man, operating the machine gun, aimed it directly at the limo windshield. One of the men shouted in Arabic and pointed.

"They want us to get out of the car," Ahmed said.

"Your Harvard education help you figure that out?" Sharp asked, looking suspiciously at Ahmed. "Are you working with these guys?" Sharp pushed him in the shoulder. "How the fuck did they know we'd be here?" Sharp asked, raising his voice. Ahmed looked straight ahead and wouldn't answer.

Three of the masked men opened fire, pouring bursts of ammunition into the grill of the limo. Smoke appeared from underneath the hood and the engine died. The fourth man, who appeared to be their leader, walked to the passenger side, looked at Sharp and pounded on the window with the butt of his rifle. He shouted again, gesticulating with his hand. Bill glanced into the back seat. Buck, his assistant and interpreter were piled together on the floorboard. Melissa whimpered softly.

"They want us to get out of the car, Mr. Secretary," Bill said to Buck. He received no answer.

The leader pointed to the truck mounted machine gun. Bill watched the gunner prepare to fire and dove for the floorboard. He knew the limo's bulletproof glass would never hold up under large caliber ammunition fire. The men stepped away from the limo before the 50 caliber erupted, putting a burst of ammunition through the front windshield. The windows exploded sending glass shards and blood flying everywhere. Bill looked over and saw Ahmed's head was a mass of bone and blood, his body slumped over the steering wheel. "Bye, bye, you fucking martyr," he said. Bill peeked over the dashboard and saw the leader take the sidearm from his belt and walk to the passenger side of the limo. He kept shouting in Arabic which Bill couldn't understand, but the message was clear. Bill kicked at the door, finally opening it enough to exit. The leader pulled down the mask which covered his nose and mouth. He motioned with his sidearm at Bill and pointed toward the ground. Bill saw the toothless grin of his attacker. "Go see a dentist, you towel-headed motherfucker," Bill growled before someone hit him from behind with a rifle butt. Bill's knees buckled and he collapsed to the ground where the leader kicked him in the stomach.

Buck, his aide and the interpreter were forced from the limo, punched and kicked until they stopped struggling. All four were forced to the pavement, in a row on their knees facing the leader. The other masked men walked back and forth behind the group.

The leader nodded to his men and stepped aside. Bill heard the first pistol shot, so close that the sonic blast stung his ears. His head immediately ached, but that was the least of his problems. Even with his head bowed, he saw the splatter of blood on the ground in front of him. You fucking bastards. Acker, the interpreter, fell forward onto the ground and Bill stared at his limp body. The next shot was even closer and the force of the sound drilled through Bill's skull, but it was Melissa's limp body falling forward that caused Bill's anger.

Bill saw the shadow of the man who stepped behind him. He turned his head and looked into the man's eyes. "You better make sure I'm dead or I'll kill every last one of you motherfuckers," Bill hissed. He felt the blow to his head, then saw nothing. He struggled to remain conscious, but a second blow ended that hope.

Buck was hit over the head as well and knocked unconscious. Black bags with drawstrings were put over their heads, tightened in the fashion of a noose and their hands were tied behind them. Sharp and Buck were lifted up and thrown into the bed of the pickup. The masked men climbed in around them while the leader rode in the cab with the driver. Sharp regained consciousness briefly, bouncing around the truck bed as the vehicle drove straight across the desert toward the Lebanese border. I'm not dead. Buck must be alive, too. Sharp rose up slightly before being struck again in the head with a rifle butt. Everything went black as he slumped back onto the truck bed.

William Sharp, an American diplomat working out of the United States Embassy in Damascus, Syria, and Nicholas Buck, the Under Secretary for Political Affairs at the United States Department of State, were taken captive on Thursday, September 22nd, 1988.

# Chapter One

*Thursday, October 13, 1988, three weeks later*

STEVE TILTON, AN Associate Director for the Intelligence Directorate at the Central Intelligence Agency, left Dulles International Airport Thursday morning bound for Freeport, the largest city on Grand Bahama Island. Upon his arrival, he took a taxi to one of the beachfront resort hotels where he checked in under his real name. He had nothing to hide even though his trip was unannounced. Neither was the secret nature of his trip a concern. He was there to simply ask a question.

He deposited his bags in the room, an upper floor suite with a beautiful view of the ocean which he ignored. Tilton immediately left the room and took a different taxi through the small downtown area to a small office on Logwood Avenue. There was no signage on the white, one story brick building announcing the firm's name or what kind of business it conducted; none was needed. It wasn't the type of business that advertised its services. Those who needed the firm's assistance knew of it and those who didn't overlooked the quiet, unassuming business that operated out of the premises. It was quiet and unassuming because the office was merely a contact point for people seeking the services of the Security Associates of the Bahamas, a security firm with a clandestine mission.

Steve was the son of a prominent Boston area insurance executive and as a young man, had all the advantages of a privileged life. His family was politically well connected, he attended the best schools and he used his family connections to find employment in the CIA. It wasn't just family connections that made Steve successful, though. He turned out to be a brilliant man, someone whose ability to analyze data was only exceeded by his ability to manipulate the political environment he worked in. It helped, too, that he was attractive, tall with striking blue eyes, short gray hair and an award winning smile. He was what people referred to as one of the CIA's fair haired boys.

Tilton paused briefly in front of the building. Such a beautiful place. Well, not this block, but the island. Such a cliché she'd retire from CIA to a Caribbean island. She had always liked Key West. *I should have predicted she'd end up somewhere warm and sunny.*

The "she" in Steve's thoughts was Laura Messier, his former wife and one time field agent at the CIA. He'd divorced her in a fit of anger after some nasty business in Moscow the previous spring that had embarrassed Steve and nearly cost him his job. He'd not seen her since.

Steve wasn't sure he was in the right place; the building displayed no street number. He looked up and down the street wondering if the taxi had dropped him at the correct address. He tried peeking inside the thick glass window beside the door, but the blinds were shut. He pushed inward on the door and found it locked. Blinds on the inside of the door prevented a look inside. He thought about knocking, but found a sloppily painted over button mounted next to the door. He pushed it and heard the buzzing sound from somewhere inside. A pleasant feminine voice answered over a small speaker above the door. "Can I help you?"

"I'd like to speak with Jack Mason," Tilton said, looking above the door to speak into the microphone.

"Do you have an appointment?"

"No."

"Mr. Mason is unavailable."

"My name's Steven Tilton. He'll want to see me."

"One moment."

Steve stepped back from the door and looked around. He eyed the security cameras underneath the awnings. Good idea considering how many people want her dead, he thought.

Hearing the buzz over the intercom, he stepped to the door and pushed. It opened easily and he entered to find an office that smelled like freshly cut wood. The construction must be recent, he thought. The light brown interior with plush tan carpeting looked sparse. An attractive young woman sitting behind an L-shaped desk smiled and said, "Mr. Mason will be with you in a minute. Can I get you something to drink? Coffee? Soft drink?"

"No thanks."

Steve sat down in one of the plastic chairs that lined the room. The receptionist returned to her work and ignored him. The room was silent, except for the occasional sound of the woman typing.

Jack Mason was a retired CIA field agent who came to work for Laura Messier following the incident in Moscow. He'd become inadvertently drawn into the incident and decided later it was time for a change. He'd taken on too much risk over a distinguished thirty-five year career and at his age, nearly 60, enough was enough.

Jack appeared in the lobby a few minutes later. "Steve," he said smiling. "How the hell are you? It's been months."

The two men greeted each other warmly. "Retirement's treating you well, Jack. You look great."

"Come on; let's go back to my office."

Jack led him down the hallway and into the first office in a row of closed office doors. Steve noticed another security camera at the end of the hall. "Sit the hell down and tell me all the gossip out of D.C.," Jack said.

They sat in two chairs in front of Jack's desk, chairs that looked exactly like those in the lobby. A cheap steel desk painted green was piled with paperwork. Jack never was the office type. A field man, through and through. Steve quickly glanced around Jack's office. No windows. Just a small cubbyhole in a non-descript building with no street address. Good cover. The walls were painted white, much like the exterior of the building. The carpet in the building looked new. They haven't been here long, Steve thought. The only distinguishing aspect about the room was the photos of Jack standing beside four different Presidents of the United States. Damn impressive. How many people can say they stood next to four presidents?

Steve spread his arms out and smiled after sitting down. "Nothing much to tell, Jack. Just the same shit over and over every day. You know how it is."

Jack smiled at that. "It's good to know nothing changes. Your visit is interesting timing. Moldova's here."

Steve's body became tense and his eyes narrowed. "Leo Moldova?" he asked with an element of surprise in his voice.

"The same. I thought you boys would have known about it. He's out at the compound meeting with Laura right now."

Leo Moldova was one of the Assistant Directors of the KGB.

"They want their plane back," Steve said as though it was obvious.

"That's my guess," Jack said flatly.

Laura had arranged the defection of the head of the Soviet Navy during the incident in Moscow. Admiral Arkady Tonov commandeered a jet which they used to escape the country. It ended up in Laura's possession and she refused to return it. The $50,000 bribe that had been paid to the Head of the Soviet Civil Aviation Department to sign a receipt for the Dassault Falcon 50 jet aircraft came from a joint account Steve held with Laura. The jet was worth millions.

"There's more to the story here, Jack."

Jack laughed at that. He knew exactly what Steve was referring to. "Relax Steve, no one will ever know. Forget about it."

That assurance did nothing to ease Steve's worry. "It wasn't a legal transaction, Jack."

"Not that the Soviets ever cared about legalities," Jack replied.

It's my ass on the line here, Steve thought.

"Laura kicked their asses and they're still pissed off about it. As it happens, the plane isn't even on the island at the moment. It was pointless for Moldova to come."

Steve shook his head back and forth in disgust. "I would imagine the discussion could get confrontational."

18

"You used to love that about her if my memory's correct. If you're not here to talk about Moldova, what brings you to our neck of the woods?"

Steve leaned forward and looked straight at Jack. "Nicholas Buck," he said softly.

Jack looked down at the carpet and fell silent. When he spoke, it was almost imperceptible. "Nasty piece of work that was," he said slowly. "The Syrians got caught with their pants down. Us, too." Jack looked up at Steve. "He's probably dead by now, Steve."

"We don't think so."

"Wasn't there someone else taken as well?"

"Yes, an embassy employee."

Jack looked at Steve with the skeptical look of a customer at a used car lot. "Why would you think he's still alive?"

"Buck knows things. It would take time to debrief him."

Jack gave Steve a look of disbelief. "You mean torture him, don't you?"

Steve gave Jack a blank administrative stare that betrayed no emotion. "Yes."

Jack looked at the white brick wall, thinking. They can't find him. He considered what the conversation meant. After a moment, he looked back at Steve. "What makes you think she'll help her ex-husband?"

"This is business, Jack."

"She's not going to look at it that way. I don't mean to get between the two of you, but you should have never divorced her, not over the Russian mission."

"She went on an unauthorized mission that resulted in the deaths of seven people. It amounted to a clandestine attack on the Soviet Union. The diplomatic ramifications were a nightmare. The only reason she's not in prison is the Attorney General stepped in to stop the prosecution. You know how strict the CIA is. I was told to either resign or divorce her."

Jack gave Steve a look of disbelief. "That prosecution was bullshit, Steve. It was a French mission. Why didn't you tell CIA to go fuck themselves?"

"Because I'd have lost my job and I'd be back in Boston selling insurance. This is my career, Jack."

There was silence in the room for a moment before Jack leaned forward and lowered his voice. "You don't go against your family, Steve. I don't think she'll ever get over it."

At that point, Steve looked like an attorney on the verge of losing his case. "Look, I'm not here representing myself; CIA Director Bates sent me. Buck's kidnapping has national security implications. She has the standing necessary in the Muslim world to find him. She may be the only person who can."

"Langley must be pretty desperate to send you down here. You're the last person she wants to see."

"I'm hoping we can lay our personal feelings aside, Jack. We've got no leads, none. There's been no claim of responsibility and the Syrians have no clue what happened. The political pressure in D.C. is mounting so, yes, I'd say we're desperate."

Jack took his time considering Steve's words. When he finally spoke, he shook his head. "About Buck, you may be wasting your time. Some militia group has him up in the mountains somewhere. He'll probably never be found alive. Having said that, if anyone can find him, it's Laura

Messier. She's really good, as you know. But you've got a big hill to climb to persuade her to help. She's not going to be able to separate business from her personal life with you. You're asking a lot."

"I'd like to try. Would you make the call?"

Jack stared at his friend again before he made his decision. "She might be able to use your assistance with Moldova. The more political muscle he sees, the sooner that conniving little bastard will go away. If you're willing to help with Moldova, perhaps she'll listen to what you have to say about Buck. I'll make the call."

Jack leaned over his desk, turned the phone around and dialed the number. Steve could only hear one side of the conversation.

"Rick, I need to speak with Laura."

Steve assumed Jack was speaking with Rick Williams, another CIA employee who left the agency to help Laura start her business.

"I know she's in a meeting, damn it." Jack got irritated and raised his voice. "I'm telling you I need to speak with her." After another moment's wait, Jack said, "Steve's here. Tell her Steve's here." This time his follow-up was instant. "Tilton. Who the hell do you think I mean." He put his hand over the mouthpiece and spoke to Steve. "Hang on Steve. It'll be a minute." Jack waited several minutes, then spoke again.

"Rick, I'm bringing him out to the compound. She should hear what he has to say." Another wait. Jack raised his voice again. "Jesus Christ, Rick, of course I pre-interviewed him. Put Jean on the phone." Steve knew Jack meant Jean Broussard, the former French Intelligence man who was Laura's partner. "Okay, don't put Jean on the goddamn phone. I'm bringing him out. End of story."

Jack slammed down the phone receiver, looked at Steve and smiled. "That went well."

"I take it she doesn't want to see me?"

Jack smiled. "Let's wait a few minutes before we drive out there."

The receptionist stuck her head inside the door. "Mr. Mason, you've got another call."

"Thanks, Maria. Can you bring Mr. Tilton something to drink?"

"Of course," she said.

Jack rose. "Steve, I'm going to take this call in another room. Wait here and I'll be back in a minute."

"Soft drink or coffee. What would you like?" the receptionist asked.

"Diet Coke would be fine."

"Coming right up."

When Jack returned, he sat behind his desk and looked at his watch. "Before we go out to the compound, I've got a question for you." He leaned forward and put both elbows on the desk and folded his hands in front of him.

"Can you find out if there are any Soviet subs in the vicinity?"

Steve thought for a minute. "I suppose I could. Why do you want to know?"

"One of our locals took his fishing boat out this morning and saw something strange in the water. He said it looked like a depth marker, except it was black; it swiveled back and forth and had a glass lens on top of it. That sounds like a periscope."

"You suspect Moldova brought some company?"

Jack leaned back in his chair. "I don't think it's a coincidence."

"You got a phone I can use?" Steve asked.

Jack pushed the desk phone toward Steve. "Use this one."

"You record anything in here?"

"No. You need a scrambler?"

"No. I do need some privacy, though."

"I'll go grab a cup of coffee. Come back to the kitchen when you're finished. Last room down the hall."

After his call, Steve found Jack in the kitchen making sandwiches. "Turkey with Swiss okay?" Jack asked.

"Sure."

"One of the perks of the job. Free lunches. That's more than I ever got at CIA." Jack set two sandwiches and chips down at a folding table pushed next to the wall. "What'd you find out?"

"Akula class," Steve said as he sat. "We believe it to be the Bratsk. It entered Bahamian waters yesterday. It's being trailed by the Los Angeles class Buffalo. The information is twelve hours old."

"Interesting timing don't you think?"

"I do."

"Could they launch a special ops team?"

"I'm not an expert on subs, Jack."

"Steve, I've got to place another call. I'll be right back. How's the sandwich, by the way?"

Steve looked up and smiled. "Anytime I get a free sandwich, Jack, I'm not about to complain."

Jack walked back to his office, shut the door and placed a call to a small computer repair shop in San Jose, California. "JP Computing, can I help you?"

"Postl? It's Mason. Do you still have your backdoor into the CIA mainframe?"

"Sure. What do you need?"

"I need an order for documents. The request must come from Steven Tilton, Associate Director. I need copies of all relevant material on a man named Nicholas Buck. Have the material sent by courier to National Airport by 9:00 a.m. tomorrow morning. Address the package to the attention of Island Airlines and leave it at the counter in the private aircraft terminal."

"I'll do it right away."

The next call was placed to the St. Pete-Clearwater Airport in Florida.

"Island Airlines, Svetlana speaking."

"Svetlana? It's Jack Mason. I need a favor."

"Hello Mr. Mason."

"A package will be waiting at National Airport tomorrow morning at 9:00 a.m. It'll be at the counter in the private terminal. I need Dmitri to fly it down here. It's urgent, otherwise I wouldn't ask."

"Hang on a moment." Svetlana returned to the phone a couple of minutes later. "I talked with Dmitri. You'll have the package by noon tomorrow."

"Thanks."

Jack returned to the kitchen a couple of minutes later. "You ready?" he asked Steve. "Let's go out there now." Jack paused for a moment. "Hang on a minute. I've got to tell the secretary we're leaving."

Jack walked to the front of the building. "Maria, I'm taking our visitor out to the compound. I may be gone the rest of the day. Don't let anyone in the building."

"Yes, Sir," Maria said.

"No one," Jack said sharply. He watched as concern settled on her face. "Nothing to worry about, Maria. Just don't let anyone in."

"What do I do if someone buzzes?"

"Don't answer."

Jack began to walk away and thought better of it. He turned around. "Take the rest of the day off, Maria. After we've gone, lock the place and go out the back," he said with a feigned smile.

Maria knew that look. There could be trouble on the way, she thought.

Jack walked back to the kitchen. "I'm parked in back, Steve. Let's go out the back door."

Four parking stalls were behind the building next to a dumpster. Jack's car, an old red Triumph Spitfire, was the only car parked there. Jack had parked it over two spaces to prevent another car from coming close to his baby.

"Geez, Jack, what a great car. A Triumph, isn't it?" Steve asked, walking around to the passenger side, inspecting the car with a measure of admiration.

Jack beamed at Steve's praise. "Yep, a '76 Spit. Bought her as soon as I got here. She runs like a bat out of hell."

"Damn. Retirement's treating you well."

"I figured as long as I was living in a British Commonwealth country, I should have one of their roadsters," Jack said as he climbed in. The top was already down and Steve had a notion to lift his leg over the door, but didn't. He squeezed himself into the seat and looked for seatbelts. "If you're looking for belts, this one never had 'em. What the hell; it's time to live a little."

The engine fired up, Jack revved it a few times and backed out of the parking spot. "I've seen you drive, Jack. It's a wonder you're still alive."

Jack smiled at the banter. "No worries. It isn't like D.C. down here. There won't be much traffic on the way out."

It was a beautiful day on the island, sunny and warm, without a cloud in the sky. Jack accelerated to full speed once they got out of the city and the only traffic eastbound was an occasional construction vehicle which Jack passed easily.

"Lots of construction going on over here on the East End," Jack said, passing another truck. He pointed toward the southern coast. "People buying up coastline and building homes."

"I can see why. It's beautiful."

"Nassau's pretty much already developed. It won't be long until this entire area's developed, too," Jack said waving his arm back and forth.

Traveling east past High Rock and then a large oil terminal, Jack slowed and turned right onto an unmarked road. "You've never been out here, have you?" Jack asked looking over at Steve.

"No, this is the first time."

"Laura and Jean bought a couple hundred acres between the road and the ocean. I don't know what they paid for it, but it must have cost a fortune."

"I'll bet."

Jack pulled up to the guard house where two local police cars and one black government sedan were being checked through the gate. The gate was a long steel bar that lowered over the driveway, operated electronically from inside a guard shack. One guard stood inside the shack while another stood outside and checked identification. "Jean brought his staff over from Paris," Jack said, pointing to the guards. "Twelve ex-military. The place is pretty damn secure."

"Impressive," Steve said, looking at the security fencing that ran in both directions.

Jack pulled the car up to the gate. "Good afternoon, Paul."

"Who do you have with you today, Mr. Mason?"

"Steve Tilton, CIA."

The guard bent over and looked at Steve through the driver's side window. He turned and gave a thumbs up sign to the guard in the shack. "Go ahead, Mr. Mason." The bar raised and Jack drove through. Once through the gate, they quickly caught up to the police cars slowly moving up the drive. Jack had to slam on the brakes. "Come on people. Move it," he said to no one.

"What's that?" Steve asked, nodding at a one story building with a small parking lot in front. "Looks new."

"That's the barracks for the full-timers. Pretty nice. Most of them live there."

They passed another large building with utility vehicles parked in front. It had a garage door style opening. Jack nodded toward it as they passed. "That's Rick's area. He keeps all his construction toys there. It's also the armory."

"Nice," Steve said.

"I don't know if you can see it, but behind the garage is the firing range and training area." Steve looked back as they passed the building. "Takes a lot of money to keep this place running."

"I'd imagine so."

"Not many private facilities like this one."

They arrived at the main house, a large two story home, painted white, with a porch that ran the length of the structure and wrapped around the sides. It reminded Steve of the old colonial style buildings in Key West.

They parked in the circle drive behind the police cars and watched the occupants in the black sedan exit the vehicle and walk toward the house. "She's pulling out all the big guns today," Jack said, nodding toward a tall man in light brown slacks and a flowered print shirt. "That's the Prime Minister." They watched Rick Williams hold the door for Sir Edmund Davies. "Now, it's our turn," Jack said, opening the car door. Jack and Steve slipped inside the front door.

The entire group stood in the foyer where Rick towered over everyone else. Standing at 6'5" with a huge frame, he looked every bit like the Marine officer he formerly was. He motioned them forward. "We're meeting in the conference room." Rick led the visitors down a hallway to the rear of the house and into a room that doubled as a dining area. A long table with eight chairs stood in the middle. "Everyone, please take a seat," Jean said, gesturing toward the table.

Sitting on one side of the oblong table was Leo Moldova and his interpreter. Laura and Jean Broussard sat at one end. The Prime Minister and his aide sat opposite Moldova and Steve Tilton sat at the other end of the table. Rick Williams and Jack Mason stood against the wall near the door.

She's unbelievably beautiful, Steve thought, seeing Laura for the first time in months. More attractive than I've ever seen her. She's been growing out her hair. With light brown hair that fell below her shoulders, she wore a flowered halter top, yellow shorts and sandals. Steve noticed that Laura completely ignored him. She's still pissed off.

The Russians were immediately outnumbered. The Prime Minister sent a clear message of disrespect by failing to acknowledge Moldova. Davies had a commanding presence and took control of the meeting, looking straight at the Russian. "Mr. Moldova, I'm Sir Edmund Davies, the Prime Minister of The Commonwealth of the Bahamas. Your presence in our country is unannounced. The Soviet Union's interests are represented by the Swiss Consulate in Nassau and they have no record of your arrival. Please state your business in the Commonwealth."

Moldova, a small man with a receding hairline and an intense manner, whispered to his interpreter. It was his interpreter who spoke across the table. "This is a private matter, Mr. Prime Minister."

"A private matter?" Davies asked rhetorically. "You land a Soviet government aircraft in my country and call it a 'private matter'? Mr. Moldova, you're welcome to come to the Bahamas on a commercial flight and enjoy our great weather and beautiful beaches as a private citizen. However, if you land a government aircraft inside our jurisdiction, it's official business. I apologize for being so direct, but I insist that you state your business."

The interpreter whispered to Moldova who spoke softly in return. The interpreter spoke again to Davies. "We are here to discuss the matter of a stolen jet aircraft in the possession of Laura Messier that we wish returned to the Soviet Union."

Davies opened a briefcase he carried with him. He withdrew a file and set the briefcase back on the floor. He opened the file and slid a piece of paper across the table. "You mean this aircraft?"

Moldova picked up the paper and studied it. "Yes. This is it," he said in English.

"I'm amazed that you've suddenly learned English, Mr. Moldova. According to the laws of the Commonwealth, this aircraft," Davies said, jabbing at the paper with his finger, "is legitimately owned by Laura Messier and properly registered in the Bahamas."

"Mr. Prime Minister, pardon the interruption. I'm Steven Tilton, Associate Director of the CIA. Would you mind if I spoke?" Steve asked.

"Please, go ahead," Davies said with a nod.

Steve addressed Moldova in a hostile tone of voice. "Assistant Director Moldova, the aircraft you've referred to is properly registered with the Federal Aviation Administration in the United States and its ownership by Laura Messier is beyond dispute."

"I see," Moldova said indignantly.

"There is another matter to discuss," Steve continued.

Both Davies and Moldova stared at Tilton.

"Go on, Director Tilton," Davies said.

"As of noon yesterday, an Akula class Soviet submarine we believe to be the Bratsk was spotted inside the twelve mile nautical limit in the territorial waters of the Commonwealth of the Bahamas. The sub is being trailed by a United States Los Angeles class sub and we have a Navy destroyer steaming toward the sub as we speak. Our intent is to force the sub to the surface and board her."

Davies became visibly upset and slammed his hand on the table. "Mr. Moldova, we will not tolerate a violation of the sovereign territory of the Bahamas. The Law of the Seas grants the right of safe passage for vessels to pass through our Economic Zone, but does not give them the right to encroach inside our territorial waters without the expressed permission to dock at Nassau. No request has been made, nor permission granted. Get the hell out of our country, Mr. Moldova, or I will give the United States permission to take whatever action they deem necessary to defend our territorial waters. And, I'll have you arrested and charged with espionage. I suggest you accompany our local constables back to Freeport International Airport and leave the country within one hour. Do you understand?"

Moldova's face turned a bright red. He hesitated for a moment.

"Mr. Moldova, I expect an immediate answer," Davies yelled.

Moldova pushed his chair away from the table and simply said, "Yes." He and his interpreter rose to leave. Jean motioned toward Rick, "Rick, would you be kind enough to escort Mr. Moldova to his car?"

"I'd be happy to." Rick stood and gestured to Moldova. "This way, please."

Moldova and his interpreter were turned over to the custody of the local police outside the house and Rick watched as they exited the driveway.

# Chapter Two

*Friday, October 14, 1988*

STEVE TILTON AWOKE the following morning to the sound of the ocean through the open sliding door. Both Steve and Jack stayed at the compound overnight and took upstairs bedrooms on the ocean side. The double decked porch on the back side offered a spectacular view. For the first time in months, Steve was at peace. He stepped out onto the porch and caught a glimpse of the water on the horizon beyond the trees. Just like Key West, he thought. You never appreciate those times until they're gone.

Steve found Jack in the kitchen helping himself to a breakfast spread laid out on the table. "It's self-serve around here, Steve. Dig in," Jack said, between mouthfuls of eggs, potatoes and ham. "Juice is on the counter." He pointed to the coffee pot. "Coffee's over there."

"Where is everyone?"

"Jean made a run back downtown."

"Where's ..." Jack interrupted him.

"She's down at the beach, Steve," he said flatly, as though it were none of Steve's business.

Jack gave Steve a hard, cold stare. It was an embarrassing moment between the two.

"I think I'll take a walk down to the beach."

"You do that," Jack said coldly. Steve stiffened at the remark. Jack saw the reaction and reconsidered his tone. "Look, I'm sorry. I shouldn't have said it that way. We're

32

just a little protective of her. That's all." Jack pointed toward the back door with his fork. "Go ahead."

"Okay," Steve said quietly. He left through the kitchen door and searched until he found the path to the beach.

The path wound its way through thick tropical foliage, its route through the underbrush designed to spare the larger plants and trees. In a few places, the foliage grew over top the path to make a canopy. Bird calls pierced the air as he walked, giving Steve the impression he'd entered another world. And then there was the ever louder sound of the ocean. Traveling what he thought was about halfway, he found a hut with screened windows and a thatched roof that looked to be newly constructed in a style that was reminiscent of what he judged might be a South Pacific native hut from a long ago century. He entered the screen door and found a bed, chair and end table made entirely of cane. A lantern rested on the end table. Steve looked at the books stacked on the table. Mostly history and philosophy.

"Vixen! Stop!"

Steve recognized Rick's voice and exited the hut where he came face to face with a snarling Doberman Pinscher. Steve froze.

"Vixen! Stop girl! He's okay. Sit!" The dog sat down, but her muscles quivered and gave Steve the impression she'd strike if he made any movement at all.

Rick came up the path from the opposite direction and petted the dog.

"Sorry, Steve. I heard someone coming down the path, but Vixen got the jump on me."

"That's one hell of a security system you guys have," Steve said.

"She's got four of them. Gives them the run of the place. I'd hate to be an intruder and run into one of these," he said with a chuckle, looking down at the dog.

"Scared the shit out of me."

"Yeah, I know. They scare the bejesus out of all of us. Come on," Rick said, gesturing down the path. "I'll take you down to the beach." The path was wide enough for only one, so they walked single file with the dog following, swaying its head back and forth as though it was searching for prey.

The two men knew each other well and were comfortable in each other's presence. Their conversation seemed to belie the fact that they hadn't seen each other in months.

"It's quiet here," Steve said. "I can't hear much, except the birds and the ocean."

"You get used to it. The underbrush blocks the sound from the highway. Sometimes we hear horns from tourist ships pulling out of Freeport on their way to Nassau, but other than that, the only sound we hear is Dmitri on his approach to the airstrip across the road." Dmitri Polzin was Laura's pilot who escaped the Soviet Union along with Arkady Tonov.

"I've seen sat photos of the strip. Pretty nice."

"The government leased it to us and in return, we gave them landing rights. We refinished the runway when we arrived. It must have cost her a fortune, but it's damn convenient to have access to the plane in minutes."

The men walked out of the underbrush onto the wide beach, pausing at the edge. Other than a few spots of seaweed here and there, the beach was picture perfect. The gentle waves washed upon sand that looked as clean as anything Steve had seen in a photo. Near the water, Laura stood facing an old man, both of them wearing white robes and black belts. Laura was blindfolded.

Rick and Steve stood and watched. "She flies these martial arts specialists in from New York," Rick said. "She's taken to working out blindfolded.

The combatants walked around each other, gauging distance and position, stalking each other. An occasional flurry of punches would erupt, the old man would attack while Laura would give ground, then they'd stop and the two would begin stalking each other again.

"She's the best in the world, isn't she," Steve said staring at Laura.

"Some say she can't be defeated. The Olympic Committee tried to get her to participate in the Taekwondo competition at the games, but she turned them down. She'd have easily won the gold in either the men's or women's division."

Watching Laura, Steve gradually became aware that this wasn't the woman he knew back in D.C. She was different and Steve was at a loss as to how to explain it. The concern showed on his face. "How is she, Rick?"

Rick looked at Steve and understood his meaning. He waited before he spoke as though struggling to put his thoughts into words. "She isn't doing well." Rick paused again, unconsciously scratching his chin. "She's sort of withdrawn from everyone and everything, Steve. She spends a lot of her time alone in that hut back there."

"What's wrong?"

Rick leaned against the nearest tree and thought for a moment. "Hell, I don't know. I'm not a shrink. Maybe the Ilitch killings did something to her. She's been different ever since. That and the divorce."

Laura had gone to Moscow to stop the KGB's top assassination team. She killed four men, then three more at the airport before escaping the country.

Steve grimaced at hearing that. He looked at the ground. Rick saw his reaction.

"I'm sorry, Steve. I didn't mean it that way."

"I know what you meant."

"Look, I understand why you divorced her. She just still loves you, that's all. You may be the only man she's ever loved."

Hearing that, Steve looked away to avoid being seen with emotion in his eyes. He finally said, "I miss her."

Rick tilted his head toward Steve and changed the subject. "Jack told me this morning why you're here. Jean's going to be back this afternoon. I think we're planning to discuss it over dinner."

"I have to get back to D.C. in the morning. I'll need an answer by then."

Rick stood up straight and put his hands in his pockets. He seemed to adopt an administrative tone. "Just so you know, Jean will run the meeting this evening. She lets him do the administrative stuff." He shook his head and shrugged. "She probably won't say much. She's become unpredictable." Rick suddenly relaxed as his comments became personal again. "We've done two missions since we started and Laura's not gone on either of them."

"She'll have to do this one. She may be the only one who can."

"Jean said the same thing this morning. Who knows, maybe it'll bring her back to reality."

"It's a tough mission," Steve said.

Rick chuckled and gave Steve a wry smile. "Aren't they all?"

# Chapter Three

IN HER EARLY thirties, Laura still looked exactly as she had on the runways of Paris and New York as a fashion model. Wearing a white bikini over which she draped a white chiffon wrap, she moved around the table with the grace of an angel, putting her hand on an arm here, a shoulder there, as she leaned between the men to set bowls and platters of food on the table. Laura insisted on serving dinner herself, eschewing the help of an older woman who served the compound. She's one of the most beautiful women I've ever seen, Steve thought. So talented; one of God's special people.

Dinner was served on the back porch at dusk. The fading sunlight gradually gave way to the soft light of the suspended lanterns that gave the porch an intimate, relaxed feel. After a leisurely dinner of roast chicken, vegetables and salad served family style, Laura topped off the meal with strawberry shortcake and whipped cream. She was silent during the meal, preferring to attend to the needs of those she entertained. She seemed to defer to Jean who drove the conversation, acknowledging each person by asking questions and engaging in small talk. After she'd cleared the table and served coffee, Jean said, "Shall we get down to business?"

"Yes, definitely," Jack said.

Steve had the feeling it was his turn to speak. He looked around the table at the familiar faces. Jack Mason, Rick Williams, Jean Broussard and Laura were all trusted friends. He'd never met Pierre Thibault until this evening. Thibault looked to be in his mid-forties, with a muscular build, dark hair and eyes that darted quickly from person to person. He looked like he could take care of himself in a fight. Thibault was quiet during dinner, seemingly content to listen to conversation rather than participate in it. Jean put both elbows on the table, folded his hands in front of him and leaned forward.

"You have a proposal for us, Steve?"

"Yes, but I need to share classified information." He addressed Pierre. "I'm sorry, Sir. I'm not familiar with you." Pierre began to speak, but Laura waved him off.

"Pierre is our Lebanon expert, Steve. He came to us from Jean's staff in Paris. He's French ex-military, survived the barracks bombing in '83 and has traveled extensively in the country. How long were you stationed there, Pierre?" she asked.

"Two years, Ma'am."

"He's a trusted friend and ally, Steve. Cut the horseshit and tell us why you're here."

She has changed, Steve thought. She's as cold as ice. "As you probably know," he began tentatively, looking around the table, "two Americans were kidnapped three weeks ago in Damascus, Syria. Nicholas Buck is the Under Secretary for Political Affairs at the State Department and William Sharp is a State Department employee working out of the embassy in Damascus. We've been unable to find them."

Pierre looked at Laura. "Would you mind, Ma'am, if I said something?"

"Please, Pierre. Speak your mind. You know the area better than any of us."

"Monsieur Tilton, there were people killed in the abduction, yes?" Pierre asked in heavily French accented English.

"That's right. There were three. Buck's aide Melissa Clarke, Buck's interpreter Harry Acker, and the driver, a Syrian who worked for the embassy."

"Aren't you forgetting the other Syrians who were killed," Jean said sharply. "I assure you Assad hasn't forgotten."

"Yes, of course," Steve replied, somewhat embarrassed at the omission. "Four Syrian guards accompanying the group were also killed."

"Is that it?" Laura asked pointedly.

Steve wasn't sure what she meant, so he looked directly at her and replied, "Yes."

"Aren't you leaving out the truck driver whose truck blocked the road?"

That question caused Steve to hesitate. She knows more than she's saying. Steve looked down at the table. "I'm sorry. I neglected to include him."

"Why?"

"We can't confirm his identity."

"What you mean is the Syrians aren't giving you that information."

Steve hesitated so Laura continued. "The Syrians have blocked you from information you need to run a decent investigation. Is that correct?"

Steve wasn't accustomed to being so severely questioned. "Yes," he replied tersely.

"Let me ask you this," Laura continued. "Did you bring pictures of the scene where the attack took place?"

"No," Steve said defensively, sounding as though he was unprepared for this line of questioning.

Laura glanced at Jean. "Jean?"

Jean reached into the briefcase beside his chair and withdrew four photos. He slid them across the table. "Can you confirm this as the scene of the attack?"

Steve's eyes grew wide open as he studied the photos. "Where did you get these?"

Laura ignored the question. "What about statements from eyewitnesses who saw the escape vehicle. Reports seem to indicate it headed westbound on the Damascus-Beirut Highway. Is that correct, Jean?"

"Yes, that's our information. Are you in a position to confirm that, Steve?"

"Those are the reports we've gotten."

"Did you bring those reports?" Laura asked in tone a prosecutor might use.

"No, I didn't," Steve said, shocked at the animosity in her voice.

"Why not?"

"Because the file is classified."

Laura looked at Jean again. "Jean?" Broussard reached into his briefcase, withdrew a thick file and laid it on the table.

"You mean this file?" she asked.

Jean pushed the file across the table. Steve thumbed through its contents. He looked at Laura with anger in his face.

"How did you get this?" he asked sharply, pointing to the file.

"CIA isn't the only organization capable of clandestine activities, Steve." Laura followed that comment with something spoken in French. Jean smiled at her comment.

"By stealing this file, you committed a federal crime," Steve said sharply.

"Is that a threat?" Laura asked raising her voice. She rose and slowly walked around the table in the same stalking manner she used in her martial arts workout earlier in the day. Rick recognized it immediately and stepped in front of her. "Stop it!"

"Get out of my way, Rick, or I'll put you down," she hissed.

"No, you won't. What you're doing is wrong. Take a seat." Laura checked herself and sat down, but she was furious.

Jean, who remained calm during the exchange, merely smiled. "Monsieur Tilton, if we were able to obtain this file so easily, would it be difficult to imagine that Buck's meeting was leaked in advance?"

"Leaks are a separate issue," Steve replied.

"I don't mean to contradict you, Monsieur Tilton, but the issues are linked," Jean continued. "Any plans for a rescue could be leaked as well.

Rick Williams laid his hand on Steve's arm. "We're only trying to make sure no one gets killed in a rescue attempt. We assume that's why you're here, right?"

Steve leaned forward and spoke to Jean. "We never found the ambassador kidnapped in '85. He turned up dead a few months later, his body thrown in a ditch outside Beirut. This time," he said looking around the table, "we're going to send a clear message to those who would harm our diplomatic personnel. We're going to find our people and prosecute the criminals. You have sources that are not available to us. If you can help us find them, we'd appreciate it. As for a rescue, we can do that ourselves."

Laura began to speak, but Jean stopped her. "Please, allow me, Mademoiselle."

"Okay, go ahead," she said bitterly.

"That's your proposal, Monsieur Tilton? You want us to assist you in locating your people?"

"Yes," Steve said emphatically. He nodded toward Laura. "She may be able to locate these people using her own sources. Once we have that information, we'll take it to the Pentagon and plan a rescue. And we need your answer quickly."

"Oh, you'll get a quick answer," Laura said in anger as though she'd heard enough. "Go fuck yourself!"

Jean put his hand on her arm. "Mademoiselle, please."

"Sorry. Go ahead."

Jean turned back to Steve. "You must understand that our sources aren't exactly friends. Let's just say their interests and ours are aligned from time to time. If they provide us with information that your government uses to mount a military style rescue, our sources would become enemies. We'd be unable to pursue any further work in the region."

"Are you willing to sit by and allow our diplomats to be tortured and killed?" an astonished Steve Tilton asked.

"Sure," Laura said with a shrug.

Jean intervened again, this time forcefully. "Mademoiselle!"

Laura sat back in her chair, looking away as though she'd heard enough, but she allowed him to continue.

"Monsieur Tilton, you ignore the political nuances of the region," Jean continued. "The perpetrators of this crime do not consider themselves criminals. They see themselves as patriots. They have the support of the community who hides them. Here's what that means in real terms. The entire population will resist you if you attempt a rescue."

Steve started to speak, but Jean raised his hand. "Forgive me, Monsieur Tilton, please allow me to finish." Jean turned to Rick. "Rick, would you mind informing Mr. Tilton what a rescue might look like in a sovereign territory where the United States has no assets?"

Rick was a former Marine Captain with combat experience. Trained at Quantico, he'd served as the Commander of the Marine Guard unit at the American Embassy in Paris before joining the CIA. No one doubted his expertise in military ground operations. "Sure," he replied to Jean. Steve," he began politely, "any rescue the Pentagon might execute would use special ops personnel. You might be able to gather the information you need beforehand from sat data, but there'd be many unknowns. Most likely, the hostages would be moved or killed before you reached them and the entire population would fight when you arrived. With so many Syrian troops in the country, you could end up fighting Syrian regulars."

Jack spoke with the inflection of a friend giving advice. "Steve, there's only one way to rescue those hostages. Go in there as friends. It must be someone the kidnappers trust."

"That is her value," Jean said nodding at Laura. "She's got standing in that community as you well know. She could bring those hostages out with a minimum of casualties and honestly, at the end of the day, her actions could be seen in the Muslim world as a humanitarian gesture. Everyone could claim a victory."

Steve thought for a couple of minutes and the group allowed him time. Others had come before them seeking solutions in difficult circumstances. He looked down at the paperwork on the table, struggling to phrase his words without provoking further argument. "The United States government will never waive its right to rescue those hostages," he finally said.

"We're not asking the United States to waive any rights, Monsieur Tilton," Jean replied. "If you're seeking our help, we're simply asking you to stand aside and allow us to work without interference."

"That's the answer you'd like me to give to Bill?" Steve referred to Bill Bates, the Director of the CIA.

"If you're serious about enlisting our aid, we'll give you a document to take to your Director," Jean said. "It will outline the conditions under which we're willing to help. We insist that the knowledge of this proposal be limited to those who need to know. With all due respect, we need to avoid security lapses. We've taken the liberty of checking you out of the hotel. The rest of your belongings were brought to the compound and you'll stay here this evening. Dmitri is bringing the plane back to the island in the morning and he'll fly you back to Washington."

Steve understood the security issue, something he managed on a daily basis. Bates had authorized an internal investigation into leaks at the State Department and CIA regarding the Buck meeting. He nodded his head in the affirmative.

"I'll take the document back to Washington and you'll have the Director's decision tomorrow," he said.

Now, can we all relax and enjoy the rest of the evening?" Jack asked. "Rick, why don't you and I go down to the beach, get a bonfire going and get drunk. You coming with us, Steve?"

Rick rose and slapped Steve on the back with a smile. "Come on, Steve. Just like old times."

Steve felt the tension drain away. She won't be involved, he thought. "Give me a minute to change."

"Pierre, you in?" Rick asked.

"Someone's got to keep you guys out of trouble," he said. "I'll meet you down there. I've got to go back to my quarters first."

The group went their separate ways, each left to his or her thoughts, content to leave the work ahead for another day.

# Chapter Four

*Saturday, October, 15, 1988*

CIA DIRECTOR BILL Bates drove in from home on Saturday to meet Steve and learn the result of his trip. He leaned back in his chair and studied the contract Jean had given Steve. "This agreement's a joke," he said, briefly looking up at Tilton who sat in front of Bates' desk. "It contains none of the protections the feds need. This couldn't make it through a GSA audit." He paused a second, throwing the agreement on his desk. "Hell, it wouldn't even pass muster with our people downstairs. Who the hell does she think she is?"

Tilton didn't know quite what to say so he said nothing.

Bates leaned over his desk, put his elbows on the desktop and rubbed his face. "Can she even find Buck?" he asked looking up at Tilton.

Tilton scratched his head wondering how to answer. "Hell, Bill, how would I know?"

"To even consider this, I've got to kick it upstairs. Five million isn't something that can be overlooked. They want to know today?" he asked in disbelief.

"A signature and 2.5 mil today."

Bates got a mischievous grin on his face. "You say they've got their plane waiting at National?"

"The pilot's hanging out in the terminal right now waiting for a signed contract and a wire transfer form."

"Let's impound their plane as collateral," he said with a smile, leaning back in his chair.

Steve grimaced. "Let's not, Bill. She's got the AG over at Justice protecting her."

"Who? Middleton?" Ron Middleton was the Attorney General of the United States. "He's a fucking idiot," Bates said with disgust, rolling his eyes.

Middleton protected Laura last spring after the Moscow incident. "He might be an idiot, but he's an important idiot." Tilton waited a few seconds before continuing. "Here's the way I see it. We're being stonewalled by the Syrians, Arafat says he doesn't know anything and we can't go in there ourselves. We've got nothing, Bill."

"That's true," Bates said. "Go on."

"If we hire an honest broker, someone who has ties in the region, we can say we've done all we can. If she finds Buck, we look good. If she doesn't, it's on her. Either way, it's a smart move. Look at it this way. At least you've got something to tell the White House."

Bates smiled, leaned back and slapped the arm of his chair. "That's a damn good idea. I'll get the White House to sign off on this." Bates picked up the phone and dialed the White House Chief of Staff.

"White House Chief of Staff's office. May I help you?" the pleasant female voice said.

"It's Bill Bates calling for Landon."

"One moment please." After a few seconds she connected the two. "The Chief of Staff is on the line. Go ahead please."

"Bill, what do you have for me?"

"Landon, we've got a lead in the Buck kidnapping. We want to hire an honest broker to go in there and try to get him out."

"Who's the broker?"

"Remember the name Laura Messier?"

"Of course. The President loves her."

"She's got contacts in the region and we have reason to believe she can find him. She wants a 2.5 million dollar payment. Will you guys sign off on it?"

"Hang on a minute. I'll walk in and ask the President."

There was another short delay before he came back on the line. "Bill, the President loves the idea. You have something for us to sign?"

"I'll send it right over."

"He wants to sign it himself."

"You'll have it in a couple of minutes."

It took another half hour for the contract to be signed and returned to Bates' office, during which time Bates arranged for a payment to be wired to an account in the Grand Cayman bank specified in the contract. Bates' secretary photocopied the signed contract and handed a copy to Tilton.

"The money will be wired this afternoon," Bates said. "Are you hand delivering the contract?"

"That's what they want. No phone calls."

"Stop at finance and get a copy of the wire transfer."

Tilton smiled before he walked out. "You want me to say hello to her for you?"

"Are you fucking kidding me? Tell that bitch I hate her fucking guts."

Tilton laughed out loud at that. "I think she already knows that."

"Get the fuck out of my office, Tilton."

Tilton drove back out to National, handed the contract to Dmitri Polzin, Laura's pilot, and told him the money would be in the account by the end of the business day.

Everything I do with her is hard, he thought walking back to his car. How can I love her so much and hate her at the same time?

# Chapter Five

*Sunday, October 16, 1988*

THE WORKING GROUP for the rescue mission held its first meeting in the dining room of the main house at the Bahamian compound. Laura served Rick, Jack, Jean and Pierre a lunch she prepared herself and the meeting began as she cleared the table of dishes. "Has everyone had a chance to review the CIA file?" she asked carrying an armload of dishes to the kitchen.

"It doesn't tell us anything," Rick said.

"Why is that?" Laura asked, walking into the room again.

"CIA doesn't have assets in the region," Jack answered. "They've relied on Syrian Intelligence."

"Syrian intel is very good. Assad has informants everywhere," Laura said over her shoulder on her way back to the kitchen with the remaining dishes.

"The Syrians don't have enough information," Rick said. "The evidence was burned, there weren't any witnesses and there are about a dozen groups that might be responsible."

"And no group has claimed responsibility," Jean added. "It was an audacious crime so close to the Palace. Well planned and professional."

"Here's what I think," Laura said, returning with a pitcher of iced tea. She leaned between the men, filling their glasses while they talked. "CIA hasn't looked very

51

hard for these guys because they're afraid of what they'll find. You see where I'm going with this, don't you?" she asked, looking at Jean.

"Of course, but for the benefit of the others, continue your thought."

"The U.S. may have been trying to strike some kind of deal with the Syrians. I don't know what that deal could be. Maybe they want to secretly back the government in West Beirut and accept Syrian troops in the country. Who knows? But, if they discovered the Syrians were responsible for the kidnapping, it would blow up whatever deal they were negotiating. On the other hand, if they found one of Arafat's groups responsible, well, they need Arafat at the table for negotiations with Israel, so they don't want to alienate him, either. They blame it on the Shia because it's politically expedient."

"So Buck becomes a casualty of the peace process? Is that what you're saying?" Rick asked.

"Unless they find someone stupid enough to do the investigation for them," Laura said sarcastically.

"Like us?" Rick asked.

"Like us," she said, nodding her head. "Politics be damned," she continued, raising her voice. "Let's find these guys because it's the right thing to do. If any of us were in their place, we'd want someone to go to hell and back finding us."

The table grew quiet as no one knew quite how to respond to her comment. She's reacting to her own captivity in Gaddafi's headquarters, thought Jean. Laura finally took a seat at the table. "By the way, what are we doing to protect Postl?" Jack Postl was a young Czech man, a computer expert, who had previously worked in the

Kremlin. She brought Postl out of Moscow along with a Soviet naval officer and his son.

"After he broke into the CIA computer system and copied the file for us, we rented another apartment for him out in San Jose," Jack replied. "We paid to have him moved. He left no forwarding address. We think he's safe for the moment."

"What the hell's he doing out in California these days?"

"He opened a computer repair shop, but spends much of his time breaking into computer systems. He calls it 'hacking.'"

Laura leaned back in her chair and thought for a moment. "I always felt that kid had larceny in his heart," she said with a smile. "We're going to need him. Make sure we pay him well."

"I've got that covered," Jack said. "I talk to him every week."

"Okay. What are the names of the American hostages again?" Laura asked.

"Nicholas Buck and William Sharp," Jean reminded her.

"That's right. Who has them?"

"I don't think that's the question we should ask," Jean replied.

"Why not? We find out who took them, we'll know where to look."

Jean pointed to the file on the table. "That was the CIA's approach. We could debate that and never come to an answer."

"What do you suggest?"

"Find where they've been taken. In other words, do some good old fashioned detective work. Pierre, would you explain?"

Thibault, by nature a quiet person, was reluctant to express an opinion. "Come on, Pierre," Laura urged him. "Speak up. It could save the lives of the people at this table," Laura said. "Maybe your own."

"Mademoiselle, the only realistic possibility is that they're being held close to the border just inside Lebanon," Pierre began. "The kidnappers wouldn't risk holding them in Syria because Assad has too many informants. They wouldn't travel very far into Lebanon because the local militias set up roadblocks to collect tolls from travelers. They're being held along the border in a spot that doesn't attract attention."

"Jean, do we have a map of Lebanon?" Laura asked.

Jean dug into his briefcase and produced a large map and spread it out on the table.

"Show us, Pierre."

Pierre stood and leaned over the table, tracing a path along the Damascus-Beirut Highway with his index finger. The others stood to watch. "My guess is they traveled along the Damascus-Beirut Highway and turned off somewhere before the border crossing. If they went to the north, they'd be in Shia territory. That's the CIA narrative. I believe that to be wrong."

"Why?" Laura asked.

"There are Syrian military outposts all along the route they'd take north into Shia territory. That route would be risky considering how far they'd need to travel."

"And they'd want to avoid the border crossing itself because their vehicle would be searched, right?" Laura asked.

"That's correct."

"What if they went south?"

"They'd be in Druze and Maronite held territory," Pierre replied. "Those groups aren't known to be terrorists."

"They wouldn't hold them in Damascus, would they?" Laura asked.

"That'd be the worst place to keep them."

"I'm not sure what you're telling us, Pierre," Laura said. "They didn't just vanish."

Pierre paused and looked around the group before continuing. "Here's what I think they did. There are several dirt roads that cross the border right here," Pierre said, circling the area just south of the Damascus-Beirut Highway border crossing. "They're too small to be shown on the map, but they're used by smugglers to avoid the border crossing. That's Sunni territory. It's hilly terrain and the Syrian military never goes in there because the population's hostile. There are small farms back in those valleys. It'd be a perfect place to hold hostages."

"You're saying CIA is wrong to suggest Shia involvement?" Laura asked.

"Yes, I do. The CIA only knows that area through reports. They've never been back in those hills. Whoever took the hostages either lives back in there somewhere or has friends in the area."

"How could CIA be wrong?" Laura looked around and saw amusement in the faces of her colleagues. She smiled. "Stupid question, I guess."

Jean replied. "Mademoiselle, your CIA views the world from a global point of view. Pierre's knowledge of the area exceeds your experts in Washington."

Laura glanced at Pierre. "I thought you were stationed in Beirut, Pierre. How'd you come to know this area?"

"Back in '83 when we were bombing the Bekaa Valley, we had a plane go down back in those hills. We took a platoon in there to search for the pilot. We were ambushed constantly by militia fighters shooting at us from the hills. Those people have weapons and they don't like outsiders," Pierre said.

"Arafat might have information that could help us," Jean suggested.

"Arafat's in Tunis, Jean," Laura replied. "How could he possibly know anything?"

"Arafat's money supports many of the Palestinian groups. That doesn't buy him control as much as it buys him information."

"Arafat wouldn't do this, Jean. He's a statesman."

"I don't believe he'd have approved the kidnapping had he known about it in advance," Jean replied. But, after the fact, he's as likely to know where they are as anyone."

"Why wouldn't he talk to the U.S.?"

"He can't be perceived as working with the Americans, Mademoiselle," Jean said. "With Arafat's blessing, though, you could be the intermediary that obtains their release. Arafat would look like a peacemaker and the gesture would be seen around the world as a contribution to the peace process."

"Pardon me, but why would Arafat speak to Laura?" Jack asked.

"The Mademoiselle is perceived in the Arab world as something like a warrior princess. Reputation is important in that part of the world."

"What the hell is a warrior princess?" Rick asked.

Jean smiled. "With all due respect, Rick, you should study history."

Oh God, here it comes, thought Laura. "Jean, please stop."

Jean glanced at her, smiled and continued. "History is replete with instances of famous warriors who were women, going all the way back to ancient times," Jean said. "In the Arab world, Queen Zenobia united the Arab world in the Third Century. During the Battle of Uhud, legend says the Prophet Mohammed's life was saved by a woman warrior named Umm Ammarah. We have our Joan of Arc in France. You have your Annie Oakley. The Mademoiselle has that kind of reputation. Arafat will speak with her because of it."

Laura, who had been looking down at the table, lifted her head. She had tears in her eyes. "That's not the reason, Jean and you know it."

Jean hesitated seeing her tears. "I apologize, Mademoiselle. I've pushed you too far," he said tenderly.

"What?" a confused Jack asked. "What are you talking about?"

"It's a private matter," Laura replied. The room became silent as the group watched Laura struggle to put her feelings into words. She finally said, "I can't ..." she hesitated a moment, then shook her head and said, "I'm sorry." She looked away, staring down the path toward the ocean.

The meeting had come to a halt. The silence only lasted a minute but it seemed longer. It was Jean who finally spoke. He gently rested his hand on Laura's arm. "Mademoiselle," he said softly.

Laura rose from the table, dabbing at her eyes with a napkin. "Please excuse me, everyone. Carry on without me." She left the meeting and walked down the path toward the hut near the beach. Rick rose to follow, but was stopped by Jean. "Give her time, Rick. You were there. You saw what happened."

Rick hesitated and then decided Jean was correct. "Yes, I was," he said sadly.

"Old wounds cause pain," Jean said softly. "Shall we continue?"

Rick sat again in his chair. "Let's move on."

Jean hesitated, thought for a moment and then looked around the table. "Gentlemen, I think we should take a break. Let's reconvene at the dinner hour. Rick, can you ask the cook to prepare an evening meal for us?"

"Sure."

"Let's give the Mademoiselle time to rest. I need time to study the file, anyway. Something's missing. I've yet to discover it, but perhaps another reading will enlighten me. Can we meet again here this evening at seven?"

The group nodded their assent. "Very good," Jean said with a wry smile, as though he possessed a measure of confidence that Laura lacked. "Have a relaxing afternoon and we'll meet here again this evening." He picked up the file and walked into the house.

# Chapter Six

DINNER WAS SERVED on the porch as the house was still uncomfortably warm from the heat of the day. Laura entered through the double doors from the living room wearing a white sheath dress cut above the knee. Her make-up and hair were exquisitely prepared and the men dared not stare at her longer than to acknowledge her presence. All except Jean. "Mademoiselle, you are a vision of beauty and elegance this evening. You make me wish I were thirty years younger."

The men stood while Jean seated her at the table. "Thank you, Jean. You do know that I like older men, don't you?" she asked teasingly.

"If you don't stop flirting with me, Mademoiselle, I shall have a heart attack straight away and fall dead on the floor." That brought much needed laughter to the table.

"Well we can't have that, can we," she replied in kind. "Welcome everyone and I apologize for this afternoon. My emotions overcame me. I'll try to avoid that this evening."

"There's no need to apologize," Jean said. "Isabella," he shouted, hoping the cook would hear him from the kitchen. The older woman peeked out the door. "Yes, Mister Jean?"

"Please serve the first course."

"As you wish, Sir."

"I should really help her, "Laura said.

"No, you won't," Jean said, putting his hand on her arm. "She brought her lovely daughter, Sofia, to help this evening. Relax, Mademoiselle. May I pour you a glass of wine?"

Jean had set two bottles of expensive Chardonnay on the table and he kept Laura's glass full during dinner. "You've been such a gentleman this evening. I think you must have bad news to share."

"Nothing of the sort. Not when the most beautiful woman in the world is sitting at my table. Tonight, I must keep you smiling."

Laura laughed. "Okay, now you've gone too far. Let's get on with the meeting."

"As the Mademoiselle commands," Jean said, bowing his head in mock deference. "I never argue with a woman who could kill me with one blow."

"And I will if you don't get on with the meeting," she said to laughter around the table.

Jean's gift of manipulation had served him well during his years working for French Intelligence. Even those he investigated had no clue of his methods and many thought him to be their best friend. In one short conversation, Jean managed to focus Laura on the task at hand while setting the entire table at ease. The ending to the afternoon meeting was forgotten.

"I'm coming to the conclusion that someone inside the American Embassy in Damascus leaked information about Buck's meeting to the kidnappers," Jean began. "There is nothing in the file to suggest the embassy staff was closely investigated. A few questions were asked of the Ambassador, but the CIA investigation seems routine."

"You're referring to locals who work at the Embassy?" Rick asked.

"Anyone who had access to the embassy schedule, but especially the locals. This attack took planning."

"The file contains very little about the driver," Rick noted. "He's identified as Ahmed Kalami, but there's no age, residence or next of kin listed. All we know is he was a Syrian who worked for the embassy. In Paris, we'd never assign a local to drive VIPs. We always assigned Marine guards. And if it were a politician, we'd have a chase car accompany them."

"It sounds like the Embassy disregarded their own security procedures," Jean responded.

"Any experienced American driver, say a Marine guard for instance, would have done everything possible to avoid a trap. At the first sign of trouble, he'd have turned around and gone the opposite direction. Hell, he'd have headed straight across the desert if he had to. This driver, apparently, did nothing."

"Let's say for a minute that you're right and we implicate the driver. He wouldn't have been the only person involved. There would have been others."

Isabella walked onto the porch. "Mister Jean, Sofia and I are finished cleaning the kitchen. May we be excused for the evening?"

"I'm so sorry, Isabella. I neglected to release you." Jean rose and pulled a hundred dollar bill out of his pocket and gave it to her.

"Mister Jean, please keep your money. Miss Laura pays us well."

Laura got up and walked over. "You keep that Isabella. The dinner was extraordinary this evening. If you serve meals like this over at the barracks, I may have to start eating over there." That brought laughter to the group. Isabella blushed and looked down.

"You're welcome, Miss Laura. I'll put this away for Sofia's college expenses."

"No, you won't," Laura said. "We're going to pay Sofia's college expenses. You needn't worry about that. You take that money and buy something nice for yourself."

"Miss Laura and Mister Jean, thank you so very much."

The group moved to the cushioned furniture on the front porch. Laura turned on the front lights. "Would anyone like a drink? The bar's open." The men helped themselves and made their way, one by one, back to the front porch and sat down.

Jack Mason began talking of the incident again. "So, this Bill Sharp fellow checks out a car at the Embassy to travel to the airport and pick up Buck. There's no American driver and no chase car. It's a violation of their security procedures. That sounds suspicious. What do we know about Bill Sharp?"

"He's ex-military," Rick said. "In fact, he's Delta Force. He's good, Jack. He would be above suspicion in my opinion."

"That could be useful in a rescue," Jean observed.

"I'd expect he fights as well as me," Rick said.

"Well, since you're a pussy, Rick, I don't have much hope for Mr. Sharp," Laura quipped. The entire group erupted in laughter. Rick turned red faced.

"I guess I let myself in for that one," he chuckled. He paused, waiting for the laughter to die away. "Truthfully though, I'd expect Bill Sharp to put up quite a battle in an interrogation. Those Delta guys are tough dudes."

"That may be the thing that's keeping them alive," Laura said. "I think it will be a pleasure to finally meet Mr. Sharp. I'd like to stick an M249 in his hands and say 'Go to work.'"

"It may come to that, Laura, because getting out of there will be a problem," Jean said. Jean turned to Rick. "Rick, would the employment records for locals working in the embassy be kept on site"

"They would. In Paris, we didn't pass those records on to Langley."

"Why would the embassy allow a local to drive someone as important as an Under Secretary of State?" Jack asked. "That sounds insane."

"The obvious answer is they were understaffed," Rick answered. "But the driver had to have gained their trust somehow."

"How does one do that?" Jack asked.

"Maybe he spoke excellent English, came from a politically connected family, something of that nature. Maybe he was even educated in the States," Laura suggested.

Jack leaned forward and looked straight at Laura. "If he was educated in the States, there'd be a visa for him. That's something we can look up."

"Jack, I want you to take the plane and go out and get Postl," Jean said. "Drag him back by the shirt collar if you have to. Set him up in a D.C. office somewhere close to a trunk line where he gets a good computer connection. Have Postl search visa records, education records and anything else of relevance. If the driver came to the States, there's a record of it somewhere."

"I'll contact Dmitri and leave in the morning."

"There's one more thing we need in Washington, Jack. Stop by Langley and tell Monsieur Tilton we'd like to see satellite photos of the area south of the border crossing."

"No problem," Jack said.

Jean turned to Rick. "I've got a tough job for you and Pierre. I want you to go to Damascus, wave a copy of the contract in the Ambassador's face and tell him you want access to their employment records. I'd like you to review records for the driver, the person who assigned the driver and anyone else who might have had access to the embassy schedule."

"What if they won't accept the contract as documentation?"

"It was signed by the President of the United States for Christ's sake," Laura said. "Tell them to call the White House. And they can mention my name when they do it. The President's a friend."

"Okay," Rick said. What kind of political clout does she have, Rick asked himself.

Jean looked back and forth between Rick and Pierre as he talked. "Have Maria in the office set up your travel. You'll want to fly to Paris and talk to …" Jean thought for a moment. "Who do you know at DST, French Intelligence?"

"Henri Thomas and I worked together on the Libya thing," Rick said.

"Yes, I remember now." Jean tapped the side of his head with his finger. "I'm getting a little foggy up here. Meet with Henri and have him explain DST's message system. I'll set up some way to send messages back and forth through DST. Henri may have some ideas, too. We'll route your travel through, say Athens, then on to

Damascus. The purpose of your visit will be to interview the American Ambassador. You won't have diplomatic credentials, but that should get you through Customs. Once you're through Customs, check into the Omayad Hotel downtown. That's where the diplomats stay. Have Henri make the reservation for you."

"Okay."

"Call DST from time to time and leave messages about your progress."

"Got it."

"Start with the driver. If you find an address, watch the residence for a few days. Many of those families live together. If the driver was connected with the kidnappers, we may see someone visit the family. Terrorist groups often subsidize the families after the death of a martyr. If you see a male who doesn't belong, follow him. Now this is important." Jean paused to attach a sense of importance to his next comment. "Let Pierre take the lead on that. He knows the territory. If you follow someone onto those dirt roads, be careful. If the hostages are held back there, lookouts will be posted."

"Don't worry, Jean. I'll keep him out of trouble," Pierre said, smiling and cocking his head toward Rick.

"What about other locals who had access to the embassy schedule?" Rick asked.

"Investigate them, too. But, remember, if you follow someone back on those dirt roads, the last thing we want is to have you taken hostage."

"How often do you want us to check in?" Rick asked.

"Every day," Jean said. "If we don't hear from you, we'll assume you're in some kind of trouble."

Jean turned to Laura. "And Mademoiselle?"

Laura knew what he'd suggest and she was reluctant to hear it. "You've got an equally difficult job," Jean said. "I'm afraid Monsieur Tilton is right. You must visit Yasser Arafat."

"I understand," she said, resigned to the fact that it was unavoidable.

"Not yet, however. First, I must take a short trip to New York."

# Chapter Seven

*Monday, October 17, 1988*

JEAN SEARCHED THE jewelry district in Manhattan on Monday for a particular size and type of stone that might help Laura gain access to Arafat. The inclusion and transparency of the emerald he searched for didn't matter as much as the size and color. He was told the largest emerald in New York could be found at Mankiewicz Jewelry on 47th Street, west of 5th Avenue. Jean found the shop, pressed the buzzer and watched an old man with a miniature magnifying glass strapped to his head make his way through the shop and talk through the door. "May I help you," he said in a loud voice, looking up from his hunched over frame.

"I'm looking for a piece of jewelry I've been told may be in your shop," Jean said equally loudly.

The man looked at Jean momentarily as though judging his intent before unlocking the door. "Just a minute," he said. The man unlocked a series of locks on the door and Jean stepped inside. He immediately locked the door behind Jean and they walked through a dusty, utilitarian workshop with only one filthy display case upon which lay a felt cloth blocking the view of various rings and pendants piled inside. Mankiewicz turned around, looked up at Jean and simply said, "What are you looking for?"

Harold Mankiewicz had balding hair, a thick Eastern European accent and a slightly detached manner that left

67

Jean wondering if the man ever sold anything. Grossly overweight, he waddled more than walked and his dirty blue apron revealed that he preferred to work on jewelry rather than sell it. When Jean told him that he'd heard Mankiewicz owned the largest emerald in New York, the man shrugged and said it wasn't a highly graded stone, but he'd be happy to show it. "I'll be back in a moment," Mankiewicz said, before walking into a back room that apparently served as a workroom. When he finally emerged after a lengthy wait, Mankiewicz laid the stone upon the felt cloth and immediately began pointing out its flaws. Jean, however, was more interested in its bright green color and oval shape. It's the right color. The shape's correct, too. "How many carats is it?" Jean asked.

"It is an 80 carat stone. Anything larger would be considered a museum piece."

Jean asked if a gold setting could be fashioned around it and attached to a gold necklace. Mankiewicz shrugged and said he could have the work finished late the following day. Jean gave him a check for $25,000 as a deposit and left on a second errand.

Jean's next stop was the French Consulate where he showed his French passport and DST identity card to the attendant. He asked to see the Consular General and was directed to the second floor office of Charles Dubois. French Consular Generals are veteran businessmen who are posted to various countries to promote trade. The posting in New York was highly coveted. Dubois, a trim, tanned, gray haired gentleman in his late fifties, was known as much for his social skills as his business acumen. "Mr. Broussard," he said extending his hand, "so nice of you to visit us. How may I assist you?"

"Good afternoon, General. Thank you for seeing me. I need to call the DST in Paris using a secure line. It must be during Paris business hours so I'm hoping you can arrange something for tomorrow morning."

"Of course, Mr. Broussard, we'd be glad to assist you. We open at 8:30. Would that be convenient?"

"Yes, excellent."

"You may use the phone here in my personal office." He turned slightly and gestured toward the phone on his desk. "I'll inform the staff. I'm arriving at the office late tomorrow, so you'll have my office to yourself."

"Thank you, General," Jean said.

The General shook Jean's hand firmly and rested his opposite hand on top of Jean's forearm. He inched forward, too close for Jean's comfort. "Always happy to assist the Intelligence Services of the Republic of France."

Jean headed for the elevator, taken aback at the General's close body contact. That handshake may work for his polo friends, but it seems gratuitous. Too much cologne and sun tan lotion for me.

The following morning, Jean arrived precisely at 8:30 and was shown to the General's office where he inspected the phone before placing a call to Jacques Martin, the DST Associate Director, in Paris. Jean found a small electronic device in the receiver he judged to be an eavesdropping device on the line. He removed it and looked around the room. The room needs a complete sweep, he thought. He placed the call.

"Jean, so good to hear from you," Jacques said after the switchboard operator had proven Jean's identity and connected the two. It was early afternoon in Paris. "How's life in the Bahamas?" Jacques asked.

"I'm as busy in retirement as I was in Paris. How are things back home?"

"Quite busy as I'm sure you can imagine. We certainly miss the efforts of the Mademoiselle and yourself. How can I help you today?"

"Jacques, the Mademoiselle and I will be conducting a mission soon. We'd like to use the DST as a way to communicate between us. Can you set something up?"

"Absolutely. I'll set up a special telephone line for you to send and retrieve secure messages. What can you tell me about the mission?"

"Jacques, I'm not on a secure line at the moment. I'll call you from a secure location later and explain what we're doing."

"Very good."

"I'm also sending a couple of men your way in a day or two. Could you possibly have Henri help them?"

"It's as good as done."

"You've been most generous. Thank you."

"Phone me tomorrow from secure and I'll give you a pass code for the line."

"Thank you, Jacques."

"You're welcome, Jean."

Late that afternoon, Mankiewicz pulled the finished piece from a drawer behind the display case and laid it upon the felt cloth for Jean's inspection. The emerald had become a show piece. "It's quite lovely. You've done a wonderful job," Jean said.

"She must be a very special woman."

"Yes, she is."

Mankiewicz presented Jean with a bill and expected a complaint about the price, but Jean only smiled.

"I'll return with a check from J.P. Morgan shortly. Would that be satisfactory?"

"Of course," the dealer said.

Jean returned with a cashier's check in hand about an hour later and slipped the elongated jewelry box into the breast pocket of his jacket, shook hands and left. Mankiewicz was confused as to why anyone would carry a necklace worth over $100,000 in his pocket on the streets of New York and decided to follow Jean out of the shop to watch him walk away. By the time Mankiewicz walked around the display case and stuck his head out the door, Jean had already disappeared. Strange, Mankiewicz thought. A Frenchman walks in, pays full retail for an expensive stone without haggling, walks out with the piece in his pocket and disappears. He looked at the check. 'Security Associates of the Bahamas.' Never heard of them.

# Chapter Eight

*Tuesday, October 18, 1988*

LAURA HAD CREATED a private charter service for her Dassault Falcon 50 earlier in the year after she ended up with the jet used to escape Moscow. Dmitri Polzin had piloted the Falcon during the escape and brought his wife, Svetlana, out of the Soviet Union along with him. Laura hired them to operate the charter service. Dmitri and Svetlana turned out to be industrious small business operators, attracting a number of wealthy clients in New York who they ferried across the country. The business made a considerable amount of money which they split with Laura and the enterprise had worked well for all concerned. Plus, Jean and Laura had access to the plane whenever they wished.

Dmitri and Svetlana met Jack Mason at the airstrip across the highway from the compound early Tuesday morning for a cross country trip to San Francisco. "Good morning, Jack," Dmitri said with a smile, bounding down the airplane stairs. Dmitri was in his early forties, a tall, fair haired Russian man with blue eyes and broad shoulders. "Are we ready to leave?"

"Hi, Dmitri. Yes, let's get on our way."

"You have just the one carry-on?"

"Yeah, this one bag is it."

"Go ahead and bring it aboard. Svetlana will stow it for you."

Jack boarded the plane and was greeted by Svetlana, an attractive young Russian woman with a terrific personality. She spoke surprisingly good English, although her speech had a definite Russian accent.

"Hello, Mr. Mason. Can I get you coffee?"

"That would be fantastic. Black please."

Dmitri followed Jack up the stairs and brought a co-pilot out of the cockpit. "Jack, I want you to meet our co-pilot, Pete Franklin."

"Nice to meet you, Pete. Thanks for helping out today."

"My pleasure, Sir."

"We've hired Pete full-time," Dmitri mentioned. "The FAA insists we use a co-pilot on every flight and Pete's worked out quite well."

"Nice to have you with the firm, Pete," Jack said, extending his hand.

Pete Franklin, a retired commercial pilot, had the look of a military pilot, which was his background before he flew the big people movers. Tall and muscular, with short gray hair, he looked every bit the professional pilot he turned out to be.

"It's going to be a long flight, Jack," Dmitri said before returning to the cockpit. "We'll be refueling in Oklahoma City later this morning, so relax. I think Svetlana's serving food later. You can watch a movie on the screen up there," he said, pointing to a screen mounted beside the aisle, "and we'll get going in a minute or two."

They arrived in San Francisco mid-afternoon, West Coast time, and upon deplaning, Jack apologized to Dmitri. "I'm sorry about the quick turn-around. I'd like to head back as soon as I return with Postl."

"We'll have the plane refueled, Svetlana's going to re-stock the galley and we'll be hanging out in the terminal when you get back. Come find us and we'll be ready to go."

Jack took an expensive taxi ride out to San Jose and thought about how to approach Postl during the trip. He figured since Postl grew up under Communist rule in Czechoslovakia, an authoritarian approach would be convincing. Postl was no pushover, though. He was a large man and extremely bright. Jack decided to count on Postl's fear of authority to convince him to cooperate.

The driver found the shop easily and the bell hung above the doorframe rang when Mason entered. He paused and looked around. JP Computers was an attractive storefront space that contained displays of desktops along one wall, a row of stools in front of the long glass case and a peg board behind the counter from which hung various computer parts. Mason waited at the counter for a couple of minutes and when no one appeared, he walked around the counter and through a doorway. Mason found Postl hunched over a work table in the back room. Postl looked up, surprised to see Mason. "Mr. Mason! I didn't hear you enter. You should have called to let me know you were coming."

"Sorry about that, Jack. I was in a bit of a hurry this morning."

"What can I do for you?" Postl pushed his chair back from the table and turned to face Mason. "Would you like to sit down?"

"Sure."

Postl dragged a chair from across the room and set it next to his work bench. Mason sat down and looked Postl in the eyes. "Jack, I'm sorry, but we've got to bring you back to the East Coast for a couple of weeks."

Postl had anticipated what Mason might say and was prepared with an answer. "Mr. Mason, I can't leave the shop unattended. I've got customers waiting for repairs. I'm sorry, but it's quite impossible."

It was the answer Mason expected. He adopted a friendly tone of voice which belied the threat contained in his words. "Postl, I'd like you to reconsider your answer. Laura and Jean are sending you $5,000 a month and it doesn't seem like they're getting very much for their money. I strongly suggest you close your shop and come with me."

Postl shook his head side to side. "Tell Ms. Messier she'll have to wait until I have time. Whatever work she needs done, I can do it from here. Now, if you'll excuse me, I've got work to do. I'm sorry you made the trip for nothing."

Mason smiled; he expected Postl to resist. "You're certainly not required to come with me, Jack. However, you've broken into a classified computer system and the government's looking for you. The intelligence services take that kind of breach seriously. Once they find you, which they will …" Mason hesitated to allow the effect of the threat to be understood, "they'll see that you're a recent defector from the Soviet Union. You'll be arrested and charged with espionage. That's a twenty year prison sentence in a federal institution."

Postl became frightened. Mason could see it in his face. "You and Ms. Messier have tricked me into doing illegal things," he said, panicked. "I'll go to the police and report you."

Mason chuckled. "Well Jack, yes, we did ask you to do something illegal." Mason leaned back and smiled. "But we've got a contract for the work we're doing and we're entitled to the information. We just needed it a little quicker because lives are at stake. I'm sure the government will understand our position. Who do you think they'll throw in jail, Ms. Messier or you, a Soviet defector?"

Jack didn't answer. "When the government does find you, Jack," Mason continued, "we won't lift a finger to help. You'll be on your own."

Mason watched Postl consider his comment. Postl began nervously tapping a pencil on his workbench. He looked embarrassed. Mason continued. "However, if you like, we can call the police. You'll go off to jail and I'll find someone else to do the work."

Uh ..." Postl stammered, "this isn't fair."

"Jack, fairness isn't the issue. We're paying you very well, a lot more than you made at the Kremlin. You've got everything Ms. Messier promised you before you left Moscow. We're not going to force you. It's up to you whether you want to help."

"I need some time to decide."

"You've got about ten seconds. As soon as I walk out the door, the money stops and our relationship is ended."

Postl began to understand the discussion wasn't a negotiation. "How long did you say I'd be gone?"

"A couple of weeks, Jack. Consider it a business trip."

"When would we leave?"

"Now, Jack. Right now. Pack up what you need here," he said pointing around the shop, "let's stop by your apartment and get the hell out of here before you're caught."

"Okay, I'll do it, but you're going to have to pay me extra."

"No problem. I knew you were a smart guy. Let's get going."

Postl scrambled to pack the equipment he'd need into empty cardboard boxes he found in the rear of his shop and was ready to leave about fifteen minutes later. After stopping by his apartment a few blocks away, the two were on their way back to the airport.

# Chapter Nine

*Wednesday, October 19, 1988*

MASON AND POSTL returned to Washington in the early morning hours the next day. It took Mason until Friday to find Postl a small office in downtown D.C. and have the phone company run a suitable data line into the office. During the delay, Mason checked them into separate rooms at the Watergate hotel. In the interim, he traveled out to Langley for a meeting with Steve Tilton. Steve met him in the lobby.

"Jack, I didn't know you were coming."

"Sorry. I was in town on other business and needed to ask a question."

"Sure. Come on up to the office."

"How's it feel to be back?" Steve said on the elevator ride up to the seventh floor.

A wry smile came to Jack's face. "I'm lucky to have gotten out before I needed the deluxe package at the local mortuary."

Steve chuckled. "Yeah, it can be a real pressure cooker around here."

Steve led Jack into his office and shut the door. The two sat in front of Steve's desk. "What can I do for you?"

"I need satellite photos."

"Sure. Where?"

"The area just south of the Damascus-Beirut Highway border crossing from Syria into Lebanon. The highest resolution you can give me."

That's the area they're looking at? Steve asked himself. We considered that already. Steve didn't want to appear uncooperative so he made a concession out of professional courtesy. "I should be able to come up with something. We do surveillance for the Israelis in southern Lebanon." Steve leaned forward. "You have a reason to look there?"

"Nothing solid. At this point, it's an educated guess."

"What are you looking for exactly?"

"Dirt roads south of the border crossing. We want a look at the farms in the area."

"Drop by tomorrow afternoon; I'll give you whatever we have. Anything else?"

"That's it for now."

Once Postl had established an office, Mason checked out of the Watergate and gave Postl one final admonition. "Before I leave, here's a company credit card for expenses," Mason said. "Don't go wild and crazy, Jack. No strip clubs, bars or a new wardrobe. Just put everyday expenses on it."

"What about cash?"

"You should be able to get cash advances on the card, too. Small amounts only. This isn't a vacation."

"Okay," Postl said. "What am I supposed to be doing?"

"You're looking for records on Arabic males who came into the country on student visas. Check foreign exchange programs, school records, visa records, anything you can find."

"From what countries and over what time period?"

"Let's say Lebanon, Syria, Egypt and Saudi Arabia. Start with the last five years and see what you come up with."

"There'll be hundreds, just so you know," Postl said.

"Then you'll be buying a lot of printer paper. We'd like you to print the lists."

"A lot of that stuff won't be posted on computers."

"Just get whatever you can find."

"One more question. When do you want it?"

"We need it now, Jack."

"Okay. I'll get to work."

"One more thing," Mason said, turning around before he left. "Pick up the phone when we call."

The following day, Mason stopped by Langley again and met Steve one more time. "Were you able to get the sat data for me?"

"They didn't have much," Steve said, pulling a file out of one of the drawers in his desk. He spread one photo onto his desktop.

"When was this taken?"

Steve turned the photo over. "A week ago." He flipped the photo back. "Do you mind showing me what you're looking for?"

Jack stood over the desk and studied the photo. "This resolution isn't what we'd like, but at least it shows the dirt roads," he said, nodding at the photo.

Steve walked around the desk, reached over and pointed to faint lines on the photo. "You mean these?"

"Yes, exactly. See that?" Jack asked, pointing out what looked to be a small farming operation.

Steve opened the middle drawer of his desk and fished out a hand held magnifying glass. He leaned in, turned the photo around and studied it. "The big building looks like a barn."

Jack nodded. "That's the kind of place we're looking for. Rick and Pierre are going over there to have a look."

"Is Laura going to meet with Arafat?" Steve asked, changing the subject.

Jack immediately looked up. "She doesn't want to, but Jean is pushing for it."

Steve gave Jack a questioning look. "You don't think he'll meet with her?"

Jack nodded, "We think he'll meet her." He shrugged his shoulders. "We're just not sure Arafat knows anything."

"Maybe not. But he wants to move the peace process forward. We've heard Arafat plans to accept UN 242. Getting those hostages released would go a long way toward what we want to see from him."

"Politics is your thing, Steve. When I was in the Secret Service, I never cared what political party presidents came from. I'll leave the political stuff to you guys."

Steve smiled as he got up from the desk and walked around to shake Jack's hand. "All right, we'll leave the politics for another day. You need anything else?"

"There is one thing. We need visa records for Arabic males who came into the country on student visas at some point and returned to their home country in the past few months."

"Jesus, Jack, there have to be thousands. Are you looking for a specific person?"

"No, but let's cut the search down. Just Lebanon, Syria, Egypt and Saudi Arabia. Limit the search to entry in the last five years."

"That's still going to be a lot of people."

"True, but they'll be from wealthy families. Easier to locate. We're trying to triangulate a number of sources, Steve."

"The FBI would be the source for that. I'll see what I can dig up, though."

Jack scooped up the picture and gently folded it over without putting a crease in it. He laid it in his briefcase. "Thanks. I'll keep in touch. If you need to talk, call the office in Freeport. I'll get back to you."

"Will do," Steve said. "Good hunting."

# Chapter Ten

*Sunday, October 23, 1988*

RICK WILLIAMS AND Pierre Thibault waited until their colleagues returned to get one last briefing before they left for Paris and then on to Damascus. Jack laid the satellite photo on the dining room table in the main house and the men stood over it, studying.

"This is what I remember," Pierre said, circling the area south of the border crossing with his finger. "We should take this with us."

"If you're searched at Customs in Damascus and they find this," Jean said, holding up the photo, "they'll take it from you. You could be thrown out of the country."

Rick and Pierre looked at each other. "What do you suggest?" Rick asked.

"Create a small hand drawn map of what you think's important. Write no words that identify the area. Fold it and put it in your billfold. If it's discovered during a Custom's search, concoct a story around it that will satisfy them."

Laura walked into the room and began studying the photo. "If you guys try and follow someone back on those roads," she said, circling the area with her index finger, "you'll be noticed."

Rick pointed to the surrounding area. "You're right," he said. "We need to watch where those roads intersect with the Damascus Highway."

Laura studied Pierre and Rick. Pierre's reactive, she thought. He responds to immediate threats. Good in a fight. Rick's had officer's training. He's strategic, patient. "I don't mean to tell you guys what to do. If it were me, I'd photograph cars that go in and out."

"Good idea. Who knows, we might get lucky," Rick replied.

"If you find something interesting, ask the Embassy to send the film to Washington. Send it to Steve Tilton, for his eyes only."

"We'll do it," Rick said.

"Remember, if the hostages are back there somewhere, they'll be moved if their captors see anything unusual," Jean warned. "Keep out of sight."

"Syrian military uses the Damascus-Beirut Highway, too," Laura added. "Make sure they don't see you taking photos. They'll think you're terrorists."

"What about weapons?" Pierre asked.

"No weapons," Jean said. "Have Henri create some sort of official identification that gives you the authority to be there. That may not fool the police in Damascus, but it might help you outside the city."

"Anything else?" Rick asked.

Laura and Jean looked at each other. "I think that covers everything," Jean said. "Let's go to work, everyone."

# Chapter Eleven

AS THE MEETING disbanded, Laura laid her hand on Jean's shoulder. "I need a word." Jean stopped and turned around.

"Certainly, Mademoiselle. What's on your mind?" The two waited for the others to leave and then sat down at the table.

"I think you should stay here to communicate with those guys," she said, meaning Rick and Pierre. "We need to stay in constant contact."

"You mean not travel to Tunis?"

"Yes. There's nothing you can do over there to protect me. You're of greater value here."

Jean looked away. Are her language skills good enough? He began speaking in Arabic. "You'll be faced with language difficulties."

"I'm not fluent like you," she replied in Arabic, "but Arafat speaks English well enough. We'll be able to communicate. He won't harm me, Jean."

Jean leaned forward, putting his elbow on the table, cradling his chin in one hand. He considered the risk. Can she handle him? He's successful because of his guile. "I shouldn't think so. Do you know where to stay?"

"As you know, I've never been there. I was thinking of staying in the Diplomatic Quarter."

Jean nodded and switched back to English. "That would be safest. There's a hotel there on a hill that looks out over the city. I've forgotten the name. The clerks speak French; they're accustomed to diplomats. And you certainly speak Arabic well enough to communicate with taxi drivers."

"How do I get in to see him?" she asked, meaning Arafat.

"I'll make the appointment with his press office. He'll probably meet you at his headquarters in Hammam Chott. He'll recognize your name. I don't think there'll be a problem."

"Are we tipping off foreign intel services by getting on his calendar?"

Jean tilted his head, thinking. "I'll call Mossad and request they shadow you. They'll protect you."

"The Libyans?"

"They've been acting with restraint lately. It would be unlike Gaddafi to mount an attack there. Tunis is off limits."

"Even to the Russians?"

"If they meant to harm you, they would have already tried. Moldova being here was a good sign, I think."

"So, visibility may be the better strategy?"

"Precisely. I have something that may help you." Jean pulled the jewel from the breast pocket of his coat. He laid the box on the table and opened it. "Wear this when you meet him. It will offer you a measure of protection."

Laura smiled. "You know, I'd get mugged wearing that in New York."

Jean shrugged his shoulders as though his next comment would be obvious. "In Tunis, people will understand the stone's meaning. It will give you a bit of stature."

Laura laid her hand on Jean's, leaned over and kissed his cheek. "Thank you."

Jean took her hand and kissed it. "I would be honored to serve as your assistant in Tunis, Mademoiselle, but you're quite right. I should stay here and coordinate our people."

"It's settled then?" she asked.

"It is," Jean said, patting her hand.

# Chapter Twelve

*Monday, October 24, 1988*

LAURA LEFT THE following day on a commercial flight from Freeport to JFK, then on to Paris De Gaulle. She arrived late the following morning, spent the next night in Paris at the Renaissance Hotel and stopped by DST Headquarters to speak with Jacques Martin the next morning before leaving for Tunis. Jacques met her in the lobby of the ornate, centuries old building. He smiled broadly as he approached Laura.

"It's good to see you again, Mademoiselle." He air kissed her on each cheek.

"It's good to be back in town," she replied. "You know how much I love Paris." Laura was comfortable with Jacques. He'd been posted to Tripoli, Libya, during her mission there and helped her escape the country. They worked closely together during the Moscow mission.

"You have an open invitation to come back. We'd love to have you work for us."

"One of these days, I'll take you up on that."

Jacques was a career intelligence officer with a distinguished past. A slim, tall man, early fifties, with gray hair and wire rim glasses, he had academic credentials and a long list of professional accomplishments. Now the Assistant Director of the DST, Jacques had previously served with distinction as head of DST operations in several Middle Eastern capitals. He knew his way around the region; a smart and experienced diplomat.

They entered Jacques' office, a bright and airy space with high ceilings and oversize windows, across the river from the American Embassy.

"Let's sit at my coffee table. Jean tells me you're paying a visit to Arafat."

"We intend to ask for the Chairman's help in finding the American hostages in Lebanon."

Jacques gave her the patient smile of an experienced administrator. "He may not know where they're held, Laura. We approached him a few months ago about a French doctor and his nurse who worked for an international aid group in the camps. They were taken by unknown parties and haven't been seen since. Arafat professed to have no knowledge of them."

"I'm sorry to hear that. Perhaps I've overestimated his willingness to help."

"It isn't that he's unwilling. He lacks the daily intelligence on the ground in Lebanon. Arafat's focus is on the bigger picture. We hear he's going to accept Resolution 242 next month. He seems to be working toward a big agreement with Israel, something like the Camp David Accords."

"Accepting Israel's right to exist would definitely push the peace process forward."

"We think so. He's under pressure to produce something for the hundreds of millions in support he gets from his friends."

"But you don't think he can help us?"

"It depends on how he perceives you. France is a state actor. What few assets we have in the region are known publicly. Arafat and France can only help each other in the public arena. As an individual, you have the ability to take action in places a state actor could not. If Arafat sees you as someone who could be successful, he might want to attach himself to that success."

"So you think it's worth a trip?"

"I do. I would lower your expectations, though. He's a savvy politician. He may offer you token help, something he can deny, but use later if you're successful."

"I'll keep that in mind. Were you able to help Jean set up a communications link?"

Jacques nodded his head in the affirmative. "Yes. We created the phone line, put an answering service on it and gave him the details."

"I trust you'll remain confidential?"

Jacques reached over and took her hand. He looked her squarely in her eyes. "Absolutely. You're among friends here." He leaned back and smiled. "Can you stay for lunch?"

Laura looked at the clock behind Jacques' desk. "I'd love to, but I've got a flight this afternoon. I should be getting out to the airport."

"Very well. Let us give you a lift. You remember the way to the back driveway, don't you?"

"Of course."

"I'll have a car waiting."

Laura rose to leave. "Good luck," Jacques said. "Take care and keep in touch, Mademoiselle."

"Always."

# Chapter Thirteen

*Wednesday, October 26, 1988*

THE AIR FRANCE flight landed at Tunis-Carthage International Airport mid-afternoon after a two and a half hour flight. Laura carried only a small bag and went directly to Customs where she used her own passport. She declared nothing and stated the purpose of her visit to be a meeting at PLO Headquarters. The clerk stamped the passport and after a brief inspection, Laura made her way into the terminal where she found a young American man wearing a light brown khaki sports coat and tan pants holding up a sign that read "Messier."

"Hi, I'm Messier," she said smiling.

"Laura Messier?" he asked.

"Yes. Do you need to see identification?"

"No, Ma'am. My name's Don O'Malley, American Embassy."

"I was wondering if you guys would show up."

"Always happy to help. Here, let me carry your bag." He picked up the bag and motioned with his free arm. "This way, Ma'am."

Laura followed Don out the arrival doors where Don had temporarily parked the black Embassy sedan at the curb. He started to open the back door. "If it's okay, I'd rather ride up front with you," Laura said.

"Sure. Let me stow your bag in the trunk and we'll be on our way."

As they pulled away from the curb, Don nodded toward a group of men congregated on the sidewalk outside the arrival doors. "If I hadn't been here to meet you, you'd have been besieged by those men. They want to carry your bag and hail you a taxi in exchange for a tip. They would have literally ripped the bag from your hand. Tunis is notorious for travelers getting hassled on the sidewalk."

"I'm glad you were here. You know where we're going?"

"Sheraton Towers. It's not far, Ma'am."

During the short trip, Laura discovered that Tunis was Don's first post in the Foreign Service. He was right out of the UCLA graduate history program and intended to make a career out of the Foreign Service. Don pulled into the Sheraton driveway, stopped at the front door and helped Laura from the car. He carried her bag to the check-in desk, waited until she had checked in and accompanied her upstairs. "Will there be anything else, Ma'am?" Don asked once he unlocked her door.

"You've been fantastic, Don. Thanks."

"Oh, you'll see me again. I'm taking you to see Arafat tomorrow. We have the appointment time listed as 2 p.m., so we ought to leave by noon."

"Terrific. I'll see you tomorrow?"

"Yes. I'll be waiting in the lobby. Have a great evening." Walking out the door, he turned around and said as an afterthought, "If I were you, I'd stay in the hotel this evening."

"Thanks for the advice. I intend to do just that."

The following morning, Laura checked out of the Sheraton and found the pleasant young man waiting in the lobby. Wait 'till he's been an FSO for a while. He'll lose the eager look, she thought as she walked toward him, smiling.

"Good afternoon, Ma'am," Don said nodding. "The car's right outside." He picked up her bag. "You're going straight to the airport after the meeting?" he asked as they walked outside.

"Do you mind dropping me off?"

"Not at all. That's why I'm here. Do you need your bag up front?"

"I'll need to open it right before the meeting so just put it in the back seat for now."

It was a long but pretty drive through the city and suburbs eastbound to the seaside headquarters of the Palestine Liberation Organization. "Tunis is a lovely city," Laura said during the trip.

"Yes. It's a city steeped in history with many architectural gems. In this climate, they've been well preserved."

"It was originally a walled city, wasn't it?"

"Yes, Ma'am. Battles have been fought around here for thousands of years. It's an amazing place."

"What's the procedure once we get to Arafat's?"

"I'll escort you to the gate where you'll check in with a guard. After that, you're on your own. I've never been inside."

"I guess the Israeli bombing leveled the place," she said.

"Pretty much. Dozens of people were killed. I wasn't here then, but they say the whole place was rebuilt. Just a few months ago, the Israelis assassinated one of Arafat's associates, so there'll be a lot of security."

Don pulled up the drive to a grouping of white buildings protected by a high wall with a decorative gate that served as the entrance. Laura could see one main building right inside the gate along with a partial view of other buildings in the complex. The tops of trees could be seen between the buildings. "We're here," Don said, pulling the car to the curb. "PLO Headquarters." He looked at his watch. "We made pretty good time, too. You're ten minutes early."

"Before I go in, I've got to put on a piece of jewelry." She reached for her bag and removed the jewelry box and a headscarf. Pinning the emerald necklace into her hair so the jewel lay on her forehead, Laura wrapped the headscarf around her head and over her shoulder in the style of a hijab. She turned to Don. "How do I look?"

Don's eyes widened seeing the large emerald. "Wow! That's an incredible stone. It must be worth millions."

"It's expensive, but hardly worth millions," Laura said shrugging off the appraisal. "I have a bit of standing in the Muslim community and I'm hoping the emerald will remind people of it. The Chairman will understand what it means. I'll probably sell it after this. It brings back bad memories."

"If you don't mind me saying so, you look absolutely beautiful," Don said sheepishly.

"Thanks. You'll wait here?"

"Yes Ma'am, I'll be here whenever you're ready."

Laura took a moment before she exited the car. She closed her eyes. Concentrate on every movement, especially his eyes. No one can hide everything. She opened her eyes and looked over at Don. She smiled, "I think I'm ready."

"Good luck," he replied.

Laura emerged from the car wearing a light tan pant suit and low heeled tan shoes with the jewel prominently displayed on her forehead. The obligatory white headscarf gave the impression she was a wealthy Muslim woman. She walked across the street toward the entryway and the guards standing on either side came to attention. They wore military uniforms with green berets and black high-top boots. Russian made AK-47s hung over their shoulders. The jewel had its intended effect. They treated her with a measure of respect she wouldn't have enjoyed otherwise. She spoke Arabic.

"I have an appointment with the Chairman."

The guards looked at each other as though they were unaware of Arafat's schedule. "May I have your name please?" one guard asked politely.

"Asila Gaddafi."

Both guards raised their eyebrows in surprise. They bowed slightly. "I'm sorry to inconvenience you, Mrs. Gaddafi, but we must check the Chairman's schedule before we allow you inside. One moment please," one guard said before walking into the building. Almost immediately, he walked halfway back and motioned for the other guard to bring Laura through the gate. They accompanied Laura down a shaded walkway and into the large, white building. Once inside, a clerk rose from his desk and walked around to meet her. He bowed deeply. "We're honored to host you, Mrs. Gaddafi. Thank you for coming. May I show you to the Chairman's office?"

"Yes, please," Laura said, holding her head high with an air of superiority.

The guard objected. "We must search her purse," he said to the clerk.

The clerk spoke harshly in response. "Can't you see Mrs. Gaddafi wears the great emerald of Libya? You will not search the purse of the wife of Leader of the Libyan People. She is a trusted member of the Islamic community. Go back to your post."

"Yes, Sir," the guard replied. He saluted the clerk and walked back outside.

The clerk looked at Laura. "I apologize, Mrs. Gaddafi. We've had security issues lately and the guards are overly protective."

She smiled, "I understand."

Laura was led to Arafat's office, a beautifully decorated room with many pictures of Arafat standing alongside world leaders hanging on the walls. The airy room was painted white with floor to ceiling windows at one end that overlooked a patio. A colorful red oriental rug in the middle of the room and two red padded chairs on either side of an end table along one wall gave the room a relaxed ambiance. A sliding door which led to the patio was open. The draperies fluttered in the cool breeze off the sea.

Arafat sat behind his desk at the opposite end of the rectangular room. He wore a plain green military uniform with a white and black kaffiyeh hanging about his head. Arafat always managed to look as though he'd not shaved in several days. He smiled broadly when Laura entered. He rose from his desk, walked over and took her hands in his. "Welcome, Mrs. Gaddafi," he said in English. Your beauty and grace exceeds that of every woman alive."

Laura towered over the diminutive man. At 5' 9', she was several inches taller. Height doesn't equal stature, she thought. "You're most gracious and kind, Chairman," Laura responded.

Arafat spoke briefly to his clerk in Arabic. "That will be all."

"Yes, Chairman." He left the room, walking away briskly.

Arafat motioned toward the padded chairs along the wall. "Shall we make ourselves comfortable?" He put one arm behind her back and led Laura to the chairs. A kind, gentle look in his eyes, she thought. He shows none of the cunning that is his reputation.

"May I offer you refreshment?" he asked.

"No, thank you, Chairman. You're gracious to ask."

After they had seated themselves, Arafat smiled. "Your husband prays to Allah every day that you will return to him."

"With all due respect, Chairman, Muammar can pray for the rest of his life and I'll never return."

Arafat was amused at the answer. He began laughing. "I told him the same thing. He was stupid to try to capture you. You are like a beautiful bird that refuses to be caged."

"Indeed."

"But you wear the stone of Libya upon your head."

"It isn't the great jewel of Libya, but something smaller. I wore it as a way of introducing myself."

"Its effect is becoming on you. It gives one the impression you're a queen."

"If you would accept a gift, I would like to donate the stone to the children of Palestine." Laura removed her scarf, unpinned the stone and handed it to Arafat.

Arafat accepted the stone and studied the jewel for a minute. He finally looked up with a sincere expression of gratitude. "This is a rare gift to the Palestinian people, Mrs. Gaddafi. It will support food and medical care for thousands in the camps. I will accept it on their behalf. You have shown me that you are a kind and generous woman." He dropped the stone into his pocket.

"It is my honor to make such a contribution, Chairman. I support the right of the Palestinian people to control their own destiny."

Arafat nodded. "You are right to support the cause of the long suffering people of Palestine, Mrs. Gaddafi. Or should I call you Shewolf?"

It was Laura's turn to laugh. "You're familiar with the name?"

Arafat gave her a sly grin. "Who isn't? You are the famed assassin who killed Gaddafi's man and the KGB's best. You are what we call in the Muslim world a warrior princess, a woman who is both beautiful and dangerous."

"My cause is one of peace and justice, Chairman."

Arafat hesitated before answering. "There are rumors you separated yourself from the American government. That was a wise thing to do for one interested in peace. You no longer bear the stain of America's injustice around the world. Yet, you arrived today in a U.S. Embassy car." He motioned toward the door leading to the front entrance. "How is it possible that you donate so generously to the Palestinian cause, yet ally yourself so closely with the United States?"

"I sought American help with traveling about the city today. I do not represent them," Laura replied.

Laura saw a slight crinkle in Arafat's eyes as though he tried to avoid a smile. "It is good to hear you say that. I would not have spoken to you otherwise."

"I appear before you today on a mission of mercy."

That statement raised Arafat's interest. He looked directly at her. He doesn't know why I'm here, Laura thought.

"Is there any other kind?" Arafat responded.

Laura smiled at that statement. "No, Chairman, there isn't. I represent the mothers of two men who were recently taken from their families. I wish to fall upon the good and peaceful nature of the Palestinian people and ask for their safe return."

Arafat suddenly realized Laura's purpose. "Ah, you mean the men who plotted with Assad to suppress the legitimate rights of the Palestinian people?" he asked.

There was no way to sugarcoat this. "Yes," she replied.

Arafat was surprised by her direct answer. She could see it in his face. "Why would I help such men?"

This would be the key answer. Laura hesitated to heighten its effect. "Because Allah is Al-Ghaffur."

Arafat nodded and smiled. "Yes, Shewolf. Allah is the Oft-Forgiving."

"Chairman, children should not grow up without knowing the wisdom of their father. Mothers should never bear the loss of their sons. Although the Palestinian people have borne that grief countless times, peace must start somewhere. I will give you this oath, Chairman. I will exact a pledge of repentance from these men for the sins they've committed against the Palestinian people. Should they repeat their sins, let them suffer the penalty of Allah Himself, for He is exalted and the Lord of Retribution."

Arafat looked away and considered her answer. The man is impossible to read, she thought.

"Shewolf, you have answered well," he finally said. "Had the Americans approached me in this manner, I would have helped them. They are a Godless people."

"Chairman, there are good men in every culture and country. It is those men, such as yourself, who will lead our world toward peace."

Arafat cast his gaze downward, still pondering the matter. When he looked up at Laura, he had tears in his eyes. This is one of the most sincere people I've ever met, Laura thought.

"You have come before me today with the true humility of a peacemaker. You understand that no mother should lose a son, whether it's a Palestinian or Zionist mother. No child should lose a father. I shall help you, Shewolf, in the interest of peace. Walk with me to my desk and let us study a map."

Laura followed Arafat across the room where he rummaged around his desk, pulling a map of Lebanon from underneath a pile of paperwork. He spread the map on top of his desk and pointed to an area in northeast Lebanon. "Here is where the men are being held."

That's Shia territory, she thought. The same information CIA has.

"I'm sorry I cannot be more specific, but I lack the information necessary to give you a precise location. But, I will give you this." He opened a desk drawer, pulled out a gold coin and handed it to Laura. "This coin grants you safe passage throughout the country, even in Shia held territory. People recognize that it comes directly from my hand. Whenever you are stopped, show this coin and you will be allowed to pass unharmed. That is the best I can do."

What was it Jacques said? He'll give you enough help that he can take credit if you're successful?

Laura stepped back and bowed her head. "On behalf of the families of these men, I humbly thank you, Chairman, for your help."

"I have one request of you, Shewolf."

"Yes, Sir?"

"The men who took this action are patriots to the cause of a free and self-determining Palestinian people. Approach these men with the same humility you've shown me, with an olive branch in one hand and that coin in the other."

"I thank you for your wise counsel, Chairman. Inshallah. I wish you a long life and much happiness. Alhamdulillah.

"You're most welcome, Shewolf. You have something the Americans lack and that is honor. I wish you safe travels. You're welcome in my house whenever you choose to visit." Arafat took her hand and kissed it. He walked with her arm in arm to the front gate where they parted. She looked back at him over her shoulder as she crossed the street. Arafat waved and smiled. He's a talented man, she thought, waving before turning back toward the embassy car. He's not going to be too happy, though, if I have to kick the hell out of the kidnappers.

# Chapter Fourteen

*Saturday, October 29, 1988*

TWO DAYS LATER, Laura arrived home at her Bahamas compound. She changed clothes and walked down the path to her hut where she slept the rest of the day. At dusk, Jack Mason walked down the path and woke her, knocking on her screen door. "Laura, sorry to disturb you."

Vixen slept beside Laura's bed. She'd heard Jack coming down the path and was standing at the door, panting. Laura opened her eyes and looked toward the door. "That's okay, Jack. What's up?"

"Dinner's being served at the house if you're hungry."

"Tell them to put out a place setting for me. I'll come up."

Laura appeared on the back porch ten minutes later wearing jeans, a top and sneakers. Jean and Jack were the only ones present. "Wine, Mademoiselle?" Jean asked holding a bottle above her glass.

"Lots of it, Jean. Where are Rick and Pierre?" she asked, sitting down at the only empty place setting.

"They left for Damascus yesterday."

Laura looked puzzled. "I thought they were going to wait until I returned."

"We received some news yesterday," Jack said. "Postl found a student visa for Ahmed Kalami."

Laura leaned forward. "The driver?"

"Yes."

"Where'd the visa originate?"

"Syria," Jack said, as Isabella set the main course of roast beef on the table.

"Did the visa application list an address?"

"In Damascus. We assume it's his parent's address."

"Do we know where he went to school?"

"Harvard University."

Jean reached over and filled Laura's glass. "Thanks, Jean." She turned to Jack again. "How does a kid get from Damascus to Harvard?"

Jack gave her a slight smile. "Connections."

"You mean he's got family in the States?"

"Either that or his parents are rich."

Laura sipped her wine and thought for a moment. "That means we can find a record of him."

Jack leaned forward and put his elbows on the table. He looked straight at Laura. "That's exactly what it means," he said. "That's why Rick and Pierre left for Damascus. It's a legitimate lead."

Laura leaned back in her chair. "So let me get this straight. Boy genius Ahmed comes to America, attends Harvard and goes home to Syria to take a driving job? Does that sound right to you?" Laura asked.

"Nope."

"Me either. Do we know where he lived in Boston?"

"Not yet," Mason replied. "Postl says he needs access to a terminal connected to the university system to break into Harvard's student records."

"Like a terminal at the university library or something?" Laura asked.

Jack nodded yes between mouthfuls of food.

Laura looked down at her dinner. She hadn't touched it yet. "Do you find it odd none of this is in the CIA file?"

"Perhaps it's those political considerations you mentioned earlier," Jean suggested as something of an explanation. "The Americans want to avoid blaming the Syrians in the interest of diplomacy."

"And Assad doesn't want to investigate it because he doesn't want the blame," added Jack.

"They're going to let this fall through the cracks, aren't they?" Laura asked rhetorically. "Buck and Sharp will never be found and they'll be forgotten in a few months." She looked back and forth between Jean and Jack. "So why hire us? Why in the hell would they send Tilton down here to make a big deal about finding them?"

"It's called 'political cover,' Laura," Jack said. "They want to give the appearance they've done everything they can."

"The hell with them. Let's find these guys and we'll start by tearing Kalami's history apart. There's got to be a clue in his past we can use."

"I agree," Jean said flatly.

Laura glanced at Jack. "Do you want to take Postl up to Boston or should I?"

Jack shook his head no. "It's your turn. He's not my favorite person," he said with a smile.

Jean and Jack watched Laura begin to laugh. "I'll do it. I've grown quite fond of him."

After dinner, Isabella cleared the dishes from the table. "Miss Laura, you've not touched your food. You didn't like it?"

Laura looked up and smiled. "I'm sure it was delicious, Isabella. I just got off a plane and I'm not very hungry right now."

"Would you like me to wrap it and put it in the fridge?"

"That would be fine. Are you serving coffee?"

"Coming right up," Isabella said carrying an armload of dishes.

"Thanks."

Jean put his hand on Laura's arm as she reached for her wine glass. "How was your trip to Tunis? You haven't said a word about it."

Laura looked at Jean. "Arafat was everything you told me he'd be. Smart, savvy; he's an impressive man."

"And what did he tell you?" Jean followed.

"I think he told me the truth as far as I could tell. He was hard to read."

"That's what I've heard about him. I've not had the pleasure of meeting the man."

"His information is the same as CIA's. He thinks they're being held in Shia territory, although he said he doesn't always get accurate information."

Jean shook his head in agreement. "Arafat has an impossible job. No one can control all the factions in Lebanon."

"He did offer me help, though." She pulled the coin from her jeans and handed it to Jean.

Jean held the coin up to reflect the porch light off its surface. "I've heard these exist, but I've never seen one." He laid the coin on the table between them.

"What is it exactly?" Laura asked.

"I've heard Arafat gives these to his lieutenants when they travel. The coins give them safe passage wherever they travel in the Muslim world. This is a valuable gift," Jean said, tapping the coin with his index finger.

"I hope so because I traded the jewel to get it," she said with a smile.

Jean threw his head back and began to laugh. He slapped one hand on his knee. "Mademoiselle, you should have been born in the Middle East. You have the instincts of a trader."

Laura waited for Jean's laughter to subside. She pointed to the coin. "This gives us a certain amount of prestige in the region?"

Jean cocked his head to one side, thinking. "The coin means we're a friend of the Palestinian people. It's been said these coins are passed directly from Arafat's hand."

"So we use it as an introduction of sorts?"

Jean nodded his head. "Yes. Everyone accepts his money, so they'll speak with us. However, not everyone wants peace. Whether we can use Arafat's influence to negotiate a hostage release," Jean shrugged his shoulders, "depends on who we're talking with."

# Chapter Fifteen

*Friday, October 28, 1988, one day earlier*

RICK WILLIAMS AND Pierre Thibault left Freeport on a commercial flight the day prior to Laura's return. They changed planes at JFK and caught a connection to Paris. Due to the time change, they spent an extra day in Paris with Henri Thomas at DST Headquarters getting briefed on the communications system they'd use to stay in contact. Henri had his technology people create false identities for the two which were sewn into the lining of their baggage. "Come into the country using your real passports," Henri said, "but check into the hotel with the false passports we've put in the lining of your luggage. While you're in country, operate on your false identities."

"Okay," Rick replied.

"If you're going to conduct surveillance along the Beirut-Damascus Highway, you need a reason to be there. I've given you ID cards from the Syrian Ministry of Transport that match your false identities. I also included a letter from the Transport Minister giving you the authority to be out in the field researching traffic. That highway is in a constant state of disrepair due to heavy military traffic. Everyone is annoyed by road repairs, even terrorists. Those IDs should get you through a roadside interrogation."

"What do we say if we're stopped?"

"Tell them you're planning future repairs. They might shoot you because you're from the Ministry of Transport," Henri said with a laugh, "but they won't suspect you of being spies."

Rick rolled his eyes. "That's encouraging."

"Believe me, there isn't a better cover for you," an amused Henri told Rick.

"That's probably right. Thanks, Henri, you've been a big help."

"Call me if you get in trouble. We have people in Damascus."

"We appreciate the help."

"Good luck," Henri said as the men stood and embraced. Rick and Pierre left for Damascus the following morning.

After an uneventful flight, the men cleared Customs at Damascus International Airport without incident. The airport was busy and long lines at Customs pressured officials to clear passengers quickly. After a brief examination of their documents, Rick and Pierre walked through the terminal to the street, hailed a taxi and traveled downtown to the Omayad Hotel.

They used the restroom before they approached the hotel check-in counter and tore the false identities from the lining of their bags. They provided the false passports at the counter and received their room keys. The hotel kept their passports in a locked drawer underneath the counter. It was late in the day by the time they'd settled in their rooms, so they decided to pay their first visit to the American Embassy the following morning.

# Chapter Sixteen

*Monday, October 31, 1988*

PIERRE AND RICK entered the Embassy of the United States shortly after 8:00 a.m. and walked to the window in the lobby.

"Good morning, gentlemen," the young American female clerk said with a smile, "and welcome to the United States Embassy."

Rick and Pierre slid their real passports underneath the thick glass that separated the counter from the office area behind. "We're here to conduct an investigation into the disappearance of two United States citizens, Nicholas Buck and William Sharp," Rick said. "We were sent under contract with the Central Intelligence Agency. We wish to speak with Ambassador Franklin Brooks."

The clerk studied the passports carefully. "Mr. Thibault, you're a citizen of France. Is that correct?"

"Yes, Ma'am."

"Why are you helping investigate the disappearance of U.S. citizens?"

Rick spoke before Pierre could answer. "Mr. Thibault is a Middle East expert who's assisting with the investigation."

"Would you mind waiting a moment? I'll be right back."

"Certainly," Rick replied.

She took the passports into a room behind the office where Rick could see a man seated at a desk. He glanced at Rick through an open doorway as he listened to the clerk explain the situation. After studying their passports, he handed them back to the clerk who walked to the window.

"Mr. Williams, do you have an official document giving you permission to conduct an investigation?"

"Yes." Rick dug into his bag and pulled out a manila folder that contained the contract. He pushed the folder underneath the glass barrier.

"Thank you. I'll be with you in a moment." She took the contract back to the man in the back room. He thumbed through the document, stopping on the signature page. He spoke to the clerk and she returned to the window.

"I'm sorry, but we must verify these documents with Washington. They're seven hours behind us so we won't receive confirmation until tomorrow morning. If you'd permit me to make a copy of the document and your passports, we'll have the matter resolved tomorrow."

"The document's classified so after you copy it, we ask that you secure it."

"Of course." She stepped away a third time, returned and slid the contract and passports through the tray underneath the glass barrier. "We'll see you tomorrow, Mr. Williams?"

"Bright and early. Have a good day, Ma'am."

"You, too."

Walking across the lobby toward the exit, Rick heard his name. "Williams!"

Rick turned around and saw a friend walk toward them. "Well, I'll be damned. What's up, Coxie?"

"What the hell are you doing here?" Tom Wilcox asked, smiling broadly as he approached.

Rick and Tom hugged as though they were long lost brothers.

"Pierre Thibault," Rick said, "this is Captain Tom Wilcox, United States Marines."

Wilcox held out his hand. "Nice to meet you Mr. Thibault." He looked back at Rick. "I heard your name behind the counter and I couldn't believe it. I decided to come out and see for myself. It's great to see you, man."

Tom Wilcox was a large man, 6' 3", with a short Marine haircut and the square jawed look of a soldier. In his mid thirties, with blond hair and green eyes, his Marine Service C uniform was familiar to Rick.

"It's good to see a friendly face, Tom. To answer your question, we've been assigned to investigate the disappearance of Nicholas Buck and Bill Sharp."

Wilcox looked around the lobby. He instantly became serious and motioned with his head. "Walk with me a minute." He led them into an interview room off the lobby, shut the door and leaned against a desk. "It's about time they sent someone over here."

"What do you mean?" Rick asked, puzzled by Tom's reply. "No one showed up to investigate?"

"Oh, they sent one lardass over here right after it happened," Wilcox said, shaking his head in disgust. "He spent about ten minutes with the Ambassador and left. We haven't heard a thing since."

"I'm hoping to spend a few days here, Tom, if I can get past the clerk."

"Glad to hear it." Wilcox nodded toward the lobby. "Don't worry about those people. Folks have gotten a little

111

nervous since the kidnapping. Once they get the okay from Washington, you'll be in good shape. Where are you guys staying?"

"The Omayad."

"Good. That's the best place for you. It's where we put our people."

"If there's one more thing I could ask you?"

"Anything. I'm head of security here," Wilcox said.

"Fantastic, Coxie; it's a well deserved promotion. We're looking for some wheels. Off road type vehicles."

Wilcox thought for a moment. "Hang on a minute. I've got a name for you." Tom left the room.

Rick spoke to Pierre. "We caught a break. Coxie and I go way back, all the way to Quantico. He'll fix us up."

Pierre nodded. "Good."

Wilcox returned with a business card, handing it to Rick. "There's a Brit in town who deals in foreign imports. Ryan Madigan's the name. You tell him I sent you and he'll get you whatever you want."

"Thanks, man," Rick said. "You're going to make things a lot easier for us."

"Not a problem, Rick. Bill Sharp was well liked around here. He's a Delta Force guy. Good dude."

"We're going to try to get him back."

Wilcox slapped Rick on the back. "Good to hear it. We should get together one night while you're here."

"Count on it."

"We'll see you in the morning?"

"Yep. Thanks, Coxie."

"You bet."

# Chapter Seventeen

*Tuesday, November 1, 1988*

AFTER A TAXI ride across town to Madigan Motors, Rick and Pierre found a luxury car dealership that catered to the elite of Syrian society. The showroom was filled with high priced imports. They walked away after signing a contract for two new Range Rovers. Rick used the Paris communication system for the first time, leaving a message for Jean to wire transfer an exorbitant amount of money to an account Madigan specified. "Look, blokes and frogs," Madigan explained again after Rick finished the call. "I can't do anything about the price. I must ship these things here from Britain. The destination charges are in the thousands. Plus, I've got oil sheiks who pay above sticker price for new luxury cars and leave them in the hotel lot after their visit. I do the best I can."

Rick wasn't pleased with the price, nor being called a "bloke." Pierre was equally uncomfortable being referred to as a "frog," a slang term for the French used by the British during the Napoleonic Wars. Nevertheless, they trusted that Laura and Jean would consider the price to be the cost of doing business. Madigan promised to have the vehicles ready as soon as the wire transfer was completed. Rick and Pierre walked out of the showroom where a taxi waited for them. I'd like to punch that Brit right in the chops, Rick thought as they climbed in the cab.

Rick looked at Pierre. "How come I feel like I just got my butt kicked in there?"

Pierre shook his head spread his hands apart. "That's because you did. That guy had us over a barrel and he knew it. He's the only dealer in town. Let's hope Laura and Jean understand what we're dealing with here."

# Chapter Eighteen

*Wednesday, November 2, 1988*

RICK AND PIERRE arrived at the Embassy the next morning shortly after 8:00 where they encountered the same clerk at the counter. "Good morning, Mr. Williams," she said with a smile.

"Hi. I'm sorry. I didn't get your name yesterday," Rick replied.

"Nancy. Nancy Murdock from Billings, Montana."

"It's nice to meet you, Nancy Murdock from Billings. Do you need our passports again?"

"Yes, please. If you'd just slide them under the window, I'll get you going this morning."

She took the passports into the back room again and showed them to the same man. Rick watched him study the passports and could read his lips as he said, "Okay." Nancy returned to the window. "If you'd walk down to the door to your left, I'll buzz you inside and have you sign the visitor roster."

Once Rick and Pierre signed in and had their visitor badges, they were told to report to a security station where a young Marine corporal sat at a desk in the hallway. "Good morning, gentlemen. My name's Corporal Richard Hunt. Captain Wilcox told me you'd be here this morning."

"Is Captain Wilcox available?" Rick asked.

"No, he's not in yet. What can I do for you?"

"We'd like to start by speaking with Ambassador Brooks."

"Let me call up to his office and get you on his schedule."

Richard picked up the phone, talked briefly, then hung up and looked at his watch. "It's 8:30 now. The Ambassador can see you for a few minutes at 9:45. Is that satisfactory?"

"That'll be fine. Where can we find your personnel records?"

"Walk down this hallway," Richard said pointing to his left, "take your first right and you'll find it. It says Human Resources on the door."

"Can we go down there now?"

"Yes, Sir. The clerk's name is Lisa."

Rick and Pierre found the personnel office where Lisa greeted them warmly. "Hi. Can I help you?"

"My name's Rick Williams and this is Pierre Thibault. We're here to investigate the disappearance of two Americans, one who worked here."

"Captain Wilcox told me you'd be here this morning. So sad to lose Bill Sharp. He was a friend to everyone. We've been in a state of shock since it happened."

"We think he's still alive."

Lisa gave Rick a look of disbelief and hope. "After all this time?"

"Yes, Ma'am, we do," Rick said with confidence in his voice.

"I'll do everything I can to help you."

"I need to see the employee files on all the local people who work in the building."

"Sure, I've got them right here." Lisa reached for manila folders stacked at one end of the counter. "Captain Wilcox told me you might want to look at them, so I gathered them yesterday. There are only seven."

Rick looked at Pierre and whispered. "Good old Coxie." He turned back to Lisa. "Is there a place we can sit down and have a look at them?"

Lisa pointed to an empty desk behind the counter. "Sure. Walk around the counter and you can use the empty desk back there." Lisa gave them a friendly smile. "If you'd like a cup of coffee, feel free to use the cafeteria in the basement. You can bring your coffee up here if you like." She pointed with her hand. "Turn right out the door. The stairs are at the end of the hallway and the restrooms are before you get to the stairs. Let me know if you need anything."

"Thanks, Lisa," Rick said.

The first thing they noticed was the file for Ahmed Kalami was missing. Rick rose and walked over to Lisa's desk. "Lisa, sorry to bother you, but we noticed Ahmed Kalami's file is missing."

"Oh yes. Ambassador Brooks has Ahmed's file in his office."

"Why?" Rick asked.

"The Foreign Service pays a death benefit to the beneficiary of each employee killed in the line of duty. Ambassador Brooks and his secretary are handling it."

Rick walked back over to their desk. He looked at Pierre after he sat down. "Did you hear that?" he asked quietly so Lisa couldn't hear their conversation.

"Yes," Pierre answered, nodding his head.

"I wonder who the beneficiary is."

"Good question."

"Brooks will know," Rick said.

Of the other six files, two were local men who worked part-time. Rick walked back to Lisa. "Sorry to bother you. These two part-time gentlemen? What do they do?"

"They're listed on the payroll as external sources."

"You mean like informants?" Rick asked.

"That's my understanding. They call Mr. O'Dell periodically. We never see them here at the Embassy."

"Mr. O'Dell is the Station Chief?"

"His title is CIA Chief of Damascus Station."

"Thanks," Rick said before returning to the desk.

"These two guys," Pierre said, pointing to the two files, "wouldn't have access to anything?"

"No. Lay those aside for now."

They moved to the next file. "This fellow here," Rick said, holding up a file, "is building and grounds."

"A maintenance man?" Pierre asked.

"Every Embassy has someone like that," Rick responded.

"It doesn't sound like he'd have access to anything."

"Not anything critical," Rick said. "Lay his file aside, too."

"Take a look at this one," Pierre said, handing the next file to Rick.

Rick studied the file for a minute and then walked over to Lisa and showed her the file. "Sorry to trouble you, Lisa."

Lisa smiled. "It's no trouble, Mr. Williams. What can I help you with?"

"This woman," he said pointing to the file, "Huda Deeb. She works at the Ambassador's residence?"

"Yes. She's the residence housekeeper and cook."

"Does she come into the Embassy on a regular basis?"

"I don't see her very much," Lisa said. "She reports directly to the residence each day."

"How about picking up her paychecks?"

"The Ambassador takes them home and gives them to her directly."

"Thanks," Rick said. He walked back to Pierre. "Put Huda Deeb in a suspect pile."

Pierre picked up the next file and looked at the name. "Rick, take a look at the name." He handed the file to Rick.

"Bingo," Rick said under his breath. "Safa Kalami." Rick took the file to Lisa. "Sorry to keep pestering you, Lisa, but this woman ..." Rick showed her the file, "is she related to Ahmed Kalami?"

"Safa? That's his sister."

"She's the cleaning lady?"

"Was the cleaning lady."

"What do you mean 'was'?"

"The poor woman was so distraught after her brother was killed, she quit. I haven't seen her since."

Rick looked at his watch. "We've got to meet the Ambassador in a few minutes. Can I take these files upstairs?"

"Sure, not a problem."

Rick walked back to Pierre. "Definitely put her in the suspect file."

Pierre picked up the last file. He opened it and showed it to Rick. "This woman's kitchen help."

Rick walked back to Lisa. "What can you tell me about …" He looked at the file again to remind him of the name. "Nadira Bahar?"

"She handles the kitchen downstairs."

"She has regular hours?"

"Yes. I haven't seen her today, but she's probably down in the kitchen."

"Thanks." Rick walked back to Pierre. "Put her in the suspect pile, too."

"Here's who we've got," Pierre said. "Nadira Bahar, the cook; Safa Kalami, the cleaning person and Huda Deeb, the housekeeper at the residence." Pierre smiled. "It sounds like a murder mystery, doesn't it?"

Rick grinned. "Yeah, the butler did it. Who's that French detective in the movies? You know the one I'm talking about?"

"The guy with the funny hat?"

"Yeah, that's the guy."

"Inspector …" Pierre thought for a moment. " … I can't remember his name."

Rick looked at his watch. "Okay, Inspector Thibault," he said to Pierre, "it's 9:35. Let's go up to Brooks' office." Rick rose and walked over to Lisa's desk. "We're taking three files up to the Ambassador's office if that's okay."

Lisa gave Rick her best administrative smile. "Sure. Which ones are you taking?"

Rick looked at the names. "Bahar, Kalami and Deeb."

"Okay. Make sure I get them back at some point."

"Will do. Thanks, Lisa."

On the way to Ambassador Brooks' office, Pierre looked at Rick. "I got it."

"Got what?"

"Inspector Clouseau."

Both men looked at each other and began laughing. "That's it!" Rick exclaimed. "Oh my God, is that guy funny or what?"

"He's the best."

"We better pull it together before we go in Brooks' office," Rick said, adopting a more serious tone. "Put your game face on, my friend."

# Chapter Nineteen

RICK AND PIERRE stood together outside Brooks' office for a moment before entering. "Are you ready for this?" Rick asked, nodding toward the heavy, finished wood door with Brooks' nameplate on the wall beside it.

"You mean ready to hear a lot of bullshit?"

"That's exactly what I mean."

"Sure, why not? I listen to you guys at the compound every day," Pierre said, stifling a laugh.

"I should have known better than to ask. Just let me do the talking in there, okay?"

"I always do, little brother," Pierre said with a smile. "I'd rather let you embarrass yourself. You're pretty good at that."

Rick chuckled. "Thanks buddy. I appreciate your support," Rick said cynically.

"Anytime."

Rick and Pierre walked into the Ambassador's office precisely at 9:45. While the rest of the building looked like a typical government building with off-white walls, linoleum flooring and overhead florescent lighting every few feet, the Ambassador's office was distinctly different. Mahogany paneled walls, wood floors and leather chairs gave the office an upscale feel. It looked much like a D.C. law partner's office. The room even smelled like wood. Floor lamps in the corners warmed the florescent lighting in the ceiling and Brooks sat in a high backed executive chair behind a large wooden desk with beautifully carved sides and ends. The walls, decorated with pictures of Brooks posing with Middle Eastern leaders, gave one the impression he was an important man.

Franklin Brooks stood and walked around his desk. "Excuse me," Rick said immediately after entering. "We're here to see the Ambassador. I'm Rick Williams and this is Pierre Thibault," Rick said.

"It's nice to meet you gentlemen," Brooks said in a deep, resonant voice. He firmly shook hands with both men. "I'm Franklin Brooks."

"Very nice to meet you, Sir," Pierre said.

"Likewise," Rick added.

There were three others sitting in the office. Brooks gestured toward each one as he introduced them. "This is Paul O'Dell, our station chief, Karen O'Dell, the secretary I share with Paul, and of course, you've met Tom Wilcox, our security head," Brooks said as a way of introduction.

"Good morning," Rick replied.

"Please take a seat," Brooks said, gesturing toward folding chairs that were placed near the others in front of Brooks' desk. "Sorry about the chairs. We don't usually hold large meetings in my office."

"Not a problem," Rick said with a patient smile.

Brooks sat down behind his desk. He leaned back in his chair. "I've been told you're investigating the disappearance of Secretary Buck and Assistant Ambassador Sharp. How can we help?"

Brooks may have been a political appointee, but he seemed to be a good choice. A retired executive with an aerospace company, Brooks had worked in the Middle East selling commercial aircraft for years. Of medium build, slender with nearly white hair, Brooks had a distinguished look about him.   The guy's got a million dollar smile, thought Rick.  Probably a million dollar bank account, too.

Rick scanned the group after sitting down.  "Lisa, down in Human Resources, gave us access to the Embassy personnel files and I've brought a few with me."  Rick held up the files he carried into the office.  "We'd like to ask about some of your local employees who work at the Embassy.  The files are incomplete."

"Sure, go ahead," Brooks said, looking at his watch. "Tom and Paul would be the ones to answer those questions."

"Why is Ahmed Kalami's file missing?"

Brooks answered that question.  "We kept that file in my office after his death.  The file is technically still open until his death benefit check is delivered."

"Could we get a copy of the file?"

"Sure," Brooks said.  He opened a drawer in his desk and withdrew the file.  "Karen, would you copy this for Mr. Williams?"

"I'll do it right now," she said.  Brooks handed her the file and she left the room.

"Who'd he list as his beneficiary?"

"His sister, Safa.  The check's in her name.  We can't find her so we're holding the check."

"You're talking about Safa Kalami?"

"Yes."

Rick turned his attention to O'Dell and Wilcox.  "How do locals get hired?"

"Most were here when we arrived," O'Dell said.  "For new hires, people working here usually recommend a friend."

Rick looked at the Ambassador. "Huda Deeb, your housekeeper at the residence. There's no start date in the file. How was she hired?"

"I came here in '84 and Huda was here then," Brooks replied. "She's worked at the residence for what, Tom?"

"Over ten years," Tom said. "She's in her early sixties and is one of our most loyal employees."

"Would she have access to any sensitive material you might bring back to the residence in the evening?" Rick asked Brooks.

"I never take anything out of the office."

"Thanks." Rick looked at Wilcox. "Tom, does Ms. Deeb ever come to the Embassy?"

"I never see her," Tom said. "You hand her paychecks to her at the residence, don't you, Frank?"

"Yes," Brooks replied. "I take her checks home with me."

Karen O'Dell returned with a copy of Ahmed Kalami's employment file. "Pardon, Mr. Williams," she said. "Here's the copy you requested."

"Continue your questions, Mr. Williams," Brooks said with a hint of impatience in his voice.

"What can you tell me about Nadira Bahar?"

"Mrs. Bahar works downstairs," Tom continued. "We have a lunchroom in the basement. She comes in mornings, prepares a buffet lunch for the Embassy staff, cleans the kitchen and is gone by the end of the day."

"How did she get hired?"

O'Dell answered. "She's the wife of our long time maintenance man, Mansur Bahar. They've been here quite a while, too. Right, Tom?"

"Yes," Wilcox said. "They were here when all of us got here. We've never had a problem with either of them."

"Neither would have access to sensitive material then?" Rick asked O'Dell.

"No."

"That brings us to Safa Kalami. She's Ahmed's sister?" Rick asked Tom.

"Yes, brother and sister," Tom replied.

"How did Safa come to work for the Embassy?"

"Once again, she was here when I got here," Tom said. "You've been here longer than me, Paul. Do you know?"

"She was here when we arrived, too."

"Do you know what sort of vetting she went through?" Rick asked O'Dell.

"I have no idea," Paul replied. "As far as I know, she lives with her parents and I think she's still single, isn't she, Tom?"

"That's what she's told us," Tom responded.

O'Dell continued. "Her father's a prominent food supplier in the city. He has the contract here at the Embassy."

"Safa no longer works here. Is that correct?"

"That's right," O'Dell said. "She quit after her brother's death."

"She had access to the entire Embassy?"

"Yes, but she never had keys. We let her in and out of rooms during the evening hours when she'd be working."

"What was her job?" Rick asked.

"She cleaned the Embassy overnight," O'Dell said. "She'd empty trash cans, dust, vacuum, that sort of thing. She'd work an eight hour shift and leave in the early morning hours."

"Who unlocked rooms for her?" Rick asked.

"One of the guards let her in and out," Tom answered. "Whoever happened to be on duty. We'd use a walkie-talkie. When she'd finish a room, she'd let us know and someone would let her into the next room."

Rick turned to the Ambassador. "Safa had access to your office?"

"Yes," Brooks answered.

"Where do you keep your appointment book?"

"Here on my desk." He pointed to a leather bound album sitting on the desk.

"You keep a record of all your meetings on the calendar?"

"Most of them, yes."

"Could she have had access to the calendar?" Rick asked.

Brooks thought for a moment. "I suppose so, but I've never found my desk disturbed. I don't think she ever touched anything on the desk."

Rick turned to Wilcox. "Tom, would a security guard normally stand inside the room and watch her clean sensitive areas, like the Ambassador's office for instance?"

"Probably not. They'd typically just let her in and leave."

Rick turned back to Brooks. "Where do you keep sensitive documents?"

Brooks pointed toward a small door inserted into one of the walls. Rick had failed to notice it when he entered. "Everything goes in the safe at night," Brooks said, glancing toward the wall.

"Except the calendar," Rick added.

"Yes, that's correct," Brooks responded.

Brooks looked at his watch. "I'm afraid that's all the time I have, Mr. Williams. I'm due at a meeting. Karen, would you have Henry meet me downstairs with the car?"

Yes, Sir." Karen O'Dell left the room. Brooks looked at Rick. "You can go ahead and use my office. If you have any other questions, I'll be back this afternoon." He grabbed his briefcase and put on his suit coat which hung over the back of his chair.

"One quick question before you leave, Sir?"

Brooks hesitated as he walked toward the door. "Of course."

"Where were you on the morning of the disappearance?"

"Several of the Western Ambassadors get together for a brunch once a month. The British Ambassador was the host for this one and I attended."

"Was it listed on your calendar?"

"No, actually it wasn't. It was handled verbally between the British Ambassador and me."

"Was Buck's meeting on your calendar?"

"Yes."

"Was the meeting secret?"

"I'm not sure what you mean by 'secret'," Brooks said. "The meeting wasn't announced to the press. We were told Buck needed to be taken to the Palace for a meeting with Assad."

"I won't keep you, Mr. Ambassador," Rick said. "Thanks for your time."

"It was a pleasure meeting both of you," Brooks said, nodding to Rick and Pierre.

Rick waited until Brooks was gone, then glanced at Tom. "Do you mind if I ask where Brooks is going?"

Tom smiled. "I think I know where you're headed with this, Rick." Tom leaned over Brooks' desk and turned the calendar around. He flipped it open, finding today's date. "It says he's meeting a couple of American businessmen for lunch. That's too easy, isn't it?"

"That's my point. Kalami could have read Brooks' calendar any evening she was in here. What's it say about the day of the incident?"

Tom turned the pages until he found the day in question. "It says Buck/Palace 10 a.m."

Rick turned to O'Dell. "How did Ahmed Kalami get hired?"

"I think it was through his sister, wasn't it, Tom?"

"That's right," Tom responded. "We normally have two drivers here. One of them retired recently, so we found someone locally to get a second driver in here quickly. Safa volunteered Ahmed and we interviewed him."

"Who ran the interview?" Rick asked.

"Lisa pre-interviewed him, then he talked with me."

"What were your thoughts at the time?"

Tom thought for a moment. "His sister's a terrific person. Very friendly and a hard worker. When I met Ahmed, he had a pleasant personality just like his sister. Spoke perfect English, had studied in the States. He seemed like a good fit."

"Did you run his name through Washington?"

"No," Tom said, shaking his head. "We talked to his father. He confirmed everything Ahmed told us."

"How long had Ahmed been working here?"

Tom thought for a minute. He looked at Paul. "What would you say, Paul. A couple of weeks?"

"Maybe less," Paul replied. "He was new. The exact start date should be in the file Karen gave you."

"How's the death benefit usually delivered?"

"Honestly, we've never had a death before," Paul said. "We've been trying to get in touch with Safa because the check's in her name. Her father told us she's not living with them any longer and he has no idea where she is."

"I'd like to move on and talk about the external sources on the payroll for a minute," said Rick. "Paul, is there anything important about them we need to know?"

"There's not much to tell. One is a local politician who calls in information. The other is a local businessman. They never come to the Embassy."

"How do you meet them?" Rick asked.

"If we meet them in person, we use a local restaurant."

"Fine. What can you tell me about the emergency phone line?" Rick asked Paul.

Paul looked surprised by the question. "Well, there's not much to tell there, either. The hotline is staffed twenty-four hours a day. Any American in trouble can call the line and we'll send someone out to help."

"It's staffed by Americans?"

"That's right. Technically, they work for CIA, but they're registered as diplomats."

"I guess that brings us to Bill Sharp. What can you tell me about him?"

"Bill was the Ambassador's right hand man," Paul replied. "He knew the Embassy better than anyone. He filled in wherever he was needed. Bill was the one guy who made the Embassy run on a day to day basis."

"I don't mean to be impolite, but why are you talking about Sharp in the past tense?"

Paul stared at Rick. "You don't seriously think he's still alive, do you?"

"Yes, I do," Rick replied. "Otherwise, we wouldn't be here."

Paul became red faced, although it was impossible for Rick to tell whether that was from embarrassment or anger. He stared at the carpet. There was an uncomfortable silence in the room for a moment before Rick turned to Tom and continued. "Why wouldn't Sharp have driven Buck to the meeting?"

"We'd never allow someone like Buck to travel alone in the city with just a driver. We'd always send an extra person. Brooks left earlier that morning and took Henry as his driver, so that left Ahmed to drive and the Ambassador sent Bill along to babysit."

"And you felt that was safe?"

"With Bill along, we felt confident in the arrangement."

"Was Sharp armed at the time?"

"No. Only the guards carry weapons."

"I'm just thinking out loud here, Tom, but maybe the kidnappers thought they'd be kidnapping the Ambassador."

"That's possible, Rick," Tom replied. "I think Brooks decided to send Bill at the last minute, didn't he, Paul?"

"Honestly, I have no idea. I was out of the loop on that."

"Rick, I think that's the way that went down," Tom answered. "Brooks sent Bill instead of going himself and he decided at the last minute."

"I don't mean to make anyone uncomfortable, but I need to ask a question about Brooks. Do either of you feel comfortable giving me a straight answer?"

Tom looked at Paul. Neither seemed to want to answer the question. "What do you want to know?" Tom finally asked.

"It seems like Buck's meeting with Assad would have been important enough for the Ambassador to attend. Any idea why Brooks sent Sharp instead?" Rick asked.

Tom hesitated, thinking. "I'm not sure I can answer that. I don't really know."

"Tom, you and I have been friends for a long time. I need an honest opinion, even if it's a guess. Call it background information."

Tom looked away for a moment as though he was reluctant to give an opinion. "All right, here's my take on it, Rick. I have no idea whether this is true. It's just how I read the man."

"Go ahead."

"Brooks was a big-time dealer in aircraft before he retired. He met personally with foreign leaders. They treated him with respect. Brook doesn't get that kind of treatment in this job. My guess is Brooks planned on attending the meeting, but State told him he wouldn't be allowed in the room. I think Brooks intentionally skipped the meeting and sent Bill instead."

Rick thought about the answer. "Thanks, Tom. Your opinion will go no further than this."

"I appreciate that," replied Wilcox.

"The kidnapping was a professional job, Tom," Rick said. "Whoever did this had their operation ready and waiting for an opportunity. Do either of you know the politics of the Kalami father?"

Paul O'Dell answered that question. "I know he's supportive of the Assad regime. He's got food contracts with the government. I don't think he'd be mixed up in anything like this."

"Do you think Safa Kalami would be capable of running a surveillance op inside the Embassy?" Rick said looking at O'Dell.

"No, I don't. No disrespect toward Safa, but she's not capable of it," Paul said as though it should have been obvious. "She doesn't even have a high school education."

"What's your take on the kidnapping, Paul?"

"It's nice of you to ask," O'Dell replied. "I'm speaking personally, of course, but I've always thought Amal was behind it. Amal is backed by the Iranians. They're making a play for influence in the region and using Amal to do it."

That's the company line the CIA is using, Rick thought. "It's nice to hear the perspective of someone who's actually on the ground here," Rick said, smiling weakly at O'Dell. "Since the bodies of Buck and Sharp were never recovered, Washington assumes they've been kidnapped. But since no group has claimed responsibility, no one really knows. If you were conducting a search, where would you look first?" Rick asked.

O'Dell's immediate response surprised Rick. It's a tough question. He's not even thinking before he answers, Rick thought, while listening to Paul's response. "The local Lebanese militia groups wouldn't necessarily know who Buck was," O'Dell began. "But the Iranians would. My take is Amal took orders from Tehran and kidnapped Buck. They thought Sharp was the Ambassador so they took him, too. They took the hostages over back roads through Syria north and slipped over the border into Amal controlled territory. That is, if you believe they're still alive."

"That's sound advice, Paul. We'll look into it," Rick replied.

"I think you've got a better shot at finding them that way than looking at the Embassy employees. It's your investigation and I'm not telling you how to run it. That's just my take on it."

"We'll start with that approach and see what we can develop," Rick said.

Paul gave Rick an administrative smile, as though he thought Rick was a novice investigator. "Good. Anything else?" O'Dell asked as a way of signaling the meeting was over.

"Thanks for your time today," Rick said. "Please convey our thanks to Ambassador Brooks as well. We've got enough to get started." Rick stood up and put the folders under his arm. Pierre followed Rick's lead and prepared to leave. "We'll be in and out of the Embassy for a few days while we follow up on details. If you think of anything else, please let us know."

"You're welcome," Paul said. "If we have any questions, we'll go through Tom."

"Great," Rick said. "Thanks, again, and we'll be in touch."

# Chapter Twenty

RICK AND PIERRE asked the young girl at the counter downstairs to call a taxi. They waited outside on the sidewalk. "What do you think?" Pierre asked Rick.

"Obviously, they don't know anything. You can't blame them, really. They've got an embassy to run. It's not their job to investigate a kidnapping. During the meeting, though, I couldn't help but wonder if their offices are bugged. Perhaps, O'Dell's right. This wasn't an inside job. Whoever did this obtained their information from listening devices."

"If their offices are bugged, it would mean they were listening today," Pierre replied.

"And they're probably laughing their asses off right now because they think we didn't get any information. However, that might not be a bad thing."

"What do you mean?" Pierre asked.

"They think they're safe."

"Would you risk a kidnapping attempt based on what you overheard in a bugging op?"

"Not on that information alone," Rick replied. "I'd still want someone on the inside to verify the information. Our prime suspect is still Safa Kalami, in my opinion," Rick reasoned.

"I think so, too. If the Embassy offices are bugged, we should send our voice messages to Paris from the French Embassy, just to be safe."

"Good idea. Why don't we go see if the Range Rovers are ready? I'd like to send copies of the personnel files back to Washington. If the vehicles are ready, we can swing by the French Embassy and send the files by diplomatic bag."

"After that, we should check out the Kalami residence," Pierre said.

"I've got the address in Safa Kalami's file. Think you can find it?"

"Probably."

"Good. We can watch the residence the rest of the day and drive out to the border crossing tomorrow," Rick suggested. "If we see the Kalami woman, then maybe we've got something."

# Chapter Twenty-One

TRAFFIC WAS HEAVY during the ride to Madigan Motors and the taxi encountered numerous delays. Rick and Pierre continued to discuss the meeting.

"I'll tell you one thing O'Dell's wrong about," Pierre said. "There's no way the kidnappers traveled back roads over a hundred miles north into Amal territory. They'd have had to pass several Syrian Army installations along the way. They wouldn't risk it."

"People are trying awfully hard to convince us to look in Amal territory," replied Rick.

"Like Jean said, it's politically convenient to blame Amal."

During the conversation two motorcyclists pulled up on either side of the taxi, stopped and stared inside. "Shit," Rick said without looking at Pierre.

"I see them," Pierre responded.

"We are totally screwed if those guys attack. Don't look at them."

Pierre chuckled. "I wasn't planning on it."

The cyclists gave the men a long look, revved their engines and then drove on ahead between lanes of traffic. Rick expelled the air he was holding and then wiped his face with both hands. "What the hell was that?"

"A warning?" Pierre asked ominously.

"Those weren't the usual guys you see riding around town on motorbikes. Black leather jackets, gloves, shaded visors; those guys were militia."

"Well funded, too, nice machines," said Pierre.

"If Jean made that wire transfer and we get those cars, we've gotta drive straight back to the Embassy and get Coxie to give us some protection."

Mad Ryan Madigan the Deal Maker, as the sign said, walked through the showroom with open arms when they entered. "You blokes are all set. The transfer came through early today, we've prepped your vehicles and they're parked out back."

"What about tags?" Rick asked.

"You've got thirty days to register them with the local authorities. Come out back and I'll show you where they are."

They followed Madigan to a fenced lot behind the showroom where two new black Range Rovers sat, still dripping water from being washed. "Pierre, you check that one; I'll do this one."

The men looked under the cars, looked around the engine compartments and then felt underneath the dashboards. "I think they're clean," Pierre said.

"Either that or we'll be blown to shit once we drive off the lot."

"These cars have been totally secured, gentlemen, if that's what you're worried about. Come back inside and I'll give you the titles and sales receipts."

After the transaction was finished, the men drove the cars off the lot and headed to the French Embassy where they sent copies of the employment files back to Washington inside a diplomatic bag. After completing that task, they traveled back to the American Embassy where they parked in the circle drive and walked inside to the counter. The young woman recognized them. "Mr.

Williams," she said nodding to Rick. "Mr. Thibault, so nice to see both of you again."

"We need to speak with Captain Wilcox."

"Of course." She left the counter and used a phone on a desk behind the counter.

It was only a minute or two before Tom came out of the door adjacent to the counter. "What's up, guys?"

"Is there somewhere we can talk?"

"Sure. Let's use the interview room again."

Rick related the story of the motorcycle intimidation. "It sounds like someone knows you're here," Tom said.

"Damn straight, it does."

"What do you want to do?"

"When's the last time you had Brooks' office swept?"

"For bugs?"

"Yes," Rick replied.

"I can't remember. It's been a long time."

"I'd get Paul's guys going on it. If I were you, I'd do the other offices, too. If there's some kind of security breach, we've gotta find it."

"I'll get Paul going on it right now," Tom said.

"We need some protection, Tom."

"You mean weapons?"

"Exactly."

"Follow me." Tom led them downstairs to a small armory. He looked among the shelves until he found two pistols. "I can give you these M1911s."

"You got extra mags for them?"

"I can come up with a few." Tom found two detachable magazines for each of them. "They're only single stack. We don't have a large selection. I can give each of you a couple of boxes of 45 ACP cartridges."

Rick inspected the weapons. "These look good. Thanks."

"No problem. You shouldn't open carry them through the lobby. Hang on a minute." Tom found a canvas bag. "Put everything in here."

Rick and Pierre secured the weapons and the mags in the bag and zipped up the top. "Thanks again, Coxie. You just saved our lives."

"Not a problem, Rick." He slapped Rick on the back.

"I've got one more question. Do you know your way around the city?"

"Of course. What do you need?"

"We want to drive by the Kalami residence and we need to find a Transport Ministry facility."

Tom thought for a minute. "Let's walk back upstairs and I'll grab a map." Wilcox found a map and spread it out on a table in the interview room. "This is what we give to visitors. What's the Kalami address?" Rick opened the file and pointed to the address. Tom took a pen from his shirt pocket and traced lines on the map. "Here's where you are now," he said, circling the Embassy. "The Kalami residence is here." He traced a route through the city. "It should be easy to find. I was there once. The house sits on an entire block. It's one of the nicest homes in the city."

"How about the Transport Ministry?"

Tom studied the map. "There's one right here," he said, finding it on the map. "Along the Beirut-Damascus Highway northwest of the city." He pointed on the map as Rick and Pierre watched. "As I recall, you can see it from the highway. They park construction vehicles there."

"Thanks, Tom. We'll check it out."

"Good. Now get the hell out of my Embassy and let me get back to work," he said with a laugh. "I've got pretty ladies in the office I've got to guard."

Rick saluted Tom. "With pleasure, Sir."

Rick and Pierre talked walking out of the Embassy. "You want to do a drive-by on the Kalami residence?" Pierre asked.

"How about we take one of the vehicles back to the hotel and ride in one car."

"Okay by me," Pierre agreed.

After dropping Rick's vehicle off at the Omayad, Pierre found the Kalami residence easily, just a short distance northwest of the hotel. They found a walled compound that encompassed an entire block. "I was afraid of this," Pierre said as they slowed in front of the residence. "You can't see inside."

They passed the front entrance, a heavy wrought iron gate that opened electronically. "Slow down," Rick said. "I'll look up the driveway." He could see a black Mercedes parked in the circle drive at the front door of a nicely kept home. Pierre stopped momentarily in front of the gate. "Man," Rick said, whistling. "That guy's got money."

"Let's drive around the block," Pierre suggested. On the back side of the property, a doorway had been cut into the wall that looked to be used for trash removal. Pierre stopped and studied the wooden double doors that had been built into the opening. "We could climb the wall next to the door and look around."

"And get arrested?" Rick asked, looking over at Pierre. "No thanks. Let's drive around to the front and watch for a while."

The two watched the front entrance to the Kalami residence until dark and observed no activity, no traffic in or out of the residence. Pierre finally looked at Rick. "This is pointless. We're not going to see the woman, Rick. She's gone."

The streetlamps along the street had turned themselves on, lights showed through the windows of the residences and the neighborhood had settled in for the evening. "You're right. If I was involved in a kidnapping, the last place I'd go is back home. I suppose we could ring the buzzer and ask the father if he's seen his daughter," Rick said.

"What's he going to say, Rick? Thanks for killing my son? Can we leave now?" Pierre asked.

"We might as well. All we're doing here is advertising the fact that we're looking for someone. Maybe we'll come up with something tomorrow near the border crossing."

# Chapter Twenty-Two

LAURA AND JACK Postl entered Harvard University's Widener Library to roam among the stacks and special collection rooms hoping to find a student or faculty ID. After a half-hour of walking among the study areas without success, Laura finally spied a printed grade report used as a bookmark. She quickly memorized the student name and ID number and replaced the grade report.

"I've got what you're looking for," Laura told Jack, who wandered around the library, amazed at the collections.

"This is an awesome place," Jack commented, walking around like a tourist.

Laura grabbed him by the arm. "Yeah, it's one of the five best libraries in the world. We're here on business, Jack."

"Okay. Where's the ID?"

"I didn't steal it," she said, rolling her eyes. "I memorized the information and returned it. Where do we need to go now?"

"I need to find a computer terminal in a place that's not too busy. It must be connected to whatever enrollment system they have."

They walked around the library until Jack spotted a row of computer terminals. He sat down while Laura walked around the stacks. He accessed the software interface and immediately got up and found Laura. "Those terminals are restricted to the library catalog. We need to find an administrative office."

They left the library and walked across the campus until they found what appeared to be an administrative building. Upon entering, Laura studied the office listing in the lobby and headed up the stairs where they discovered a row of administrative offices on the second floor. Fortunately, one office was empty and the door was left standing wide open. Laura wrote the information she'd memorized from the grade report on scratch paper and handed it to Jack. She looked up and down the hallway and saw no one. "I'll serve as lookout. One knock means trouble. Now close the door and get to work."

Ten minutes later, a disheveled older man with gray hair and glasses walked down the hallway holding a soft drink and a sandwich that looked to have been purchased from vending machines. He stopped in front of the door. "Professor Woods?" Laura asked, looking at the nameplate on the door.

He nodded. "Why are you standing outside my office?"

Laura gently knocked once on the door. "I want to sign up for student advisement."

"This isn't student advisement. Who told you to come here?"

"Financial Aid."

"You're in the wrong department. Let's go in my office and find out where you're supposed to be."

The professor tried to open his door and found it locked. "Oh dear. I'm afraid I've locked myself out. Wait here and I'll find security to open it."

The professor walked down the hallway and disappeared. Laura knocked on the door again with more force. "Jack, it's time to go."

Jack opened the door with a smile. "Let's go."

Laura and Jack walked briskly down the hallway. "We've got about two minutes before security arrives," Laura said. "Let's get lost in street traffic," Laura said as they exited the building. "You walk on ahead of me and I'll follow you. Enter the first coffee shop or café you see. I'll meet you there."

They walked off campus into Cambridge where Laura saw Jack enter a sandwich shop. She entered and found him in line at the counter. "What'd you find out?"

"Based on the name 'Ahmed Kalami,' I found he's no longer a student and his last address listed was this." He handed Laura a piece of scratch paper.

"Come on. Let's go," Laura said before leaving the shop.

"Can I get a sandwich first?"

Laura grabbed him by the arm. "Eat later." She pushed him out the door, stepped to the curb and flagged down a taxi. "You know where this is?" Laura asked the driver, handing him the address.

"On Somerville Avenue? Sure."

"Take us there."

It took no more than ten minutes. The driver pulled to the curb at a storefront. The lettering hand painted on the front window said, "The Crescent Society," above a half crescent moon. Laura asked the driver to wait. "Hold my partner ransom. If I don't come back, he's yours."

The driver laughed. "You got it, lady."

Laura entered the storefront and was met by an older woman wearing a hijab. "May I help you," she asked with a friendly smile.

"Yes, Ma'am. I'm looking for an apartment for an Islamic student my husband and I are sponsoring at Tufts University. I was told you might be able to help."

"We do provide financial assistance to promising young Islamic students, but your student must fill out an aid application to be considered." She reached underneath the counter and handed Laura several pages of forms. "Please have your student complete the application and return it to this address." She laid a full color brochure on top of the forms and pointed to the address printed on the first panel of the tri-fold. "We have a number of resources available for students, including opportunities for prayer at one of our associated mosques. If I could have your name and phone number, I'll have someone call you."

Laura wrote a false name and number and left it with the woman. "Thank you so very much. I'll wait for your call."

"You're welcome. Thank you for helping our students."

Laura walked out and climbed in the taxi. "Let's get out of here."

The driver looked in his rear view mirror. "Where to now, lady?"

"Downtown Four Seasons."

# Chapter Twenty-Three

*Wednesday, November 2, 1988*

LAURA AND JACK traveled back to D.C. early the next morning. Grabbing a taxi at the airport, Laura dropped Jack at the office Mason had rented for him. "I'll call you later today," Laura said before Jack exited the car. "I might need you so don't leave the office until I call."

"What if I get hungry?"

Laura sounded angry when she spoke. "Get yourself some carry-out and wait for my call, Jack."

"Aren't you going to give me some cash?" Jack asked.

"It's called 'per diem,' Jack and no, I'm not. You've got a credit card. Use it. I'm late for an appointment."

The driver retrieved Jack's bag and deposited it on the sidewalk. Jack grabbed it and knocked on Laura's window. She rolled it down. "You're worse than the Soviets, you know," he said.

"I've got an appointment at FBI Headquarters. I can't be late."

Laura watched Jack walk inside the building. *He's still having trouble adjusting to life in the States. Be patient.*

The driver got into the taxi and looked in the mirror. "Where to now, Ma'am?"

"FBI Headquarters, J. Edgar Hoover Building. You know where it is?"

"Yep."

Laura arrived at the J. Edgar Hoover Building with ten minutes to spare before her appointment. She entered the lobby and told the officer at the Information Desk she had a scheduled appointment with Dan Jenkins. He picked up the phone, talked briefly and hung up. Looking at Laura, he said "Assistant Director Jenkins will meet you here in the lobby."

Jenkins walked through the lobby minutes later and smiled seeing Laura. They hugged each other tightly. "It's so good to see you," he said whispering in her ear. They parted, but still held hands. "How have you been?" he asked.

"I'm doing well, Dan. And you?"

"You know me. I'm always doing well." Dan stood back and looked her up and down. "You look fantastic."

Laura looked down, embarrassed. "I really should say something about not calling."

Dan waved her off. "Don't worry about it. It's just good to see you." He nodded toward the elevators. "Come on; let's go up to my office." He glanced at his secretary on the way through his outer office. "Bette, would you hold my calls?"

"Yes, Sir."

Laura looked around Dan's office at the pictures from his twenty years with the bureau. He'd enjoyed a fine career and was rumored to be a candidate for the Director's job. He must have been a college baseball player, she thought looking at a couple of team pictures hanging behind his desk. In his late forties, tall with dark hair that had begun to gray at the temples, Dan had a friendly manner about him, eyes that crinkled at the corners when he smiled. The two had served together in Paris and had a strong affection for each other. Dan had been transferred back to Washington before Laura left Paris, but they reconnected after Laura's mission to Moscow. Dan stepped in to protect Laura from CIA Director Bates following the mission. He motioned toward two brown leather chairs that sat along one wall. Dan sat beside her and spoke gently, remembering how vulnerable she'd been following the divorce. "How's Steve? Is he still over at the agency?"

"Yes," she said nodding her head. "I've seen him only once since the divorce."

"Will you guys ever get back together?"

"Probably not."

Dan was silent for a moment, wondering whether to ask the next question. "Do you still love him?"

Laura was slow to answer. Dan could see the tension in her body. I've gone too far, he thought. "I'm sorry. That was a rude question."

She looked down at the floor. "Not everything is a yes or no answer, Dan."

"Sorry," he said again. "That's the FBI agent coming out in me."

I've come to realize," she said speaking softly, "that Steve will sacrifice anything to further his career. Even his marriage."

Dan put his hand on top of hers. "Some men are like that, Laura. And when they finally get that big job, it's a hollow victory. They can't come home to a loving family every evening. Steve will finally realize someday that the job is worthless without the other."

Laura smiled as though Dan had put her feelings into words. "As smart as he is, Steve's a slow learner, I guess."

"Divorce is never about one thing, you know."

He's right, she thought, nodding her head. "I recognize that I made mistakes, Dan. What can I do about it now?"

"You can change. You remember our last conversation walking out of Langley?"

"Of course. Change takes time, Dan."

"If you ever need to talk, just pick up the phone. I'm not going anywhere."

"Are you seeing anyone?" Laura asked awkwardly. The question came without thinking.

Dan laughed. "I'm seeing you right now."

Laura smiled. "You know what I mean."

"I'm thinking of asking out a lovely woman who lives in the Caribbean."

She put her hair behind her ear to give her a few seconds before answering. "You never know. She might accept."

"Good." Dan relaxed and leaned back in his chair. "Now, what can I help you with today?"

"I need to pull the bank records for a non-profit organization."

Dan thought for a minute. "That's a tough one. I'd need evidence of serious criminal activity that I could take to a federal prosecutor."

"It has national security implications, Dan," she said pointedly.

"I see." Dan watched her for a moment as an interrogator might during an interview. "Are you working on a mission?"

Laura pulled out a copy of the contract and handed it to him. "I'm working under a contract."

Dan scanned the contract, talking while he read. "I figured Bates would come to his senses about you." He stared at the signature on the last page. "I see the President signed this himself." He handed the contract back. "You've got friends in high places. What's the mission?"

"I'm working on a rescue of Nicholas Buck, Dan."

Dan's eyes widened. "The Under Secretary of State who was kidnapped?" he asked, surprised.

"That's him." Laura looked directly at Dan. "There's a charity in Boston called The Crescent Society. Their bank records may lead to the kidnappers."

"What evidence do you have they were involved?"

"We suspect Buck's driver may have been working with the kidnappers. He accepted money from The Crescent Society while he was here in the States. They're an organization devoted to Islamic causes. We think some of their money may fund a terror organization."

"All right, give me a day to do a preliminary investigation. What's the name of the non-profit again?"

"The Crescent Society. They have an office in Boston."

Dan wrote down the name. "I need as much hard evidence as you can give me. Are you going to be around for a day or two?"

"I can be."

"Where are you staying?"

"Nowhere yet."

"Stick around for a day. Let me know where you're staying and I'll call you tomorrow."

"Thanks, Dan. You're the best."

They stood and hugged. Dan kissed her on the cheek. "Can you find your way out?"

"Of course."
"Okay.  I'll call you in the morning."

# Chapter Twenty-Four

LAURA CHECKED INTO the Watergate and called Postl from her room. "Jack?"

"What took you so long?"

"I need printed copies of Kalami's Harvard enrollment and his address."

"I might be able to do it remotely. I'm not sure." Jack said.

"I need it tomorrow."

"I'll see what I can do."

Early the next morning, Laura phoned Langley and left a message for Steve. She caught a taxi and paid for a long trip out to McLean where she walked in the CIA lobby. It was the first time she'd been in the building since her resignation months ago. She stopped and looked around the lobby. I don't feel the same attachment I felt before, she thought. I guess I really am gone. She walked to the counter and informed the clerk she had a meeting with Steve Tilton. The clerk had no idea who she was. Large organizations have short memories, she thought. The clerk asked her to sign in, gave her a Visitor's badge and then asked that she wait in the lobby. Steve showed up in the lobby thirty minutes later with an apology. "I'm sorry, Laura. I didn't check messages until now," he said red faced.

"I was beginning to think you didn't like me," she said, unable to resist the sarcasm.

Steve ignored the insult. He put his hands in his pockets and gave her a short shrug of the shoulders. "Well, we can't have that now, can we? Come on upstairs."

Steve led the way to his office, a trip Laura had made countless times. There was a sense of unease between them as they took the elevator to the seventh floor. Fortunately, they weren't alone and it was convenient to stay silent. Steve shut his office door behind them and picked up a file that lay on his desk with the name "Buck" scribbled on the cover. He opened it, withdrew a copy of Kalami's visa and handed it to her. "Can I see the rest of the file," Laura asked.

Steve gave her a look of frustration. "You've seen it. It's the one you stole."

"So much for security, I guess."

"We took steps to prevent that sort of thing when I returned."

"Good. I'll have our computer guy break in again to show you how bad your security really is."

Steve showed a flash of anger. "You want to throw insults at each other or do you want to work?"

"Can you make me a copy the visa?" She handed it back.

"Sure. Anything else?"

"If you have anything Rick sent from Damascus, I'd like a copy of that, too."

"I'll get it for you."

"When did Kalami leave the country?"

"Unfortunately, we don't have a record of it. INS has him listed as still being in the States."

"I'll skip the reference to security."

Steve gave her a look of anger. His face turned red and he started to speak, then thought better of it and stopped. He gave her his best administrative smile. "Anything else?"

"Yes, there is. Can you reprogram a satellite for me?"

Steve's mouth opened halfway. "You're kidding, right?"

"No, I'm not. We need surveillance on a general location and we need it several times a day."

"Can't you put eyes on your places of interest?"

"We can't get within a mile of that vicinity, Steve."

"Is that the location Jack Mason asked about?"

"South of the Damascus-Beirut Highway border crossing."

"I already gave him what we had," Steve said. He'd reached the end of his patience. "Damn it, Laura, we can't cover every inch of territory over there just because you think there might be a terrorist there."

"We've got a pretty good idea they're there, Steve. It's not a wild guess."

"You've got to understand something." Steve had been leaning on his desk, looking down at Laura who was seated in a chair. He leaned forward to make a point. "We have little control over satellite coverage. That's a cross jurisdictional issue and we can't just order up coverage anytime we want. It's the NSA's call and they have to get the Pentagon and JPL involved. It's a huge deal, Laura. If you've got some hard evidence, I'll run it by the Pentagon and we'll see."

"Or, I could just call the President."

Laura meant it as an insult, but Steve leaned back, looked at the ceiling for a moment and then looked back and grinned. "You know, that's not a bad idea. If you called the White House and the President issued an order, those guys would be running around like crazy getting it done."

Now that Laura had physical distance between herself and Steve, she relaxed. Please keep your distance, she thought. "I'll make the call when I get back to the Watergate."

"What are you doing for dinner?" Steve asked, abruptly changing the subject.

Laura felt her body tense again. Relax. Deep breaths. "Steve, I've got some critical calls to make this afternoon. I'll probably take dinner at the hotel this evening. Thanks, though." She gave him a polite smile.

Steve's face became red as he showed his embarrassment. "I'm sorry. That wasn't appropriate. Anything else?"

"I'd like to take a copy of Kalami's visa with me."

"Of course. Hang on a minute." Steve took the file and the visa request into his outer office and returned with the copies. "Here's the visa along with some material Rick sent me."

Laura skimmed the pages. "Perfect. I'll get out of your way and let you get back to work."

"You need me to walk you downstairs?"

"Nope. I've done it a million times."

She stood to leave and Steve wisely put space between the two of them. "Call me with your progress."

"I will."

# Chapter Twenty-Five

*Wednesday, November 3, 1988*

RICK WILLIAMS WOKE up to a knock on his hotel room door. Thinking it was the maid service, he took the 'Do Not Disturb' sign and opened the door to place it on the door handle. That's when he noticed the business card pushed underneath the door. He picked up the card and read a handwritten note.

"Vroom, Vroom. Mossad"

He picked up the phone and called Pierre's room. "I got a note under my door."

"Me, too," Pierre replied.

"From Mossad?"

"Yes. Mine had a motorcycle drawn on it. It just said 'Mossad.' How did they know?"

"I have no idea. Let's talk about it downstairs. I'll meet you in the coffee shop."

Rick and Pierre ordered bagels and coffee at the hotel restaurant and sat down at a small table. Rick looked at the foot traffic in and out. "I'm getting paranoid. I'm watching every single person who comes into the restaurant."

"Relax," Pierre replied. "Mossad could be helpful. They've got resources here. We should talk to them."

"If Mossad knows we're here," Rick said," who else knows?"

"We can't worry about that. The Israeli's are friendlies, Rick."

"All right, I'll let it go. We need a camera and field glasses to watch those roads this morning."

"Let's find one of those electronic shops," Pierre suggested. "We should take lunch with us, too. We may be out there all day."

"I was thinking of taking along equipment to support our cover, a traffic counter if we can find one. If we stretch one of those pneumatic tubes across the highway, we'll look like real Transport employees."

"Where do we find one of those?"

"Transport offices would have them. I wonder if those IDs Henri gave us would fool a Transport worker?" Rick asked.

"Only one way to find out."

The men took one of the Range Rovers, stopped for supplies and headed out of town on the Beirut-Damascus Highway. Pierre drove. "Look for a highway construction facility," he said. "I've got my hands full dodging military trucks. They think they own the damn road."

The highway was busy; Syrian military vehicles moving in and out of Lebanon slowed civilian traffic. Pierre looked over at Rick in the passenger seat. "The border crossing's only about thirty kilos away, but with this traffic, who knows how long it will take. You finished loading the camera?"

"I think I've got it figured out," Rick replied. "There." He pointed to his left. "That looks like the transportation facility Tom mentioned. Let's stop."

Pierre exited the highway and pulled into a construction yard filled with backhoes, large piles of gravel and a warehouse. They found the Transport office inside the warehouse. "Let me do the talking," Pierre said.

A gruff, overweight maintenance worker sat behind the counter on a stool and asked their business. Pierre showed him his Ministry of Transport ID and the letter from the Minister.

"Why doesn't anyone ever tell us you people are coming out here?" the man muttered, showing the frustration many construction workers feel at seeing bureaucratic paperwork.

Pierre smiled. "Just doing our jobs," Pierre replied in Arabic.

"What do you need from me?"

"A traffic counter."

"They should have given you that downtown."

"They told me to come here."

"Give me a minute," the man said, reluctant to get up off his stool and do any meaningful work. He came back minutes later with a long rubber tube and a small black box which attached to the end of the hose. He threw them on the counter. "Make sure you return it."

"We'll have it back in a couple of days."

"You need to sign for it," the man said reaching underneath the counter for a clipboard. He threw it on top of the equipment.

"Do you have a pen I can use?" Pierre asked.

"Praise Allah, none of you people are ever prepared," he said taking a pen from his shirt pocket and throwing it on top of the clipboard. Pierre signed for it, picked up the equipment and started to leave.

The man shouted at them. "Wait a minute. I need my pen back."

Pierre turned around, walked back to the counter and laid the pen on the counter. "Sorry."

Pierre threw the equipment in the back of the Rover and they pulled back on the highway. "I guess those IDs really do work," Rick said.

"If we can fool that guy, we can fool anyone."

After driving toward the border for about fifteen minutes, Pierre looked to his left across the terrain. "The highway runs parallel to the border at this spot. Lebanon is only a couple of clicks to the south."

"We've passed a couple of roads that head in that direction. Should we start with those?" Rick asked.

"Let me show you the border crossing first." They followed a Syrian personnel carrier. "Those are Syrian regulars ahead of us," Pierre said. "They're probably on their way to Beirut." The canvas on the back of the truck flapped in the wind, sometimes exposing the soldiers sitting in the rear.

"I've sat in my share of those vehicles," Rick said. "It's not a lot of fun."

"This is the main route the Syrians use to bring troops in and out," Pierre continued. Pierre slowed his vehicle to put space between the personnel carrier and the Range Rover. "We should be coming up on the border anytime now."

They saw a large sign ahead written in Arabic. "The border is a kilo away. You want to see it?"

"Yes," Rick said. "Will we be able to turn around when we get close?"

"I think so, but I've never approached the crossing from this side before."

"What would happen if we tried to go through it?"

"I'm not sure. Let's turn around before then," Pierre replied.

Rick finally saw the border crossing ahead, a building that stretched over the roadway with bays where cars pulled in to be checked through by the authorities. The longest line was to the side where military vehicles were being waved through without a search. "I've got a bad feeling about this," Rick said. "Don't go any farther. Turn around whenever you can."

Pierre turned left onto a road that led into a small village adjacent to the crossing. He drove only far enough to turn around and then headed back the other direction on the highway. "What do you want to do?" he asked.

"I see what you mean about the kidnappers turning off the highway before the border crossing. They'd have never made it past." Rick looked out over a landscape that reminded him of the American Southwest. Small trees and shrubs grew up amid the rock outcroppings. "Let's pick a road that looks like it gets a lot of traffic."

"None of them get a lot of traffic," Pierre said, pointing across the barren landscape at the hills in the distance. "You wouldn't go back in there unless you lived there. That's rough territory back in those hills. Rough people, too."

"Thinking like a kidnapper, that'd be a great place to hide."

"The best."

As they approached one of the roads leading off the highway, Pierre began to slow down and signaled with his right blinker. "The one just ahead of us is one we should watch."

Rick looked off to his right. "Go ahead and pull off."

Pierre turned right onto an unmarked road that was paved for only a few hundred yards before turning to gravel. Pierre drove to the end of the paved section and stopped. "There's nothing between here and the border," he said pointing ahead. "Anyone traveling down this road means to go across into Lebanon. I'm afraid to go any farther out of fear of being seen. See that tree line we just passed?"

Rick looked back through the rear window and pointed at the trees. "Can we pull off the road behind those trees?" Rick asked.

"We bought the damn off-road package, Rick. If we can't take this thing off-road, we might as well return the Rover to Madigan and get our money back."

Rick laughed. "Okay, let's do it."

Pierre pulled back and forth on the narrow roadway until he'd turned the vehicle around and drove the Range Rover down into a gulley, up over a bed of rocks and managed to get behind the trees. He pointed the car toward the highway. "Just in case we need to leave in a hurry," he said with a grin.

"I agree," Rick replied. He looked around. "Let's pull the equipment out of the back and lay it on the ground in case anyone sees us." Rick pointed to the bushes that grew between the trees. "We can sit among those bushes. Bring the glasses and the camera."

The two men found a vantage point where they could clearly see the road and the highway a couple of hundred yards away. "This look okay to you?" Pierre asked.

"It's a good spot. We can make a quick exit and we'll see anyone who approaches."

"You got the camera?"

"Camera, field glasses and my trusted M1911," Rick said. He patted the weapon tucked inside his belt.

"Let's take pictures of every vehicle that comes by. I'll take first watch. Two hours on and two off until sunset," Pierre suggested.

"Fine by me." Rick handed the camera and glasses to Pierre. He leaned back against a tree and closed his eyes.

At dusk, Rick and Pierre packed up and left for the city having remained undiscovered the entire day. They were dusty, thirsty and ready for a trip back to civilization. They'd taken a number of pictures of vehicles traveling the road that day, of which only two were unusual, a late model black Mercedes sedan with darkened windows and an old Toyota Corolla occupied by four men with weapons.

# Chapter Twenty-Six

*Thursday, November 3, 1988*

THE FOLLOWING MORNING, Rick and Pierre stopped by the American Embassy to see whether Paul O'Dell could develop the film. Paul looked up from his desk. "What do you know, it's our professional investigators come to visit."

Rick ignored the insult. "Were you able to sweep the Ambassador's office?"

Paul grimaced. "As a matter of fact, we did. You were right, the office was bugged. We checked all the offices on this floor. Mine was bugged, so was Sharp's."

"Who did it?"

"We can't tell. The devices were of unknown origin. They were probably installed when Brooks had the renovation done on his office."

"What are you going to do about it?"

"Brooks wants to let the matter drop."

Rick looked surprised. "Drop? He's not even going to mention it to Washington?"

"Nope. He just said sweep his office once a month from now on."

Rick put his hands on his hips. "Does that sound right to you?"

Paul threw his pen on the desk, leaned back and looked Rick in the eyes. "Rick, he's the boss. There's nothing I can do about it."

Rick nodded his head. "I understand that, but ..."

Paul raised his voice and cut him off. "Rick, there's nothing else to say. The issue's been decided."

"We do what we're ordered even if it's wrong?"

"This is the government. We follow orders," Paul said, shrugging his shoulders. "You're a military guy. You understand it."

"Would you mind if I asked a question?"

"The bugging issue is closed. Anything else, I'd be glad to help."

"Why haven't you questioned the Israelis about Buck?"

Paul pushed his chair back from the desk and crossed his legs. That's all I need this morning, he thought, another long conversation. "That's not our call, Rick."

"Aren't you in a position to put pressure on Washington to do something?"

"If I don't keep my mouth shut, Karen and I will be back in the States looking for work," O'Dell said pointedly.

"Or the next victims of a kidnapping."

"Look, I'm not going to argue the dangers of working in the Middle East. Everyone understands the risks." He leaned forward and put his elbows on the desk. "All right," he said as though he surrendered the argument. "The Israelis weren't informed of Buck's meeting with Assad. My guess is they don't have a clue where Buck was taken because they weren't watching."

Rick thought about what might be gained by telling O'Dell about the Mossad contact. He decided to ask questions instead. "Why doesn't Washington bring them on board now? Mossad appears to have assets here."

"Rick, that's above my pay grade," O'Dell said, raising his voice again. "I'm not going to tell them how to run an investigation. All I know is you're here kicking around the dust trying to follow cold leads. Buck and Sharp are dead. Get used to the idea."

Rick equaled O'Dell's intensity and his voice could be heard echoing down the hallway. "Put yourself in their shoes. If you were captured, I'm sure you'd appreciate a couple of guys like us coming to find you."

O'Dell stood up, his anger overcoming his good sense. Only the desk separated the two men from being nose to nose apart. "If I'd been captured, I'd appreciate experienced investigators, not clowns like you guys coming in here waving a goddamn contract!"

Rick made a move to reach across the desk and Pierre stepped in to stop him. "Whoa, big guy," he said, putting his arm in front of Rick. "We gain nothing by fighting among ourselves. Back off." He gave Rick a slight, but firm shove. Rick, who towered over the much smaller O'Dell, took a step back. Pierre looked at O'Dell. "Both of you! Back the fuck up!" O'Dell backed away, finally sitting down again.

There was silence in the room as both men struggled to gain control of their anger. "Mr. O'Dell, are you going to send those listening devices back to Washington to have them analyzed?" Pierre asked.

"Brooks vetoed the idea," O'Dell replied in a more reasonable tone of voice. "We destroyed them."

"You don't think there's a connection between the kidnapping and those listening devices?"

"Are you trying to suggest we're responsible for Buck and Sharp's disappearance?" O'Dell asked bluntly.

"At this point, we're just asking questions, Mr. O'Dell."

"We're subjected to surveillance every day, Mr. Thibault. It's not exactly a stable region, if you haven't noticed."

Pierre conceded the point. "We're just trying to help." Pierre looked at Rick, hoping he'd keep quiet before he continued. "We watched the Kalami residence two days ago looking for the girl," Pierre said.

"I'd be careful about that if I were you," O'Dell shot back. "Kalami's politically connected. One phone call from him and you could be thrown in jail for a very long time."

"We noticed a black Mercedes in the driveway."

"Good for him. He deserves to drive nice cars."

"We saw an identical Mercedes traveling down one of the back roads into Lebanon yesterday."

Paul O'Dell was surprised. He seemed to struggle to formulate his next comment. "Unless you can show me proof that car belonged to Kalami, I can't comment on it."

"We took surveillance photos," Pierre said. "Could you develop the film for us?" Pierre reached into his pocket and handed the small, sealed tube of film to O'Dell.

Paul studied the tube. "We should be able to do that for you. Tomorrow soon enough?"

"Great."

"What's on the film?"

"We photographed traffic," Pierre said. "Photos of trucks and cars."

"Is the Mercedes in one of the photos?"

"Yes."

"Perhaps we'll be able to read a plate number. I'll send the film out. It should be ready tomorrow morning. Anything else?"

"Nope. I hope we're still friends," Pierre said with a hint of a smile.

"We are," O'Dell said, although he didn't sound as though he meant it. "I know you're just trying to do your job. We'll give you as much support as we can."

It was during the trip back to the hotel that Rick and Pierre discussed the conversation. "Is it just me or did you find the conversation with O'Dell weird?" Rick asked.

"He doesn't seem all that concerned about the kidnapping."

"He should be. He could be next."

"Here's a question for you. Do you think our hotel rooms are bugged?"

"I didn't think of that," Rick said. He looked over at Pierre. "We should assume they are."

"This spy shit's a little harder than I thought," Pierre said with a smile.

"Damn straight about that," Rick replied.

# Chapter Twenty-Seven

*Friday, November 4, 1988*

STOCKING UP ON supplies before the return trip to their surveillance spot the next morning, Pierre bought more of everything, film, water and food. They were silent during the trip outbound from the city. There wasn't much to say when looking forward to another long day in the hot sunshine of the desert. As they approached the road, Pierre put his left blinker on and watched in his rear view mirror as the car behind them did the same. "We've got trouble. The car behind us is turning left, too. I'm going to pull onto the shoulder as though we're turning around."

"Put it in reverse so they see the back-up lights. They'll probably drive on by."

Pierre completed the turn, pulled off the road and began to back up. The car that followed steered around them and disappeared around a curve. "Did you see those guys?"

"I tried not to look, but I think it was another four guys with weapons," said Rick. "Shift change at the kidnappers?"

"Maybe. It could be nothing, though. Everyone carries weapons out here. I do need to pull back on the highway just in case they stopped around that bend and are watching us."

"Good idea," Rick replied.

Turning back toward Damascus, the men drove several miles toward the city to avoid turning around in view of military vehicles. "Best not to make a spectacle out of ourselves," Pierre said with a smile.

"Maybe we ought to drive another car out here tomorrow."

"Oh, you mean like the other black Range Rover?" Both men laughed at their naiveté.

"We're terrible spies," Rick said.

Pierre turned around at a fueling station and headed back out of town. Upon arriving at the intersection, they turned and pulled into the same spot they used the day before. Pierre unpacked the field glasses and camera from a bag on the rear seat and handed them to Rick. "You've got first watch."

"Thanks, man. I appreciate your enthusiasm."

"Just doing my part to save men I never heard of," Pierre said with a wry grin. "By the way, take the hose and stretch it across the road. Let's see if we can get the traffic counter going. If anyone stops, we'll at least look like we know what the hell we're doing."

During the morning hours, there was little traffic on the road in either direction. The few vehicles that traveled the road took no notice of the traffic counter and drove over the hose without slowing. Rick took a photo of the same black Mercedes sedan, hoping the sun provided enough light to see the faces of the driver and front seat passenger through the windshield. There was no chance to get a photo of the license plate, but Rick thought there might be on the return trip, especially if the car had to stop at the intersection for traffic.

The men traded watches every two hours and during the afternoon, both men photographed a number of old cars and pickup trucks that looked well past their prime. Weapons couldn't be seen in most, but they snapped pictures of them anyway. Pierre was on watch when the Mercedes drove around the curve toward the highway at the end of the day. "Rick," Pierre yelled turning around toward the Rover where Rick was napping, "I'm going to step into the open to get a photo of the license plate. Cover me."

Rick stepped out of the car and moved behind the bushes to watch. The sedan came to a complete stop at the intersection and Pierre walked forward into the open, stood and began taking photos one after another. "Get down," Rick screamed. "There's another car coming."

The sedan made its right turn and sped away toward Damascus, but Pierre was seen by the fast approaching car that followed. The men in the car held their weapons out the windows and began firing around Pierre. He stood still, held his hands up and waited for them to pull up. "Stay calm, Rick," Pierre shouted. "We fooled the Transport guy earlier. Let's talk our way out of this. Hide the weapons."

Rick threw both M1911s into the brush behind the Rover. "I'll come out when they drive up."

The green car of a make and model Pierre didn't recognize stopped in the middle of the roadway next to Pierre. All four men clumsily exited the car holding AK-47s and ran toward Pierre, their weapons pointed directly at him. "What are you doing here?" one of the men screamed in Arabic. The men looked angry and agitated.

Dressed in loosed fitting pull-over shirts, homemade pants and without head coverings, the men seemed nervous and excitable. Unpredictable, thought Pierre. "Who are you?" the man screamed again.

These guys aren't fighters, Rick thought, watching from behind the bushes. They haven't secured the area; they aren't even holding their AKs properly. Walking with their fingers on the trigger mechanism. They're just as likely to shoot each other. Rick pointed at the men as he stepped out of the bushes. "What's going on here," he said loudly in English.

The men reacted immediately, turning their attention to Rick. "Put your hands in the air," another of the men shouted at Rick.

"I have no idea what you're saying," Rick bellowed back. He kept walking toward the men with anger in his voice. "We're Transport employees. We're working."

The men understood nothing of what Rick said, but responded to the perceived threat by firing into the bushes. "Put your hands up or we will kill you," the first man said to Rick in Arabic.

Pierre replied to the men in reasonably good Arabic. "My friend doesn't understand what you say. I'll talk to him."

"Rick," Pierre said in English, "they want you to put your hands above your head." At that point, Rick did as Pierre asked.

Their leader motioned with his weapon to one of the men who walked over and grabbed the equipment at Rick's feet. He unplugged the traffic counter from the hose and walked back to the leader. "What is this?" the man asked Pierre.

"Traffic Control equipment. We're from the Transport Ministry in Damascus. We measure traffic and inspect roads," Pierre said. "Here's my ID." He began to reach into his pocket.

One of the men ran forward and shoved Pierre to the ground. "Remain still. Give me your ID."

The man took Pierre's billfold to his leader. "Him, too," he said, motioning to Rick. The man walked to Rick, put the barrel of his AK underneath Rick's chin, reached around and pulled the billfold from his pocket.

I could waste you right now, motherfucker, Rick thought. After taking you down, I could take the rest of you assholes, too.

"Don't do it, Rick," Pierre said softly enough that Rick could hear, reading Rick's body language.

The man took Rick's identification to the leader, who seemed confused by the Transport IDs. "Why are you taking pictures" he asked Pierre.

Pierre rose to his feet. "The Ministry wants photos of cars and trucks. They need the vehicle weight load on the roadbed. We're getting ready to pave this road from highway to border," he said, pointing from the highway along the road toward the Lebanese border.

"Guard these men," the leader said to one of his men, pointing to Pierre and Rick. The two were watched at gunpoint while the leader and the others huddled together and engaged in an animated discussion. The leader passed the traffic counter around for inspection. After they'd come to a decision, the leader separated himself from the others and walked toward Pierre. "We're taking you to the Imam. He will decide what's to be done with you. Where's your vehicle?"

"Behind trees," Pierre said, pointing behind them.

"Why are you hiding your car?"

"If we park the car on the roadway, traffic slows down. Ministry wants to know the speed of traffic. We park the car where it can't be seen," Pierre said.

The leader ordered one of his men to drive the Range Rover out onto the roadway. The man severely scraped the undercarriage as he pulled onto the roadway. Pierre grimaced. Ouch! There goes one of the Rovers. The front bumper sustained damage. The leader ignored the damage and motioned for Pierre and Rick to get in the back seat of the green car they had driven to the scene. The leader entered the driver's side door while one of his men climbed in the front passenger seat, turned around and pointed his weapon at them. "Do not move or I will kill you," he said. The other two men drove the Rover and both cars turned around and headed toward the Lebanese border.

# Chapter Twenty-Eight

RICK AND PIERRE were driven what they estimated to be fifteen miles into Lebanon over a rough gravel road to a group of buildings set some distance off the roadway. The vehicle turned into a long driveway and stopped in front of two small concrete block houses, side by side, approximately 200 yards off the roadway. Lots of armed guards around, thought Rick, looking around at the scene. What is it? A militia headquarters? Rick counted two guards standing at the entrance to the driveway, four more in front of the buildings. Ten, counting the men in the cars, Rick thought. All carrying AKs.

In front of the buildings, the gravel driveway widened into an area for parking. Four vehicles were haphazardly parked there, including two white pickup trucks. The buildings were square, one story structures with flat metal roofs and they seemed to face each other. Neither building had windows that looked out toward the road.

A wooden fence about eight feet high had been constructed between the buildings with a gate in the center. The fence was attached to the corner of each building and was constructed of poles which looked to have been taken from trees in the area. Lumber supports were nailed across each section of fence. Every eight feet of so, a larger pole had been sunk into the ground to serve as an anchor for each section. The gate was actually two gates that swung inward. They were propped open with buckets. Rick saw more men inside the open gate carrying weapons. No barn, no farm equipment, no livestock, just armed men everywhere, thought Rick.

The leader and his man in the front passenger seat exited the green car and held their weapons on Rick and Pierre. "Get out," the leader shouted. Rick and Pierre climbed out of the vehicle, Rick towering over the two men who had taken them hostage. "This way," the leader said, swinging his weapon toward the open gate. Two guards inside the gate walked outside and stood on either side with AKs pointed at Rick and Pierre. If I were to start something right now, they'd be shooting each other in the crossfire, Rick thought.

Pierre, reading Rick's thoughts, whispered, "Easy, big guy."

# Chapter Twenty-Nine

*Thursday, November 3, 1988, one day earlier*

LAURA LEFT THE Watergate early the next morning and stopped by Jack Postl's office. She found the door locked and rapped several times. Jack answered looking like he'd slept in his clothing. "You scared me," he said. "Come on in." He motioned toward an extra chair near his computer station.

Jack's computer monitors were lit and the machines churned with a sound as though they were processing information. Laura saw the monitors display computer code, long strings of numbers and letters interspersed with all manner of quotation marks and asterisks. Pastry and a half filled coffee cup sat by the computer keyboard.

"I stopped by to see if you'd been able to print Kalami's Harvard records."

Jack picked up several pages lying on top of his printer. "Here's what I was able to print for you."

Laura scanned the material. "Good work, Jack. What are you doing now?"

"I found where the Islamic charity keeps their bank account. I'm trying to hack into their bank's computer system."

"The reason we keep you on the payroll certainly isn't cleanliness, Jack," she said with a smile, picking up the remnants of several fast food meals strewn about the tables and throwing them in the waste basket.

"Sorry about the condition of the place, Ms. Messier."

"Just kidding, Jack. Good idea on the bank records. Keep up the good work." She turned to walk out the door and stopped, holding up the Kalami paperwork. "Thanks for this, Jack. It's important. I appreciate the help."

"You're welcome."

Laura walked out on the street and hailed a taxi. "I need to go to the J. Edgar Hoover Building. Can you find it?"

"Sure," the driver said before pulling away from the curb.

I'm too hard on Jack. We wouldn't have gotten this far without him, she thought.

Laura walked into the FBI Headquarters and asked to see Dan Jenkins. The clerk phoned upstairs, hung up and said, "Assistant Director Jenkins asked that you meet him in his office. Do you know where he's located?"

"Yes, I was there yesterday."

"Please sign in." The clerk pushed a clipboard across the counter. She provided her driver's license, signed and printed her name. She clipped the pass to her clothing and headed toward the elevators.

Laura entered Dan's office and found him reading at his desk. He tossed a copy of The Washington Post on his desk. "I got your message. What have you got for me?"

Dan motioned toward chairs in front of his desk. She sat and opened her bag and pulled out a stack of paperwork. "Okay," she said, putting the papers on her lap and thumbing through the pages. "Here's the CIA report on the kidnapping incident." She handed it to Dan.

"Do you mind if take a minute and read it?" Dan asked sitting down beside her.

"Go ahead. Take your time."

Dan spent a couple of minutes reading. "The name of the driver is identified as Ahmed Kalami, a Syrian local who worked at the Embassy," Jenkins said while still reading. "He's the focus of your investigation?"

"At the present time, yes."

"There's no background information about him."

"That report came from Syrian Intelligence," Laura offered. "CIA relied heavily on their investigation." She handed him two pages of employment documentation. "We were able to obtain parts of his employment file from the embassy in Damascus."

"CIA didn't obtain them as part of their investigation?"

"No. We sent our people over there and they sent them to us."

"I wonder why CIA didn't include them in their report," Dan said, still studying the information.

"I don't know," Laura answered.

He glanced up at Laura. "They didn't consider it might be an inside job?"

"Again, I don't know."

"That's one of the first things I'd have considered," Dan said, shaking his head. "It seems strange they wouldn't follow that angle."

"There could be political considerations at work."

Jenkins paused to consider that suggestion. "That might be worthy of a separate investigation. What else have you got?"

She handed him a third set of documents and said, "Apparently, Kalami was in the States at some point and attended Harvard University. Here's a copy of his visa and Harvard enrollment."

Dan examined the documents and looked up at Laura. "This is good; I can use this."

"The address listed on his Harvard enrollment isn't his residence. It's actually an Islamic non-profit named The Crescent Society. We don't know where he lived."

"Kalami could have used that as a post office drop. Students sometimes continue to use their parent's address as their official residence."

"We suspect Kalami received funding from this organization. That, by itself, wouldn't be unusual, but we suspect The Crescent Society funds individuals and groups that engage in terrorism. We believe Kalami was sent back to Syria to conduct a terrorist operation."

"Are you saying that Kalami intentionally drove Under Secretary of State Buck into a trap?"

"That's our premise, yes."

Dan laid the paperwork on his desk and changed the subject. "Let me share what we've found. This is off the record, by the way," he said as an afterthought.

"I understand."

"I pulled the tax returns for The Crescent Society yesterday. They have a number of chapters around the country. The national organization solicits contributions from corporations, usually those that do business in the Middle East. But each individual chapter also solicits donations. Apparently, local donations fund their local operations, but we suspect the excess is sent to their headquarters in New York City. The literature says the organization funds educational and medical expenses for an underserved Muslim population overseas. We'd like to find out if that's true."

"We think the money trail could lead to the kidnappers," Laura responded.

"Possibly. We asked agents in some of our local offices to attend their prayer services last night. They heard radical Islamic clerics promoting violence as a means of political change. The clerics got their people fired up and then they passed around the collection plate."

"Can you do anything about it?" Laura asked.

"Unless they advocate specific acts of violence, we can't do anything about free speech. But if the money's being used to fund illegal activities, then we've got an obligation to investigate it. Based on what we heard last night, we want to know more. The problem is," Dan said, looking at Laura, "this is going to take time. If you're looking for hostages, you don't have that kind of time. We'll try to get a warrant, but a judge may want to see more evidence. Are you going to be in town?"

"I'll be around for a few days. CIA's trying to get satellite coverage over an area we believe to be the location of the hostages. Apparently, it takes some time to reprogram those things to photograph a specific location."

"I've got all I need from you. I'll keep you updated."

Laura stood to leave. Dan followed her to the door. "What are you doing for dinner this evening?" he asked.

"I've got to run out to Langley right now, but I should be back by five or so."

Dan laughed. "I'll pick you up at the Watergate around seven."

"Perfect."

# Chapter Thirty

"GOOD AFTERNOON, MS. MESSIER," the clerk said at the check-in counter in the lobby of CIA Headquarters. "Are you here to see Associate Director Tilton again?"

"Yes. Can you check me through?"

"I'll call up to Director Tilton's office and let him know you're here." The clerk walked down the counter to a phone and came back almost immediately. "He's on his way down."

Laura looked at the name tag. "Greg Smith?"

"It's an honor to meet you, Ma'am."

"An honor?" Laura asked with a look of confusion. "What are you talking about?"

"We studied your mission to Tripoli when I was at The Farm."

Laura looked concerned. "If you did, it'd be a breach of confidentiality," she said.

"Well, they didn't actually say it was you, but that was the rumor."

"What was your specialty at The Farm, Greg?"

"I trained as a field agent. First in the rankings for both weapons and hand to hand."

"I see they've put you on ice for a while."

"I've been working here nearly a year. I wonder whether I'll ever get out from behind this counter."

"Be patient. They put me in an administrative job for two years. Besides, don't be too anxious to become one of those stars on the wall." The wall on the opposite side of the lobby displayed a star for each CIA employee who'd been killed in action.

"It's hard to keep training when you don't know your future."

Laura thought for a minute. He's just like me. "I let my training slip when I worked admin, too, Greg. But keep it up. I can tell you from experience; it's training that will save your life out in the field."

"Laura!" She heard her name from behind. She looked over her shoulder at Steve, who stepped forward and kissed her on both cheeks.

"Since when did you become a Frenchman?" Laura asked, surprised at the greeting.

"I had an epiphany yesterday."

She looked back at the clerk. "It was nice speaking with you, Greg Smith. I'll remember your name."

"Are you flirting with the hired help now?" Steve asked as they walked toward the elevators.

"What are you talking about?" Laura asked, not understanding what he meant.

"The kid at the desk," Steve said, nodding back toward the lobby.

Laura became a bit annoyed. She stiffened and backed up a few inches to look at Steve's face. "That kid could probably kick both our asses, Steve. He's the future of the agency if you haven't noticed."

Steve held up his hands. "Relax, will you? I'm just making conversation."

After entering Steve's inner office, he sat down at his desk and folded his hands in front of him. He leaned forward as Laura sat in front of him. "Your phone call yesterday to the White House Chief of Staff shook things up. What the hell did you tell him?"

Laura adopted an administrative tone of voice. "I told him we needed a little help."

"I see." He leaned back in his chair. "Well, whatever you said sent our friends over at the Pentagon into panic mode. They received a direct order from the President."

"And?" Laura asked with a lift that conveyed the impression she expected results.

"Two satellites began taking pictures this morning. Each will make three passes during daylight hours and you'll have the first group of photos to look at late this afternoon."

Laura nodded slightly. "Thank you."

"I haven't told Bill yet. With that request, you've created an expectation that you'll produce something. That's the impression the White House has. It's dangerous to leave people with that kind of expectation, Laura. If you fail to find Buck now, you're going to lose all credibility. You'll be persona non grata around Washington."

"You think I care about that?"

"You should," Steve suggested.

"No offense intended, Steve, but you're sounding more and more like a politician these days."

"I'm just telling you the reality of the situation. What people think of you is important." Steve shifted to another subject. "Now fill me in on what's going on."

"You just kicked my ass and you want information?"

Steve shook his head and laughed. "Well, yeah, that's my job."

"Okay, here's my answer. No comment."

"All right, off the record then."

"This is for your ears only."

Steve became agitated. "Bates wants updates, Laura," he said with stress in his voice. "And you can't blame him. He's spent two and a half million on this, he's had satellites reprogrammed, he's gotten the President involved. We need to justify this, Laura. Let's start with Tunis. How did that go?"

"I gave Arafat something and he gave me something in return."

Steve rolled his eyes in frustration. "So you were able to speak with him?"

"Yes, of course."

What exactly did he give you?"

"I gave him a hundred thousand dollars and he gave me permission to look for Buck inside Lebanon. And he gave me a pretty good idea of Buck's location."

"We thought he didn't know where Buck's being held," Steve replied, puzzled at Laura's comment.

"He doesn't. It's what he didn't say that brings me to my present conclusion."

"And what conclusion would that be?"

"We're looking in the right place."

Steve knew from her expression he'd get nothing else. He sat silent for a couple of minutes, staring at her. She stared right back. "I'll have the first group of photos in my office after six," he said.

"It'll have to be tomorrow morning. For now, let's keep this between you and me."

"I can't hold Bill off forever."

"That's not really my problem, Steve." Laura gave him a cold, impersonal smile. "I'll see you tomorrow morning."

Laura rose and walked out. That woman is fucking scary, he thought, watching her walk out his door.

# Chapter Thirty-One

*Friday, November 4, 1988*

TWO GUARDS WALKED out from inside the gate and pointed weapons at Pierre and Rick. "We're bringing them to talk to the Imam," the leader said to the guards. The men motioned Pierre and Rick through the gate into a courtyard area where Rick saw a third building which looked like a storage shed, equidistant between the two houses. The exterior fence stretched completely around the three structures, attached to the back walls. The front doors of each building opened onto the common area.

The courtyard area looked similar to a working farmyard except for the numerous armed men who stood outside the buildings. A few goats and chickens roamed freely about the yard and two women washed clothes in large pans set on a wooden platform beside a well that had been dug in the middle. The women stared at the two strangers briefly before resuming their work. Pierre and Rick were taken to the building on the west side where guards held them outside. "Wait here," the guard said before walking inside.

Rick immediately began counting men, studying weapons and judging how to best mount an attack on the compound. Twenty-five men, all armed, probably more inside the buildings, he thought. It's likely they have scouts outside the walls. We could crash the gate with a vehicle, but we'd be in a firefight immediately. Probably best to hit them from several sides. Attack the gate on foot while a vehicle crashes through the fence along the back to put men at their rear. Bring a couple of ladders, climb onto the roofs to rake the courtyard with machine gun fire. Throw grenades in the windows. They think they're well defended, but they're not. Five or six of us could overwhelm them.

"Stop looking around," Pierre whispered.

"Quiet," one of the guards said before slamming the butt of his rifle into Pierre's stomach. Pierre saw the blow coming and tightened his abdomen. The blow bounced off as though the man had hit the wall of the building. Pierre smiled slightly. I'll make you pay for that, he thought.

The leader, who had entered the building, appeared in the doorway and motioned the men forward. Rick and Pierre were pushed through the door into an interior room that served as a foyer with three connecting rooms, one in front of them and the one on each side. They were led through a doorway into the room directly ahead where a man sat cross legged on the floor along the far wall. "Sit please," the seated man said in English. The lead guard tried to force Rick to the floor with the butt of his rifle, but Rick dodged the blow and put the man flat on his back with a quick punch to his face. "Enough!" the seated man shouted. Dressed in a black robe with a white turban, the man held up one hand, "Stop!" The guard stumbled to his feet holding his face.

The seated man had a distinguished look about him. He wore a closely cropped gray beard that made him look older than his real age, his late fifties. He sat on Persian rugs which overlapped each other, completely covering the room's concrete floor. As Pierre and Rick adjusted their vision to the low light, they saw that the man sat on a large decorative pillow with bowls of food resting on the carpet in front of him. He was in the midst of taking his evening meal. Two large candles burned on pedestals, one on each side, giving him the look of a priest.

The man motioned for them to sit on the other side of the carpet. "Please, sit," he said in English, pointing to the space directly across from him. "May I offer you food?"

Pierre and Rick sat down and crossed their legs. "No, thank you," Pierre responded angrily in Arabic.

"Come now. You are honored guests," the elder said, continuing to speak English. He spread his arms out wide and smiled. He looked up at the guard standing behind Pierre and Rick. "Ask that food be brought to our guests."

He looked back to Pierre. "You may speak English if you wish." Pierre and Rick said nothing. Both were breathing heavily from the rough treatment at the hands of the guards. The elder smiled, began eating again and spoke in English between mouthfuls of meat, cheese and bread.

"You believe you've been taken prisoner?" He waited for a response. Failing to hear one, he answered his own question. "You are not prisoners. We protect the people in this area from those who wish to do them harm. You have been brought to me so I may find out whether you represent a danger."

Pierre and Rick still said nothing.

A young woman entered the room with two trays which held plates and cups. She lowered herself to her knees and set the trays in front of Pierre and Rick. She poured tea into the cups from a pitcher that rested in front of the Imam. "Thank you, Safa," the Imam said to the woman.

The woman bowed her head slightly, rose to her feet and left the room. "Now, please enjoy our hospitality," the elder said. "If you reject it, our people will become offended. Take your evening meal with me."

Pierre and Rick looked at each other. Pierre nodded to Rick, then reached for a bowl and served himself. He passed the bowl to Rick who took a small portion and set the bowl back in its place. The elder waited until both men had taken portions from each bowl and began to eat.

# Chapter Thirty-Two

"MY NAME IS Imam Kassem. I hold a doctorate in economics from Harvard University and have taught at the university in Beirut." He raised both arms, palms up and looked at the ceiling. "However, it is my study of the Koran that caused Allah to appoint me leader of this community. It is this abiding faith in Allah which protects our people from harm and it is my job to pass Allah's judgment and mercy upon those who sin against our people."

Arrogant little prick, Rick thought.

The Imam picked up the Transport IDs which the guard had laid in front of him. "Your identification seems to be in order, but you are not Syrian. Where are your passports?"

"They are …" The Imam held his hand up and interrupted Pierre. "I wish to hear your associate speak."

"The hotel kept them," Rick said in English.

"Which hotel?"

"The Omayad in Damascus."

The Imam looked at the guard standing behind them. He held out the IDs. "Take these IDs, call the hotel and confirm their identities."

"Yes, Imam," the man said. When he walked forward to take their identification, Rick had the urge to punch the man again.

The Imam looked at Rick. "While my assistant confirms your identity, tell me where you're from."

"I'm from the United States."

The Imam wagged his finger at Rick and grinned. "Yes, I knew that as soon as you walked in the room. And you?" Kassem pointed at Pierre.

"I'm from France."

The Imam pointed his finger in the air. "I could tell from your one sentence in Arabic. You speak our language very well, by the way."

Kassem had a calm demeanor, his body posture and gestures were relaxed. He took his time, thinking about each question between bites of food. His eyes, though, communicated much; squinting or widening, in response to the answers he heard.

The guy's cagey, Rick thought. He fights with words, not weapons.

Kassem looked back at Rick. "Why are foreigners working for the Syrian Transport Ministry?"

"We came into the country at the invitation of the government to advise them on future repairs to the Beirut-Damascus Highway."

"They don't have experts in their Ministry who do that?" The Imam seemed genuinely confused.

"The government believes the problems that exist with the highway and the proposed repairs demand more experience than the Transport Ministry can provide."

Kassem thought about that answer. He ate for a few minutes, causing Rick to wonder whether his answer was believed. "What is your education," Kassem asked Rick.

"I graduated from the University of Georgia with a degree in structural engineering."

"Where did you do your graduate work?"

"Georgia Tech University."

"So you build buildings?"

"Among other things. I also work on roadways, bridges and other infrastructure projects."

Kassem looked at Pierre. "And what's your expertise?"

"I'm a construction manager."

"A general contractor?"

"Yes," Pierre replied.

The Imam looked back to Rick. "Why would a construction manager travel with you during a design phase?"

"He speaks Arabic," Rick replied.

The Imam seemed amused at the answer. "I understand," he said, nodding his head. "Communication is key in every industry. Let me ask you this. How did the Syrian government come to hire you?"

Rick motioned toward Pierre. "We work for an international architectural firm in London. Our employer sent us to Syria."

The man returned with the IDs. "Excuse me, Imam."

"Yes, Abdul. What have you found?"

"The men are registered at the Omayad Hotel and their passports are being held there."

"Thank you."

Kassem turned his attention back to Rick. "And what is the name of this firm that employs you?"

"International Design Consultants."

"And where is it located again?"

"London, England," Rick said.

"Abdul?" Kassem looked at the guard standing behind Rick and Pierre. "Take these IDs and call this firm in London. Find out whether these men are employees there."

"Yes, Imam."

The Imam handed the IDs to his man and then returned his attention to Rick. "Tell me about these proposed repairs."

Rick shrugged as though the answer was obvious. "The heavy military equipment the Syrians use is tearing up the highway. It wasn't built for that kind of traffic."

"Elaborate, please. How so?"

I'm going to have to make this shit sound good, Rick thought. "The Beirut to Damascus Highway was built with a four inch concrete base, perfectly fine for passenger cars and light truck traffic. But to support heavier loads, it needs a six inch base."

"Like the expressways around Boston?"

"Yes, those are six inch base construction."

"So, you plan to add another layer of concrete?"

"No. Concrete doesn't adhere well to concrete."

Kassem thought for a moment. He rubbed his chin. "I wasn't aware of that." He paused as though he didn't believe Rick. "What is your solution then?"

"I'm going to recommend filling the cracks with tar, then adding a four inch layer of all-weather asphalt on top. That will protect the concrete from further erosion."

"Asphalt will support military traffic?"

"It will extend the life of the roadbed until money can be found for more extensive repairs. Asphalt adheres well to concrete and it's an inexpensive temporary solution."

Kassem considered his next line of questioning. He ate for a few minutes as though time wasn't a concern. Pierre and Rick sat silently, looking down at their food. Kassem noticed. "Is there something wrong with your food?"

"Forgive us," Rick responded. "We mean no insult. We are under a great deal of stress at the moment."

Abdul returned again with the Transport IDs. "Forgive the interruption, Imam."

"What did you find out about these men?" he asked.

"It is a real company headquartered in London. I was transferred to the Personnel Department. They confirmed the men are employed by the company and are currently working in Damascus, Syria."

Thank you, Henri, Rick thought.

Abdul handed the IDs back to the Imam.

Kassem resumed his questioning. "My associate told me you are driving a luxury SUV. I wasn't aware that the Transport Ministry owned such vehicles."

"Our company in London rented the vehicle for us," Rick replied.

"I see. Tell me, why were you watching our road instead of the highway?"

"The government wants to pave the roads that intersect with the highway between Damascus and the border. In both directions, north and south. Asphalt is cheap and it fits within their budget. The last two days, we've been studying your road, counting traffic and measuring the weight of motor vehicles to make a design recommendation that meets the needs of the local population."

"And that's what this equipment is for?" Kassem asked, pointing to the traffic control equipment the guards had brought inside.

"That's what we use to measure traffic," Rick answered.

Kassem ignored the hose and picked up the counter. "How does this work?"

Rick leaned across the food and reached to point out its features and was immediately hit from behind. "You do not touch the Imam," the man said.

Rick looked around at the man. "Fine, asshole," Rick said. "You explain it."

Kassem interceded between the two men. "Abdul, let him explain himself." The man moved back against the wall. Kassem nodded at Rick. "My apologies. Please, go ahead."

"The traffic counter is connected to the tube via the connection on the side of the device." Rick pointed to the connection. "The tube is filled with air and the control device has a small air pump inside powered by a nine volt battery that is housed in the bottom of the unit."

Kassem flipped over the unit. "This door here," Kassem said, pointing to the battery compartment.

"Yes," Rick replied.

Kassem opened the door and found the battery. "How long does the battery last?"

"About twelve hours," Rick replied. "We must replace it every day."

"I see." Kassem snapped the battery door shut, turned the box back over and pointed to the read-out. "What do these boxes tell you?"

"The number of vehicles and their approximate weight."

"Does the box retain the numbers? If I turned it on, would it reflect the recorded numbers from today?"

"No, unfortunately, it does not. We must record the numbers before we turn the unit off."

"So there is no way to prove your story is true?"

"Not with that equipment. It's not of the quality we'd use in the United States."

Kassem thought for a moment. "Let me give you the benefit of doubt. What are your recommendations for our road?"

"Based on my observations, I'll recommend a two lane, six meter wide paved surface with a gravel base. We'll build a three meter wide gravel shoulder on each side. The surface will be a four inch layer of asphalt."

"Is the current roadway wide enough to accommodate that width?"

"If we include the gullies on each side, yes," Rick answered. "There should be enough room without harming the trees and bushes on either side."

Kassem thought about that and resumed eating. It was a few minutes before he posed the next question. "How much will it cost to pave our road from the highway to the border?" Kassem asked.

"I don't estimate costs. I offer recommendations and let the government and the contractors figure out pricing."

"I see."

The woman came into the room. "Imam, are you done with the evening meal?"

"Yes, Safa. It was excellent as usual." Kassem looked at Pierre and Rick. "Are you gentlemen finished?"

"Yes, Sir," Rick said. "Thank you for your hospitality."

Kassem looked at the woman. "You can go ahead and remove the dishes and remaining food. Make sure the guards are properly fed."

"Yes, Imam," the woman said.

Kassem waited while the woman made several trips back and forth to remove the dishes and remaining food. Kassem looked at the man standing behind. "Abdul, why don't you take your evening meal in the kitchen? I do not believe these men are a danger to me."

"Yes, Imam," the man said and left the room.

"Now that we can speak privately, I have a complaint." Kassem waited to allow the sentence to have its maximum effect. "What upsets our community is this!" He raised his voice for the first time and picked up the camera and held it in front of Pierre and Rick.

Rick nodded. "Imam, that's a common complaint wherever we go. People don't like to be photographed."

Kassem shook the camera in front of them. He shouted, "Why is this necessary?"

"The traffic control equipment doesn't give us all the information we need. We must record what types of vehicles use the roadway. Are they single or double axle? Wide wheel base pick-up truck or narrow passenger car? A car with four passengers can weigh more than an empty pick-up. To recommend the safest roadway at the most efficient cost, we need that information."

Kassem screamed at them. "But you photograph the passengers! It is an invasion of privacy. Do you know what the government could do with that information?" Kassem looked as though he wanted to hurl the camera against the wall.

Rick remained calm. I've trapped him, he thought. "The government never sees the photos."

Kassem's mouth opened wide. He was shocked by the answer. "What?" he asked excitedly. "How could this be? You're lying to me!"

"No, Sir, I'm not. Our research is proprietary. All the underlying documents, including photographs, are brought back to Britain where the information is compiled into a report. The client only sees the final report."

Kassem had spent nearly an hour setting up Pierre and Rick and found himself at the end to be confused. "You're telling me you don't show the photos to the government?"

"No, Sir. We develop the film, count the vehicle types and put the photos in our luggage when we leave. The government only sees a final report which is written in Britain after we return."

"What would happen if I destroyed the film?"

"If you were to destroy the film, our research would be incomplete. We'd have to spend another day here."

"Where are the photos kept before you leave?"

"We keep them in our hotel room. Once they're developed, we run our totals and usually throw the photos in our luggage with the rest of the material. We could put them in the hotel safe if you'd like."

Kassem paused to think. Rick decided to avoid overselling the idea and allow the Imam time to digest the material. When Kassem spoke, it was as though he'd made a decision. He looked at Rick. "You make no copies?"

"No, Sir. We only work with originals."

"I have made my decision. If you return here at any point in time, my men will kill you. If you make copies of the photos, you will be killed. If any part of your story turns out to be false, you will be killed. Whether it's here or in Britain, we will find you."

"Yes, Sir," Rick said.

"Abdul," the Imam shouted. The man ran into the room quickly. "Yes, Imam. Do I put these two with the others?" he asked in Arabic.

"No," Kassem said harshly. "You will return their equipment, including the camera. You will release them and follow their car back to the highway. Do not harm them, but if you see them here again, kill them."

"Yes, Imam."

The man looked down at Pierre and Rick. "Follow me." Rick and Pierre rose to leave, but Kassem stopped them momentarily.

"One question before you leave. What is the mascot for the University of Georgia?" Kassem asked Rick.

"They're the Bulldogs, Sir."

"And Georgia Tech?"

"The Yellow Jackets."

"Go in peace. May Allah shower his blessings upon you."

"We wish you the same, Imam," Rick said.

# Chapter Thirty-Three

IMAM KASSEM IMMEDIATELY picked up the phone after Rick and Pierre left the room and dialed a private number at the Embassy of the Islamic Republic of Iran in Damascus.

"Yes?" the voice answered in Persian.

"I need help with a problem," the Imam said in Arabic.

The man recognized the Imam's voice and switched to Arabic. "How can we help you, Imam?"

"Two men visited us today. They work for the Syrian Transport Ministry. I do not trust them. I wish for you to eliminate them."

"Why didn't you do it yourself while they were there?"

"The Syrians would come looking for them."

"What's the reason for your distrust?" the man asked.

"They're not Syrian. They claim to be advisers brought in by the Ministry to assist with building roads."

The Iranian laughed. "The Syrians have finally realized they do not know how to build roads."

"One was American," Kassem said.

"Americans do work in Syria, you know."

"I suspect an American arriving here is more than a coincidence."

The Iranian paused before speaking again. "Perhaps you are right. However, killing Americans presents problems for us."

"If you do not help, I will deny you further access for interviews," Kassem said sharply.

There was another pause as the Iranian assessed the threat. "Where are the men at the present time?"

"They are driving back to Damascus as we speak. They are staying at the Omayad Hotel under the names Simmons and Larson."

"Room numbers?"

"404 and 406."

"Consider it done."

"There is one more thing," Kassem mentioned.

"Yes?"

"They have film and photographs in their rooms I wish to have destroyed."

"We'll eliminate your problem," the man said.

"You're a good friend of the Palestinian people."

"Our representative will arrive again tomorrow morning for another interview. We expect your full cooperation."

"You shall receive it."

"Salam," the man said. The line disconnected.

# Chapter Thirty-Four

TWO IRANIAN MEN arrived at the Omayad Hotel within an hour of the phone call. They were clean cut, wore conservative suits and looked very much like the businessmen they were not. They proceeded downstairs to the employee locker room where they found a maid storing cleaning materials in a closet at the end of her shift. One man served as a lookout while the other came from behind and hit the woman sharply on the head with the face of a clothing iron he found on an adjacent cart. The woman fell forward into the closet, unconscious. Pulling a weapon from his shoulder holster, he quickly screwed on a suppressor and fired two rounds into the woman's head. He found her pass key, took it off the ring, closed the door and jammed a different key into the door lock and broke it off. He made sure the door was locked shut before he wiped everything he'd touched with a handkerchief.

The men took the elevator to the fourth floor, donning black gloves before the elevator door opened. They found room 404 where one man knocked gently. When he didn't receive an answer, he let himself into the room and handed the pass key to his associate who walked down the hallway to room 406 and entered the room in the same fashion. Both men closed the draperies and positioned chairs in a direct line of sight with the room doors. They withdrew their weapons, screwed on the suppressors and waited.

# Chapter Thirty-Five

ABDUL DROVE HIS car back to the highway while Pierre and Rick followed in the Rover. A white pick-up followed. After the Rover turned toward Damascus and sped off, Kassem's men turned around and headed back to the compound. Pierre and Rick traveled a kilometer, checking the rear view mirror to make sure they weren't followed. "We've got to go back and find the weapons I threw in the brush," Rick said.

Pierre turned around and pulled off the highway well before the intersection. They ran across the highway deep into the brush and looked for the weapons. It was nearly dark by the time they found both M1911s. They returned to the Rover, turned around and headed back toward Damascus.

"Where did you come up with that bullshit back there?" Pierre asked.

"You mean at Kassem's place?"

"Yeah. You had me totally convinced you knew construction."

"I worked for my uncle during the summers when I was in school. He was in construction."

"We were in some pretty deep trouble until you began talking."

"I guess you never know when something you did in the past might help you," Rick said.

"Thank your uncle for me the next time you see him."

When Rick and Pierre arrived at the hotel, they talked briefly in the hotel parking lot. "We should walk away from the car," Rick said. "Bring the camera and nothing else. Let's check out."

"Should we take our personal items in the rooms?" Pierre asked.

"No," Rick said. "I think we walk away from the rooms, too. You've got your room key?"

"Yes."

"We'll turn them in at the desk and leave. Where's the other Rover?"

"It's parked one level up," Pierre replied.

"Let's get the hell of here while we can."

As Pierre and Rick approached the hotel check-out, the manager walked from behind the partition and spoke with the young woman working the counter. "Fatima, I'll take care of these gentlemen. You go ahead and take a break."

"Thank you, Faraj."

Faraj smiled as Pierre and Rick approached the counter. "Good evening. May I help you?"

"We'd like to check out please."

"Of course. May I have your names and room numbers?" Faraj pulled their paperwork, took their keys and produced a receipt after receiving payment. "One moment and I'll retrieve your passports."

"We're late to an appointment. Can we pick them up later this evening?"

"Of course. I'll put them in the drawer here at the counter. They'll be here when you return. I hope you had a pleasant stay."

After the two had left the counter, the man picked up the phone and dialed a number. "They've checked out."

"As well they should," the voice said. "Find two other European men staying at the hotel. Replace their information with Simmons and Larson."

"As you wish, Sir."

"Shalom."

# Chapter Thirty-Six

PIERRE CHECKED THE second Range Rover thoroughly before starting the engine. He found the Rover untouched. "Stand away from the car, Rick, just in case we missed something. If this thing explodes, one of us should survive." Rick climbed out and walked a few meters away. After the car started without problems, Rick returned. "We're heading to the American Embassy?" Pierre asked.

"Stop at the French Embassy first. We've got to send a report to Tilton. Then let's head over to the American Embassy."

The French Embassy was closed for the evening, but the two were allowed in the back gate and ushered into the DST Operations room. Rick wrote his report along with a diagram of the Kassem compound. The information was sealed in a bag with a "Top Secret" label on it and transported to the airport by a diplomatic car where it would be sent to Washington on the next flight out.

The American Embassy was also closed for the evening so the Rover pulled around to the back gate where a guard stood in a shack inside the gate. Rick got out of the car, walked to the fence and waved. The guard talked into his walkie-talkie. "I've got a car at the gate. Requesting immediate assistance."

"We'll send someone over," the man on the other end of the line replied.

The guard left the shack and walked to the fence. "Can I help you?"

"My name's Rick Williams. My partner," Rick gestured toward the Rover, "Pierre Thibault and I need immediate access to the Embassy. It's an emergency."

"I'm familiar with you Mr. Williams. Go ahead and pull through."

The guard walked back into the shack, pressed a button and the gate slid open. Another Embassy guard appeared and directed the car through the gate. After the gate closed behind them, Rick exited the automobile as the guard approached. "What's the problem, Mr. Williams," the second guard asked.

"We request immediate shelter in the Embassy."

"Step this way, Sir."

Rick looked back at the car. "Don't worry about the car," the guard said. "Leave the key in it and we'll park it for you." Both men were escorted into the building where the head of the evening guard conducted a short inquiry. "What's the problem, Mr. Williams?"

"We encountered some difficulty today. Can you call Captain Wilcox for me?"

"I already have, Sir. He's on his way here as we speak."

Rick smiled. "Thanks for the help."

"Are you here for the rest of the evening?"

"I'm afraid so."

"We'll have someone show you to a room upstairs. You're free to use the kitchen. There should be leftovers from today's lunch. No phone calls until morning."

"I understand," Rick said.

# Chapter Thirty-Seven

TOM WILCOX ARRIVED a half-hour later. He looked at the clock as he entered; it was almost 10:00 p.m. He found the evening guard officer in their small Operations Center. "Where are they?" he asked.

"We put them in a room upstairs for the evening."

"What did they tell you?"

"Not much, Sir. They said they sought sanctuary in the Embassy this evening. They requested to speak with you."

"Thanks. I'll go upstairs and interview them."

Rick heard the knock on the door. "Evening, Rick," Tom said with a hint of a smile when the door opened. "You boys get yourselves in trouble?"

Rick grinned. "You could say that. Come on in and we'll explain it."

The room was arranged similar to a hotel room with two double beds, a desk, chair and a bathroom that adjoined the room. Rick and Pierre sat on the end of the beds while Tom pulled a chair close by. "We had a nasty incident with an Imam today," Rick began. "We were conducting surveillance along a side road near the border and were captured by four armed men. We were driven into Lebanon to be interrogated. They released us, but we saw some interesting things while we were there.'

"Like what?" Tom asked.

"Safa Kalami was there for one. The walled compound was guarded by a platoon size group of armed men for another."

"Were you threatened?"

"Aside from the fact that the Imam told us we'd be killed if they saw us around there again?" Rick answered his own question. "One of the Imam's goons wanted to hold us. Asked the Imam if he wanted to put us with what he called 'the others.'"

"What do you suppose he meant by 'the others?'"

"I'm not sure," Rick replied. "But forty men seems excessive for guarding an Imam."

"What do you want to do?" Tom asked.

"We've sent a report back to Washington. While they decide what they want to do, we'd like to stay here for a few days. Our lives could be in danger. We checked out of the hotel for safety reasons."

"Good idea. You're welcome to stay here."

"Do you guys have some clean clothes for us? We left everything at the hotel."

"I'm sure we can come up with something. Get some sleep and we'll talk more in the morning."

# Chapter Thirty-Eight

AFTER WAITING TWO hours, the Iranian assassins returned to the hotel lobby counter asking the whereabouts of two friends they expected to meet for dinner, a Mr. Simmons and Mr. Larson. The young female clerk looked for their names in the file. "Yes, Mr. Simmons is in room 608 and Mr. Larson is in ..." she thumbed through the file, "... yes, here he is. He's in room 712. You can use the house phone over there ..." she pointed to a phone on the wall across the lobby, "... to call their rooms if you like."

The Iranians gave the woman a pleasant smile. "Thank you," one of them said. They walked halfway across the lobby. "Those idiots gave us the wrong room numbers. We're lucky. We could have killed the wrong people," the first man said.

"Let's go to 608 first," the man's partner said.

They found room 608, looked in both directions and found the hallway empty. They took the pass key, gently unlocked the door and entered. A German businessman had finished showering and was using a towel to dry himself in the bathroom. He'd left the bathroom door open and saw the men immediately. "Can I help you?" he asked, upon seeing the men.

He was immediately shot four times, twice in the chest and twice in the head. Killed instantly, he fell backwards into the tub, the shower curtain crashing down on top of him. The men searched the room for film and photographs without success so they gently closed the door behind them and took the elevator to the seventh floor.

They found room 712 and waited for an elderly couple at the end of the hallway to step into an elevator before entering the room. They gently opened the door and found the occupant lying on the bed watching television. The man began to rise from the bed and was shot immediately, also four times, twice in the chest and twice in the head. He fell back onto the bed, dead. The men searched through his luggage, finding a camera and several rolls of film. After one of the men put the camera and film in his coat pocket, they gently closed the room door and left the hotel. "What are we supposed to do with this stuff?" the first man asked, pointing to his pocket.

"Destroy it," his partner replied as they walked along the sidewalk.

He opened the small plastic film canisters, exposed the film and tossed the camera and film into a dumpster in an alley. They walked to their car parked two blocks away and returned to the Iranian Embassy.

The hotel counter manager, Faraj, asked the female clerk about the two men who had just left the hotel. "Did those two gentlemen check-in?"

"No, Sir. They needed to find friends in the hotel."

"Were you able to help?"

"Oh yes, Sir. I looked up the names and gave them their friend's room numbers."

"Very good."

Faraj walked to the counter, waited until he was alone, replaced the Simmons and Larson registration with the original guest information and then discarded the Simmons and Larson paperwork.

# Chapter Thirty-Nine

*Friday, November 4, 1988*

LAURA AWOKE TO the sound of the shower. She immediately bolted upright in bed. Relax, she told herself. You had a flashback. It was a memory of Laura's time trapped in Muammar Gaddafi's personal quarters. She unclenched her fists and lay back on the pillow. Dan Jenkins came out of the shower, walked over and kissed her. "Good morning, sweetie."

"You getting ready to leave?"

"Sorry. Today's a workday."

Laura watched him dress. He sat on the bed beside her. "Here," she said, "let me do your tie for you." She sat behind him on the bed, put her arms around him and tied a single Windsor.

Dan smiled and turned around to look at her. "How do you know how to tie a tie?"

"I was in the CIA, remember?" She kissed him flush on the mouth; one of those long kisses that last seemingly forever.

"I've got to go," Dan said, pulling away from her.

"Thank you for last night. I had a good time."

Dan leaned over and brushed the hair from her eyes. "I did, too. Can I call you today?"

"Leave a message at the hotel. I'll be gone much of the day."

"Once again, I'm sorry about the prosecutor. There just wasn't enough to take before a judge."

"It was a long shot, Dan. Thanks for trying."

Dan gathered his suit coat and looked at her. "I'll call later in the day. Bye."

The door swung shut and Laura was alone. Hotels suck, she thought. Impersonal, lonely. She looked at the clock; it was 7:15. The blinking light on the phone told her she had a message waiting. The message can wait. She called room service, ordered a light breakfast and hopped into the shower. Drying her hair with the bathroom door open, she heard the knock of room service at her door. With an oversized towel around her, Laura let the server carry in breakfast. She signed the slip and turned on the television softly to put sound in the room. After dressing in jeans, a sweater and sneakers, she poured herself coffee and sat down at the desk to munch on an English muffin.

"And in international news," the television news broadcaster said, "three people were murdered at a downtown Damascus, Syria hotel overnight." The station cut to footage of an ambulance parked in front of the hotel. It was after dark, police had cordoned off the front of the hotel and the video showed emergency personnel wheeling covered bodies out the front door. "Two European businessmen were killed in cold blood along with a maid in a brazen attack at the Omayad Hotel." Laura's eyes locked on the television screen. "Police say the killings appear to be a random act of violence. The Syrian government has not issued a comment on the incident. Now, for sports, let's turn to …"

Laura stopped listening. She stared at the blinking light on the phone. Picking up the receiver, she pushed nine for messages and heard the recording start. It consisted of two bell tones and nothing else. Jean's got an emergency, she thought. Call from secure. Shit! Laura slammed the phone down, grabbed her bag and looked out the window; it looked cloudy and cold. She dug into her luggage, found a light jacket and hurried downstairs. Laura ran out of the Watergate, found a taxi waiting and asked the driver to take her to CIA Headquarters.

# Chapter Forty

LAURA APPROACHED THE counter at Langley where she found a familiar face.

"Good morning, Greg Smith. I'm here to see Director Tilton."

"I haven't seen him yet this morning."

"How about Roger Wilson?"

"Let me call up to Chief of Staff Wilson's office."

Greg Smith returned a minute later. "Mr. Wilson said to come on up."

She hesitated and looked at Greg. Competent, cooperative, she thought. "You know ...," she said, folding her hands on top of the counter and leaning forward, "I remember the day Roger called me in and gave me my first posting overseas. It'll happen for you, Greg Smith."

"Thank you, Ma'am."

Laura walked in CIA Chief of Staff Roger Wilson's office where his secretary looked up. "Go on in, Ms. Messier. Roger's waiting for you."

She pecked on the door, opened it and stuck her head inside. "Am I interrupting something?"

Roger looked up from his desk and held his hands up. "Don't shoot! I give up," he said, laughing. He rose and walked around the desk.

Laura walked in the office. "Hi Roger."

Wilson gave her a hug. "It's so good to see you, Laura. How long has it been?"

"Two and a half, three years maybe?"

"Come." He motioned toward a chair in front of his desk. "Sit." Roger returned to his chair, sat back and put his feet up on the desk. He locked his hands behind his head. "Imagine! The famous 'Shewolf' sitting right here in my office. My word! You've got every bad guy in the world afraid of you. When you sat here in my office in, what was it, 1980? None of us figured you had that kind of potential. You've distinguished yourself, young lady."

Roger was one of the veterans of the seventh floor at Langley. In his late sixties, short, with gray hair and slightly pudgy, Roger had survived about every scandal that had taken place over the years. Directors might come and go, but the agency simply couldn't run without Roger Wilson. He had no enemies, had dirt on everyone, but never, ever, revealed what he knew. "Are you here to see Steve?"

"Yes, but he's not in yet. So I thought I'd bother you for a few minutes," she said with a smile.

"It's no bother. Are you taking a look at sat photos this morning?"

Laura immediately tensed and gave Roger a look of concern.

"Relax," Roger said with a laugh. "Reprogramming satellites is a big deal. Bates found out and had a sit-down with Steve yesterday."

"This can't go beyond the seventh floor, Roger."

"Don't worry. Bates knows there's a lot at stake."

"I need a little information."

"From me? Sure. What can I tell you?"

"What do you know about Greg Smith?"

"You mean the kid downstairs in the lobby?"

"Yes, that's him."

Roger looked at the ceiling, thought for a moment and looked back at Laura. "Graduated from Princeton with a degree in history. Football star. He came to us like you did, answered a blind ad in the student newspaper. Trained as a field agent at The Farm. High scores in weapons training. He's green, Laura. We put him downstairs to give him some seasoning like we did with you. We'll put him in the field when the time's right."

Amazing memory, Laura thought. "Married?"

"No, not that I know. I think he rents an apartment in Falls Church. Why are you asking?"

"I believe Steve's going to force me to take someone along on a mission. It has to be someone who'll follow orders.

Roger put his feet down and leaned forward. He lowered his voice. "He's not ready, Laura." Roger's tone was serious.

"Can he fight?"

Roger chuckled. "Oh, I guarantee he can do that. I just don't know how he'd react under pressure. You never know until your life is threatened. You, for instance," Roger said, nodding toward Laura, "thrive on that kind of pressure. Greg Smith? We don't know that," he said. "You'd be better off taking special ops personnel with you."

"The problem with those guys is they're trained to fight their way in. I infiltrate and fight my way out. It's a basic difference in the way we go about our jobs."

Roger cocked his head to one side and thought about the difference for a minute. "I see your point. You want me to pull Smith's file and go over his psych evals?" he asked.

"Would you mind?"

"I'll have a profile ready for you in an hour."

"Thanks, Roger." Laura looked at her watch. "Steve might be in by now. I'll stop wasting your time and run down to his office."

"Stop by after you're done."

# Chapter Forty-One

LAURA WALKED DOWN the hallway and into Steve's outer office. "Hi Linda. Is he in yet?"

"He just arrived, Ms. Messier. Why don't you go on in?"

"Thanks."

Steve walked out of his doorway as Laura walked in. They nearly collided. "Linda, could you ..." he shouted. "Oh, I'm sorry, Laura. I didn't see you. You want coffee?"

"That'd be great."

"Linda, could you call downstairs and have the cafeteria bring up coffee for us? Order something for yourself, too."

"Sure."

"And hold my calls please."

Steve motioned to Laura. "Come on in." Laura walked in and looked around Steve's office. The higher up the political ladder you go, the more windows you have, she thought. He's got a complete wall of 'em. He's so talented in ways I'm not. He deserves what he's earned. She stood in the middle of his office and noticed the satellite photos spread over Steve's coffee table. A magnifying glass rested on top. He's studied photos for years. Listen to him; he knows what he's talking about.

Laura took off her jacket. Steve pointed toward the door. "You can hang your things on the back of the door if you like."

"I'll just throw them over the sofa, thanks."

Steve watched her stare at the photos. "I've got something to show you," he said, nodding toward them.

"Mind if I use your phone first? I've got to make a call from secure."

"Of course." Steve picked up the phone and had the call routed through a special switchboard that distorted the conversation beyond recognition. If someone on the other end had an identical piece of equipment, the conversation could be decoded and sounded normal. Jean had the necessary equipment at their location in the Bahamas. Laura understood from Jean's message that he wanted to talk using the scrambler.

Steve waited until he heard the transfer and then the dial tone. "You're ready." He handed the phone to Laura.

"We can put this on speaker if you like," she offered.

"Thanks. I'd appreciate it."

There was a knock on Steve's door. Linda poked her head inside. "Steve, you've got coffee service out here."

"Thanks, Linda." He turned to Laura. "Go ahead. I'll retrieve the coffee and be back in a flash."

Laura dialed the number to the main house at the compound in the Bahamas. Jean answered. "Hello, Mademoiselle."

"Is it bad news?"

"Are you secure?"

Steve brought the coffee tray into the office and set it on his desk.

"Yes, secure here. I'm sitting with Steve Tilton. You're on speaker."

"Good morning, Monsieur Tilton."

"Morning, Jean."

"Mademoiselle, not bad news, no."

"I heard about the murders at the Omayad last night. Are they okay?"

"Pierre and Rick are fine."

"I was worried sick, Jean. I heard the news this morning."

"We suspect the killers intended to murder Pierre and Rick. However, I've been assured this morning both are safe in the Embassy."

"What are you saying? The killers murdered the wrong people?"

"That would be the assumption," Jean said. "I'm not quite sure how that could happen. It might be a coincidence."

"I don't believe in coincidences."

"Neither do I, Mademoiselle. Rick left a detailed message for us with Jacques in Paris. I retrieved it this morning." Jean went on to explain Pierre and Rick's incident with Imam Kassem the previous day.

"And you suspect a connection between Kassem and the hotel murders?" Laura asked.

"I think they're connected, yes. Rick has written a report on Imam Kassem which the French Embassy sent to CIA in a diplomatic bag for Steve Tilton's eyes only. You should read it."

Laura looked at Steve. "When would that arrive, Steve?" Laura asked.

"They're seven hours ahead of us. I doubt it's here yet, but I'll check."

"Rick said he enclosed a map of Kassem's facility," Jean continued. "That may give you a clue as to what to look for in satellite photos."

"What would be important enough about meeting Kassem to be killed over?"

"That is a key question," Jean said. "Further, why would an Imam need a forty man garrison guarding him? And where is the money coming from to pay them?"

"I'm working on a possible financial trail as we speak."

"Good. We need every piece of evidence we can find."

"The sat photos are in Steve's office now," Laura said. "We're just sitting down now to study them. Hopefully, Rick's report will help."

"In the meantime, I've asked Pierre and Rick to stay inside the Embassy for now."

"I think that's wise," Laura responded. "I'll call you once we've reviewed Rick's report."

"I'll wait for your call." The line clicked off.

Laura turned her attention to Steve. "Ready to look at photos?"

Laura sat on the sofa, leaned over the table and began studying. "Would you like coffee?" Steve asked.

"That would be great. Thanks."

Steve prepared Laura's coffee the way he knew she preferred it. He poured a cup for himself and set both cups down on the table. Laura smiled. "You remembered."

Steve laughed. "I watched you make coffee every morning for a couple of years, Laura. Of course I remembered."

Laura blushed. Any mention of their marriage caused her embarrassment. She avoided eye contact. "Thanks," she said, looking at the photos. She finally looked up at Steve standing on the other side of the table. "I was nearly assassinated once by someone who poisoned my coffee," she said as she raised her cup.

A memory came to Steve and his face showed the poignancy of it. "You don't trust me?" he said in a teasing manner.

Laura relaxed hearing his comment. "It takes a while to get past things," she said with the hint of a smile.

"The attempted poisoning or other things?"

Laura looked out the window at a gray and cloudy fall sky. "Everything, I guess," she said softly after some hesitation.

Steve walked around and sat beside her on the sofa. "Then let's get past them," he said gently.

The moment was not lost on her. He's making an effort, she thought. "Can we move on to the photos?" she asked abruptly.

"Of course."

"You've been looking at these things for years," Laura said. "Walk me through them."

"Okay," Steve said. "Here's the general area," he said, holding up a wide angle photo. "There are several shots like this one. I took the liberty of stacking them all together." Laura scanned each one briefly.

"What am I looking for?"

"Changes from one photo to the next."

"You mean like traffic?"

"Sure." He picked up a photo. "Look at the border crossing here," he said pointing at the photo. "See how the traffic has built up?" He riffled through the photos and picked another. "Now look at this one," he said handing it to her. "The traffic is far less. Look at the time stamp." Laura looked at the time printed at the bottom right of the photo. "11:02:61; the other one is, what …" she looked at the first photo. "07:49:77; this one is rush hour," she said, pointing to the earlier photo. "That's the cause of the traffic change."

"Correct," Steve said. "Not only that, look at the composition of the traffic; it's different. That's the kind of change you're looking for. Anything of interest you find, we can send the photo back and have them increase the resolution of the particular area you'd like to see."

Laura looked at Steve. "You've already studied these?"

"Late yesterday afternoon."

"Why don't you show me what you've found," Laura said.

"All along these dirt roads south of the border crossing," Steve said, tracing their path with his index finger, "you see a number of single dwellings. Some have small plots of tilled ground around them, others are just homes. During the middle of the day, you don't see cars parked there. Those homes are probably occupied by locals who work in the villages or on larger farms in the area. I'm ignoring those because they don't have the infrastructure we're looking for."

"Okay," Laura said, nodding her assent.

"I took the liberty of circling a couple of spots of interest," Steve continued. "Spots that have the kind of infrastructure that would support larger numbers. This spot, for instance," he said pointing out a grouping of buildings, "is some kind of large agricultural operation." Steve had circled the spot with a red pen. Laura laid her finger inside the circle.

"Here?" she asked,

"Yes. Be careful, that's a dry erase pen. It smears easily."

Laura laughed. "Those years I'd arise in the mornings to find you at the kitchen table studying photos, I had no idea what you looked for."

"You learn a few tricks over time," he said, chuckling. They looked at each other and made another connection, this time borne of memories. Laura's body tensed and she looked away, fighting the feeling of comfort between them. "Uh …" she stammered, trying to regain her focus, "tell me what you see."

Steve moved the magnifying glass over the spot. "Of the four buildings you see here, this one is probably the residence," he said, pointing to one of the structures. "The larger one here," he pointed to another, "is likely a barn. You can see ruts where vehicles pull in and out of that shadowed area on one side. That shadow could be an open barn door. The trucks parked in front and alongside that building? Its harvest time for olives; they could be in the midst of a harvest. The two smallest buildings are probably storage areas of some kind."

"Okay," she said, trying to concentrate on the photo rather than their close proximity. She could smell a hint of his cologne, the same kind he'd always used.

"Behind the buildings," he continued, moving his finger back and forth, "are rows and columns of trees, probably fruit or olives trees. You see more ruts where trucks pull into the orchards. The hills on either side of this valley funnel moisture into the valley creating a natural irrigation system. They've got a nice operation going. There are certainly enough buildings around to hold hostages. Lots of vehicles, too. Notice the route into the valley isn't direct. The roads go around those hills so there wouldn't be a lot of traffic back in there. They could put spotters in the hills and have sufficient warning of approaching vehicles."

"Bottom line, what do you think?"

"It looks like a successful farm operation to me. Judging from the photos, the people who live there work hard from dawn to dusk. I doubt they'd have time to get themselves mixed up in hostage taking. But, it's a possibility."

"What about the second circle?" Laura pointed to a second spot.

"That's two residences that face each other with a small building in between to the rear. You can see they form a triangle."

"Yes, I see that."

"There are several interesting things about this place." Steve slid the magnifying glass over it. "For one, they've got fencing around the perimeter, probably to keep livestock penned in. Goats, chickens, perhaps a cow. The third, smaller building at the back could be an animal feed area. See that spot right in the middle?"

"This?" she asked, pointing to a small, dark spot between the buildings.

"Yes. I'm guessing that's a well. It'd have to be a deep well because that area isn't low like the valley area in the first spot. It'd be expensive to drill there. Those people have some money."

Laura looked at Steve and smiled. "How do you know these things?"

Steve blushed, unaccustomed to receiving praise from her. "I've looked at thousands of photos over the years."

"Anything else?"

"Yeah, there's more. You see the wide lighter area in front?"

"Yes."

"That's gravel they've hauled in to widen the driveway. Take a look at the cars. Four of them at midday. That would indicate a lot of people live there. Either they don't work or they work there during the day. It could be a place where several generations of the same family reside. That's common in that part of the country."

"That makes sense," she replied.

"You don't see farming around the place so they could be merchants who own shops in the surrounding villages."

"How far off the highway is it?"

"You mean the Damascus Highway?"

"Yes."

"It's, maybe, fifteen miles or so inside Lebanon," Steve replied. "That would put it about twenty miles off the highway." He moved the lens across the photo. "There's another analysis that would explain what I see at that location." Steve looked at Laura. "It could possibly be a militia headquarters."

"Bottom line, what do you think?"

"That's the place that raises the most questions. I'd like to see photos at all times of day in high resolution. I'd like to see who comes and goes. Maybe we can pick out some activity in that courtyard between the houses."

"Let's do it," she said.

"I'll take these downstairs and have the tech people get to work. We'll also have a new set in an hour or so."

"Where will Rick's report end up?"

"It'll go to Foggy Bottom first. State will send it over tomorrow."

"Would it be there now?" Laura asked.

Steve shrugged his shoulders. "Maybe. Let's call and find out. If they have it, let's drive over and pick it up."

Steve called the Department of State, got transferred around several departments and was finally put on hold. He put his hand over the receiver and looked at Laura. "They're looking. It might take a few minutes."

"I've got to run down to Roger's office for a minute."

"Okay. I'll stay on hold here."

Laura walked back to Roger Wilson's office where the secretary recognized her. "Mr. Wilson left this envelope here for you." She picked up an interoffice envelope.

Laura walked to the desk and retrieved it. "Thanks," she said.

Steve had just hung up the phone when she returned. "Well, it's there," he said. "You want to take my car?"

"Would State give it to me?"

"The report? Sure. It'll be waiting for you at the counter in the lobby."

Steve tossed her the car keys. "Don't mistreat the Jag please," he said, teasing.

She smiled. "You know I will. Did you park in your usual place?"

Steve shook his head in mock disgust. "Yes. Just don't wreck it. Insurance and registration are in the glove box. I'll ride herd on the tech boys while you're gone."

# Chapter Forty-Two

*Saturday, November 5, 1988*

THE BLACK SEDAN traveled out of Damascus toward the Lebanese border the next morning following the murders at the Omayad. Headed toward Imam Kassem's compound, the sedan made its way over nearly twenty-five kilometers of bumpy, degraded roadway inside Lebanon. It's no wonder these people drive such terrible vehicles, the passenger thought, bouncing around the back seat. The passenger was a distinguished officer in the Ministry of Intelligence of the Islamic Republic of Iran, or MOIS, as it's often referred to in the West. Lieutenant Colonel Samir Rajavi worked directly for the Minister and was responsible for all interrogations conducted by the Ministry. He'd come to his present position by virtue of his work interrogating Iraqi prisoners during the Iran-Iraq war where his methods were quickly adopted throughout the Ministry. Offering prisoners the opportunity to escape torture through cooperation led to more accurate information and Rajavi's approach had revolutionized the interrogation practices used by the government of Iran.

The condition of Kassem's hostages was of concern to Rajavi. Their physical and mental health had deteriorated to the point where it was nearly impossible to gain further information. Kassem's men, inexperienced in interrogation techniques, had tortured the hostages without mercy, leaving only one of the four physically and mentally

230

healthy. In addition, security at Kassem's facility was becoming a problem. Two strangers had been brought there the day before and it was only a matter of time before the entire hostage operation was exposed.

When Rajavi stepped from his vehicle that morning, he wondered how many more interviews could be accomplished before he put his own life at risk. *I need to rid myself of this amateur, Kassem. He knows nothing about the art of hostage manipulation. Only a few more trips are needed before I'll have extracted every piece of information I need from the Americans held here.*

"Good morning, Imam," Rajavi said, bowing slightly while standing before Kassem.

"Good morning, Colonel. Please sit," Kassem said, gesturing toward a chair opposite him. Kassem had chosen to bring two chairs into his room to accommodate the Colonel, who refused to sit on the floor. "Have you taken care of the problem I mentioned yesterday?"

"My men eliminated the threat to your security. Be advised that the Syrians will investigate the hotel deaths. The incident may not be over."

"Were they Transport Ministry employees?"

"How could I know that?"

"I thought your men would have investigated them."

Rajavi laughed. "Imam, with all due respect, assassinations in downtown hotels are risky. We will do no investigation."

"What about the film?"

"It was destroyed. You gave us the wrong room numbers, though."

"I gave you the room numbers they provided," Kassem protested. "The men must have lied to me." Kassem felt a sense of anger at his own gullibility. He looked away and thought for a moment. "That makes their visit even more suspicious," he said looking back at Rajavi.

"The mistake was bringing them here, Imam," Rajavi said with disgust in his voice.

Kassem ignored the statement. "Did you bring a donation this morning?"

Rajavi smiled and withdrew a check drawn on a secret account in Dubai. "Here is your money. I urge you to kill the hostages before you're discovered, Imam. Dump their bodies along the highway somewhere close to Beirut to draw attention away from yourself."

Kassem became angry. "Do not tell me what to do with the prisoners, Colonel. They'll be killed at the proper time!"

That statement concerned Rajavi. He stared at the Imam, thinking. Has he sold access to someone else? Is that why he's keeping them too long? "You've sold access to the Russians?"

"I gave your government first access to the prisoners as a courtesy for your contributions to the Palestinian cause. After the Russians interview them, they'll be disposed of."

The man's an economist. Always looking for money, Rajavi thought. "If you'd permit me a comment, Imam, you're a brilliant economist. You've achieved great success raising the living standards of the people you serve. However, you're not a spy or a military man. You're keeping the hostages too long. Rid yourself of them before you're discovered."

"The Syrians are no threat, Colonel. Their interests lie along the coast and in the Bekaa. The Americans have quit looking. We're safe for the present time. However, I appreciate your wise counsel, Colonel. We are close to being finished."

"The Americans have not stopped looking, Imam. They're looking in the wrong place. You're probably right about the Syrians, but the danger is the Zionists. They have a strong presence in Damascus. If they find out you're here, you're in danger."

The Imam rolled his eyes with sarcasm. "Zionists, Zionists; that's all I hear people speak about. They were pushed out of Lebanon and I see no presence of them here."

Rajavi decided to give up. The man's consumed by his own brilliance. It will be his undoing. "As you wish, Imam. The government of Iran is grateful for the access you've provided. You've been most accommodating. A few more trips and I will have finished my work. Today, I wish to speak to the hostage named William Sharp."

I will be happy to rid myself of Rajavi, Kassem thought. He's a peasant wearing a uniform, just like the rest of the Iranians. Glorified goat herders. The Imam nodded. "He'll be ready for you at the shed in a few minutes, Colonel."

"Thank you. Praise Allah," Rajavi said.

"Allah be praised," Kassem replied.

# Chapter Forty-Three

*Friday, November 4, 1988, a day earlier*

LAURA ARRIVED BACK at Langley with Rick's report after an hour's wait at the State Department. "Sorry it took so long," she said returning to Tilton's office. "They were still looking for it when I arrived."

Steve looked up from his desk. "Not a problem. These were just returned now," he said, holding up the photos. "You go over the report; I'll study the photos."

Laura sat on Steve's sofa and read Rick's report, turning over each page on the coffee table to keep it in order. Enclosed were pictures Rick had developed and the diagram he'd drawn of Imam Kassem's property. After she'd finished, she walked to Steve's desk. "You find anything?' she asked.

Steve, still studying the photos, looked up from the magnifying glass. "We can see far more detail in these. The place we looked at earlier continues to raise questions."

"How so?"

"Sit across from me and I'll show you." Laura sat down in one of the chairs in front of Steve's desk. He turned one photo sideways and slid the lens over it. "See that black car?"

"Yes."

"It looks expensive, like a Mercedes. So, I said to myself, 'maybe the owner of the place is rich,' but the car isn't there in the evening like someone who leaves and returns from work. It stops during the day for a couple of hours. Take a look."

Laura looked at several photos, one which showed the black car present and another where it was not. "See the time stamp?" Steve asked.

"It shows up around ten and leaves in the afternoon."

"An expensive car back in the countryside like that is unusual. I want to see if it shows up tomorrow."

Laura slid a photo toward Steve. "This is from Rick's report."

Steve took a look at the photo of a black sedan from the rear. The license plate was clearly visible. "Same car?" she asked.

"Could be. Where and when was this taken?"

"Two days ago. The dirt road is the one that leads to the location we're studying. Can you read the plate?"

Steve ran the lens over the plate. "No. Let's take it downstairs. Maybe the tech guys can clean it up." He set it aside.

"Another strange thing about this place," Steve continued, "is the number of men walking around doing nothing. They seem to be carrying weapons as though they're guards. Here, look."

He slid the photo between them. Laura pushed the lens across the photo. "See the two standing on either side of the entry opening to the yard?"

"Yes," she said as Steve pointed with his index finger.

"There are two in front of each building also," Steve said. "One in front of the shed and plenty of others outside the fence. That's a lot of men standing around doing nothing."

"Which begs the question why they're there."

"Exactly," Steve said.

"You have a yellow highlighter?"

"Hang on a minute." Steve opened the middle drawer of his desk, rummaged around for a minute and found one. "Here," he said, handing it to her. She highlighted a portion of Rick's report.

"Look at the diagram Rick sent us. Look familiar?" She handed it to Steve.

He studied it for a moment and then looked up. "Shit! It's the same place we're looking at." He put the diagram and one of the photos side by side. "They're nearly identical."

"Now, read the highlighted section of the text," she said, handing a page to Steve.

Steve read aloud. "The guard says to the Imam, 'Should I put them with the others?'" Steve raised his eyes and met Laura's. "That's about as close as we can get to a confirmation without actually seeing a hostage."

"When will the next batch of photos be ready?"

"Tomorrow morning."

"We might get lucky," she suggested.

# Chapter Forty-Four

*Saturday, November 5, 1988*

WILLIAM SHARP'S DETERIORATION was clearly evident after six weeks in captivity. His physical and mental health was failing. His captors knew it; he knew it. He'd learned in Delta Force training that everyone breaks at some point and there was no shame in divulging information in order to survive. In Bill's mind, he'd already determined that he'd die. The United States didn't negotiate with terrorists and even if a rescue was possible, Bill doubted anyone knew where he was located. Remembering the CIA station chief that had been kidnapped a few years ago and found dead in a ditch some months later, Bill anticipated he had only a few more weeks before he suffered the same fate. In Bill's mind, his choice was simple; die after giving them information or die withholding it. Despite his congenial manner, Bill Sharp was one of the toughest individuals his military commanders had ever seen. He'd made his choice soon after his capture. These motherfuckers can go to hell, he thought every day.

Three armed guards rousted Bill from a dirty mattress on the floor. Judging the angle of the sunlight coming through the window, he knew it was late morning. As the guards tied his hands behind his back, Bill had a few seconds to survey the scene. The French doctor was near death. He lay on a dirty mattress without moving. The

237

nurse had received better treatment, but only because she'd been raped continually by guards. She was delirious. Buck had been beaten to the point of death in spite of revealing all that he knew. Just wait, Bill told himself. I hope you motherfuckers make a mistake. If that happens, I'll send a few of you towel heads to that precious God of yours.

Bill was pushed from behind toward the door. He stumbled on the doorstep and fell to the ground outside. One guard shouted at him while another tried to kick him in the groin. Bill blocked the blow by turning to his side slightly. "Fuck you, asshole," he said. He rose to his feet and with a guard on each side holding his arms and a third leading the group, they marched Bill across the courtyard to the shed where he knew the Iranian waited. As they walked across the yard, Bill looked up into the sky, hoping that sooner or later, an American satellite would photograph his image and someone back home would learn he was alive.

The Iranian was already seated at one end of the table when Sharp entered the room. The guards pushed him toward the empty chair at the opposite end. "Release his hands," Rajavi said in Arabic. The guards, reluctant to accept orders from anyone except the Imam, didn't respond immediately. Rajavi stood and drew his sidearm from his belt and pointed at one of the guards. "Release his hands," he shouted. The guards untied Sharp, who immediately brought his left elbow upward and caught the guard underneath his chin. The man staggered backward as Sharp wheeled on the man to his right and landed a punch flush in his face. The guard's face exploded in blood. "Stop," shouted Rajavi. The guard behind Sharp raised his rifle butt to hit Sharp on the head from behind. Rajavi fired his weapon into the ceiling. "Stop! All of you." He walked around the table. "Sharp, take a seat." Rajavi addressed the guards. "You three are the poorest excuse for military men I've ever seen."

"He hit me," the bloodied guard shouted, gesturing toward Sharp. He looked at Sharp and hissed. "I'll kill you for that."

"Fuck you, you pussy," Sharp countered.

Rajavi moved around the table and fired his sidearm again. He stood eye to eye with the guard whose nose had been broken. "That was your fault, not his," he said pointing at Sharp who had sat down. "And, no, you won't kill him. You kill him, I kill you. Understand?"

The guard backed up a step. "Yes," he said.

Rajavi laid the barrel of his weapon on the guard's forehead. "Yes, what?" he asked.

"Yes, Sir."

"Get out," he shouted. He pointed at both of them. "All of you get out of my sight. Now!" The guards fled out of the shed, bumping each other as they ran.

Sharp looked around the filthy shed with its wood plank walls, dirt floor and leaky roof. Overcome the guards, stand on the table, punch a hole in the roof and I'm gone.

Rajavi watched Sharp thinking, content to observe rather than talk. He waited nearly five minutes before he spoke, watching Sharp. He's impressive, Rajavi thought. Psychologically strong. An ability to tolerate pain. When Rajavi finally spoke, he softened his tone. "Good morning, Mr. Sharp," Rajavi said in perfect English.

A battle of wits, Sharp thought. Just like yesterday. "Good morning, Corporal Shithead."

"At this point, Mr. Sharp, I want you to understand why you're still alive. They have kept you alive so that I could interview you. After I leave the last time, you will be killed. It's in your best interest to keep my interest as long as possible."

"I heard you say that yesterday."

"Neither of our governments cares about us as individuals, Mr. Sharp. I can be replaced and so can you. We are expendable. I suggest we become partners, you and I. Let's forget we're on opposite sides. You're trying to figure out how to stay alive and I'm trying to keep my job. Let's cooperate with each other and perhaps both of us can meet our goals."

"I'm with you there. We're gonna meet each other halfway."

"You've already seen my first contribution. During our interviews, you've received better food and less punishment. Do you agree?"

"This has become a resort the last few days. The room service needs a little work, though."

Rajavi smiled. He's close to breaking. "Can I offer you something to drink?"

"Nope. I'm just fine."

"Let us begin then, shall we?"

Rajavi sat down and pulled a yellow legal pad and pen from his briefcase. He began studying his notes from the prior day of interrogations. "We haven't had much time to talk, have we? I've spent most of my time with your colleague. You and I spent yesterday talking of your military career. Where did we end our discussion?" he asked without looking up.

"You tell me," Sharp replied.

"Oh, I neglected to ask you. Have the torture sessions been halted?"

Sharp looked Rajavi in the eyes. "It's all the same to me, bro. Don't notice, don't care."

"You're lying, Mr. Sharp. I can see it in your eyes. Hope cannot keep one alive forever."

"I appreciate your concern, Corporal. I really don't mind the rough treatment. Delta Force training was tougher than this."

Rajavi had heard such statements many times, bravado from tough men ultimately broken by prolonged torture. He looked down at his notes again. "Ah, yes, here we are. We were talking about procedures at your Embassy. Could you explain them again?"

"It's like I said yesterday. All embassies operate the same. Yours, mine, all of them."

"Explain your job at the Embassy."

"I'm a gopher."

"What's a gopher?"

"A gopher is a rodent that lives in the American West. We often call someone who does menial tasks a gopher."

Rajavi smiled, "I doubt your tasks are menial, Mr. Sharp. Again, what is your job at the Embassy?"

"I'm the resident bullshitter."

"What do you mean by that?"

"My job is to persuade people to like Americans," replied Sharp.

"That's all?"

"Hey, that's a tough assignment in this part of the world. Take you, for example. You hate Americans. Nothing I can do about that. Do you know what you need to do?"

"What's that?" an amused Rajavi replied.

"Build some fucking resorts along your coast, put up some five star hotels and a couple of championship golf courses and you're in business."

The man's clever. He's trying to turn the interrogation, thought Rajavi. Perhaps his will isn't broken yet. Rajavi decided to change the subject. "Can you confirm the head of CIA Station in Damascus is Paul O'Dell?"

"O'Dell? That piece of shit's a diplomat, not CIA. He's dumber than a fuckin' doornail."

"Then who's the CIA representative at the Embassy?"

"I don't think they have one," Sharp said. He shook his head. "It's those damn budget cuts. You know how those Republicans are. They cut salaries so they can buy the latest bomber, which could wipe you guys off the face of the planet, by the way."

"How many CIA operatives reside in the Embassy?"

"None that I know of. They rely on the Israelis." Sharp pointed above him. "The U.S. does its eye in the sky thing."

Rajavi laughed. "You've got the guards here so afraid of satellites, they look into the sky before they walk out the door."

"I keep telling them to wave."

"If American satellites are as good as you claim, why haven't they found you?"

"They're probably watching this place right now."

"Why haven't they rescued you?"

"Probably killing bad guys in other places. Don't worry, one of these days real soon, you're gonna meet 'em."

"I want you to understand something." Rajavi leaned forward for emphasis. "No one is coming!" He paused to judge Sharp's reaction to the statement. "I'll say it again. No one is coming to rescue you." Rajavi waited for a reaction from Sharp and received only a slight smile in response. Rajavi looked deeply into Sharp's eyes. Sharp stared right back. He really believes he's going to be rescued, thought Rajavi. Let's not encourage further resistance. Move on.

"What's Paul O'Dell's job at the Embassy?" Rajavi continued.

"He's a paper pusher. He's not the guy you think he is."

"What's a paper pusher?"

Sharp gave him a look of disbelief. "You don't know what a paper pusher is? Everyone's got paper pushers in their office. He picks up a piece of paper from one pile and moves it to another. That's what he does all day. Boring as hell."

"How many agents does O'Dell run in Damascus?"

"Zero. The Israelis do all the work."

"I find that hard to believe," Rajavi said with a smile.

"You think those guys at the Embassy are competent? That's funny. They're like the Keystone Cops over there."

"What are the Keystone Cops?"

"Way back in the days of silent films in America. The Keystone Cops were bumbling police officers. Kinda like those guards outside."

"I see." Rajavi paused for a minute. He looked down at his notes again. "How many local contacts does he have?"

"You're talking about O'Dell?"

"Yes."

"Have you ever seen him leave the Embassy to meet anyone? The guy sits on his ass everyday inside the Embassy."

"He can run local assets without meeting them."

"If you haven't noticed, Americans aren't real popular in this part of the world. I don't see many locals wanting to work with the Americans. Besides which, O'Dell's got the personality of a two by four."

"What's a two by four?"

Sharp laughed. "It's a piece of wood. You buy it at a lumber yard, although it's often called a 'stud.' Today's studs are usually pine and grown ..."

Rajavi held up his hand and interrupted Sharp. "Stop! I've heard enough."

Sharp cocked his head and shrugged. "Hey, I'm only trying to help. We're partners, remember?"

"One moment please." Rajavi wrote on his legal pad for a few minutes. Looking up, he said, "Wait please, while I record your answers."

Sharp chuckled at that. "You better hurry. I'm late for my next appointment."

When Rajavi had finished, he laid the pen down. "I'd like to change the subject. Tell me about Franklin Brooks."

"The Ambassador?"

"Yes," Rajavi replied.

"Not much to tell. Brooks is a business guy. He got rich screwing people. I guess they sent him over here to screw Syrian businessmen for a while."

"We've heard rumors about a new construction project in Damascus financed by American investors. Would those plans be secured in Brooks' office safe?"

Sharp shook his head. "Listen, there's nothing valuable in that safe except the menu to the only carry-out Chinese restaurant in Damascus."

"What's the combination to the safe?"

"You think I know that? By the way, chicken and pea pods is a good choice."

Rajavi decided to explore a different line of questions. "What's discussed at the Western Ambassador's breakfast once a month?"

"The best golf courses in Dubai."

Rajavi frowned. "Mr. Sharp, you're not trying hard enough."

"If you don't mind me saying, you're asking stupid questions. Paul O'Dell is an idiot. So is Brooks. They don't know anything. Look at it this way. The government can't get qualified people to work over here. No offense, but who the hell wants to go to Syria?"

"What was Buck's meeting with Assad about?" Rajavi asked.

"You'll have to ask Buck. I wasn't in the room."

"They've beaten him too badly. He's incoherent. He talks nonsense."

Sharp smiled at that statement. "He talked nonsense before you guys got a hold of him. He's a politician. No one understands those guys."

"I find it hard to believe you didn't know the subject of the meeting."

"You think they tell me anything?"

Rajavi stared at Bill. "Yes, I do."

Sharp decided there was no risk in telling the truth. "I have no idea what they discussed. I sat in another room the entire time. In fact, I didn't even find out about the meeting until the day of."

"What do you believe the meeting was about?"

Sharp shrugged his shoulders. "Your guess is as good as mine."

"How did the kidnappers know about Buck's meeting?"

"That's a good question. It was probably a leak in Washington. No one can keep a secret there."

"You've been seen in Damascus taking meetings on behalf of the Ambassador. Why does the Ambassador send you instead of going himself?"

"I told you. I'm the biggest bullshitter he's got," Sharp said with a smile.

"Holding meetings at the ambassadorial level isn't bullshit, Mr. Sharp."

"All ambassadorial meetings are bullshit. What planet are you from? You know how these meetings go?" Sharp asked rhetorically. "I'll tell you. You meet people and you tell 'em what they want to hear. End of story."

Rajavi scratched his head. "I find that hard to believe."

"Hey, I didn't ask you to believe it. I'm just telling you like it is. If you worked in an embassy every day, you'd know I'm right."

Rajavi thought for a minute before continuing. Sharp's clever, he thought. It's as though he draws energy from the lies he tells. "The Ambassador was supposed to be in the car on the day of the kidnapping. Is that your understanding?"

"Probably. Brooks is one lucky son-of-a-bitch."

Rajavi laughed at Sharp's answer. "You'd rather Brooks was here now?"

"Nah. Brooks is a fucking pussy. He couldn't take it."

"And you can?" Rajavi leaned forward, interested to hear Sharp's answer.

"So far, this is like a visit to the country club."

Rajavi thought for a moment. Most prisoners pretend to be tough. This one actually is. "Where was Brooks the morning of the kidnapping?"

"I have no clue. He was gone when I arrived for work."

"What could be more important than meeting Assad?"

"Probably that Ambassador's brunch."

"What happened to Buck's notes from the meeting?"

"You mean during the kidnapping?"

"Yes."

"I have no fucking clue. Ask the idiot in the building across the yard," Sharp said. "Saving Buck's notebook wasn't high on my priority list at the time."

Rajavi sat back and stared at Sharp. "You're not going to give me anything, are you?"

"Look, I'm telling you what I know."

"Mr. Sharp, if I believed that, you'd already be dead."

"Would you like to hear some valuable information?"

"Please," Rajavi said. "My patience isn't unlimited."

"These friends of mine? You don't want to be here when they show up. They're gonna walk in here like it's the OK Corral and kill everyone."

"What's this OK Corral?"

"American history over a century ago. The Wild West. Four guys stood in the open against twenty bad guys and killed them all."

"And you think that's going to happen here?"

"I'm sure of it."

"Mr. Sharp, no one is going to rescue you. If you'd like to get out of here alive, there is only one way. Give me the

247

information I want. If the information is valuable enough, I'll swap you for Palestinian prisoners the Zionists hold."

"Fantastic."

"I want you to think about what I just said. It's your ticket to freedom. I've got business elsewhere for a few days, but I'll come back one more time. If you refuse to talk next time, I'll shoot you myself."

"Could I make one request in good faith?"

"Certainly, Mr. Sharp."

"Could you ask them to put more bugs in the food? That shit's pure protein."

Rajavi laughed. "I'll be back next week for one last visit, Mr. Sharp." Rajavi rose and walked toward the door. "Guards!"

"Yes, Sir," one man said walking in the doorway.

"I'm finished with the prisoner."

Lieutenant Colonel Samir Rajavi walked back into Kassem's office. "I need one more interview with the prisoner named Sharp."

Kassem nodded. "Of course. It will be the same fee as today. When will you come?"

"Sometime next week. I'll contact you the usual way. I have a request of you."

"Yes?"

"Kill the hostages after I've finished my interviews. It's dangerous to keep them."

Kassem smiled. "I'll keep them alive as long as I wish, Colonel."

# Chapter Forty-Five

*Saturday, November 5, 1988*

LAURA AWOKE FEELING the pangs of loneliness. The Watergate Hotel seemed sterile and cold compared with her home on Grand Bahama Island. Walking out of the hotel front door into the cacophony of the urban landscape, Laura focused her mind on the task at hand. Get your act together, she thought. How did you feel in Gaddafi's captivity? You've got a debt to pay.

Her first stop was Jack Postl's small office downtown where she rapped loudly on the door. "Hi Ms. Messier, I'm glad you stopped by," Jack said, answering the door. I didn't know where to reach you."

She entered, took off her coat and laid it over the back of a folding chair. Jack's computer terminals were alight with all manner of symbols, letters and numbers which told her exactly nothing.

"Sorry, Jack. I forgot to tell you I've been at the Watergate for the last few days."

"I made a breakthrough late last night. It took a long time, but I was able to finally hack the bank infrastructure. I'd never done that before. It makes fascinating reading. Do you how much some of these politicians have in their checking accounts?"

Laura grimaced. "No Jack, I don't want to know. What have you found out about The Crescent Society?"

"They're a pretty big operation for a non-profit no one's heard of. They've got locations in Boston, New York, here in Arlington, out in Chicago and on the west coast in Los Angeles. They're basically a fund raising organization that funnels money through one of the big New York banks and sends it overseas."

"Where do they send it?"

"Grand Cayman."

"How much?"

"In the first nine months of this year, over three million," Jack said looking pleased with himself.

"And you can't tell where it goes from Grand Cayman?"

"No, unfortunately."

"Maybe we can get at this another way. Their tax return is a matter of public record somewhere. I think their non-profit and tax exempt government filings are available, too. Can you find that information for me?"

"I'll certainly try."

Laura looked around the office. "How are you doing otherwise?"

Jack looked as though he didn't understand the question. "You mean am I having a wonderful time in Washington? No, I'm not. It sucks here."

"Stupid question, I guess."

"I'm doing this out of loyalty to you and Mr. Broussard."

"Hopefully, you're doing it for the money, too. It's a job, after all. For goodness sake, don't steal money from bank accounts. That would land you in some serious trouble."

"I understand. You're paying me well enough. When I arrived here, I had dreams of getting a job with one of the big IT firms in California. Wow, was I wrong. The people are so advanced, I'm thinking of going back to school to catch up. Maybe I'll get a degree in IT from Berkeley."

"If you want to do that and still work for us, Jack, we'd be happy to pay the tuition for you."

Jack's eyes brightened. "That would be wonderful."

"We support our people, Jack."

"That's very nice of you. Thank you."

Laura laughed. "Well, don't thank me yet. We're going to continue to ask you to do things for us, but we want to make sure you reach your goals, too."

"Thanks."

"We'll have a chance to talk later. Right now, I'm on my way to CIA." She wrote a note on a piece of scratch paper lying on Jack's computer table. "Here's the phone where I'm staying. Call me if you lay your hands on the tax filings."

"Will do."

Laura took another expensive taxi ride out to Langley where she walked to the front counter to get a visitor's pass. "Good morning, Greg Smith."

"Good morning. Please sign in. Director Tilton's expecting you."

"I meant to ask you, Greg Smith. Do you work out on a regular basis?"

"I try to."

"We should work out together while I'm in town."

"What do you mean?"

"You had pretty good scores at The Farm. I'd like to see what you can do."

"Sure," he said with a grin. "It'd be a nice test of my abilities to go up against a real field agent."

Laura smiled to herself. He has no clue. "Good. I'll be in touch."

Laura walked down to the cafeteria to purchase a cup of coffee before going up to the seventh floor. I'm glad I'm out of this trap, she thought, looking around the dining area. The nine to five crowd; I couldn't do it.

She entered Steve's office where his secretary casually looked up. "He's expecting you, Ms. Messier."

Steve looked up from his desk as she walked through the door. "Good timing; the photos are on their way up. Let's set up on the coffee table." Steve brought over a desk lamp and two magnifying glasses. He moved two chairs in position so they could both study the photos.

The photos arrived fifteen minutes later and Steve eagerly opened the thick padded envelope. "I took the liberty of asking them to isolate the location we looked at yesterday. They're supposed to give us the highest resolution possible." He split the stack in half. "You take the top half." They leaned over the coffee table and began their work.

"Look at this," Laura said, handing Steve a photo almost immediately. "It's that black car. Early in the morning."

"Oh, that reminds me," Steve said. "The guys downstairs were able to identify the plate. It's registered to the Iranian Embassy in Damascus."

"Think this is the same car?" she asked holding up the picture.

"Only one road in, one road out. Not much traffic. Yeah, I'd say there's a good chance it's the same car."

Laura glanced at Steve. "What would bring an Iranian Embassy car all the way out there?"

"Maybe another photo can tell us," Steve said.

They returned to their study, but it was only a minute later when Laura stopped and stared. She looked at a sequence of three photos taken seconds apart, shifting them back and forth. She focused on one of the three, staring at it several minutes before Steve noticed. "You've got something?"

"Take a look." She pushed the three photos across the table.

Steve studied them silently, comparing each one under the lens, back and forth. He moved the photos under the lamp to gain more light to see the images. When he was sure, Steve slowly looked up and said softly, "That's a hostage, Laura."

"Yeah," she said quietly, almost to herself. "That poor man." She pointed at the photo. "His hands are tied behind his back with an armed guard on each side of him."

"He's being walked across the courtyard," Steve said, pointing to the man in the photo. "Look at the last photo. He's looking into the sky as though he knows there's satellite coverage."

"He wants us to see his face," Laura said.

Steve studied the face with his magnifying glass. "It's not Buck. Buck has sandy hair and glasses."

"Maybe he lost his glasses."

"No, the hair's too dark. William Sharp, maybe?" Steve asked.

"That would be my guess."

"And the Iranian would be there to do an interrogation?"

"Seems likely."

"Are we jumping to conclusions?" Steve asked. "What are we missing?"

Laura leaned back in the chair, mulling over the evidence. "I can't think of any other explanation." Laura leaned forward again and pointed to the photos. "Look at how the guards hold him by his arms while they're walking. Does that seem right to you?"

Steve looked away for a moment, thinking. "Let's try to put this in context. Rick said something about the number of guards in his report. Let me find the report." He walked to his desk, rummaged around his desk until he pulled the report out from under a pile of paperwork. He began thumbing through the pages. "Here it is," he said, walking back to the table. "'A platoon sized guard unit' he says. If it's not a hostage situation, why do these people need so many guards?"

Laura had been looking at the rest of the photographs. "Would you take a look at something else?"

"What have you got?" he asked, sitting down again.

"One of the last photographs shows the sun shining on the building on the left. There's a sign above the door. Can you make it out?"

Steve looked through the magnifying glass. "The writing appears to be Arabic. We'd never be able to read it. There's a logo underneath the writing."

"What does the logo look like to you?"

Steve squinted into the lens. "A scythe maybe. Without the handle?"

"Or a crescent moon?"

Steve shrugged. "Could be. Why's that important?"

"Ahmed Kalami received funding from an Islamic organization here in the States called The Crescent Society when he attended Harvard. That organization sends millions overseas. That could be how they pay their guards."

"Or they could receive money from Arafat."

"Possibly. I don't think Arafat has any idea where all his money goes."

"I can't see any income generation at that location. No farming, no livestock, no commerce."

"Bottom line. What do you think we've got?" Laura asked.

"My best guess is we're looking at a militia operation that's holding hostages," Steve said, "and there's reason to believe Buck and Sharp are there. If they are, we know Sharp's still alive."

"Next step?"

"We've got to kick this up the ladder. Let's gather this together and walk down to Bill's office."

"I'm not meeting that asshole," Laura said bluntly.

Steve's posture collapsed. His shoulders sunk, he put his head down and then grimaced when he looked back at her. "Laura, get over it. This is your research; you developed this. Everyone comes together when it comes to foreign policy. You know that."

Laura bristled at the thought of meeting Bill Bates. "Tell Bates to go fuck himself. I'm not going and that's final. Besides, I want to follow up on the financial angle."

Steve began collecting the materials and shook his head. This is exactly why she'll always be on the outside looking in, he thought. It's a huge personality flaw.

"Okay, if that's what you want, I'll explain it the best I can."

"The admin stuff is your strength, Steve." she said, "Do your job."

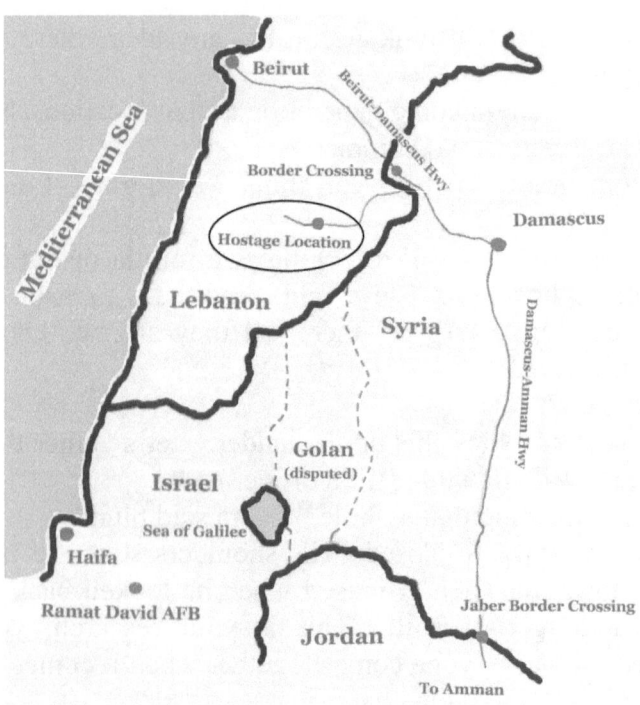

# Chapter Forty-Six

LAURA TOOK ANOTHER long taxi ride back into the city where she stopped again at Jack Postl's office. Luckily, he'd just returned and they met in the hallway as he opened his door. "Hi Laura," he said with a nice smile and bright eyes.

"You certainly are cheerful this afternoon," she replied as he opened the door and led her into his office.

"I've got something to show you," he said. Jack slammed the door shut, peeled off his coat and threw it on a small table in the corner. He opened his briefcase and spread several documents on a folding tabletop. Laura dragged a folding chair to one side while Jack pulled his office chair over from in front of the computer. "There's a foundation office in town that keeps track of information on non-profit organizations. It's open to the public; anyone can look at the information. Here's what I found on The Crescent Society." He handed Laura the first document. "This lists the office holders and board members for The Crescent Society."

Laura scanned the list and one name caught her eye, John Kassem. The home address was somewhere in Boston. "I wish we had this information while we were in Boston. We could have checked out this guy's address," she said pointing to Kassem. "I'd be willing to bet he's not there."

"This information is several years old. He may have updated his address in a later filing."

"What else have you got?"

Jack handed her The Crescent Society's latest tax return. "They're not required to release everything, but here's a list of grant recipients. One of them is a Crescent Society chapter in Yanta, Lebanon."

Laura had a mental image of a map of Lebanon in her mind. Yanta was a small village close to the hostage location. "This is great material, Jack. Can you make copies for me?"

"Sure. I leased a copier so I can do it right here." Jack spent a couple of minutes changing the settings. "Okay, here you are," he said, handing her the paperwork.

"You just put another nail in the coffin," Laura said with a smile.

Jack looked confused. "What does that mean?"

Laura laughed. "It just means it's important. You've done a terrific job, Jack."

"Anything else?"

"What about the bank records? Can you copy those, too?"

"Already did. Here," he said handing her more paperwork.

Laura returned to the Watergate, checked her messages and returned Steve's call before the end of the business day. "What'd the asshole say?" she began the conversation.

"That's a nice way to begin a conversation," Steve replied, his voice dripping with sarcasm.

"Steve, I'm in no mood for games."

"Bates and I are going to the White House tomorrow to brief the President. Congratulations. You've done a fine job."

"I'm loathe to compliment you, Steve," she said reluctantly, "but you've been a critical part of this effort."

"All options will be on the table in the discussion tomorrow, Laura. I have no idea what they'll decide. I'll give you a call after the meeting and let you know."

"Okay. Good night."

# Chapter Forty-Seven

LAURA SHOWERED AND ordered dinner from the room service menu. She anticipated the knock and when it arrived, she opened the door to find a waiter had pushed a dinner cart to the door. "Yes, Ma'am. You ordered dinner?"

"Put the tray on the desk, please," she replied.

Instead of carrying the tray into the room, he pushed the cart inside and allowed the door to close behind him. Laura immediately sensed alarm. It was something about the way he pushed the cart. He struggled getting it inside the doorway.

He was an older man with graying hair, small of build and well groomed. He looks like a professional, she thought. A professional what? She noticed the name 'Wilson' on the lapel of the hotel jacket. Hard sole dress shoes. That's not the kind of shoe people wear working on their feet all day.

She watched the way he walked; the way he clumsily set the tray upon the table. Instead of taking the cover off the dinner plate, he turned and said, "Would you sign the ticket, Ma'am? The meal will be charged to your room."

"Hang on a minute while I get my purse. I've got a couple of bucks for you."

"There's no need, Ma'am. Just sign the ticket." He held the room service ticket out toward her.

Laura walked around the bed to pick up her purse which she'd thrown up against the pillows after arriving back at her room. She slipped one hand underneath the pillow and found the Sig Sauer P226 right where she'd left it before she'd told housekeeping that her room didn't need cleaning. The suppressor was already screwed onto the barrel. She picked up the purse with one hand and the pistol in the other, hiding the pistol behind the purse as she walked slowly around the bed toward the man. She threw her purse on the bed, exposing the pistol which she pointed directly at the man's chest.

"Don't move," she said harshly. "Don't even blink. Leave your hands where I can see them." The man didn't seem surprised to see a gun.

"How'd you know?" he asked with the hint of a smile.

"Lie face down on the floor." The man didn't move. Laura fired a shot close enough to his head that he could feel the breeze as the round flew by him and embedded itself in the outer wall. "The next one goes in your brain," she said. This time, he slowly lay down.

Laura walked behind him to the window and pulled down a panel of the sheer curtain. She tore the fabric with her teeth and ripped a long strip from top to bottom. She moved behind the man and kicked him. "Spread your legs apart." After he'd done that, she said, "Put your hands behind your back." She laid the gun on the bed, put one foot on the back of his neck and tied his hands firmly behind his back with the curtain fabric. She searched him, pulling his billfold from his back pocket. Laura picked up the weapon again and pointed it at his head. "Now roll yourself over and sit up against the wall. This isn't the time for imagination, my friend. Do as I ask and you might live through the night." He managed to flip himself over and squirmed into a sitting position against the wall.

"What now?" he asked.

"Shut the fuck up," she replied.

Reading the identification in the billfold, she said, "You're a diplomat?"

"Mossad would be more accurate," the man replied.

"It was a yes or no answer. If you insist on talking, I can render you unconscious if you like?"

She picked up the phone and dialed Steve's home in Georgetown. "Hello," Steve said.

"Steve, its Laura. I need to speak with Operations at Langley immediately. Set up the call. Have them call room 1417 at the Watergate."

"What's wrong?"

"No time, Steve. Just do it. I'll explain later."

She hung up and looked at the man. "Now, we wait."

"Take a look at the dinner ticket, please," the man said.

Laura walked to the desk and studied the dinner ticket. On top rested a business card. She read it aloud. "Neal Steiner, Embassy of the State of Israel, Washington, D.C. You're a little lost, aren't you, Mr. Steiner."

"I'm here to help."

"Really?" she asked with a wicked, cold smile. "Thank you for that. I appreciate it."

The phone rang. "Yes?"

"Ms. Messier?"

"Speaking."

"Your access code?"

"47994."

"This is Langley Operations. How can we help you this evening?"

"I need to check the credentials of a Neal Steiner, Israeli Embassy here in Washington. Fax his vita to the

Watergate Hotel and ask them to deliver it to room 1417. This is important; have them slide the material underneath the door. I don't want to be disturbed."

"Yes, Ma'am. I'll do it right away."

She hung up the phone and turned to the man, "Now we wait again."

"The men you sent to Damascus are amateurs," Steiner said.

Laura walked over and kicked the man in his face. The back of his head slammed into the wall and the force of the two blows stunned him momentarily. "You want to live through the rest of this evening?" she asked rhetorically. The man took a moment to regain his senses and then he stared at her. "I have no problem shooting an intruder. Shut the fuck up," she said slowly with emphasis.

She stared at the man intently. After twenty minutes, Steiner said, "You have good concentration skills."

Laura walked around the bed so the muzzle of her weapon pointed toward the outer wall. "This suppressor is soft enough that no one will come to the room. Hold perfectly still. I only intend on wounding you."

"No, please," Steiner said.

Laura walked back in front of the man and smiled. "This is real easy. Don't talk."

Over an hour later, Laura heard an envelope pushed underneath the door. "In this situation, Mr. Steiner, it would be wise to relax while I retrieve the envelope." She walked to the door, picked up the envelope and returned to the desk chair. She opened it and read the file. She held up the picture. "Does this look like you?" she asked Steiner. He didn't answer. "Yes, I think it does. It says here you're a registered diplomat and you're Mossad's man in

Washington. Is that right?" she asked. When he didn't respond, she said, "You can answer now."

"Yes."

"It's not like you boys to come without back-up. Where are they, Mr. Steiner?"

"I didn't bring any."

"Why not?"

Steiner chuckled. "I didn't expect you to be this good."

"Do you mind if I enjoy my meal now?"

"Would you untie me?"

"No. You interrupted my evening, so I'm going to take my time."

Laura took another twenty minutes, eating a chef salad with a buttered dinner roll while continuing to review Steiner's file. After her meal, she poured herself a cup of coffee, added cream and sugar, then laid the file on the tray and looked up at Steiner. "You can untie yourself now."

"How do you expect me to untie myself?"

"You figure it out. I'll wait."

Steiner struggled with his bonds, but eventually wiggled out of the makeshift rope that bound his hands. Laura was amused. "Just continue to sit on the floor and tell me why you're here."

"I told you. We want to help."

"With what?"

"Whatever your interests are in Yanta."

"Why?" she asked pointedly.

"We thought that would've been apparent when we rescued your men at the Omayad from the Iranians."

"We must be having difficulty communicating. I asked why you want to help?"

"You're operating too close to the Golan for our comfort. We insist on being involved to avoid an escalating conflict."

"And how might things escalate?" Laura asked.

"The American military won't help because it's too close to the Syrian border. The Americans will ask Assad's permission. He'll deny it and take two companies of Syrian regulars into Yanta. With artillery, I might add. He'll be met with equal strength by the partisans and we'll be drawn in to protect our interests. We'll have another war on our hands. We wish to prevent that."

"Just for the sake of argument, what do you think we're doing in Yanta?"

"We're not sure."

"I'll stop by your Embassy tomorrow morning to discuss it. Is that satisfactory?"

"We'd be pleased to host you."

"Go ahead and rise now, Mr. Steiner. Leave immediately and remember, no sudden movements."

Steiner rose awkwardly, brushed himself off and straightened his jacket. He walked to the door. "Mr. Steiner, aren't you forgetting something?"

Steiner turned around. Laura pointed the weapon at him. "You came into the room as a waiter so leave like one. Take the cart with you."

He exited the room pushing a food cart full of dirty dishes.

# Chapter Forty-Eight

*Sunday, November 6, 1988*

LAURA RETURNED TO the Watergate from her meeting at the Israeli Embassy the next morning and began outlining a clandestine mission into Lebanon. She'd nearly forgotten about Steve when the phone rang late in the day.

"Hello?"

"Laura, its Steve."

"And?"

"You have a meeting at the White House tomorrow morning at 9:15. That's all I'm permitted to say on an unsecured line."

"Thanks. I'll call you from secure following the meeting," Laura replied.

"Good luck."

Laura returned to her planning, detailing each bullet point in the outline, aware that something important was afoot.

# Chapter Forty-Nine

*Monday, November 7, 1988*

LAURA ARRIVED AT the Northwest gate of the White House grounds the following morning at 8:45. She wore the only dress clothes she'd brought with her, a dark blue business suit. The skirt was cut at the knee and the matching jacket fell well below the waist. Three inch black heels raised her height to put her at eye level with the men she'd likely meet. Her jewelry was modest, a matching pearl necklace and earrings. She pulled her hair behind her head and held it with a clasp. Her large brown bag didn't match her outfit, but she didn't figure anyone would notice. After she'd been checked through the gate at the head of the driveway, she walked up the sidewalk to the West Wing entrance where her credentials were checked against the daily schedule of White House visitors. She was ushered into the small lobby inside and instructed to wait. Two military officers dressed in U.S. Army Service Uniforms arrived soon after and waited alongside her. All three sat in chairs stationed around the room. One officer was an older man, perhaps in his early sixties, short gray hair and appeared to be of high rank. He carried a briefcase. The second man, younger, had light brown hair and although he had fewer bars on his uniform, still looked distinguished. Promptly at 9:15, a young man dressed in a business suit walked into the lobby and introduced himself.

"Ms. Messier, General Carey, Major Jordan, I'm Tom Rankin, Assistant to the Chief of Staff here at the White House. If you'd be so kind as to follow me, the Chief of Staff will see you now."

They were led through the West Wing to a corner office at the opposite end of the hallway from the Oval Office. The Chief of Staff rose from his desk and introduced himself. "I'm Landon Mitchell, Chief of Staff to the President." Three chairs had been placed in a semi-circle around the front of the desk and Mitchell motioned toward the chairs. "Please take a seat. I apologize for meeting here in my office, but we've got a busy schedule today."

Mitchell sat behind his desk and picked up a folder with the Presidential Seal on the cover. The folder was stamped "Top Secret." "Thank you for coming today," Mitchell said, acknowledging each one with a nod. "I've been instructed by the President to inform you that a Presidential Finding was created yesterday."

He opened the folder and withdrew one piece of paper. He paused to look around the room before continuing. "This document will give you the legal authority to act within the limits specified here."

Mitchell stopped again and looked around the room. He read aloud from the Finding embossed with the Presidential Seal. "Pursuant to the Foreign Assistance Act of 1974, this Presidential Finding authorizes covert military action to rescue American hostages currently held in Lebanon. This covert military action will commence beginning at 12:00 a.m. (midnight) on Monday, November 14th, 1988, and continue until completion. Signed by the President of the United States, Sunday, November 6th, 1988."

He laid the paper back on his desk and looked at each person. "This will be a joint action taken with the Defense Forces of the State of Israel. It has been cleared at the highest levels of government in both nations. The mission is considered urgent and the President has an expectation the mission will be undertaken and completed next week. The original copy of the Finding will reside here at the White House and a copy will be taken to the Pentagon by General Carey. This mission is labeled "Top Secret" and you may not speak of it to anyone not directly involved. I would remind each of you that following the mission, the President will report your actions to both Intelligence Committees in Congress. Although your names will be redacted from the report, it's imperative that your activities fall within the limits set forth in the Finding." Mitchell looked at his watch. "Across the hall, we have a small meeting room available for," he looked his watch again, "about thirty minutes for you to discuss the mission." Mitchell rose and handed a copy of the Finding to General Carey who put it inside his briefcase. Mitchell walked around the desk and offered his hand to each person. "Good luck and may God Bless the United States of America."

# Chapter Fifty

TOM RANKIN, WHO stood near the door, stepped forward. "Please follow me, if you will." He led Laura, General Carey and Major Jordan across the hall to a small room that looked as though it could have been an office, except it contained just a small table and four chairs. "We can give you this room for a half hour or so." He left and shut the door behind him.

"Ms. Messier and Major Jordan, please take a seat," General Carey said, taking control of the meeting. He looked at Laura. "Ms. Messier, my name is General John Carey, Secretary of the Army and a member of the Joint Chiefs of Staff." He gestured toward the younger man. "This is Major James Jordan, Delta Force Combat Applications Group out of Fort Bragg, North Carolina. He's an expert in counter insurgency warfare."

Laura nodded. "It's nice to meet both of you."

The General looked at Jordan. "Major, have you ever heard of a spy known as Shewolf?"

"Yes, Sir," Jordan replied.

"What have you heard?"

Jordan hesitated, as though he wasn't expecting the question. "Well, Sir," he began, "Shewolf is a renegade French spy who hires herself out to Western governments. Her real name isn't known. The stories one hears about her are legendary. Some say she doesn't exist; she's a fictional person used by intelligence services as propaganda."

The General gave Jordan a sly smile. "Major, I assure you she does exist. She's not French, though. She's an American who previously worked for the Central Intelligence Agency. She's one of ours, Major, and she's the best in the business. The stories you hear are probably true." He motioned toward Laura. "Major, this is Shewolf."

Major Jordan's eyes widened. He stared at Laura, having misjudged her earlier. He stood up, leaned over the table and held out his hand. "Pleasure to meet you, Ma'am. Your reputation precedes you."

Laura smiled sheepishly. "Thank you, Major," she said, taking his hand.

"Indeed, Major," General Carey said. "Ms. Messier's reputation does precede her. She's highly regarded by the President. He's ordered that she lead a mission which will be named "Eagle Rescue" to rescue our hostages. And, Ms. Messier," Carey said looking at Laura, "the President has also ordered that you take four men from our Delta Force unit at Fort Bragg along with you. Major Jordan will lead those men under your overall command."

Laura suspected the government would insist on augmenting her team. She was relieved it was only four men. "Very good General. I accept."

"The Israelis will provide logistics for this mission. They should be contacting you shortly."

"They already have. I had a meeting at the Israeli Embassy yesterday, General."

"You have anything to add, Major?" the General asked.

"Excuse me, General," Laura interrupted. "Our team will meet at my headquarters in the Bahamas to discuss my plan in detail. The Major will have an opportunity to make suggestions at that time."

The General smiled. "Let me rephrase then. Do you have any questions, Major?"

"How do we travel to the Bahamas?"

"Have your men at Andrews this evening at 9:00 p.m.," Laura said. "Street clothes with personal items only. Bring whatever identification you currently have. We'll use my private jet."

"Yes, Ma'am," Jordan said.

The General stood. "Bring our people home, Ms. Messier."

"Yes, Sir."

# Chapter Fifty-One

*Tuesday, November 8, 1988*

A REFRIGERATED SEMI-TRAILER truck made its way out of Amman, Jordan, for its daily trip north on the Damascus Highway toward the Jaber border crossing into Syria. Filled with fresh produce and perishables for Damascus markets, it was fully loaded each morning, although the trailer would be slightly heavier some mornings than others, depending on what had been ordered the evening before.

The driver was aware of the trailer's contents only from the bill of lading he picked up at the Amman shipping office each morning. It wasn't his job to inspect the shipment, only to make sure he picked up the proper forms before he left the warehouse. He'd deliver to a similar warehouse on the outskirts of Damascus, have lunch while the trailer was loaded for the return trip and pick up a second set of forms before returning to Amman late in the afternoon. The trip was routine.

The driver would submit the paperwork to a clerk at the border crossing weigh station on the trip into Syria and again returning to Jordan. He'd drive onto the scale, receive a receipt and continue his trip. Receipts were given to the warehouse manager after his return to Amman. Once in a while, customs officials would search trailers at random intervals, but the crossing was one of only two between Jordan and Syria. Traffic was heavy and officials couldn't risk long lines, so most mornings if the paperwork was found to be in order, trailers were simply weighed, charged the appropriate fee and allowed to cross the border. This particular morning was no different than any other. The trailer weighed slightly more than normal, but that wasn't unusual. The truck delivered its shipment to Damascus and made its return trip to Amman without incident. It was the monotony of routine that the Israeli Mossad relied upon and their delivery was successful.

# Chapter Fifty-Two

*Monday, November 7, 1988, one day earlier*

U.S. ARMY MAJOR James Jordan's handpicked squad from The Joint Special Operations Command met at Andrews Air Force Base thirty minutes before flight time. They'd just stepped off a flight from Fort Bragg, North Carolina. From the Army's Delta Force unit, all four had volunteered to bring one of their own, William Sharp, home from captivity. Adam Wright and Nick Marshall were snipers, Carl Thomas and Jerry Stock were spotters, but Thomas was also an explosives expert and Stock a field medic.

They waited patiently on the tarmac as Laura talked with Pete Franklin, the co-pilot and Svetlana, Dmitri's wife, outside the plane. Refueling had been completed, Pete had finished his walk around and Dmitri had stayed in the cockpit to run through an instrument check. Pete looked at his watch, opened the cargo bay and motioned to Laura. "We're ready to go, Laura," he said.

Laura walked over to the JSOC group standing outside the doors leading into the terminal. "Major, we're ready to board."

"Ma'am, let me introduce you to our team before we depart."

"Of course, Major, that was rude of me."

Jordan pointed toward each man as he identified them. "Captain Adam Wright, sniper specialist," he said working his way around the half circle of men. "Captain Carl Thomas, explosives, Captain Nick Marshall, sniper, and Captain Jerry Stock, field medic. Gentlemen," he said nodding at Laura, "this is our overall mission commander, Laura Messier. You may know her by another name," he said, hesitating momentarily for maximum effect. "This is Shewolf." Eyes widened and jaws dropped as the four men re-evaluated their opinions. Jordan was amused by the reaction. "Yes, gentlemen, Shewolf is a real person and one of the most experienced operatives in the world. Be glad she's on our side."

"It's nice to meet everyone," Laura replied with a smile. "I want to thank each of you for your participation. With such expertise as we have here, I feel confident in the success of our mission."

Each man offered a greeting and a hand in friendship as Jordan stood back and watched his team take on a new measure of confidence. These men knew Shewolf's reputation, an Intelligence Star winner whose exploits had taken on legendary status.

"Well, you heard our commander, gentlemen," Jordan said to his squad. "It's time to saddle up." The men walked across the tarmac, threw their gear in the cargo bay and proceeded up the stairs into the aircraft.

Laura waited at the bottom of the stairs until the last possible moment. When Svetlana stuck her head out the door and said, "Laura, Captain says we've got to go." Laura took one last look toward the terminal doors.

"Okay. On my way up," she replied.

She bounded up the stairs, Svetlana closed the door and ramp agents backed the plane around the apron. The plane proceeded down the taxiway and waited until the tower gave Dmitri permission to access the runway. Dassault Falcon 50 tail number 1908 took off at 9:20 p.m. bound for an uncontrolled asphalt airstrip on the east side of Grand Bahama Island. Fifteen minutes later, Dmitri made his opening announcement. "Ladies and gentlemen, this is Dmitri Polzin, your captain. We'll be flying to beautiful Grand Bahama Island this evening where it's currently a balmy eighty-one degrees. Flight time will be approximately two hours, fifteen minutes. You may take off your seatbelts and move about the cabin. The weather this evening is calm; however, if we run into unexpected turbulence, the seatbelt light will come on and we ask that you return to your seats and strap yourself in. The restroom is in the rear of the cabin and Svetlana will be coming through shortly to serve refreshments. Relax and enjoy the flight. Captain out."

Greg Smith burst through the terminal doors and ran onto the tarmac. One of the ground crew walked up. "You can't be out here, buddy."

"I'm supposed to catch a flight this evening. Can you tell me where to find the plane?"

"Where's it going?"

"It's a private flight to the Bahamas."

"Left five minutes ago." He pointed to a plane rolling down the runway. "That's it taking off."

Greg hung his head and was silent for a moment. Damn, he thought. "Thanks," he said before slowly walking back through the terminal. My first mission and I messed it up. I may be stuck at that counter my whole career.

Laura's crew rarely used the Bahama landing strip at night because no runway lighting was available. As Dmitri neared the Bahama coastline, he radioed his arrival time to Jean at the Bahamian compound. Two of Jean's men drove to the airfield across the Grand Bahama Highway and a mile to the east. They dropped flares over the length of the runway along the sides and at each end. Their vehicles were positioned on either side of the apron to light the area where the plane would drop its passengers. The plane landed without incident. Dmitri wheeled the aircraft around on the apron, let his passengers off and then immediately took off again to fly back to the St. Petersburg Airport in Florida where their charter service was based. It had been a long day for Dmitri and his crew.

Laura's guests squeezed into the two vehicles and were driven to the compound where they used all the empty rooms in the barracks and main house. Except Laura. She headed straight to the hut on the ocean where she preferred to sleep. Vixen hadn't seen her in a couple of weeks and jumped around like the pup she was. After a warm hello and a licking of Laura's face, both headed down the path toward sleep and the solace of the beach.

The following morning, Tuesday, guests found a hearty breakfast served at the main house and the barracks. Jean was a superb host, making everyone feel at home and invited them all to enjoy the amenities at the compound. Business would wait until after dinner.

Rick and Pierre had returned from Damascus for the mission planning session and invited the JSOC men to the firing range and workout facility where the group bonded over friendly competition and the constant banter that accompanied it. Lunch was served on the back porch at the main house where Jean entertained everyone with stories and jokes that made the entire group feel welcome. Laura wasn't seen, however, either at the beach, the house or at her hut. She simply vanished. Rick sent a search party across the grounds during the afternoon to find her. They returned after an hour without any news of her.

Rick decided to take the two friendliest dogs, Dasher and Dancer, and conduct a search himself. The dogs bounded off into the dense undergrowth once Rick gave them permission to run free. He walked silently over the length of the beach, deciding to avoid yelling her name figuring the dogs would make enough noise to alert her attention. He peered into the dense tropical plant life off the beach and scanned the ocean for boats and swimmers. Rick saw no sign of her, no footprints in the sand, no broken plant stems where she might have walked into the undergrowth. Nothing, no sign of her anywhere.

At the far eastern end of the property where the beach ended, the ground turned marshy and Rick could go no farther. He took one final look out over the ocean before turning around. One small speck on top of the water caught his attention. Too far out for any swimmer, Rick wondered if a shallow water marker had been placed there. Thinking it was a buoy, he turned to walk the opposite direction. For some reason, he turned to cast one last gaze over the landscape and he saw the object move in an unnatural way. It can't be a rock sticking out of the water that far out. What the heck is it? He regretted not bringing binoculars along. He pulled a large piece of driftwood out of the brush, carried it near the water's edge and sat down to watch. Over the next hour, the object would disappear at times, only to reappear a few minutes later. When, at last, it disappeared for several minutes, Rick finally stopped looking and began to walk back toward the house. The dogs burst from the dense bushes, ran across the beach and bounded up to Rick, wanting to play. When Rick ignored them, they headed into the ocean to splash.

Rick kept walking until he heard the dogs barking wildly. He turned and watched them run down the beach in the direction he'd come from. That's when he saw her walk out of the ocean. She wore a white bikini. She's the most gorgeous thing I've ever seen, Rick thought. What a modeling career she could have had if she'd stuck with it. I've loved her since the first day we met and she doesn't even know it. He watched the dogs jump around her. He could hear her laughing and calling them by name. She looked up suddenly, shocked to see him. He felt embarrassed at having intruded into her privacy. She stood perfectly still. She doesn't deserve to be stared at. Rick slowly turned and headed down the beach, upset by the embarrassment he felt at invading her private space. She came down here to be alone and I show up. Looking for her was a mistake. Reaching the path, he turned toward the house without glancing in her direction. The image of her standing on the beach was frozen in his mind, perhaps it was a moment between them, perhaps not. At least she knows I care. Rick knew she was safe and like it or not, that would have to suffice.

She didn't make an appearance until immediately before dinner when she walked up to the house and headed to her bedroom for a shower and clean clothes before dinner. She spoke to no one. Rick and Jean saw her walk through the house and attributed her behavior to the routine she repeated before every mission. Laura was capable of super-human deeds in combat. Both men had witnessed her astounding feats of bravery. This particular mission promised to be as difficult as any Laura had participated in and Jean urged Rick to leave her alone. He did and both men were relieved when she made an appearance for dinner at the long table on the porch looking fresh and rested, smiling and chatting as though nothing troubled her. Rick and Jean knew her well enough to know her performance was to give confidence to their guests. Underneath the veneer of her behavior, the men could perceive the concern she felt regarding the mission.

# Chapter Fifty-Three

LAURA HELPED ISABELLA and Sofia clear the table following the group's evening meal, a flavorful dinner of roast pork, potatoes and vegetables, followed by ice cream and coffee. Jean opened the bar in the dining room and the men retrieved drinks for themselves and returned to the back porch. Laura disappeared for a moment, returning with a large artist's case containing the CIA satellite photos, diagrams she'd drawn, maps, a list of equipment she'd requested and a time table of the battle plan. Copies were distributed around the table and the JSOC men grew serious studying the material. She asked Rick and Pierre to explain what they'd seen at the compound. The JSOC men asked questions, made suggestions and slowly, over the next few hours, the plan was adjusted until the group felt comfortable with the strategy.

The plan called for speed, surprise and timing. Eight experienced men with superior arms attacking up to forty untrained men defending a poorly reinforced compound. Done well, they'd overwhelm their opponents, but if the advantages of surprise and speed were lost, the group could be overrun by reinforcements coming to the aid of the kidnappers. Men living in the surrounding area received financial assistance from the Imam and at the first sign of trouble, they'd likely converge on the compound, perhaps tripling their numbers. The group decided to consider the plan overnight and reconvene the following day to make any final adjustments before their insertion into the region.

During the afternoon meal on Wednesday, the JSOC team focused on the extraction. That was the one aspect where the group needed outside assistance. Any delay in the extraction would result in having to defend a helicopter landing zone with little shelter from the enemy. Major Jordan sought Laura's assurance that the extraction would be executed according to plan.

"You're right to focus on that, Jim. Ramat David Air Force Base is seventy-five miles away. The Israeli's will be on stand-by and we'll be picked up within minutes after we place the call."

"Explain to me again how we'll place the call," Jordan asked.

"They're giving us a satellite phone with a direct line to the base."

"What if we can't contact them by sat phone?"

"We load everyone in the vehicles and get the hell out of there."

"And go where?" Jordan asked.

"Back to the Embassy. The State Department will fly us out using diplomatic credentials."

Jordan looked at his men. "Any more questions, guys?" The men seemed satisfied with the answer. Jordan turned to Laura. "How many vehicles do we have again?"

"Three. We've got two Range Rovers and a pick-up."

Jordan thought for a moment about how many people would fit into the three vehicles. "With the hostages, it'll be a tight fit, but we can manage."

"Good," Laura said. "The only thing left to discuss is getting into Damascus. We'll fly to Paris together as a group where the French will provide us with undercover identities. From Paris, we'll travel to Damascus and use the American Embassy as a staging area."

Jordan looked around the table. The JSOC men, cognizant of the challenges, allowed Jordan to speak on their behalf. "I think that covers our questions, Laura. What time is take-off in the morning?"

"Operation Eagle Rescue will depart tomorrow morning at 08:00 hours. Dmitri will bring the plane to the strip across the road and we'll leave from there."

Jordan turned to his men. "Let's be ready to move out at 07:00 everyone. Until then, enjoy your R and R. See everyone in the morning."

The men disbanded, some heading toward the beach and others migrating to the firing range or just sleeping in the barracks. Laura helped clean the kitchen to divert her attention from the mission and then headed to her private hut at the edge of the beach where she read until deep in the night. She'd learned that missions come with many unanswered questions. The unpredictable nature of conflict forces one into an attitude of acceptance and, finally, peace. Objectives are known, but outcomes are not. She finally fell asleep willing to let fate make its decision.

# Chapter Fifty-Four

*Thursday, November 10, 1988*

THURSDAY MORNING, THE Operation Eagle rescue group left the Bahamas airstrip and traveled to Gander, Newfoundland, where they refueled for the next leg of their trip to Paris, France. They arrived at Charles de Gaulle airport in Paris during the early morning hours on Friday. Weary after a ten hour travel day, Laura's team rested at the Paris Marriott Hotel and met Jacques Martin at DST Headquarters Friday afternoon.

Jacques had prepared identities for every person in the group to gain entry into Syria without alerting authorities. Among the JSOC men, Adam Wright and Carl Thomas were Dutch businessmen, Nick Marshall and Jerry Stock were given the dossiers of English archeologists. Rick and Pierre were Canadian businessmen, and James Jordan and Laura a husband and wife on holiday. Jacques warned them to memorize the information in case they were questioned at Customs in Damascus. Commercial flight and hotel reservations were made in the names of the false identities and each of the four pair left Paris at various times on Saturday. None of the pairs saw each other at Damascus International Airport and each took a taxi to the American Embassy where their arrival had been expected. By Saturday evening, all eight mission participants had arrived safely.

# Chapter Fifty-Five

*Friday, November 11, 1988*

THE CALL CAME from the Embassy of the Islamic Republic of Iran in Damascus to Imam Kassem's compound late in the afternoon. The unidentified voice said, "Please inform the Imam that our interrogator wishes to conduct his last interview Monday morning. Be advised that he wishes to appear earlier than usual, at approximately 08:00, due to his scheduled flight back to Tehran later in the day."

"The Imam will be informed and your interview will be scheduled at the time you requested. Good day." The line disconnected.

# Chapter Fifty-Six

THE UNITED STATES Embassy in Damascus, Syria was ordered closed by President Reagan for three days to maintain secrecy for Operation Eagle Rescue. Only essential staff were permitted to gain entry and no foreign nationals were allowed access to the Embassy or its grounds. The official reason was communicated publicly as renovations to the facility. Only Ambassador Franklin Brooks and Chief of Security Tom Wilcox were briefed in advance on the mission.

The mission detachment slept Saturday evening wherever they could find a sofa at the Embassy. Even Ambassador Brooks' office was used. Laura used one of the two rooms upstairs that had a private shower. Rick and Pierre used the other, but shared the shower with the special ops men. Plenty of food was available in the small cafeteria all evening and the following day.

In the early morning hours before dawn on Sunday, a refrigerated truck delivered food supplies to the Embassy as was the usual pattern twice per week. Except, this delivery was made by a different vendor. Embassy guards were briefed regarding the change and the truck was allowed inside the back gate where the driver and his partner loaded food supplies into the kitchen. Embassy guards offloaded weapons, ammunition and equipment the Israelis had smuggled into the country. The shipment was carried into the garage area and locked. Only the Embassy guards had knowledge of the extra delivery. All were American Marines who had been briefed by Tom Wilcox.

Bulletproof glass and metal plates were delivered to the Embassy on the pretext of a security upgrade for Embassy vehicles. The State Department sent two mechanics as diplomats to upgrade the vehicles to be used in the assault. The second Range Rover had been retrieved from the Omayad parking garage and a new pick-up truck with an off-road package purchased from Madigan Motors. Using the garage area Saturday night and during the day on Sunday, the vehicles were upgraded with slightly oversized off-road tires. The factory glass in the vehicles was replaced. Mechanics cut and welded metal plates behind the grills and into the doors of all three vehicles. When Laura found small squares of leftover metal plate lying in the garage, she studied the pieces. About the right size, she thought. Heavy, small enough, it might work.

Jordan and his men unpacked weapons and supplies Sunday morning. Every item that had been ordered arrived in working order and it gave Jordan's men the confidence they needed that Israeli help was reliable. As Laura watched the men inventory the equipment, she asked Jordan for her bulletproof vest. He looked through the vests, handed her the smallest and she walked into the mechanic's shop, finding the metal plates she'd laid aside. Opening the vest top, she slid the plates behind the stiff, mesh fabric. They fit perfectly. She tried on the vest. Heavy, she thought. Restricts my movement a bit, but worth it. She decided to use them. As Jordan's men loaded the weapons, ammunition and equipment into the vehicles,

Jordan saw Laura carry the vest out of the mechanic's shop. "You upgrade your vest a little?" he asked.

"Yeah. I found some extra plate leftover from the vehicles. I stuck it in the vest."

"Good idea. Find any more back there?"

"There are plenty of pieces in the shop if you guys want to try it," she said.

Jordan called his men together and they proceeded to take a torch and cut the metal to size. Each man shoved the plate into his vest, making it far stronger than the fabric alone. One of the men picked up a hammer and pounded his chest, making a metallic clanging noise. He looked at Jordan. "Damn good idea, Major," he said. "Just don't walk in front of me with magnets." That drew a laugh from the men.

Once the equipment was loaded into the vehicles, the building was locked to keep security tight. Two Embassy guards were assigned to guard the garage and they allowed no entry, except to the assault team. None of the team spoke of their mission outside their meetings.

Laura and her team held one last meeting in the cafeteria Sunday evening to review their plan of attack. They studied maps and satellite photos of their approach. The two pairs that would attack the scouts in the hills discussed their drop-off points and traced their paths through the hills to the compound. Adam Wright would be paired with Carl Thomas and call themselves Sierra Two. Nick Marshall and Jerry Stock would be Sierra One. Rick and Pierre would drive the Rovers and call themselves Papa One and Papa Two. Jordan and Laura would drive the pick-up and be called Zulu. The precise point of each team's position right before the assault on the compound was identified and the timing for each team was reviewed. The team discussed the extraction again, noting the path each team would take to the landing zone. Finally, all were confident that the various aspects of the mission had been addressed and questions answered. Afterward, the men relaxed and slept before their insertion in the early morning hours Monday.

# Chapter Fifty-Seven

*Mission Day, Monday, November 14, 1988*

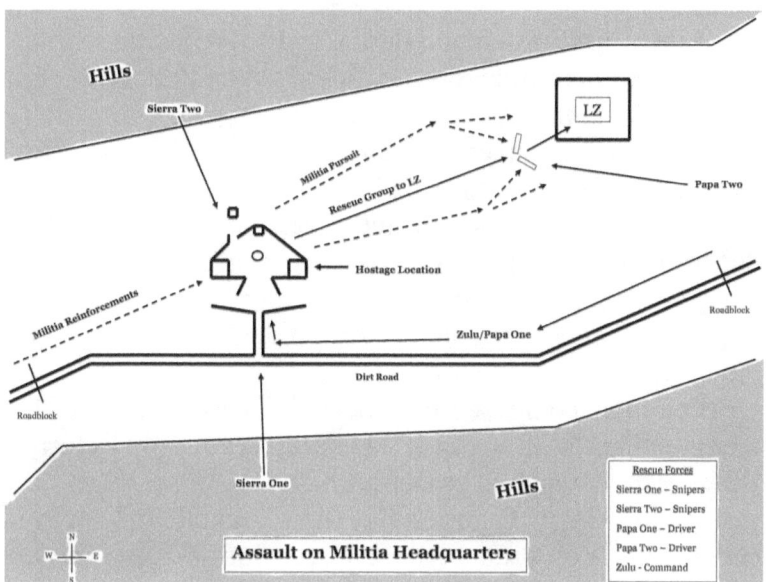

Assault on Militia Headquarters

TWO BLACK RANGE Rovers rolled out of the back gate of the American Embassy at 1:00 a.m. to begin Operation Eagle Rescue's insertion into Lebanon. Pierre drove Sierra Two (Adam Wright and Carl Thomas) under the cover of darkness to the village along the Beirut-Damascus Highway that lay right before the border crossing. The men were silent during the thirty-five minute trip. As they turned off the highway into the village, Pierre

291

turned off the vehicle lights and rolled through a village that was fast asleep. He dropped Wright and Thomas at the southernmost edge of the village, four miles north of Imam Kassem's compound. Pierre drove back to the road that led to Kassem's compound, turned and then pulled off the road into the trees at the rallying point where he awaited the others.

Using night vision goggles, Wright and Thomas walked through the barren, empty landscape toward the rocky hills north of the compound.

"So far, I haven't seen anything," Thomas said, weaving his way through the brush.

"Isn't much out here in the desert," replied Wright. "I did some reading about the area. Small mammals are about the only thing we'll encounter of the four legged kind. We'll probably see plenty of spiders in those rocks, though."

The men could see the rocky hills looming ahead of them. "That's all I need," Thomas replied. "Return to Bragg with a bunch of spider bites."

"Sorry, bro. I forgot the insect repellent." Wright chuckled. "You probably won't get a lot of respect around the base for spider bites."

The desert floor gradually gave way to the hills and finally, to the cragged faces of uplifted rock. Climbing the rugged escarpment was fairly easy for these men. Preventing the occasional slippage which sent cascades of rock down the slope was not. Nevertheless, they were alone, several miles from civilization, and the sounds of their movement went unheard by human ears.

Once at the top of the rock face, they created a position for themselves behind boulders from where they could view the valley and the compound. They radioed their progress to Pierre. "Papa Two, this is Sierra Two. Do you read?" Thomas responded.

"Sierra Two, this is Papa Two," Pierre said.

"We're in position just north of the compound on top of the escarpment, over."

"Roger that. Hold for further orders."

Rick drove Sierra One (Nick Marshall and Jerry Stock) down the road that led directly to Kassem's compound. He also turned off his lights and used night vision goggles to negotiate the road. There were no homes or buildings along the road between the Damascus-Beirut highway and the Lebanese border and Rick was able to drive to a point near the border unseen. Sierra One got out and walked the sides of the roadway toward the compound. Rick pulled off the roadway in the bushes and waited.

"Hand signals from now on, Jerry," Marshall said. "There's supposed to be a roadblock somewhere ahead."

"Roger that," replied Stock.

Shortly after crossing the border on foot, Sierra One saw movement on the roadway. Stock, leading the two, immediately held up his hand. Both men carefully moved off the roadway together into the trees to observe. Two men stood next to a vehicle parked along the shoulder. Their weapons, which looked to be AK-47s, were lying upon the hood of the car. "They don't appear to be paying much attention," Marshall said.

"Take the shot," Stock whispered.

"Distance?"

Stock pulled out a hand held triangulation range finder. The targets were clearly visible in the moonlight standing out in the open. Stock adjusted the finder until both images combined, then looked at the dial. "175," he said quietly.

Marshall took aim with his M24 with suppressor attached and gently squeezed the trigger. The muffled shot sounded louder than he'd have liked, but the round passed through both men. They fell. Marshall looked through the scope. "They're not moving, but let's be careful. You never know."

They crept up on the two men lying beside the auto. Both were still alive, but barely. Their chest wounds were bleeding profusely. The round deflected somewhat into the second man and while lying on the ground, he tried to pull his AK-47 from underneath his body. Stock put his boot on the man's arm. "Sorry, buddy. It's time for you to go meet Allah," he said in English. Stock took the pistol from his holster and screwed on the suppressor he pulled from his belt. He shot both men in the head.

"Papa One, this is Sierra One. Come in," Stock said.

"Sierra One, this is Papa One," Rick replied.

"We encountered two hostiles at a roadblock just inside the border. The threat is neutralized. Request your assistance getting the car off the road."

Rick drove to the scene and found the keys to the vehicle in the pocket of one of the men. He drove their car into the brush where it couldn't be seen. Marshall and Stock dragged the bodies off the roadway. Walking back to Marshall and Stock, Rick pointed in the distance. "See where that line of hills comes close to the road? There shouldn't be any more checkpoints until the compound. I'll take you that far, then you're on your own."

Marshall and Stock got back in the Rover and Rick drove them to a point close to where the line of hills ran along the south side of the road. "Okay, Sierra One," Rick said. "You walk from here."

Marshall and Stock exited the vehicle and walked into the hills, about two miles from the compound. Rick drove back to the intersection and pulled alongside Pierre's Rover.

An hour later, Rick heard his radio erupt. "Papa One, this is Sierra One. Come in," Stock said.

"Sierra One, I read you," Rick replied.

"We're in position south of the compound. We're on top of the hill across the road. Two hostiles directly below us guarding the road. Two more across the road guarding the compound entrance."

"Copy that, Sierra One. What's the status of the front gate?"

"Front gate is open."

"Copy. Do not engage. Hold your position until further notice."

"Roger that, Papa One," Stock said.

# Chapter Fifty-Eight

RICK AND PIERRE stood in front of the Rovers parked side by side. Rick looked at his watch; it was 2:30 a.m. "Both teams are in position, Pierre. Let's block the western approach."

Pierre talked into his radio headset. "Sierra Two, this is Papa Two."

"Go ahead, Papa Two."

"There should be a roadblock west of the compound. Eliminate the personnel and use their vehicle to block the road. Return to position and resume surveillance."

"Roger that, Papa Two."

Wright and Thomas made their way along the crest of the hill to a position about a half-mile west of the compound. "Papa Two, we've got eyes on the roadblock west of the compound. Two hostiles on the roadway."

"Engage, Sierra Two."

"Copy that."

Wright and Thomas crept toward the roadblock stopping behind a line of short trees. Thomas pulled the range finder from his belt and focused on the targets. He adjusted the triangulation until he was satisfied with the range. "We've got 225 to target, bro."

"Copy."

The men guarding the road stood together in the open roadway, their AK-47s slung about their shoulders. The moonlight cast faint shadows onto the road. Standing still in the open, they offered the sniper team clean shots. Their

M24 sniper rifles with suppressors made a muffled crack as the men fired one round each. Both guards dropped immediately onto the roadway. Wright and Thomas ran forward to the scene, checked the bodies and pulled them quickly into the brush. Adam entered the driver's side and put the car in neutral and both pushed the vehicle sideways across the roadway, before putting the car in gear and breaking off the shifter. They lifted the hood and tore the spark plug wires off and threw them into the brush. Adam tossed the keys as far as he could throw them. "Nobody's gonna find those, bro," he said to Carl.

"Papa Two, we've neutralized the threat. Road is blocked," Thomas said into the radio.

"Copy that Sierra Two. Return to your position," Pierre said.

"Roger."

Wright and Thomas walked up the crest of the hill and returned to their previous position overlooking the compound from the north. The maneuver had taken an hour.

"Sierra One, this is Papa One. Come in," Rick said.

Jerry Stock answered. "We read you, Papa One."

"Is there any movement at the compound?"

"Negative Papa One. No movement."

"Papa One out."

Rick looked at Pierre. "So far, so good. Everything's quiet at the compound."

"We caught a break when they didn't hear those rounds at the compound. There's a definite crack from supersonic rounds."

"Those guards aren't trained soldiers," Rick replied. "They're probably asleep at their posts."

"I certainly hope so."

With both sniper teams back in position and Papa One and Two at their designated location, they waited until dawn.

# Chapter Fifty-Nine

SHORTLY BEFORE DAWN, Zulu rolled up to the rendezvous point off the Damascus-Beirut Highway in the white pick-up truck. Laura and Jim Jordan got out and walked up to Rick and Pierre standing in front of the Rovers. Laura was dressed in an expensive, green colored, long sleeved silk dress with a matching Shayla, a one piece veil wrapped around her head that left her face open. The dress and Shayla were attached with Velcro down the front. The dress dragged the ground to hide the sneakers she wore. Underneath the dress, she wore pants, tee shirt, her vest and a holster from which hung two Sig Sauer P226s and extra magazines. She'd wrapped a white, gold trimmed shawl to hide any bulges from the clothing and weapons hidden underneath.

James Jordan was dressed in the uniform of a Libyan Major, complete with insignia, medals and hat. He carried a Baretta M9 pistol in a holster on his belt along with several extra clips. "Good morning, Rick," Jordan said with a smile.

"Morning, Major. Fine day for a battle."

"Definitely."

Rick glanced at Laura. "Damn, Laura," he said, "I haven't seen you wear that much clothing since, well, maybe never." That brought a chauvinistic chuckle to the men.

"Yeah, well, I've got a costume for you, too, big mouth," Laura said, looking at Rick with a smile. She walked to the truck, reached in and brought out a replica of a Libyan enlisted man's uniform. "Try this on. I guessed at the size. Don't forget the red beret."

"What's the present status of Sierra One and Two?" Jordan asked Rick.

"Sierra One has taken out the roadblock between here and the compound," Rick said while changing shirts. "Sierra Two has taken out the roadblock on the west side and blocked the roadway. Both teams are in position watching the compound. So far, there hasn't been any movement inside. The night guard is still on duty and the front gate is open."

"Good," Jordan said.

Rick's uniform was slightly oversized and he managed to pull the clothing over his vest easily. "All suited up and ready to roll, Major," he said.

Jordan and Pierre climbed into the bed of the pick-up and set the M240 machine gun onto its swivel and attached the mount into the housing welded at the base of the pick-up bed. They opened several boxes of ammunition and fed the first box into the gun. Pierre looked down from the truck at Rick. "We're all set here."

Rick climbed into the bed of the truck and tested the swivel. He checked the gun and the ammunition feed, and then counted the extra boxes of ammo. "We're good here."

Jordan looked at Pierre and Rick. "Everyone check their time. I have 6:50 a.m. Tell the teams we're approaching the compound."

Rick and Pierre radioed both teams that Zulu was approaching the compound and to be ready to engage at any time. Both teams acknowledged and prepared for the assault.

# Chapter Sixty

*07:00 Hours, Monday, November 14*

PIERRE, WEARING MILITARY fatigues and a bulletproof vest, stayed behind near the intersection at the highway to scout the road and warn the teams of incoming traffic. Jordan, with Laura in the passenger seat and Rick riding in back, drove toward the compound.

"Let's review the procedure," Jordan suggested. "We get into the compound and persuade the Imam to show us the hostages. If he refuses for some reason, we force our way in."

Laura said nothing. "This was the plan we discussed," Jordan said. "Right?"

"Yep. That was the plan," she said.

"Okay. Just confirming."

Laura gave Jordan the steely eyed look of a killer. "Major, I've learned that plans fall apart early on. Be prepared for anything."

"Roger that, Commander."

After Pierre estimated they'd have crossed into Lebanon, he radioed Sierra One across the road from the compound entrance. "This is Papa Two for Sierra One. You should see Zulu approach within minutes."

"Copy that, Papa Two."

Pierre alerted Sierra Two of the approach. "Sierra Two, this is Papa Two."

"Sierra Two. We read you."

"Zulu is approaching the compound. You should have a visual within minutes."

"Roger that, Papa Two."

After they crossed the border, Rick talked to Jordan in the driver's seat by radio. "Zulu, this is where the roadblock was set early this morning."

Jordan slowed briefly. "No sign of it now. The guys did a good job."

"You should be clear all the way to the compound," Rick said.

"Roger that, Papa One," Jordan replied.

The Sierra One team stayed on top of the hills across the road since they had to eliminate the scouts below them before advancing. Those two would be easy prey. They weren't aware of Sierra One's flanking position behind and above them and for Marshall and Stock, a 150 yard target was a high percentage shot. More difficult would be the guards across the road at the head of the driveway.

"Distance to the targets in the driveway?" Nick asked Stock.

Stock triangulated the distance. "360, Nick."

"Wind?"

"Wind is calm."

"Let's take those two first," Marshall said. "The two below us will likely turn around and look where the shots came from. We'll take them as soon as they stand."

"Got it," Stock said. Both men lined up their shots on the guards in the drive.

"Once the targets are eliminated, we've got to cross the road and move the bodies in the driveway out of sight," Marshall said.

"Roger that, bro."

Sierra Two, behind the compound to the north, made their way down from the hills and took a position right above the treetops. From that vantage point, they had a line of sight to the guards on the backside of the compound, 250 yards away. However, there were more targets in play than the Sierra One position. Wright and Stock counted six guards on the back side of the compound. After dawn, additional guards might come out the back gate to use the latrine, so there could be more outside the fence when the shooting started.

"Let's start with the gate guards and anyone at the latrine. We don't want them running back inside when the firing starts. We'll work our way out and take the targets at the corners of the building last," Wright said.

"Sounds like a plan. I feel lucky this morning."

The two men used their scopes to concentrate on the back gate and latrine.

The truck bounced its way toward the compound and during the approach, Rick covered the M240 and its extra ammunition with a tan tarp. He sat down in the bed and leaned against the cab, keeping his Beretta M9 handy, but out of sight.

Sierra One saw the guards at the foot of the hills stand up and wave to the guards in front of the driveway, signaling that a vehicle was approaching the compound. The truck passed them without incident and turned into the driveway where two guards held their hands up, motioning the truck to stop.

# Chapter Sixty-One

COLONEL SAMIR RAJAVI walked out of the rear of the Iranian Embassy into the parking lot where his car and driver waited. "Good morning, Hamid," Rajavi said.

"Good morning, Colonel. May you receive Allah's blessing this morning."

"May His blessings fall upon you as well. I apologize for the early start this morning, but I'm flying back to Tehran later today and I want to get this hostage business completed early in the day. Run inside and grab two cups of coffee for the trip."

"Yes, Sir," Hamid said, returning a few minutes later with two paper cups full of coffee sealed with plastic lids. The driver opened the back door for the Colonel and handed him a cup. "Are we ready to go, Sir?"

"Let's get underway."

The black Mercedes sedan rolled out of the Embassy gate at the height of the Damascus morning rush hour. Rajavi looked at his watch. "How long before we reach Kassem's compound this morning?"

"It will be slower due to morning rush hour traffic, Sir. We should be arriving at the compound around 9:00."

"Very good."

# Chapter Sixty-Two

*07:30 Hours, Monday, November 14*

ZULU WAITED WHILE one of the guards approached the driver's side of the pick-up truck. The second guard walked around the passenger side and looked at Laura, who kept her head down in a submissive pose. The guard on the driver's side pointed an AK-47 at Jordan and asked, "Who are you? Why are you here?"

Jordan responded in perfect Arabic. "Allah blesses you, brother. My name is Major Omar Shammas from the personal guard of Muammar Gaddafi, Leader of the Libyan People. We've come with a message for the Imam from Chairman Arafat." He handed him Arafat's gold emblem. "This coin comes directly from the Chairman and allows us free passage among his people. The Chairman is pleased with your work and we offer gifts for each of you."

The guard held the gold coin and inspected the likeness of Arafat on its face. "Who is the woman?"

"You are blessed to receive the honored wife of Muammar Gaddafi, the President of Libya. She is the official emissary of Chairman Arafat," he said, gesturing toward Laura.

The guard looked equally impressed and skeptical. "How do I know this is true?" the guard asked.

Laura held out a medium sized emerald in the palm of her hand for the guard to see. It was not nearly as large as the one she gave to Arafat nor was it in a setting.

Nevertheless, it was fairly large and beautifully cut. The sun shining in the window caused the stone to glitter in her hand.

"Who else would carry the great royal stone of Libya?" Jordan asked. "She is the Princess of Libya and cannot be touched."

"What's in the back under the tarp?"

"Her protection." Jordan slid the back glass open and turned to Rick. "Uncover the weapon," he said in Arabic.

Rick uncovered the tarp and revealed the brand new M240 machine gun. Jordan looked at the guard. "The Princess needs powerful weapons to protect her."

The guard walked behind the truck and inspected the weapon. Rick tried to look uninterested. He rubbed the sleep out of his eyes and stretched as though he'd just woken. The guard walked back to the driver's window. "That is an American weapon."

Jordan laughed. "The Chairman steals many weapons from his enemies."

The guard smiled at that. He motioned to his partner and both walked in front of the truck to confer. They looked at the emblem and talked animatedly among themselves. When they'd made their decision, the guard returned to the driver's side window and handed the emblem back to Jordan. "You may enter but show the emblem and the jewel again at the gate."

"One moment, please," Laura said in Arabic. She got out of the vehicle and lifted a basket of fresh bread, cheese and dates from behind the seat. She handed over the basket. "A gift from the Chairman for his freedom fighters," she said, before returning to the truck.

Jordan slowly moved the truck forward and as he passed the guards said, "Allah is great!"

The men smiled and pumped their AKs up and down. "Praise to Allah! Allah is great." Jordan looked in the rear view mirror as they proceeded down the driveway. The guards had shouldered their weapons and had their heads down looking in the basket to discover its contents. "So far, so good," he said to Laura.

"I should have taken them out, Major, right then and there."

"They're Sierra One targets. They'll be dead within minutes."

When the truck pulled up to the gate, Laura counted six guards, two outside the gate, two standing inside and one at each outside corner of the two buildings. The two guards outside the gate walked toward the truck and motioned for it to stop. Jordan kept the engine running and stopped several yards short of the gate. The guards walked forward, one on each side of the vehicle. The guard on the driver's side had his AK-47 slung over his shoulder as he approached. "We do not know you. Why are you here?"

Jim handed the guard the emblem. "We come directly from Chairman Arafat. That's his symbol of free passage among his people's territory. We request a meeting with the Imam."

The guard pointed at Laura. "The Imam does not meet women. If the Imam agrees to a meeting, you'll have to come alone."

"This woman is royalty," Jordan countered. "She is the wife of President Muammar Gaddafi of Libya. Chairman Arafat sent her as an emissary."

The guard hesitated for a moment. "Get out of the vehicle," he said, motioning with his rifle. Laura and Jordan climbed out of the truck, but not before Laura reached into the back for another basket of baked goods and cheese. She ignored the second guard, walked past him and around the front of the truck. The guards, struck by her beauty and authoritative posture, allowed her to do it. She handed the basket to the guard who stood next to Jordan.

"This is a present from Chairman Arafat for his freedom fighters," Jordan said.

The guard accepted the basket and handed it to a guard standing behind him. The guard looked Laura and Jordan up and down, studying every article of clothing. "Anyone can pretend to be royalty," he said. "What proof do you have this woman is Colonel Gaddafi's wife?"

Laura took the jewel from a small pocket hidden in the fold of her dress and showed it to the man. "Colonel Gaddafi is a friend of the Palestinian people," Jordan said. "Only the Colonel's wife is trusted with one of the relics of the great nation of Libya."

"I will take the coin and the jewel to the Imam. He will decide."

"You will not take the stone," Jordan said sharply. "Show the emblem to the Imam."

The guard started to speak, but thought better of it. He stopped, looked again at Laura and then said, "Wait here." He took the emblem and walked inside the gate.

Laura and Jordan waited an uncomfortably long time under the scrutiny of Kassem's men, about ten minutes. The guards stood together and whispered among themselves, occasionally glancing and gesturing toward Laura. They ignored Jordan altogether and the implication seemed to suggest they'd found another potential rape victim.

Finally, the head guard walked through the gate, striding quickly with a determined look about him. He handed the emblem back to Jordan. "The Imam will not see you. Go away."

Laura stepped forward to speak. "I urge the Imam to reconsider. I come directly from Chairman Arafat. He's given me an important message for the Imam."

"Chairman Arafat has no authority here. Leave here immediately or you will be killed."

Laura shrugged. "If that's the Imam's choice, then the rest is in Allah's hands." She ripped off the skirt and quickly drew both her P226 pistols. She shot all four guards right in the forehead with the speed of a gunfighter from the old American West.

# Chapter Sixty-Three

"FUCK!" A SURPRISED Jordan shouted. He ran back and got in the vehicle, shouting, "Rick! Engage! Engage!"

Rick shouted into the radio, "Engage! Every team fire at will!"

Laura walked forward and spread her pistols. She barely looked as she shot the men standing at each corner of the compound before walking in the gate with her pistols held in front of her. Jordan followed her in the truck as Rick stood and prepared the M240 to fire.

The guards at the head of the driveway dropped their basket and looked toward the commotion at the gate, turning their backs on Sierra One. Marshall and Stock downed them with one shot each. The scouts in the rocks below Sierra One stood up and turned around facing Marshall and Stock. They were immediately hit and downed. "Let's go," Nick Marshall said to his partner. Both men began climbing down the rocks to run across the road. Marshall stopped in the middle of the road and yelled at this partner, "In a few minutes, fighters will come streaming down that road." He pointed to the west. "Let's go down the road and set a firing position to prevent being flanked."

Marshall and Stock dragged the bodies off the driveway into the brush, then ran down the road where Sierra Two had earlier used a car to block the road. "There," Nick pointed. "They'll have to get past that disabled vehicle in the road. If we set up here, we can slow their advance."

"I'll let them know what we're doing, Stock said. He spoke into his radio. "Sierra One for anyone listening. We're setting a firing position down the roadway to the west to prevent being flanked."

Pierre answered. "Sierra One, this is Papa Two. I read you. Good idea. Keep me informed."

"Roger that, Papa."

Behind the compound, Sierra Two fired at the gate, downing two guards standing outside the gate. Wright shot a guard waiting at the latrine, while Thomas shot one at the outside right corner of the compound. The man using the latrine stumbled out pulling his pants up and Wright shot him in the back. The man at the left corner of the compound began running toward the latrine and Thomas shot him. Wright looked at his partner, "Let's advance, Captain."

"Roger that."

Both men climbed down the remaining rocks and ran toward the back side of the compound.

Laura walked into the compound and shot two women standing in the middle of the courtyard near the well. Two guards on the rooftops walked to the front edge to look down into the courtyard. Laura shot them, too, as Jordan pulled the truck inside the gate behind her. They fell off the rooftops onto the ground. Rick pushed the safety off the M240, drew the bolt back on the cocking mechanism and checked the feed tray. As soon at the truck cleared the gate, he began looking for targets.

Inside the left building, the Imam had been sitting cross legged on the floor eating his morning meal. Hearing the crack of gunfire, he looked up at his personal aide and guard. "Quickly! Hand me the phone," Kassem said. He pointed to the end table in the corner of the room. The guard stretched the cord and handed an old rotary style phone to Kassem, who made one phone call that started a cascade of further calls by his supporters. One call turned into four others, then eight and so on as the news spread that the Imam's compound was under attack. Within a few minutes, the entire community was notified. People grabbed their weapons and ran outside to either wait for rides or drive their own vehicles to the compound. Imam Kassem was their community leader and they were eager to defend him.

Inside the compound, Laura pointed to her left, giving Jordan a signal that he should concentrate on the left hand side. He left the truck idling and ran to the building on the left. Laura turned and walked toward the building on the right while Rick swiveled the machine gun back and forth in search of targets.

Guards streamed out of the building in front of Jordan and Rick sent a blast of 7.62 ammunition into them. Four fell dead before the others backed into the building. Jordan ran to the front of the building and tossed a flashbang inside the doorway. After the flash, he entered the doorway with a burst from his A4.

He stepped into the foyer and turned right into the kitchen where a woman lunged at him with a kitchen knife. He blunted the thrust with his rifle. She grabbed for the rifle and Jordan kicked her in the groin causing her to release the rifle and fall to the ground. He kicked her again and she dropped the knife. He killed her with a short burst from his semi-automatic rifle.

Jordan turned and put a burst through the doorway from which he'd come and then stepped back through to find the foyer empty. He paused, digging into his belt for another flashbang and he threw it into the room across the hall. After another burst from his weapon, he stepped in and found six guards sprawled on the floor. He raked the floor with a burst from his A4 which killed the fallen guards. After checking to make sure the men were dead, Jordan quickly moved to a back doorway that led into the room at the center of the building. He shot a short burst from his A4, then stepped into the room. He found Imam Kassem sitting calmly cross legged against the wall, his morning meal sitting in front of him on a small carpet. Kassem looked up and stared.

"Don't move," Jordan said, walking toward Kassem. "Put your hands where I can see them."

The Imam stared at Jordan without moving. "I said, put your hands where I can see them," Jordan said, louder this time. "I won't tell you again."

The Imam still didn't move. Jordan crept closer and finally stood above the Imam. Kassem withdrew a pistol from the fold of his robe and tried to shoot Jordan, but was far too slow. Jordan knocked the weapon aside and hit Kassem in the head with his rifle butt. The gun fell out of Kassem's hand and he collapsed against the wall, still conscious, but stunned. Jordan picked up the pistol and tossed it out of reach. "That almost got you killed, asshole."

He grabbed Kassem by his robe and pushed him face down to the floor. Placing his knee on Kassem's back, Jordan pulled his hands behind him and bound them with a plastic cable tie from his belt. He picked the Imam up and threw him into the corner. "Stay there and don't move."

He picked up the pistol lying on the floor and threw it to the other side of the room.

# Chapter Sixty-Four

SIERRA ONE ADVANCED to the back gate. "Papa, this is Sierra One. We're at the back gate."

Rick heard them. "Go ahead and enter, Sierra One. I'm in the courtyard."

When Sierra One entered the yard, they saw the truck parked in the middle of the yard and Rick in the back standing behind the M240. Rick put a blast from the machine gun into the doorway of the shed. "Secure that shed," he shouted, pointing to the small building on their left.

Wright turned and spoke to his partner. "Carl, cover the front gate. I'll take the shed." Thomas ran across the yard and took a position at the front gate. Wright put his back against the wall next to a window. He threw a flashbang in the window and then entered the door firing his A4. Two guards were lying on the floor struggling to regain consciousness. Both were shot immediately. Wright checked the second room and found it empty, the only furniture in the room being a table and two overturned chairs. He ran outside and yelled at Rick. "We're clear."

Laura stood with her back against the wall outside the doorway to the building on the right. Rick shot nearly a full string of ammunition into the doorway and window while she reloaded the mags in both P226s. Immediately after Rick stopped firing, Laura threw a flashbang inside. After the explosion, she entered the doorway to find the guard barracks. As many as ten guards were scattered about the room, some of them bleeding, the rest stunned by the flashbang explosion. She began firing immediately, hitting man after man. She proceeded through the room, kicking weapons away from men who reached for them. She fell forward when hit in the back by a round from an AK shot by a guard who entered from the adjoining room. Due to the metal she'd placed in her vest, the round didn't penetrate it, but the blow knocked her to the ground. She rolled onto her back and shot the man in the doorway and another who followed him. A man lying on the floor next to her grabbed her by the neck and rolled on top of her. She shot him in the stomach, then again in the chest. Blood poured out of his wounds as she pushed him off. She shot him once more, this time in the head. She rose to her knees and found several men weren't dead yet. Two men lunged at her as she fired. One man fell on top of her and she pulled the knife from her belt and plunged it into his neck. Pushing him off, she rose to her feet and reloaded her pistols while looking for additional targets. Finding no threat, she walked around the room, shooting any guard still breathing. Laura replaced the mags in her weapons yet again and checked the bodies lying on the floor. She counted twelve dead men.

Laura's back hurt from the AK round that hammered the metal plate in her vest and she had difficulty breathing. She ignored the pain. She quietly stepped to the doorway and peeked into the adjoining room. On the dirt floor lay three people covered in grime, bound at their hands and feet. Their clothing was torn and covered with dirt. Their faces showed blood stains and their hair had clumped together in a mass of sweat, blood and dirt. They weren't moving and Laura wondered if they were dead. She found a fourth man, as dirty as the others, bound and sitting up against the wall. She smiled when she saw him. "Would you be William Sharp by chance?" she politely asked.

"You bet your sweet ass I am." He smiled broadly.

"You ready to go home?"

"What took you so long?" Sharp asked.

Laura burst out laughing. "Well, I did stop for coffee on the way in this morning."

"You didn't bring a cup for me?"

Laura walked over, slipped the knife from her belt and cut the rope tying his hands and feet. "I didn't know how much cream you wanted," she said, kissing him on the cheek.

"Boy, am I ever glad to see you," a relieved Sharp said.

"Can you walk?"

"No problem." Laura helped Sharp struggle to his feet. He pointed to the others. "This is Nick Buck over here. They've beaten the crap out of him. He's in bad shape. The two over there," he said pointing along another wall, "are a French nurse and doctor. I think they're dying."

Laura walked over and checked the pulse on the doctor. "He's still alive," she said to Sharp. We've got a medic here. I'll send him in."

Laura moved to the nurse and touched her arm. The nurse began screaming, kicking and flailing her arms uncontrollably. Laura held her down and talked to her in French. "Shush. No one's going to hurt you." Laura began stroking her matted hair. "I'm French. I've come to take you home. You're safe now." The woman stopped struggling and opened her eyes. "See, I'm a woman. I'm here to take you away from this place. We're taking you home to your family." The nurse began whimpering. "I've got to step away to tend to the others. Lie still and we'll carry you to the helicopter in a few moments."

Laura turned back to Sharp and handed him one of her P226s. "Can you handle this?" she asked.

Sharp grinned. "You don't know how much I've wanted one of these."

"Follow me." She led Sharp to the doorway, but held him back while she peeked into the guard's quarters. She found one guard on his knees. He lifted his AK, but Laura shot him in the forehead before he could aim. She turned to Sharp. "Make sure all these fuckers are dead," she said, pointing around the room. She handed him an extra mag. "And guard the others until the medic comes in."

Sharp took the weapon and an extra magazine. "You killed all these guys?" he asked, looking around the room in amazement.

"Just lucky, I guess."

"Who are you?"

"They call me Shewolf," she replied.

Sharp's eyes widened. "No shit? I thought Shewolf was some sort of legend."

Laura chuckled. "Let's save the autographs for later. Listen, the medic will be here in a minute. Don't fucking shoot him when he walks in, okay? Everyone here is a friendly now. I've got to go outside and take care of some business." Laura walked back into the yard and yelled at Rick standing behind the M240. "We're clear." She pointed into the doorway. "We got them, Rick. The hostages are in here. We need the medic ASAP."

"I'll call him up here!" Rick yelled at Wright. "Hey, Nick, we need Jerry up here right now. Run down the road and replace him." Rick spoke into his radio. "Sierra One, this is Papa One. We need Stock up here with his med kit. I'm sending Wright down to replace him."

"Roger that," Stock said.

Wright ran out the front gate and headed down the road toward Sierra One's position.

# Chapter Sixty-Five

*08:15 Hours, Monday, November 14*

FOUR F-16 FIGHTER jets from the 109 Valley Squadron at Ramat David Air Force Base in northern Israel took off one after another. They took off heading south, banked a hard 180 degrees and then arranged themselves in a diamond formation. They headed toward Lebanon to provide air cover for the helicopter rescue. As they passed the Lebanese border, they split up, two flying north just inside the Lebanese border and two circling around to the west. They were picked up immediately on Syrian radar scopes at Mezze Air Force Base. The Syrian radar operator contacted his commander.

"Sir, we've got Israeli jets in Lebanon this morning."

"Are they in Syrian air space?"

"No, Sir. They're staying on the Lebanese side of the border."

"Keep me updated on their activity," the commander replied. He hung up the phone and called his MIG fighter jet unit commander. "Commander, be advised we have Israeli aircraft activity over Lebanon this morning. Be ready to scramble the MIGs."

"Yes, Sir."

Two Israeli helicopter crews walked across the tarmac toward a Cobra gunship and a Huey Medevac chopper. They began preparations for take-off.

# Chapter Sixty-Six

JORDAN FOUND A second woman hiding in a pantry off the kitchen. He forced her into the Imam's room and sat her down next to Kassem. He tied her hands together with a cable tie. Laura walked in the front door, peeked in the kitchen, then headed into the room on the other side where she found Jordan. "We secure here?" she asked.

"These two are bound and the building is secure. The guards have been neutralized."

"We found the hostages in the other building," Laura said. "They're in bad shape. Three will have to be carried to the extraction point. Unpack the sat phone, call Ramat David and request the choppers."

"Copy that. I'll leave you with these two. Be quick about it; we've got to get the hell out of here."

Jordan ran out into the yard unpacked the satellite phone from behind the seat, placed it on the hood of the truck and placed a call to the Ramat David Air Force hotline. "Ramat David Hotline," the voice said.

"This is Operation Eagle Rescue reporting. We're ready for extraction."

"Confirm Operation Eagle Rescue is ready for extraction," the voice replied.

"Repeating, Operation Eagle Rescue is ready for extraction."

"Roger. We're on our way to the extraction point."

Laura found herself alone with Kassem and the woman. "Hello John," she said in English. She gave Kassem a hard, cold smile as she walked toward him. Kassem looked startled at hearing his first name. "That's your name, isn't it?" Laura asked.

"Hundreds of my fighters will be here in minutes. You're going to die. All of you."

"Not soon enough for you, John," she said.

Laura addressed the woman sitting next to Kassem. "And who do we have here?" she asked. "Hello, Safa," she said, answering her own question. "Does your father know you're here?" The young woman looked surprised that Laura knew her name. She looked up at Laura, but remained silent. "Yes, I know who you are," Laura continued. "Such a pretty young girl, so full of talent and love. It's a pity this man fooled you," she said, pointing to Kassem. "He's the worst kind of criminal, Safa. He persuades people to do illegal acts in the name of religion. He has no religion, Safa. None."

Laura paused to give Safa an opportunity to speak, but she didn't. Her face betrayed confusion and fear. Laura spoke again. "You betrayed everyone who ever cared for you, Safa, your family, your friends, the Americans at the Embassy who helped you. They'd have done anything for you."

Trying to come to terms with the ethics of the situation, Laura hesitated. "If I gave you to the Syrians, Safa, they'd kill you." Laura's grim expression betrayed her moral dilemma. "I don't have room on the helicopters to take prisoners and if I left you here, you'd continue to engage in acts of terrorism." Laura made a difficult decision. "You've left me no choice, Safa. And I'm sorry for that." Laura shot her in the forehead.

"You'll burn in hell for that," Kassem said.

"I didn't kill her, John. You did. Did you think taking hostages would change the policy of the United States as an honest broker in the region? Did you honestly believe the solution to the plight of the Palestinian people was to take a doctor and nurse hostage? They were trying to heal your people, John. I regret killing the girl. I'll see it in my dreams, but I don't regret this."

Laura turned suddenly and shot Kassem in the knee.

"You fucking bitch," he screamed in agony.

"That's for allowing the nurse to be raped. You're an educated man, John. What the hell is wrong with you?"

Laura shot him in the other knee and Kassem fell over onto his side. "That's for torturing the others," she said.

Kassem looked up at Laura and yelled through his pain with clenched teeth. "You will die a thousand deaths when my men get here."

She leaned in close to Kassem, took the barrel of her pistol and put it underneath Kassem's chin. She lifted his head and forced him to look at her. "Lady Liberty says hello, John." She shot him in the head and John Kassem fell dead.

# Chapter Sixty-Seven

*08:35 Hours, Monday, November 14*

THE BLADES ON the two helicopters gained speed and both aircraft lifted off the ground and turned toward Lebanon to a pre-arranged rendezvous point inside the Lebanese border about seventy-five miles away. The gunship, a Bell Cobra AH-1, manned by a pilot and gunner, contained two 7.62 mm machine guns and several seventy mm rockets, plenty of firepower to protect a medical evacuation. The Medevac chopper, a Bell UH-1 Iroquois, had room for stretchers and troops. It would be a tight fit, but authorities were confident the entire group could be extracted in one trip.

The radar operators at Mezze picked up the helicopters immediately on their screens. Their commander was notified immediately. "Are they headed toward Syrian air space?" he asked again.

"It doesn't look like it, Sir. They're headed straight north on the Lebanese side of the border."

"Thank you." The commander hung up and immediately called his MIG squadron. "It looks like the F-16s are air cover for a helicopter op they're running today. Two choppers took off from Ramat David a few minutes ago. They're headed into southern Lebanon as we speak."

"Do you have additional orders for us?" the Major asked.

"We're not going to take any action at the present time. Keep your pilots and aircraft on full alert in case they move into Syrian airspace."

"Yes, Sir."

# Chapter Sixty-Eight

RICK, STANDING IN the bed of the pick-up truck behind the M240, heard Pierre's voice over the radio. "Papa One, this is Papa Two, over." Rick pulled the headset down over his mouth. "Papa Two, go ahead."

"You've got incoming. A black Mercedes sedan is inbound toward the compound as we speak. It just passed my position. You've got, maybe, twenty minutes before it arrives."

"Roger that, Papa Two. Don't follow the sedan. We'll handle it on our end. I repeat, don't follow the sedan. Get to the extraction point and lay out the LZ on the double."

"Roger, Papa One. Papa Two out."

Pierre pulled his Rover onto the road and followed the Mercedes for a distance, making sure he was well enough behind that he couldn't be seen. Once he had traveled several miles into Lebanon, he pulled off the roadway and cut the corner, heading straight northwest across the desert toward the extraction point some 300 yards north of the compound.

# Chapter Sixty-Nine

LAURA WALKED INTO the yard to find Jordan and Rick carrying hostages on makeshift stretchers. "Are we okay here?" she asked Rick.

"We've loaded the French hostages into the back of the pick-up. Jordan and the medic are bringing out Buck next. Sharp's in pretty good shape. He'll be able to walk to the LZ."

Laura heard the crack of gunfire in the distance. "They must be taking fire down at the roadblock."

"They're going to be overrun soon," Rick said. "As soon as they fall back to the compound, we've got to move. Pierre should be at the LZ right now laying down flares for the choppers." He pointed to Carl Thomas, who was running wire from building to building. "Thomas is setting explosives to blow the buildings."

Rick nodded toward the building where the hostages were kept. "I took a look at your handiwork, Laura. How in the hell did you come out of there alive?"

Laura tapped the metal plate in the front of her vest. "The metal plate in the vest saved me. It was pretty dicey fighting those guys off."

Jordan and Stock carried out Buck on a stretcher they'd made by ripping poles out of the fence and wrapping a bed sheet around them. Sharp followed closely behind. They gently placed Buck in the back of the pick-up as Wright and Marshall sprinted through the front gate. They ran up to Jordan. "Major, they've broken through the roadblock and are coming up the fields on either side of the road," Marshall said. "We've got, maybe, ten minutes before we're overrun."

"Jordan," Laura shouted. "Get someone inside that building and gather what intel we can carry," she said, pointing to the house where Kassem lived.

Jordan looked at Marshall. "You heard the Commander. Be quick. We've got no time." Marshall ran into the house and tore open filing cabinets, sticking paperwork into his pants and shirt. "Wright, guard the front gate. I don't want anyone running up my backside."

"Yes, Sir."

Jordan looked around the compound. Thomas was unspooling wire through the hole in the fence. "You ready, Carl?" he shouted at Thomas.

"Yes, Sir," he yelled.

Jordan looked at Rick and Stock. "Rick, drive the hostages up to the LZ. Sharp," he said turning to Bill, "hop on the truck."

"If it's all the same to you, Major, I'll walk."

Stock handed Sharp an A4 from the bed of the pick-up. "Take this. You're going to need it."

Jordan yelled at Marshall. "Get your ass out here, Nick."

Marshall ran through the doorway and out into the courtyard. "Secured the intel, Major. Let's go."

Rick drove the pick-up while Stock tended to the hostages in the bed of the truck. Rick drove through the back fence and drove straight northeast about 300 yards where Pierre had laid out a landing zone with flares. Jordan surveyed the rest of the group. He pointed to Laura. "Laura, you walk Sharp up to the LZ." He yelled at

Wright. "Once we get up there," he said pointing toward the LZ, "let's spread ourselves out in a line. Make sure we don't get flanked. Let's get moving, people."

Laura and Sharp walked through the hole in the fence and headed toward the LZ. Carl Thomas headed in that direction, unspooling the last of the wire connected to the C4 explosives he'd placed on the buildings. Jordan, Marshall and Wright accompanied Thomas as they made their way slowly toward the LZ. When Thomas reached the end of his spool, he wired the end to the trigger and battery that powered it. Jordan watched the area surrounding the compound through field glasses as the Imam's men began to pour into the compound. "Jesus, they got a lot of guys. You ready, Carl?"

"Yes, Sir," Thomas said. Jordan and Wright took kneeling positions around Thomas in case they were spotted from the compound.

"On my mark," Jordan said. He watched as men continued to pour into the compound. "Wait a second! There's a black luxury sedan rolling up the driveway. Messier told me that's an Iranian interrogator. Let's wait and see if he pulls close enough to the buildings to be caught in the blast." The sedan rolled right up to the gate before it stopped. "Ready? Now!" Jordan yelled.

There was a delay of a few seconds, then one by one, each building blew up, one after another. Jordan watched the buildings crumble, the roofs cave in and after a few seconds, the group was hit with a blast of hot air coming off the explosion. Jordan couldn't see the compound or the black sedan any longer due to the dust cloud above it. The sound of the explosion echoed off the surrounding hills. "Okay, guys, let's get to the LZ."

# Chapter Seventy

*09:00 Hours, Monday, November 14*

JORDAN, WRIGHT AND Thomas sprinted to the LZ where they found that Rick, Pierre and Marshall had laid the hostages on the ground waiting for the helicopters. Pierre had pulled his Rover to the edge of the LZ to defend it against any pursuit. Rick parked the truck next to the Rover to create a barrier of two vehicles parked end to end to block the oncoming pursuit. Laura had taken over the M240 in the truck, while Pierre, Rick and Sharp stood behind the vehicles.

"We've got our guys incoming," Laura said, standing behind the M240. "Let 'em through." Jordan and his men ran past the vehicles and then stretched themselves out in a line on either side of the vehicles to prepare for an attack by the Imam's men. "Rick," Laura shouted. She threw bags of ammunition off the truck toward Rick. "Pass out the spare A4 magazines."

Rick ran up and down the line to pass out the cartridges. When he returned, Jordan had climbed into the truck to instruct Laura on loading the M240. "We're got plenty of ammo here," he said, pointing to boxes lying in the bed of the truck. "We'll try to help you load. There's a spare barrel lying there, too," he said, pointing to a long cylinder. "If that barrel overheats, it screws right off. Make sure you don't burn yourself."

Laura nodded her head. "Got it."

Jordan walked up and down the line. "We're gonna have more targets than ammo, boys and girls. Don't waste any. Laura," he shouted, looking up in the truck, "concentrate your fire in the middle. They'll probably come at us in a group. Let everyone else protect the flanks."

Sharp took a position behind the truck. He looked up at Laura. "We're screwed if the copters don't show."

"They'll show," Laura replied, not knowing how to answer the question. It was a question she'd thought of herself.

# Chapter Seventy-One

AS THE ISRAELI helicopters approached the scene, the gunship pilot saw the cloud of dust created by the explosion and radioed the Medevac. "Rescue One to Rescue Two."

"We read you Rescue One," the pilot of the Medevac responded.

"It looks like we've got fighting at the scene. The landing zone should be just northeast of that dust cloud. Go straight in and land. We'll protect your flank."

"Roger that, Rescue One."

The gunship passed to the west of the destroyed compound and fired its machine guns at the mass of vehicles clogging the road. Several were hit and men jumped out to head toward the fields. They weren't yet organized enough to mount an attack, but when they observed the Medevac hover northeast of the compound, they gained an idea of where they should focus their forces. They began to run around either side of the burning compound and head toward the helicopter landing spot several hundred yards away.

Laura, standing on the bed of the truck, heard the choppers first. She watched the Medevac come straight for the LZ. "We've got incoming copters," she yelled at the group. "I'll stay on the gun," she said to Jordan. "Get your guys ready to carry the injured.

"Rescue Two for Rescue One," the pilot of the Medevac said over the radio. "We've got a clear LZ."

"Roger, Rescue Two. You've got permission to land. We'll keep the hostiles off your back."

The pilot of Rescue Two talked to the two medics on board. "We've got injured down there. Break out the stretchers."

The Medevac hovered above the LZ kicking dust into the air. The group shielded their eyes while the copter slowly descended and finally landed. It kept its rotors slowly moving while the door slid open and two medics jumped out with stretchers. Nick Marshall and Adam Wright ran over and picked up the French doctor lying on the makeshift stretcher and loaded him in the copter. The Israeli medics carried stretchers toward the rest of the injured. Wright, Marshall and Thomas ran to help the Israeli medics.

Laura, Rick and Pierre watched as the first of the Imam's men appeared running toward the LZ. "We've got company," Rick said. "Laura, get off the truck. I'll take the gun."

Laura didn't argue. She climbed down and sought out Sharp. "You got my other pistol?"

"Here," Sharp said, pulling the P226 out of his belt. "I'll use this," he said holding up the A4 that Stock had given him.

"Get ready to fucking use it, Sharp. Here they come," she said pointing toward the first line of men who advanced on the LZ.

# Chapter Seventy-Two

THE GUNSHIP TURNED and made another pass over the line of traffic up the road. Men were streaming from their vehicles and running toward where they saw the Medevac land. They stopped to fire on the attack copter, but it fired two rockets into their midst. Several cars on the roadway exploded in a huge fireball that caught the brush along the roadway on fire. Smoke quickly enveloped the entire battle field and it was difficult for both sides to pick out targets. The attack copter swung wide to make a pass directly over the LZ. It laid down a barrage of machine gun fire across the approaching men that caused the group to momentarily halt their advance.

AK-47 fire from the Imam's men pummeled the rescue group as Laura, Rick, Pierre and Jordan sheltered behind the vehicles, popping up only to return fire into the midst of the enemy.

"Laura, I need these boxes of ammo open," Rick shouted. She hopped into the bed of the truck and pried open the boxes as Rick reloaded the M240. He resumed raking the line of men with bursts from the weapon, swinging it back and forth. Laura looked at Sharp who had appeared seemly out of nowhere. "Get your ass back to the copter, Sharp. You don't want to be taken hostage twice."

"I'm not moving an inch," Sharp shouted back, shooting at the oncoming men from between vehicles. "This is payback."

Pierre and Jordan fired over top the bed of the pick-up with their A4s while Jordan's men and the Israeli medics transferred the injured to stretchers. Laura picked up an A4 that one of Jordan's men left in the back of the truck and started shooting at the men from behind the Rover. The men were widely spaced, but there were plenty of targets to shoot at and their fire was effective.

From the vantage point of the bed of the truck, Rick saw the enemy's maneuver well in advance. He yelled at Laura and Pierre. "They're spreading out to flank us. Jordan and I will hold the middle. Concentrate your fire on the sides." Laura and Pierre turned to each side where they saw men advancing, hoping to surround the group. Rounds of enemy ammunition began to strike the Medevac. The Imam's men would kneel, fire a few rounds from their AKs and then advance a few yards and repeat the process. Rick pounded their center with the machine gun, checking the advance, stopping only to reload.

Four men made a charge on Laura's side. Rick turned the machine gun around to help her, but it was too late. She cut two of them down with her A4, but two others overwhelmed her position and she fought them both hand to hand. She kicked one man in the groin and hit the other with the butt of her rifle. The first man rose and pointed his AK at her. She saw his shoulder stiffen and she dove to her left as he fired. She pulled a pistol from her holster as she dove and shot him while lying on her back. The second man fired from his knees and Laura felt the breeze of the ammo whiz by her head as she shot him in the forehead.

The Imam's men were making a steady advance in spite of taking heavy losses. Laura looked back at the Medevac. Jordan's men were nearly finished loading the injured hostages into the copter. She turned back and began firing again. Pierre threw several A4 magazines to Laura on the left side of their position. "Here," he shouted, throwing a bag half filled with magazines, taking the rest with him over to the right.

The gunship made another pass, this time right over top of them, spraying fire on the center of the advancing line of the Imam's men. Men sought shelter anywhere they could, in gullies, under trees, behind bushes, but many were out in the open and several fell. The copter kept firing as it turned to make another pass. The men on Pierre's side fared worse. The small area between the hills and the landing zone forced the Imam's men closer together and Pierre's fire was effective. When the helicopter made a pass along the right hand side, the gunship stopped their advance. The men took positions behind trees and in gullies. Although their advance on the right had halted, the firing increased as the men on Pierre's side entrenched themselves.

Enemy rounds were hitting the vehicles hard now and Laura, Pierre, Sharp and Jordan only exposed themselves to fire their weapons. They found themselves reloading constantly. The noise from the firing and the helicopter blades made communication difficult. Rick swung the M240 back and forth continuously. The M240 barrel was overheating and Rick feared it would break down soon. He looked back at the helicopter and saw Jordan behind him motioning for the group to retreat. "Let's go," he yelled. "Let's go!"

Rick jumped out of the truck bed and shouted at Pierre and Laura. "The helicopter's loaded. Let's go." The Medevac's machine gun erupted to lay covering fire as

Rick, Pierre, Jordan, Sharp and Laura made a run for the copter.

# Chapter Seventy-Three

THE ATTACK COPTER pilot, seeing their dash from the trucks to the Medevac raked the flanks to give the group time to cover the ground, but it wasn't enough. The Imam's men, emboldened by the lack of fire by the M240 made a charge. Pierre was the first to be hit. He went down halfway to the copter. Rick and Jordan stopped to help him as Laura and Sharp turned and laid down covering fire for them. Pierre hobbled toward the copter. While Laura reloaded her A4, Rick was the second to be hit. When he went down, Bill Sharp ran to help. Together, the group slowly retreated to the Medevac where Jordan's men helped them board. Laura was struck in the back, but the round hit the metal plate in her vest. She fell forward, but managed to climb to her feet and helped push Rick and Pierre up into the copter.

The Imam's men reached the truck and claimed the M240. They turned the gun to fire on the Medevac, but the attack helicopter made another pass and fired a rocket at the vehicles. Both the Rover and the pick-up exploded in flames and smoke. Bodies flew off the truck as men were killed instantly. The men on the flanks charged straight for the Medevac, firing at will.

Jordan's men lashed Pierre and Rick inside the chopper with tethers tied to hooks inside the craft. The Medevac was fully loaded. Laura turned around to fire one last burst with her A4. Only she and Sharp were left on the ground. "Get your ass onboard, Sharp. That's an order."

Sharp hopped on and reached out to Laura. "Give me your hand. I'll hold you as we take off," he shouted. "You can ride the landing gear."

Laura pointed to the attack copter turning to make another pass. "The gunship will pick me up. Go! Go! Go!"

Sharp was still reaching out to grab Laura as the helicopter rose into the air. Laura turned away and ran back to retrieve the A4s Rick and Pierre had dropped. She dove to the ground and covered her face as the Medevac lifted off churning dust and sand into the air.

The Medevac pilot radioed the gunship. "Rescue One, we've got a full load. We've left one for you to pick up."

"Roger that. Get the hell out of there, Rescue Two. We'll get the other one."

The helicopter rose and banked hard to the north to avoid passing over the Imam's men.

# Chapter Seventy-Four

THE HELICOPTER BLADES put a cloud of sand and dust into the air completely covering Laura, penetrating her eyes and mouth. When she wiped her eyes, it only increased her discomfort. Her hands and arms were covered with fine dust; it covered her clothing and clung to her skin. Her lungs burned from inhaling the dust; she felt thirsty and remembered they'd neglected to bring water, thinking the mission would be short enough that it wouldn't be needed.

The dust cloud had one advantage. It served to hide her movements. She pushed a few cartridges into her pants, picked up two A4s and ran to her left, hoping to approach the enemy flank from the side. Laura watched the Imam's men stand and fire into the air at the fleeing Medevac, unaware that Laura had been left on the ground. She used Pierre's A4 and cut them down in one burst. When that magazine emptied, she threw the weapon down and used Rick's.

I'm not being taken alive, she thought. Not now, not ever. And that's when she decided to charge straight at them from their right flank. The attack copter saw the charge and made a pass directly over her head and hit the exposed enemy position in front of her, raking her opponents with machine gun fire and forcing them to the ground. Laura plunged into their midst, fighting like a demon, totally without fear. When the A4 ran out of ammunition, she threw it at a man and used her pistol to shoot him in the chest. With a pistol in one hand and her knife in the other, she tore into a second line of men who began to shrink from her as she passed through their line. One man grabbed her from behind and she fired at him underneath her armpit, striking him the chest. When he fell, she saw a man charge at her right and she used a flying side kick to hit him in the chin, firing at two men in front of her simultaneously.

Another man grabbed onto her hair and she slashed his wrist with her knife. He released his grip and she quickly reloaded her P226 before shooting him in the chest. Another man thrust a bayonet into her chest and it bounced off the metal plate in her vest. She stabbed him in the face and he fell away holding his face in his hands. Twice, men fired at her and missed, striking their own men in crossfire. Each time it looked as though she'd be surrounded, the gunship would rake the flanks and men would fall.

The men at the rear of the action began to shoot at the attack copter, but their fire wasn't effective. The armor on the gunship deflected the ammunition and they were unable to hit the blades or the fuel tank. When the helicopter finally hovered right above Laura's head, it returned fire in lethal amounts. Faced with a superior combatant on the ground and a helicopter gunship overhead, the horde of men began to retreat.

When the attack copter fired two rockets into the retreating men, Laura watched their lines break. The Imam's men fled the field to find shelter among the burning buildings in the compound. The helicopter followed the men, its machine gun fire cutting many of them down as they sprinted toward the burning compound. And then, the gunfire stopped and Laura stood among the corpses, more men than she cared to count. She walked among the bodies to make sure none were left alive. The helicopter pilot swung around and set the craft down fifty yards behind Laura, motor idling and blades slowly rotating, waiting for her to board.

Laura began to retreat toward the copter, wary that a wounded man might fire a round at her, but none did. There was no one left alive. Except for one man. She spotted him standing alone at the enemy's rear. She watched as he calmly began to walk toward her, slowly and deliberately. Walking around the still smoldering vehicles, he carried a white handkerchief in one hand, waving it above his head every few strides. The man looked strangely detached from the carnage and unconcerned the attack helicopter might fire on him. He wants to talk, she thought.

As she waited for the man to approach, Laura began to see the man's features. He had the purposeful walk of a military man accustomed to conflict, someone familiar with command. He wasn't Middle Eastern. As he drew closer, she recognized the uniform of a Russian soldier. She couldn't see the insignia on his sleeve, but guessed he was from one of their special ops detachments. Tall, with broad shoulders and blond hair, he looked out of place compared to the Imam's men. Looking to be in his thirties, the man wore only a sidearm which he'd holstered to his belt. Like everyone else on the field, he was covered in dust.

The field became nearly silent, except for the idling helicopter behind Laura, its blades slowly rotating. She watched the man's head move from side to side as he walked, looking at the dead bodies scattered about the field. She figured he must have been watching from the rear. He didn't seem to possess an aggressive posture so Laura did not draw a weapon. She had her P226s holstered in her shoulder harness. She'd be quick enough to shoot if he moved his hand toward his sidearm. But, he didn't. He stopped a few feet away and stood still, watching her. The flap on his holster was snapped shut so Laura felt no threat. They stared at each other.

"Congratulations, Shewolf," he finally said in English.

Laura hesitated before she spoke. "How do you know my name?"

The man smiled. "A woman who fights that well? I figured it could only be you. You've done a fine job today."

"I didn't see you," she responded.

He nodded back toward the compound. "We slipped out the back gate when we saw you enter and managed to avoid your snipers in the rocks."

"We?"

"I escorted a KGB officer."

Laura looked around and saw no one. "Where's he?" she asked.

The man turned his shoulders and pointed behind him with his left hand. "Lying back there a hundred meters or so, killed by machine gun fire from the copter," he said, glancing over her shoulder at the helicopter.

"You were there to interrogate the hostages?" Laura asked.

"Precisely," the man said, slightly nodding his head in the affirmative.

"Bad timing?" Laura asked.

"So it appears." The man looked disgusted. "Kassem was such a fool. We should have known he'd be careless."

He looked around the field. "Look at all these lives wasted. Kassem killed them with his stupidity." He eyes settled on Laura again. "Tell me. How many men did you have?"

"There were eight of us."

"Eight against a hundred and fifty armed men," he said with a chuckle.

"Armed with AKs."

The man nodded at her rifle lying in the dirt. "Yes, the AK is a superior weapon to your A4. I thought at first you'd be overrun, but the Cobra saved you."

Laura expressed her agreement. "Yes, it was fortunate timing. The extraction was slow due to the condition of the hostages. Just so you know, I regret your partner was killed," Laura said, her eyes scanning the field behind the man.

"It happens." The man shrugged and laid his hand on the flap of his weapon. Laura immediately made a move toward her holster. He saw her movement. "I'm not here to fight."

"I didn't think you were. Who are you?"

"Captain Antoly Popov, Russian Special Forces," he answered.

"We didn't know you'd be here."

"I realize that. I take no offense at your actions."

"I'm glad to hear that. I'm not sure I could kill you," she said in a moment of candor.

The Russian Captain laughed at that. "I was thinking the same thing watching you fight."

"Can you find your way back to Damascus?"

"I'm sure I'll find a car back there somewhere," he said, cocking his head over his shoulder for a moment. "Just so you know, I'll have to include you in my report. Petrovksy won't be pleased his KGB officer was killed." Petrovsky was the Chairman of the KGB. "He may want to retaliate. I'd watch for it if I were you."

"Thank you. I will."

The two of them hesitated for a moment, two enemies judging each other. "Good luck, Shewolf," he said.

"I wish you the same."

The Captain turned and walked away. Laura watched him before turning toward the copter in case he played a trick and turned to shoot. He kept walking, careful to avoid any quick movements and Laura backed away toward the copter with one hand on her weapon until she was sure of his intent. When she finally turned toward the helicopter, she ran.

# Chapter Seventy-Five

LAURA SQUEEZED ONTO the lap of the gunner in the copter, a tight fit since the Cobra was only a two man machine, but the flight was short and they landed a short distance away from the Medevac at Ramat David. She thanked the flight crew for the wonderful job of protecting the group during the extraction. Hurrying across the tarmac, Laura could see two ambulances leaving for the hospital. She ran to a third and found Rick and Pierre being attended by medical personnel. She was prevented from climbing inside to talk with her colleagues.

"I'm sorry, Ma'am. We're ready to leave for the hospital," the attendant said.

Rick lifted his head and pulled off his oxygen mask. "Come on up, Laura," he said, oblivious to the nurse's order. Laura climbed in and the nurse put his hand on her chest.

"Get off the vehicle or I'll have you arrested."

She ignored him and pushed her way through. Pierre was unconscious, but Rick was awake and responsive. "Are you in pain," she asked.

"Fuck, yes," Rick said with a smile. He nodded toward one of the IV bags hanging on a hook. "The pain reliever hasn't kicked in yet. How are you?"

"I'm fine, Rick. Don't worry about me. What are they telling you?"

"I'll be fine, Laura. I lost a lot of blood, but I'll be fine."

She glanced at Pierre and back to Rick. "What about Pierre?"

Rick smiled. "He'll be fine, too. You know Pierre; he's one tough hombre. The pain reliever probably put him to sleep."

"Where are they taking you?"

"They're going to stabilize us here, then airlift us to Ramstein with the hostages."

"I want to ride with you."

Two MPs appeared at the back of the ambulance. "Get off the ambulance. Now!"

She looked at Rick. "I guess I'll catch up with you later."

"Go. We'll be fine," Rick said.

Laura leaned over and kissed Rick on the cheek. "I can't lose you, Rick."

"You won't. Leave before they throw you in jail."

Laura got out of the ambulance and the MPs took her by the arm. She responded immediately. "Take your hands off me or I'll pull your arms out of your sockets!"

"You want to be arrested?" the MP on her left said as he tightened his grip.

"A whole fucking company of you clowns couldn't arrest me. You've got one second to take your hands off me."

Jordan and his men appeared out of nowhere. They surrounded the MPs. "You heard the lady. Take your hands off!" Jordan bumped the MP who was doing the talking. Both MPs looked around at Jordan's battle hardened men, dusty, sweaty men straight off the battlefield. They released her. "Go back to guarding the cafeteria and leave the war fighters alone," Jordan said sarcastically. "Come on, Laura" he said, motioning with his head toward the hanger nearby.

Jordan and his team walked her to the hanger. "You've had enough fun for one day," Jordan said with a smile.

"I was about to put those guys in traction," she said looking at the MPs walking away. "Rick told me they're being flown to Ramstein."

"Yeah. The medical evac plane is sitting right over there," he said, pointing across the tarmac." He looked at his watch. "The whole bunch of them will convalesce in Germany."

"How'd they find out so quickly?" Laura asked.

"Good news travels fast," Jordan answered. "This is a big deal politically. I heard the Secretary of State is leaving to travel to Ramstein. I think the news has already hit the wire services."

"Were any of you guys hurt?"

"Not a scratch."

"What happens now?"

"They've got rooms for us here at the base. You, too. The Embassy in Damascus is flying in the rest of our gear. It should be here later this afternoon. We're going to clean up, rest for a bit and then have dinner in the Officer's Club. Would you join us?"

"I'd be honored. My people should be flying in from Paris today. I'll probably fly back tonight, but I should have time for dinner."

"Good. An aide's going to show us to our rooms in a couple of minutes. A good shower will do us all some good."

"You're right," Laura answered. "I can't show up for dinner looking like this."

# Chapter Seventy-Six

THE GROUP WAS taken to a small medical facility where they received a medical check-up before being taken to rooms at the base. They found their gear waiting for them when they arrived, fresh clothes, toiletries and personal items. When Laura appeared later in the lobby for dinner, she was surprised to find all five men dressed in Class B uniforms. They looked as though nothing had happened. She was astonished the men seemed completely normal at dinner. Laura was still in a state of shock from the day's activities. However, the Delta team's banter and good-natured ribbing at dinner helped put her at ease. It was as though their mission never happened.

After dinner, they walked back to their barracks where they parted company for the last time in the lobby. "They're flying us out tonight, Laura, so we'll say our goodbyes now," Jordan said with a smile.

"Aren't they at least going to let you rest here overnight?" she asked.

"We're invisible, Laura. No one can know we were here. They're getting us out before anyone realizes who we are. When's your ride going to show up?"

"It should be here already. I wish you guys could fly back with me. My plane's a heck of a lot more comfortable than what you'll ride in," she said.

"You got that right. Those military transports aren't made for luxury. We're used to it, though. We'll sleep on the flight and be back at Bragg in the morning."

"So I guess this is goodbye then?"

"For now," Jordan said. "Before we leave, I want to tell you something. When I first met you at the White House, I'd heard of your reputation, of course, but I really didn't know how this would work out. Now that I've seen your work, I can say that you're as good as anyone we've got in Delta Force. It was a pleasure working with you. Anytime you need us, you let me know." Jordan looked at his men. "The five of us have your back, always and forever."

Tears welled up in Laura's eyes. "That means a lot to me, Jim. You guys were incredible. I've never worked with better people. It's been my pleasure to watch and learn from the best. Thank you so much for your help." Laura moved forward and hugged each man. "I hope this is allowed in the military," she said as she kissed Jordan.

"The Army's been kissing beautiful women for 200 years, Laura. Some things never change."

Laura watched Jordan, Wright, Marshall, Thomas and Stock walk down the hallway toward their rooms, talking and laughing with each other. What a great group of men, she thought.

Laura turned toward a television in the lobby. She walked over and watched tape of the President of the United States giving a statement on the hostage rescue. He thanked Yasser Arafat and the Palestine Liberation Organization for arranging the release and the State of Israel for the transfer of custody. Not one word was said about Laura, the Delta Force team or the battle they fought that morning.

# Chapter Seventy-Seven

DMITRI AND SVETLANA had kept the plane in Paris and picked her up late Monday evening flying her back to Paris where she spent the night. The following morning, she gave a full account of the rescue to Jacques Martin at DST headquarters and used the rest of the day to decompress from the mission. She took a taxi to her old neighborhood in the 7th Arrondissement where she drove by her old apartment, stopped for a cup of coffee at the shop down the street and met several of her neighbors who still lived in the neighborhood. It served to relax her and help divert the images that haunted her every night.

Laura flew on to Washington the next morning, stopping late in the day to give reports to Steve Tilton and Dan Jenkins. She provided Dan with the intel taken from Kassem's compound, including account information about his secret Grand Cayman account. Late that evening, she arrived at the airstrip across the road from her Bahamas compound. Jean and Jack Mason met her at the plane.

"It's great to see you in one piece, Laura," Jean said as they stood at the bottom of the aircraft stairs.

"It's been all over the news," Jack said. "The Secretary of State met Arafat in Brussels for a photo op."

"Nothing about us was mentioned, I hope," Laura said.

Jack laughed. "Not a word."

"Come on, let's get your things in the car and get you back to the house."

"Thanks, I'm exhausted," she said.

There wasn't any conversation on the short drive back to the main house; none was needed. Jean and Jack knew to avoid questions. She'd talk about the mission when she was ready. Once at the compound, they carried her personal items into her room and Laura fell on the bed and slept. She only appeared a few times in the ensuing days, to prepare herself a meal or walk on the beach. She rarely spoke and avoided the newspapers and the television. Life became slow again, the rhythms of life in the Caribbean returned and Laura slowly returned to normal. Jean and Jack were careful to allow her the space she needed to recover and, eventually, she did.

Rick and Pierre returned to the island two weeks later, limping and bandaged, but otherwise in good spirits. They had a recovery to make as well. Laura spent time talking with each of them, but as time passed, the memory of their time in Lebanon receded.

Only two items in the next few weeks reminded her of the episode. The first was a check from the United States Treasury in the amount of two and a half million dollars, the rest of the payment for the mission. It was money that was needed, for the group had spent heavily to fund their part of the mission. Jean handled the finances of the business and although he showed her the check, she ignored it. The second item was of interest to her, however. She received a visitor.

A stranger showed up at the front gate a few weeks later in a taxi. He provided his identification to the guards and asked to see Laura. The guards asked him to get out of the taxi; they searched him and told him to wait while they took his identification into the guard shack. The main house was called where Jean answered. "Someone at the gate, David?" he asked.

"Yes, Sir. A visitor who says he'd like to see Ms. Messier."

"What's the name?"

"William Sharp."

"Wait a moment. I'll walk down the path and find her," Jean said.

Jean laid the phone aside and walked out the back and down the path to Laura's hut. Vixen, her constant companion, lay on the floor beside her while she read one of her many volumes on history. Vixen lifted her head well in advance of Jean's approach.

"Hear something, girl?" Laura asked.

Vixen rose and pushed her nose through the screen door as Jean appeared in the doorway. He patted her on the head. "Is she there, Vixen?" he asked. Vixen wagged her tail. "Mind if I interrupt her?"

Jean spoke through the screen door. "Laura, sorry for the interruption."

Laura rose and opened the door. "You have a visitor at the gate," Jean said.

"Can you take care of it?" she asked.

"He asked for you personally. I think, perhaps, you should see him."

"His name?"

"William Sharp."

Laura didn't respond, but Jean could see the smile that came inadvertently to her face. "I take that as a yes?"

Laura nodded.

"You want me to send him down here?"

Laura walked out of the hut and headed toward the beach. "Send him down to the beach."

A few minutes later, Jean walked Sharp down the path where they found Laura sitting on the stump of a felled tree right off the beach. "There she is," Jean said, pointing down the beach a few yards. "I'll leave the two of you alone."

Sharp approached her slowly and she looked up at him when he stood before her. "You came," she said gently.

Sharp helped her to her feet and kissed her passionately on the mouth. And she let him do it. "Of course I came. I never got the chance to say thank you."

Laura took him by the hand and led him down the beach. "Walk with me for a while."

# Epilogue

IT WAS EIGHT weeks after the hostage rescue when Laura found herself sitting alone at the Eastern end of her property near the marshes.  It was a quiet, clear night, the sea was calm and a gentle breeze came off the water to cool the thick, humid air.  The gibbous moon, past full and not yet three-quarters, reflected a ribbon of light across the ocean.  Her eyes could see the faint shadows of trees that hung over the beach, of seaweed and debris that washed upon the beach.  She heard a bird pierce the quiet with a shrill cry; she turned her head and saw nothing.  The thrashing of an animal through the weeds turned her head again.  She'd become accustomed to the noises of the night; they no longer bothered her.

Sitting on a piece of driftwood, she'd begun to feel a sense of peace; the repetition of trouble free days set her mind at ease.  It was a peace suddenly broken by a distant sound that emanated not from nature, but from man.  It sounded like an outboard motor on a small craft as it came closer.  Then, it stopped.  She stood and walked to the water's edge, wondering who'd take a boat out in the dead of night.  Laura looked out over the ocean and saw nothing, so she began to walk back toward the path when she saw shapes coming out of the water onto the beach, human shapes.

Four men pulled a rubber raft out of the sea onto the beach.  She quickly moved into the foliage where she watched as the men peeled off wet suits and unloaded equipment from the raft. She silently drew the weapon from her shoulder holster and crept through the line of trees at the top of the beach until she was close enough to see their faces in the moonlight. Soldiers, she thought, watching them unload weapons.

Soldiers don't land in the dead of night with an intent to talk. Aim slow, shoot slow, she told herself. Fire before they put on vests. Fire before I know their identity. Fire before any of us is killed. Fire. She didn't have her noise suppressor so she knew her shots would wake the compound and help would come immediately.

Yet, she hesitated. Are they fishermen in trouble? One of the men turned back toward the raft and that's when Laura caught a glimpse of the bright red and gold chevron on his sleeve.

She moved forward onto the open beach, firing as she walked. The sound of her shots echoed across the water and up the beach. The men were caught by surprise. The first man was hit in the back. He fell writhing in the sand. The second man looked up at her and was shot in the face. He tried to walk a few steps, then fell into the water that washed onto the shore. The third man moved quickly toward a weapon leaning against their equipment and she wounded him in the shoulder. He grabbed the weapon and lifted it to aim. She fired twice more and he fell just outside the raft. She swung her weapon back to the first man who still moved. She followed with a second shot, this one to his head, then a third. She was just a few feet away now.

The fourth man stood motionless without a weapon, waiting to be killed. He made no aggressive move either toward a weapon or to protect himself. He just stood there silently. Laura approached him cautiously with her weapon trained on his chest. "Three left in the mag," she said in Russian.

"Yes, I know," the man replied in Russian. "I counted."

She recognized the voice. "Popov?"

"Yes, Shewolf," he said in English.

Laura motioned with her gun. "No sudden movements, Captain," she said, continuing in Russian. "Move slowly away from your weapons. Keep your hands in clear sight. If you do anything else, I'll kill you." Popov slowly stepped away from the pile of equipment, keeping his hands spread apart.

"You're a long way from home, Captain."

Laura saw a brief smile. "I'm just a tour guide this evening."

"They sent you because you know my face?" she asked.

"Yes."

"Why?"

She kept speaking in Russian while Popov spoke in English. "I do not know why, Shewolf."

"It was a mistake. We're well defended here."

Popov smiled. "I can see that."

By now, the entire compound was awake and three of Laura's guards came running down the path onto the beach with guns drawn. Three of her dogs came charging out of the undergrowth, snarling, stalking, with their teeth bared. "Stop," Laura shouted, raising her hand to command the dogs. "Stop Dasher," she shouted. "Stop Prancer; stop Dancer," she said sternly. The dogs pulled up just feet from Popov, their muscles quivering, saliva dripping from their mouths, ready to tear him apart. The guards had taught the three to be attack dogs. Vixen, however, was different. She was protective of only Laura. She came out of the brush behind her, panting heavily and sensing her owner was not in danger, walked up to Laura and sat on her haunches. Laura reached down and patted her head. "Good girl, Vixen."

The guards trained their weapons at Popov. She spoke in French to her guards. "Leon, do you have flashlights with you?"

"Yes, Mademoiselle."

"Turn them on this man, will you?"

Leon was captain of the guard for the evening and motioned toward the other two, who pulled flashlights from their belts and centered their light onto Popov. "Gentlemen, this is Captain Antoly Popov, Russian Special Forces, come to visit us." She spoke Russian again to Popov. "Captain, I'm going to ask you to slowly get on your knees and put your hands behind your head. Do it slowly if you want to live through this night." Popov dropped one knee to the ground, then the other. He clasped his hands behind his head. "Lock him up." Leon walked behind Popov, twisted his arms downward, tied Popov's hands with cable ties and shoved him hard into the sand.

Laura addressed her other guards. "Check to see that the others are dead. If not, kill them. Drag the bodies up on the beach. And inspect the equipment they've brought." She walked over and stood above Popov. She put one foot on his neck. "Don't get any ideas, Captain. You've come to my home and I intend to protect it."

"I throw myself on your mercies, Shewolf," Popov said, spitting sand from his mouth as he spoke.

"There are no mercies to be given to foreign soldiers who invade my land with intent to kill," Laura said in a vengeful tone of voice her guards rarely heard from her.

"I have a family, Shewolf."

"Says the man who would kill me in my sleep."

Laura reached down and pulled his sidearm out of his holster and cast it aside. She turned to Leon. "Search them all, including this one," she said pointing at Popov. "Leave them nothing except their clothing and shoes."

Rick limped down the path, arriving late. "What's this?" he asked, stepping up to Laura.

"This is Captain Antoly Popov, Rick. Soviet Special Forces," she said gesturing with her gun toward Popov. She ground her heel hard into his neck. "He's come to kill us."

Rick leaned down close to Popov's face. "How's that working out for you so far, Captain?" Popov said nothing. Rick looked up at Laura. "Let me kill him for you."

Laura thought for a moment. "Sit him up." Leon and his guards lifted Popov to his knees. "I've got one question for you, Captain. Would you have killed me in my sleep?"

Popov looked up at her, not quite knowing what to say. He finally said, "Yes."

It was the answer Laura expected. She smiled. "As you can see, I never sleep."

Leon walked up to Laura. "We've finished searching the others. We need to search this one," he said nodding at Popov.

Laura backed away. "Go ahead."

After the guards had searched him, Laura asked them to help Popov to his feet. "Loosen his hands." Leon pulled a knife from his belt and sliced through the tie. Popov rubbed his wrists; they'd been fastened as tightly as possible. "Leon, load Captain Popov's men into the raft."

Leon and his guards dragged the men back to the craft, lifted them over the side and threw them into the bottom of the raft. "Do they have a radio in that pile of equipment?" she asked Leon.

He searched among the equipment until he found it. "Yes, Mademoiselle."

"Bring it over here."

Leon carried a box with a microphone clipped to the side and threw it at Popov's feet. Laura motioned toward the radio with her weapon. "Call your boat. Tell them you've completed your assignment and you wish to be picked up."

Popov leaned down, turned on the radio and spoke into the microphone. No one present could understand him, except Laura. When he'd finished, he turned the radio off and stood to face Laura. "They'll meet me a half mile off your coast."

"Then you should be on your way. It'll take some time to get there. The tide's coming in."

"Thank you, Shewolf."

Laura had come to like Popov. She liked his bravery, his courtesy and his demeanor. She looked him in the eyes as she spoke. "There's such a thing as professional courtesy on the battlefield, Captain. We met each other with respect a few weeks ago in Lebanon. But there's no courtesy given at one's home. I'm allowing you to walk away on one condition. Give Petrovsky a message. Tell him it's time I dealt directly with the man who's been sending people to kill me." Popov looked at her, but didn't say a word. Laura motioned toward his raft. "Now, be gone from here."

Popov turned and walked toward his raft. He strode purposefully with pride, as though he'd walked away victorious. He pulled the raft into the water, climbed in and pulled the crank to start the engine. Once the engine started, he looked up at Laura and nodded before he turned the engine up to full throttle. She thought she saw a slight smile come to his face. And then, he gunned the engine and disappeared into the night.

### 

Thank you for reading my book. If you enjoyed it, won't you please take a moment to leave me a review at your favorite retailer?

Thanks!

Lawrence Scofield

**Follow me on Twitter:**
  http://twitter.com/LScofieldAuthor
**Friend me on Facebook:**
  https://facebook.com/LawrenceScofieldAuthor
**Favorite me at Smashwords:**
  https://www.smashwords.com/profile/view/LawrenceE Scofield

# Author's Notes

To understand the origins of violence in Lebanon, a convenient place to begin would be the Palestinian militia retreat from the West Bank into Jordan in 1967. The Palestine Liberation Organization reorganized and by 1970, campaigned for an overthrow of the Jordanian monarchy. Jordan's King Hussein resisted and the battle that ensued, called Black September, resulted in a defeated PLO retreating through Syria into Lebanon.

Once in Lebanon, the PLO resumed its violent activities against Israel and by 1982, the Israelis were forced to invade Lebanon to push the PLO northward, away from the border. A Multi-National Force (MLF) was created at the request of the Lebanese government to evacuate the PLO leadership which had been trapped in Beirut by the Israelis, this time across the Mediterranean Sea to Tunis, Tunisia. The MLF, consisting mainly of American, French and Italian troops, stayed in Lebanon after the evacuation to train Lebanese government military units. Over time, however, the MLF began to be viewed as a hostile force by various factions that opposed the weak Lebanese government.

In April, 1983, the United States Embassy in Beirut was bombed resulting in the deaths of 63 people, including 17 Americans. Islamic Jihad, an Iranian backed group, claimed responsibility. In response, the MLF was doubled in size and the American contingent increased to 1,200 Marines. Another attack followed on October 23, 1983, when two barracks housing American and French forces were bombed, resulting in the deaths of 242 American and 58 French peacekeepers. Again, Islamic Jihad claimed responsibility. The French response included bombing Iranian elements in the Beqaa Valley while the Americans added more troops in Beirut.

The Syrian military had been present in Lebanon since the late seventies and by the 1980s, their numbers had grown to over 20,000 troops. After American forces began a more active role following the barracks bombing, they came into direct conflict with Syrian troops and several skirmishes occurred. The U.S. Congress pressured the Reagan administration to withdraw American forces from Lebanon. By early 1984, American and French forces had left the country.

Attacks continued against the United States in spite of that withdrawal. On March 16, 1984, William Francis Buckley, the CIA Station Chief at the American Embassy in Beirut, was kidnapped by the Iranian backed group, Hezbollah. A video of Buckley appeared months later showing him to be severely tortured. Before his death at the hands of Hezbollah, many CIA agents in the region disappeared, presumably the result of Buckley's interrogations. Meanwhile, the U.S. Embassy, having been moved to a more secure location, was attacked again on September 20, 1984, killing 24 people, including two Americans. Most of the casualties were Lebanese. The Islamic Jihad, backed by Iran, once again claimed responsibility.

Finally, Colonel William R. Higgins, USMC, was kidnapped on February 17, 1988, while serving as Chief of the United Nations Military Observer Group in Lebanon. It may have been a mistake to assign Higgins to the position. Higgins had previously worked at the Pentagon on the staff of Secretary of Defense Caspar Weinberger and was a publicly known figure. Higgins had knowledge of a wide range of American military issues and, surely, militants recognized his potential value as a hostage. Months later, a gruesome video of Higgin's tortured body was released that showed him hanged by the neck. Higgins' body was discovered in 1991 on the outskirts of Beirut. Higgins's wife, Lieutenant Colonel Robin Higgins, later wrote an excellent volume, *Patriot Dreams: The Murder of Colonel Rich Higgins*, about the kidnapping. I recommend that book to anyone wishing to know more about the aftermath of Higgins' capture.

Against this backdrop of history, I chose to write a novel about a successful hostage rescue of American hostages using the Buckley and Higgins kidnappings as a reference. However, I moved the location of the kidnapping to Syria to completely separate the plot from the Buckley and Higgins incidents. I also used a fictional militia group as the hostage takers. The CIA's presumption in the novel that Shia elements were responsible for the kidnapping was taken from history.

Without stating a specific reason for the meeting that put fictional character Nicholas Buck in harm's way, the subject would have been the presence of Syrian troops in Lebanon, something that, in reality, was of world-wide concern. The description of Lebanon that the fictional character, Pierre Thibault, relates also has a basis in reality: the French bombing of the Beqaa Valley following the 1983 barracks incident.

One Day in Lebanon

The fruitless CIA search for Buck and another fictional character, William Sharp, in the novel parallels the inability of the Americans to find Buckley and Higgins. Combining American special operations troops with the protagonist Laura Messier gives the novel a bit of realism as any real life rescue of Buckley and Higgins would have probably used American special operations troops. The fictional mastermind behind the novel's kidnapping, John Kassem, parallels many real life Middle Eastern figures who were educated in the United States.

The novel portrays the historical figure, Yasser Arafat, as a peacemaker, which was accurate by 1988, the time of the fictional kidnapping. Arafat's recognition of the right of Israel to exist was a great act of political courage. However, Arafat's later actions as a purveyor of peace contrasts with his early history of violence, first as the leader of the Fatah organization and later, as Chairman of the PLO.

The actions taken by the Israeli Defense Forces and Mossad, the intelligence agency within the Israeli government, has a historical context as well. Beyond the Israelis' military activity in Lebanon during this time period, Mossad was responsible for many clandestine operations in the region, some of them quite violent. The fictional cooperation between the Israelis and the novel's protagonist was a logical solution to the problem of extracting the hostages.

The novel opens with the fictional character William Sharp's concern for diplomatic security. History shows there was ample reason for that concern. Attacks on United States diplomatic installations abroad increased dramatically in the early 1980s causing the Reagan administration to propose a new security agency to protect embassies around the world. In 1985, the U.S. Bureau of Diplomatic Security was created and the following year, President Reagan signed H.R. 4151, the Omnibus Diplomatic Security and Antiterrorism Act which followed the recommendations of a study by the Department of State on how to improve security for diplomats and installations. Funding for diplomatic security has waxed and waned since then with a marked increase approved by Congress following the Benghazi attack of 2012. The Congressional Research Office produced a report titled, *Diplomatic Security Funding Before and After the Benghazi Attacks* published September 10, 2014. That report can be found here: https://fas.org/sgp/crs/row/R43721.pdf for those interested in learning more.

The novel's successful rescue of the fictional characters Buck and Sharp contrasts with the outcome of the kidnapping of Buckley and Higgins. No offense is intended toward the memories of those patriots. My hope is that *One Day in Lebanon, A Hostage Rescue* will, in some small way, further the discussion of how to best protect American diplomats around the world.

Best wishes,
Lawrence Scofield
October 17, 2017

## About the Author

Lawrence Scofield holds degrees from the University of Missouri at Kansas City and Northwestern University in Evanston, Illinois. Early in his career, he enjoyed performing with major symphony orchestras and opera companies. He has appeared on Grammy Award winning recordings and has international touring experience. Following a career in the performing arts, Mr. Scofield served in the administrations at colleges and universities. After retirement, he turned his attention to the written word and now writes novels, articles and columns.

**Sneak Peek**

**From "The Laura Messier Files" Series**

# Two Days in Moscow

## A Spy Thriller

**By Lawrence Scofield**

# Prologue

THE CALL ORIGINATED from somewhere along the North African coast in the summer of 1986. Viktor Petrovsky, Chairman of the Soviet Union's Committee for State Security, sat in his office overlooking Dzerzhinsky Square in central Moscow and heard his secretary, Irina, answer the call.

"Lubyanka Building, Chairman Petrovsky's office, how may I assist you?"

"The Colonel wishes to speak with the Chairman."

"One moment, please." She put the line on hold and pressed a second line, "Chairman, sorry to interrupt you. I have the head of ..."

Petrovsky interrupted her. "Yes, Irina, I know who he is. Put him through."

"Of course, Sir."

"Good morning, Colonel," Petrovsky said after pushing the blinking button on his phone.

"Salam, Chairman. I pray Allah blesses you with health and good fortune."

"Thank you. How may I help you?"

"I have concerns about a mutual enemy, Chairman. A CIA agent named Laura Messier."

"Wait a minute while I pull the file."

Petrovsky was well acquainted with Laura Messier. She murdered two Soviet agents in 1984. He pulled the file from his credenza. "Colonel, I have the woman's file in front of me. I see she killed one of your agents last spring

1

in Paris. Why should the KGB become involved in a dispute between you and Shewolf?"

"Shewolf?" the Colonel asked. "I'm not familiar with the name."

"It's a code name we've given Messier. Her file is the largest of any agent we watch."

"Then I do not need to tell you this woman's misdeeds. I would just mention the attack last spring."

"Shewolf's involvement in that illegal act is well known to us."

"She stole the codes to the S-200 missile installations from my briefcase before the attack."

"I understand." Petrovsky hesitated before he spoke again. "What are you asking for, Colonel?"

"I want her killed."

Petrovsky laughed as though he'd been told a joke. "The problem with assassination isn't the killing, Colonel. It's finding someone to do it. It would take an extraordinary amount of money."

"How much?"

"Ten million U.S. dollars."

"I can transfer that sum immediately."

"One moment." Petrovsky withdrew a folder from the middle drawer of his desk and found the number of a Swiss bank account he used to divert funds. "Copy down this account number: 1479752230. The bank is Credit Suisse in Zurich. As soon as the transfer is made, the bank will notify me and I'll make the arrangements."

"Thank you, Chairman. You are a great friend of our nation. Salam, Chairman."

Petrovsky hung up the phone and walked into his outer office. "Irina, would you find Ivan Ilitch? I've got a job for him. And contact Yuri Volkov in Paris. Tell him to call me."

"Yes, Sir. Right away."